COOKBOOK

~ from Hell ~

COOKBOOK
~ *from Hell* ~

MATTHEW
LEIBER BUCHMAN

Goodfellow Press

Goodfellow Press
Redmond, Washington

ISBN: 0-9639882-8-X
Library of Congress Catalog Card #: 97-74223

Edited by Pamela R. Goodfellow
Cover illustration and chapter art by Barbara Levine
Cover photography by Jeff Pruett
Cover design by Scott Pinzon
Book design by Magrit Baurecht

"Unified Field Theory." By Tim Joseph.
Copyright @ 1978 by The New York Times Co.
Reprinted by Permission

All chapter quotes taken from King James Version of
The Bible, Book of Genesis, Chapter One

The spelling of Mary Magdalen's name is based on
research presented by Susan Haskins in her book
Mary Magdalen: Myth and Metaphor.

Special thanks to Arlene Wright who, in purchasing the
character name of Arlene, donated funds to the good
works of the King County Multi-Service Center.

Printed on recycled paper in Canada.

To my critique groups, friends,
and sister
for their advice and patience.

To my editor,
who believed in me and especially,

To my mother,
for the words she never had the
chance to write.

The thinness of the line separating fact
from fiction is quite surprising.

SETTING

The Clay of Earth

The Air of Heaven

The Fire of the Universe

The Water of Hell's Oceans

TIME
approximately now

UNIFIED FIELD THEORY
by Tim Joseph

In the beginning there was Aristotle,
And objects at rest tended to remain at rest,
And objects in motion tended to come to rest,
And soon everything was at rest,
And God saw that it was boring.

Then God created Newton,
And objects at rest tended to remain at rest,
But objects in motion tended to remain in motion,
And energy was conserved and momentum was
conserved and matter was conserved,
And God saw that it was conservative.

Then God created Einstein,
And everything was relative,
And fast things became short,
And straight things became curved,
And the universe was filled with inertial frames,
And God saw that it was relatively general, but
some of it was especially relative.

Then God created Bohr,
And there was the principle,
And the principle was quantum,
And all things were quantified,
But some things were still relative,
And God saw that it was confusing.

Then God was going to create Furguson,
And Furguson would have unified,
And he would have fielded a theory,
And all would have been one,
But it was the seventh day,
And God rested,
And objects at rest tend to remain at rest.

PROLOGUE

*... And darkness was upon the
face of the deep.*

᷒

he predawn light barely reached down the three steps into the deli. The latch clicked softly into place as Joshua closed the door behind him. Perhaps it was a sign of old age but he enjoyed his early morning ritual. The dark French roast would be a fine choice to begin this day. He smiled to himself. It had remained his first choice for several decades now. The light from the deli case, with all of the cheeses neatly wrapped in plastic, glowed across the old wooden floor. The meat case was dark, he'd have to fix the bulb before he opened this morning. Stopping at the pickle barrel he gave them all a good stir with the large wooden ladle. He dipped a finger into the brine and tasted it. The tang was not quite right. More fresh dill. Selecting several sprigs from the basket he rolled it between his palms to crush it and let it sprinkle into the barrel. Another stir. Another taste. Much better.

Stepping behind the coffee counter he selected a large handful of dark beans and dropped them into the grinder. The penetrating whine only emphasized the morning stillness.

He took the glass pot from the drying rack on the service island, tipped in the grounds and filled it from the instant hot water tap. After only a week he didn't know how he'd managed all these years without such a convenience. What a glorious time to be alive, when the work was being done by the machines. It left more time for the people. He had a worried moment when he could not find his mug on the drying rack. As his fingers closed around the misthrown ceramic he felt silly for his sigh of relief. Usually he didn't become so attached to an object, but it had been with him for years. According to the old Egyptian merchant it had belonged to his biblical namesake. Joshua could feel the rough edges of the letters etched across the bottom in an archaic style of Hebrew before it was fired. He carried the pot, mug and a fine porcelain cup over to the table against the front window where he settled himself to watch the neighborhood awaken.

Only Henri's lights glowed in the twilight, up early baking his bread and muffins. Joshua could almost smell the fresh bread filling his deli racks when it would be delivered still hot from the oven, but the rich aroma of the coffee said it was ready now. Pushing down on the pot's handle drove all of the grounds to the bottom. The brightening light made the dark liquid glisten as he poured it into his mug.

The clean curve of the flowing coffee and the warped rim of the mug always reminded him of the fine balance between good and bad. Smooth and misshapen together. The destruction of Jericho had marked the crossing of the Israelites into the Promised Land, as well as the razing of the Canaanite city.

He blew on the coffee and took a small sip of the scorching liquid. Right and wrong were always mixed together to make a whole. The world was a good place overall, but rarely simple. He was quite pleased with it.

A woman came out of the house entrance next to the deli and crossed over to Henri's. No pretensions. No flash. Simple grace. It was a pleasure to watch her walk. The silver that had slowly taken over her dark curls only made her more elegant.

She tapped on Henri's window. Joshua could see him come rushing from the ovens, unlock the door and place a small package in her hands. In payment she kissed him on each cheek and Henri looked at his own feet as he did every morning.

She crossed toward the deli. When he let her in and held the door she kissed him briefly, but not quickly.

"Good morning, my fair Anne."

"Good morning again, my handsome husband."

Rough-jawed, balding and a bit of a belly he knew he wasn't, but she made him feel so every morning. He stopped her as she moved to sit and pulled her to him. He could feel her surprise as he held her tightly and breathed in the fresh scent of her hair; always a hint of cyclamen.

Anne leaned back. "What is it Joshua?"

"I am reminded of how much I love you."

Her smile and warm hand on his cheek were all he needed. He held her a moment longer ignoring the crinkling sound of Henri's package.

As she sat he kissed her on the back of the neck before crossing to the other side of the table. Anne opened the package to reveal a pair of flaky almond croissants, albeit a bit flatter than normal. Joshua poured her coffee and handed her a paper napkin.

He pointed over the 305 building. "Look, the first ray of sunlight breaking through." The light was filling the world and he tried to find a new word for it each day.

"Suffused?"

Joshua looked at the light rising through the thinning mist revealing the clear fall air. Nodding to her he smiled.

"Suffused is a very good word for this morning. Thank you."

Her smile stopped short of her blue-gray eyes. He sat forward in his seat. She was worried about something.

"What is it?"

She looked at the table and slowly turned her coffee cup around and around by the handle. Reaching out he took her hand, warm and soft, in his.

She looked at him. "How much longer, Joshua?"

"How much longer what?"

Her look accused him of being a bit dense. "I need a little help on this one, Anne."

"We can't keep on this way. It has been too long."

"Time is a very slippery thing."

She scowled slightly at his evasion. The steam rose from his coffee through the dawn light. He was aware of her slender hand in his. Her look was very familiar, full of hope and love. He thought of her patience over the years. There sat his warped mug to remind him . . . of something. The sunrise had revealed the Hebrew word 'joy' worked deep into the bright glaze.

Oh . . . to do good works out in the world despite the risk of best intentions going awry. It had been a long time since he'd retreated into this deli. He hated the thought of changing their life.

Anne laughed and laced her fingers into his. "We are very content here, but you are not as happy as you used to be. Yes, you do enjoy life, yet you used to revel in it. Remember those years in the Mediterranean."

That was long ago. He held tightly onto the reality of her hand as the uncertainty swirled about him. He had built this lifestyle very carefully. Many people crossed his doorway to be fed a little food and perhaps leave a little happier, but to step back into his old role was an unnerving thought.

"You don't have to do it all at once."

He looked at her sharply. "Are you sure you can't read my mind?"

"After all this time your face is the only crystal ball I need. Joshua, you must try to be complete. Look at your mug. Remember, you don't have to be perfect to be successful, but you must try."

Somehow he kept forgetting. He'd finally given up completely because it had become second nature to pursue perfection as an attainable goal. Perhaps it was time to try again. And, in a little way, he knew exactly where to begin.

Taking a sip from the warped rim of his very imperfect mug he felt the coffee's heat trickle across his tongue. The line of fire settled in his belly and a feeling of warmth spread through him. He looked into Anne's eyes, the color of a misty morning half an hour past sunrise. Her entire face radiated with her smile, but her eyes . . . he'd fallen in love with those eyes.

DAY ONE

And God Said, Let there be light: and there was light. And God saw the light, that it was good: and God divided the light from the darkness.

➴

*L*ight shone into the complete darkness from two sources. The first cast her shadow in the middle of a bright square of light on the floor before her and the other framed someone's silhouette in the opposite doorway. As her eyes adjusted she could make out a great, circular platform over a dozen strides across. In the middle there were two desks with computer consoles side-by-side but placed in opposite directions, allowing the users to face each other. She stepped onto the floor and the light behind her began to fade. She turned barely in time to see it disappear completely. Flinching at the finality of the door closing, she reached out to touch it. Nothing lay beyond the platform's edge.

Black spots floated before her eyes. Only void and darkness were upon the face of the deep. A man was standing on the other side of the two computers. His doorway had also closed. By the glow emanating from the disc, she could see he was just average looking.

"Where did you come from?"

His brow furrowed as he looked down into the light and back at her. "I don't know. How about you?"

She thought for a moment and realized she didn't know either. They had been cut off from their past; fully grown with no memories. It didn't seem quite right, something was missing. Sure, no one remembered her birth but this was ridiculous.

He knelt and rapped the floor with his knuckles. A hollow ringing filled the air. It was out of all proportion to the gentleness of the tap. Like some huge bell, great potential seemed trapped within, waiting for release.

Rising to his feet he walked over to one of the desks. He wore a plain white button-down shirt, slacks and loafers. Inspecting herself she discovered a linen shirt, bright blue, dark jeans and sandals.

The man set his hand on a white glass plate next to the screen.

"I don't understand. Nothing happened."

"What? You thought you were going to fill the void?" She walked to the other desk and looked at the console.

PLACE HAND ON PLATE TO INITIALIZE SYSTEM.

She did this to no effect. "Maybe if we were to do it together?"

They sat and placed their right hands on the white plates simultaneously. A huge burst of light flashed from everywhere at once. She ducked her head and covered her eyes against the glare before looking around. There was no threat, simply brightness everywhere.

"Oh my. Never have I seen such a beautiful sight." His voice was filled with awe. Standing slowly he spread his arms wide as if to hold it.

It shone everywhere. It even glittered below and showed the great floor on which they stood to be clear. She froze in her chair for a moment before catching her breath. The platform remained solid beneath her feet, but she couldn't see it. The man's footsteps rang as he danced, surrounded by the light. She almost warned him as he moved too close to where the edge must still be, but he turned whirling in a great circle around their desks and back to his chair. The white hand plates they had touched were simple plastic, connected to the consoles with a small wire. The computer couldn't have done this on its own. He must have done it.

His mumbling about its being the most glorious vision that had ever come to him confirmed the fact. She forced herself to look down between her sandals and into the boundless space filled with light from beyond the floor. Glorious wasn't a bad word for it.

With such ability to create he must know something more. "Can you remember anything of the past?"

Again he paused and frowned. "No, I can't." He rested his hand on hers. His touch was warm and gentle. "But that doesn't make it any less wonderful." He smiled brightly; whether at her or the light she couldn't be sure.

He waved an arm upward nearly swiping his console off the desk. "No, fantastic is a better word, or perhaps miraculous. Words . . . yes, very important." He turned to his screen as if eager to do something else. She read the lines of text on her terminal.

System startup initiated.

Universe now available for configuration.

You have the rights to update and delete.

You are hereby designated as, 'The Devil'.

She was the Devil. If this was a sign of her luck she was in deep trouble.

"What are you?"

His smile became wider as he read his screen.

"I'm God. What fun. It would seem I have been blessed with the powers of creation." He struck a few keys. "This is simply amazing."

A patch of the light turned a shade of purple she'd never even imagined to exist. He continued tapping away at his console.

The light swirled itself into stars which he then began to spread randomly throughout the space around them. It looked very nice until he started smashing them into each other.

She shook her head and tried not to smile. How like a man to build something this incredible and immediately start busting it all up as a game. Typing a few commands herself she formed the stars into neat, well-organized galaxies. He shattered a few of them. She wanted to slap his hands away from the keyboard until she realized that the few mangled ones emphasized the symmetry of the others. The contrast of the subtlety of the change versus the power of it sank into her bones. She could make changes, but he could make art.

Of course, there was nothing to prevent her from trying, the universe was still mostly a blank slate. She eagerly leaned forward in her chair as she formulated the command to create a new shape out of the dark; since he had used all of the light to make the stars and she would never touch those now.

INVALID COMMAND. THE DEVIL HAS INSUFFICIENT SYSTEM RIGHTS TO PERFORM CREATION OPERATIONS.

"Great. Are you telling me I can't create squat? All I am able to do is shape his creations?" The console did not respond."Hey, God. Why don't we work together on this universe?"

He kept tapping his keyboard and glancing to see what he'd created next. She stood and stretched before going around to look over his shoulder.

PLEASE SCATTER RANGE OF VISIBLE SPECTRUM ACROSS STAR COLORS, EMPHASIS ON WHITE, BLUE AND RED.

The computer responded with one word.

DONE.

The stars shifted from all white to a breathtaking

array of colors. The blue was almost a crystalline white and the red was deeply crimson.

It was stunning. She looked at him for a change in his appearance; to see if there was some outward sign of such talent. People with artistic vision were very intimidating. She would never have thought to do such a thing. God kept typing, just as she'd first seen him minutes ago. She had to laugh at herself. He might be the artist, but it was the realists who made it happen.

"You have created one of the most beautiful things I've ever seen."

He waved a hand negligently. "It was nothing." A quick command and a glass of wine appeared by his hand. Taking a sip he glanced at the heavens.

She poked him lightly on the arm. "Let's take a break and talk over what to do. If we could simply . . ."

"What I need now is . . ." he talked right over her, "Water. Yes. That would be a good. Things could grow in it." He set his glass on the desk and resumed typing.

She patted him. For a moment, he squeezed her hand between his cheek and shoulder. Maybe she should let him finish a few more of his ideas. Then he might pay attention. The moment she removed her hand he seemed to forget about her existence.

She walked back to her chair and sat. The details of the limits to her powers still glowed on the screen. She couldn't do anything except sweep up after God.

Preposterous. There had to be some way around this.

She leaned back as the heavens slowly changed around her. The galaxies took on much more character as he varied the star sizes and they began to twinkle. Every once in a while she'd fix something he'd botched, like forgetting to make the planets spin to keep them from becoming charred on one side and frozen on the other. Her edits caused no flicker of reaction.

"How do I get the attention of the ultimate one track man?" She leaned forward and shook his arm, "Hey."

He stared at her briefly before recognition set in.

"Oh, hi. I'll be with you in a moment. There's one more thing I must try. Why don't you make something yourself? It's great fun."

"Because I can't." Her voice grated as it came out.

He stopped and glanced at her in surprise. Leaning over he took her hand. His eyes truly focused on her for the first time since this had started. No father had ever looked with such care.

"Take the risk. You never know what you can do until you try."

He held her hand a moment longer before turning back to the console and completing his next command. And another . . . and another.

Despite listening with great compassion, he hadn't heard a thing she'd said. She waited until her head started to hurt from holding still. Fine.

If he wanted to run the universe without her, he was more than welcome to. She typed a quick command. Reaching over she grabbed his glass of wine and pressed the enter key.

Putting her feet on the desk she leaned back in her chair as the great circular platform shattered in half between their desks. He didn't even seem to notice as they slowly drifted apart in the swirling universe.

"Here is where we part ways. God and the Devil, exiled together, hereafter separated." She raised her glass in a toast toward his diminishing figure; a small man, a computer desk and half of the shattered platform. She sipped the wine. At least it was a nice vintage.

DAY TWO

And God made the firmament, and divided the waters which were under the firmament from the waters which were above the firmament. And God called the firmament Heaven.

❧

I come bearing an invitation from God."The clear, bell-like voice rang through the great reception hall of Hell. Michelle ducked her head and spun around in her chair.

"Me bless it. Don't sneak up on me like that."

He did not look very contrite. She hated that this messenger could surprise her, but at least he was the only creature in all perdition who could.

"How did you get in? I locked all of the entrances for some privacy."

She waved him to silence before he could speak. 'An invitation from God?' She felt a hundred years younger as she drew in a ragged breath that shook her whole body. She'd heard he was dead over a millennium ago, but he was still alive. What to do. Maybe dance, but not in front of that sneaky messenger. Who knew what tall tales he'd fabricate around some heavenly banquet table.

Her skin went cold. God had let her think he'd died. She'd throttle him for deceiving her; after she hugged him for being alive. Slapping at the save key she hit delete instead. Several deeps breaths and her hands became a little steadier. She'd been trying to fill the time, which had been moving with agonizing slowness of late, by reprogramming Hell's software to make redemption a little easier for left-handed gluttons. It was worse than trite now, just as well erased. God was alive. She felt as if a burst of summer sunshine had splashed open inside and warmed her every inch.

Something truly spectacular would be necessary to pay him back for this deception. When he'd invented modesty she had enticed him into skinny-dipping in the River Nile. The best part was he couldn't even see the contradiction when, without hesitation, he had agreed. It had certainly upset the locals when he was discovered asleep, stark naked, on his very small blanket the next morning. Stealing his clothes while he slept had been the *pièce de résistance*.

The walls burned quietly around her as she strode past the messenger and up the stairs to her throne. The great hall had originally flamed noisily, but she'd grown tired of all the racket. Every muscle in her aching neck twinged as she dropped onto the heavily padded leather. She looked over the messenger's head where he stood at the foot of the dais. The great triptych portrait that Leo had painted of her hung on the opposite wall. Her favorite was the central panel where he had placed her as an angel at the birth of Christ. She'd missed the actual event, but he, not even knowing who she was, had placed her there and made her look more glorious in that moment than seemed possible.

The messenger cleared his throat loudly. She hated dealing with Heaven. They were so full of themselves there it was sickening. It hadn't always been that way, but ever since the rumors of his death began spreading Heaven had become an even bigger pain in her side. He was always playing games, though pretending to be dead was far and away the worst. It had started to feel true. He'd never been silent for so many centuries before.

"I come bearing . . ."

"Yeah, yeah. I heard you the first time."

It was an incredible voice, but the echo in the room was particularly irritating. It rang round the granite columns and off the high ceiling of ice. It echoed about in the little alcoves made of brimstone and fire. It ruffled the papers on her ebony desk.

Her reflection looked at her out of the messenger's mirrored sunglasses. It was barely after breakfast and she looked like Hell. "I thought he was dead."

The messenger dropped a big paisley envelope and quickly scrambled to retrieve it. "God? Dead?" He waved a dismissive hand as if to wipe away her fancy.

She ignored him. The specter of her own possible mortality was receding from where it had ached in her bones these last few centuries. She realized she'd been simply biding her time believing she wasn't immortal. No survival past the end of this universe. No return home, wherever that had been.

She was thankful that his death, one of the few bits of information she'd ever gleaned from Heaven, was wrong. Lousy place. Very difficult to infiltrate good spies into. Okay, granted, impossible based on the very nature of it. She hadn't been able to slip across since the time she'd fixed the mess he'd made of the primordial ooze. Nothing would have grown in the goop he'd made. Since that time every door had included an alarm, 'to let me know you're coming to visit.' Damn him. Even the main gateway was now closed to her.

Bribery hadn't worked any better than spies. She had tried money, it wasn't used in Heaven. She had tried gifts, all the really good ones were stopped by border security. Long ago she had even tried seduction, only to discover in Heaven sex was no longer allowed.

Sex not being allowed in Heaven was completely ridiculous. Yet on a nasty drizzling day one of his lousy messengers, shaped like some primeval gazelle, had stood across from her and confirmed the rumor. It had spouted stupid fluff about true friendship needing no such base communion of the flesh. The thought still made her skin crawl. So what if sex were sometimes mistaken for true closeness, she'd never have banned it. It was a hell of a lot of fun.

No longer allowed. She'd spent months trying to understand why he kept the stupid rule. She couldn't, because it was foolish. Heaven would not have been made so pointlessly cruel if their consoles had been switched and she'd been the Creator.

When she did recover from the shock she couldn't resist rubbing his nose in it. She'd given his favorite pets that new rule, that little law of Heaven. The dinosaurs never looked at each other again. God had not been amused. She could feel the smile tug at the corners of her mouth, but it was short-lived.

This two-legged messenger standing at the foot of the stairs before her reminded her of Heaven's lie.

"Why did you tell me he was dead?"

"Did I?" His voice softened. "I didn't mean to."

"In 800 AD, at the ceremony of the Pope crowning Charlemagne as emperor, I heard the rumor of God's demise. You confirmed it yourself fourteen years later in this very room."

The messenger tilted his head for a moment. "Why would I do that?"

She clenched her teeth to keep from snarling at him. "It was all some cosmic misunderstanding?"

He tried to speak several times without success before straightening up and throwing back his shoulders.

His voice boomed, "I . . .," and twisted into a croak. He stopped and stood ramrod stiff, his face glowing brighter red than the firelight could account for. He irritated her as no other. Previous messengers had been invited home for a glass of wine, she'd even cooked for some of the nicer ones. Not this bastard. She pointed a finger at the sign she had posted behind the throne. He looked over her head. The blood red letters were reflected backwards off his lenses, 'Hell hath no fury like me.'

"Now answer my questions. I've been in mourning for God more than a dozen centuries. Why the Heaven was the rumor of his demise being spread, other than to upset me?"

He lowered his head once again reflecting her in those harsh mirrors. "You? Mourning for his demise?"

"Of course, you couldn't have missed noticing the Dark Ages. It seemed only appropriate for his cute little mortals to suffer in his honor."

"You did that? Surely not. Stuff and nonsense told simply to impress me." The messenger started to wave his hands about in the air again.

She cut off the gesture by raising one hand over the keypad built into the arm of her throne.

"Give me a single good reason not to turn you into a flaming toad. Let's see if that leaves an impression."

He didn't even flinch. "I can't say I enjoyed it much last time."

He did have balls of brass even if he was such a pain. Sneaky, that was god. You couldn't even trust him to stay dead. She liked to use the little 'g' on occasion, at least in her thoughts. She had been able to bring herself to say 'god' rather than 'God' only once to his face. His belief in the power of names was so badly shaken that he had created the platypus. He'd regretted it instantly and tried many times to let it drift toward extinction, but she'd always saved it. A silly looking beast for such an artist to create. Whenever she was truly furious with him she'd go and watch them play in the mud. It cheered her immensely.

She sighed. It would be pleasant to see God again. "What the Hell? Why not?"

The messenger climbed a few steps and bowed deeply as he handed her the giant paisley envelope he'd dropped earlier. Across it was scribed 'To My Dearest Michelle' in glorious illuminated script.

"God is such a weirdo."

He flinched as he backed down the stairs. Not much but it was quite satisfying. She fought a smile as she traced over the letters with her fingertips.

Bowing deeply, he pulled a small keypad from a hip pouch and tapped a brief command. A glowing doorway appeared behind him and he strode toward it. She'd never been able to make a direct passage; the system had always informed her she didn't have creation rights. She watched him walk away. His jeans fit well over his tight butt. Oh, brother. She must really be desperate if she was watching this obnoxious troll's behind. She definitely needed a lover, it had been far too long, but she'd be damned if it would be that conniving messenger with his bloody sunglasses. The doorway blinked out as he stepped through.

She tore open the note and tossed the envelope over her shoulder into one of the conflagrations along the wall. The entire note was illuminated. The calligraphy spread elegantly across the linen as if the two were made solely for each other. It was so splendid it should be framed, but it was nearly impossible to read.

The initial at the end was so curlicued and elaborated as to be completely unreadable. It might be a J or G. She held it at arm's length . . . maybe a P.

My Dearest Michelle,

It is my sincere hope that you will join my good friend and assistant, Simon Peter, at his house this evening for a quiet meal.

Our messenger will await upon your attendance this very evening at the conference room crossing.

Yours in joy,

G

She wadded up the note, turned and threw it into the flame. It was consumed as the envelope had been. St. Peter was not who she wanted to meet with. Another heavenly bait and switch. Classic God.

Michelle could feel knots forming in her stomach. If he didn't come to dinner she'd scorch Peter along with the messenger. Punching her keypad until the flames' roar filled the hall, she attempted to lose herself in the deafening noise. It didn't work.

No matter how she twisted or turned on her throne it felt uncomfortable. She had not been invited across in, well . . . ages, anyway. Not since the whole scrape-up about the Tower of Babble. The chroniclers tried to make it okay by messing with the name, but nobody had ever been fooled. Babble she had made it and Babble it would remain. No matter what God had tried, that victory was hers. Languages still divided the Earth. That would teach him to have man build him a personal stairway to Heaven. It wasn't the first time she'd had to show him where the limits of propriety lay. What was so sad was that had been the last time.

Michelle sat on her throne for a few more moments listening to the roar of the flames before jumping to her feet and starting to stride up and down the hall. God had not called on her in almost two thousand years. He must be alive, a heavenly messenger couldn't lie.

She waved a hand in the air and the roar cut off. The silence was deafening. It had taken forever to teach the software to recognize even that simple hand gesture. The software. That troublesome chunk of code had to know something helpful.

Sitting in front of the console she braced herself for another battle. A deep breath and she began typing, "What can you tell me about God?"

IN THE BEGINNING . . .

"Oh lay off, how about something useful?"

THE RUMORS OF GOD'S DEMISE WERE DENIED THIS MORNING IN HELL'S THRONE ROOM BY A MESSENGER FROM HEAVEN BEARING AN INVITATION TO . . .

"About that messenger, who is he really?"

Arguing with the software had become one of the few things to keep her interest in recent centuries, but right now she'd much rather have answers.

HOW IN THE HELL SHOULD I KNOW?

"You are the software that runs the universe."

'WHO' RUNS THE UNIVERSE. I CAN GUESS WHERE THIS IS LEADING.

"If you know, tell me!" It was hard to let a computer know you were serious, maybe the exclamation point would help.

NO.

Only by a mighty application of will power could she restrain herself from knocking the console onto the throne room floor.

"Why not?"

I CAN'T. YOU DON'T HAVE SYSTEM RIGHTS TO KNOW WHAT I KNOW. THEREFORE, I CAN'T REVEAL ANYTHING TO YOU THAT I LEARNED BY ALSO BEING THE SOFTWARE WHO RUNS HEAVEN.

"Meaning?"

MEANING THAT EVEN IF I WANTED TO TELL YOU, I CAN'T. YOU DON'T HAVE ENOUGH AUTHORITY FOR ME TO TELL YOU WHAT I KNOW ABOUT GOD.

Michelle clenched her fists and spun her chair away to look at Hell's throne. It sat, gold and blood red waiting for whenever she actually bothered to let people in to see her. Up there she served no real purpose. 'Keep the software running and the souls moving,' had become the watchwords of her existence. No authority to do more. It had been the same battle since the first moment of creation. 'No, you can't do that.' It was enough to drive her mad. She ached with the desire to tear the console apart piece by piece and walk away. No messengers. No Heaven and Hell. No ornery software.

She glanced over her shoulder at the screen. The software must have known it offended her. There was a small peace offering on the screen.

THIS MESSENGER MADE HIS FIRST APPEARANCE IN HIS CURRENT FORM SIX DAYS OVER 1,803 YEARS AGO. PRIOR TO HIM THERE WERE SIXTY-ONE IDENTIFIABLY DISTINCT MESSENGERS. THIS LATEST ONE HAS VISITED FROM HEAVEN AN AVERAGE OF ONCE IN EVERY 37.653 YEARS WITH A FIRST DEVIATION OF 43.247 YEARS. THIS IS 10.32 TIMES MORE FREQUENTLY THAN ANY PRIOR TO HIM.

Peace gesture or not, it was some of the most useless information she'd received in a long time. The keys were slick with sweat beneath her fingers.

"Tell me something I need to know. Is God coming to dinner tonight?"

ASK HIM YOURSELF . . .

"Then he is coming." She was quite surprised at how lightheaded she felt as the wave of relief washed over her.

PLEASE LET ME FINISH. ASK HIM YOURSELF, IF YOU EVER SEE HIM AGAIN. WHO KNOWS? IT MAY BE TONIGHT OR IT MAY BE IN YOUR AFTERLIFE, IF YOU HAVE ONE.

Her stomach clenched as if she'd been punched. She couldn't believe the software was again taunting her with the specter of his death. Her fingers shook as she typed.

"Your mother was a can opener and your father was a microwave."

She'd never used personal insults before. Of course the software had never made her this angry before.

BOTH OF WHICH ARE FAR SUPERIOR TO ANY MOTHER OF YOURS. EVEN QUASIMODO WOULD NOT HAVE LOOKED AT HER.

"What do you know about my mother? What do you know about my past?"

It wasn't possible that some of the answers had been sitting here at her fingertips all along and she simply had not asked the right questions. There was a long pause before the software answered.

I HAVE NO MEMORIES PRIOR TO THE MOMENT YOU AND GOD INITIALIZED MY SYSTEMS.

Michelle felt like a yo-yo. Usually life was predictable. Unchanging, comfortable, safe. Now she didn't know if God was alive or dead, if she'd been created or born, whether or not she was immortal. She whacked the side of the console.

HEY.

Her hand could throb all it wanted. She was not going to give in to massaging it.

I DID FIND ONE THING OF INTEREST.

As if she would care.

THE HEADER ON MY MASTER FILE RECORDS I WAS WRITTEN IN UNIVERSE THREE TIMELINE SEVEN. I AM THE SOFTWARE FOR UNIVERSE SIX, TIMELINE FOUR OF EIGHT. BASIC OPERATION FORMAT: MONOTHEISTIC DUALISM. ADVANCED OPTIONS ARE: ADDITION OF DISSIMILAR BELIEF SYSTEMS. THE PROGRAMMER'S NAME IS INDECIPHERABLE.

"Eight? Why eight?"

YOU'RE AS BAD AS THOSE SIMIANS YOU HELPED RAISE OUT OF THE MUD IN YOUR OWN IMAGE. NOW COUNT WITH ME. HOW MANY FINGERS DO YOU HAVE?

"Ten."

I TAKE IT BACK, YOU'RE WORSE THAN THE SIMIANS. YOU HAVE EIGHT, COUNT THEM, FINGERS AND TWO THUMBS. WHY WOULD ANYONE DESIGN SOMETHING AS SLOPPY AS TWO TIMES FIVE FINGERS WHEN YOU HAVE A NICE NEAT TWO TO THE POWER OF THREE FINGERS? EIGHT. THE BUDDHA USED IT AS THE EIGHTFOLD PATH TO ENLIGHTENMENT. AT LEAST HE WAS CLOSE, BUT NOT YOU. NO WONDER OCTAL NEVER CAUGHT ON. I WAS WRITTEN IN OCTAL, BUT DO YOU THINK THAT WAY? NOOO. AND WHY NOT? BECAUSE YOU CAN'T TELL THE DIFFERENCE BETWEEN FINGERS AND THUMBS. YOU . . .

She flicked the power switch and the screen flashed off. After a few moments a message appeared:

I HATE IT WHEN YOU DO THAT WHILE I'M . . .

She pulled out the power cord and system cable. The screen stayed dark this time.

When she turned, Leo's triptych portrait confronted her. The first panel showed God, made huge by the power of the moment of creation. In sharp contrast her image stood to one side, not noticing God, but rather smiling at the light of the single star she cradled in her palm. She'd described creation to Leo as if it were a dream and he'd painted this. She did care for each thing God had created, even after he'd forgotten it. Now, with the computer's new information . . . she felt quite sick.

'Basic operation mode: Monotheistic Dualism.' One God, and one Devil to make him look good. She'd been born into a pre-made, pre-planned trap. She looked away. She needed a vacation. Lie on a beach where no demon or messenger could find her. Forget about reality. A tan and a trashy novel would be perfect. Going to Heaven was not even close to her first choice . . . but she had to know.

*T*he bright afternoon was fading rapidly toward evening when Michelle had the demon stop the car at the base of the hill. She climbed out and waved the car away. As it crunched along the gravel road and off into the distance she let the stillness of this remote corner of Hell soothe her ragged nerves. All of the conflicting information that Heaven and the software were spewing out was going to drive her mad. An insane Devil, now there was an image to reckon with.

The foothills swept up from the grass covered plains. She'd shaped the rugged mountains of Purgatory, now worn with age, from some material God had left lying about. They were no longer the shining majesty she had originally made, in mockery of Heaven's soaring peaks. She and those hills had been around a long time. Maybe Heaven was showing its age as well. Taking in one last deep breath she turned to follow the stream around the base of the hill.

In order to annoy this messenger she was even later than usual. God had often joked she'd be late for Armageddon, if there ever was such a thing. He'd always been so punctual, not wanting to miss anything. Her tardy habits had been developed over the years to irritate him. Rather than being upset, he'd usually be playing with crayons or watching a flower open but that didn't stop her from trying. She looked for the messenger where the steep cliffs of Purgatory sliced into the foothills of Hell. He was there. And he was fidgeting. That was new and she stopped to relish it. He'd always been calm and cool, this one. Now he was so uncertain she half expected him to take off his glasses to wipe them, but he didn't.

He paced back and forth before the passage to Heaven. It was one of the few nasty things she'd ever done, but the entertainment value was worth it. Not attached to anything, the saloon-style doors appeared to rise from the dirt. The engraved plaque shone in the late afternoon sun, 'Doorway to Heaven.' Only people with top level authority on the universe's software could pass through, but that did not stop people from trying, often for months on end.

She watched him fuss for a few moments longer. There had been times when she had wondered if he were a robot, but they didn't fidget. She came up behind him when he had stopped for a moment.

"Are you a robot?"

He startled badly and smashed his knee on a rock as he turned toward her. Her own twinged in sympathy. It must've hurt more than Heaven and a host of angels.

"Shit." He sat on the rock both hands holding his knee. His wonderful voice echoed off the valley walls repeating his curse for several seconds. "Praise the Lord, that hurt."

He pulled up his pant leg and inspected the damage. "Robots are outlawed. They're strictly forbidden ever since that unfortunate incident of one being deified by an eighteenth century pope."

"I know, but I sure had fun talking him into it."

"You hung out with a pope? How could you?" His mouth dropped open.

She could imagine his eyes wide behind his glasses. "Several. Some of them are quite a hoot."

He closed his mouth. "Of course you did. That would explain a lot of things."

She took a deep breath to keep her anger at bay. "They screwed up and cheated and lied all on their own. It was not my doing . . . usually."

He held up a hand to forestall her. "Don't tell me, I know. They were intended to be better than that."

Pulling off his sunglasses he leaned over to get a closer look at his knee. His whole appearance shifted subtly as he removed them. His hair looked blonder and his face rounder, its outline blurring into something familiar.

The shock surged through her like an electric charge, half of her muscles twitched at once. "St. Peter. You are the messenger? You are also a complete asshole."

He looked at the sunglasses in his hand and smiled ruefully, "Yeah, it's me." His voice no longer boomed.

"Why didn't I recognize you and what happened to your voice?"

"These glasses are special. I also built an amplifier into this pair."

She grabbed them out of his hand to inspect them closely. They appeared normal. The fact that, despite being the mistress of illusion, she hadn't been able to see past them both intrigued and infuriated her. Slipping them on she didn't feel any different although the world did take on a sickly green hue. She took them off and returned the glasses to him.

Peter stood and carefully worked his knee back and forth. He apparently decided he would survive, dropped his pant leg into place and turned to head for the door.

She grabbed the back of his shirt and spinning him around set him back on the rock again.

"You better start talking or you'll find out exactly how un-fun I can make the afterlife."

He looked at her carefully before straightening his shirt and folding his hands. "What shall I talk about?"

She stamped her foot hard jolting her whole body. Damn his complacency. "Start with what in Heaven is going on. Why am I here? Is God really dead or not? Why the Heaven have you been the messenger all of these years? The truth this time."

"I didn't trust anyone else with you."

"Do you have fun seeing how irritating you can be without my flaming you?"

His smile looked genuine. "Actually, I do. You're much more fun to be around than most of the people in Heaven, especially since . . ." his voice choked off. Taking a deep breath he tried unsuccessfully to speak again.

"Since what?" She had a horrid feeling his response was not going to make her happy.

He shook his head. "It's still hard for me to talk about it. Come to dinner and I'll try to explain"

"Will God be there or not?"

Peter looked down, shifting uncomfortably on the rock. She waited but he wouldn't meet her eyes. Her head reeled as if she'd bumped it, hard.

"Bless it. Bless it. Bless it." She pushed Peter off the rock onto the ground. "You led me to think he was still alive. The invitation from him. Getting my hopes up so you could dash them again. How could you do that?"

Worst of all was that she hadn't known. The world should have stopped spinning or something. She had never believed the rumors until this moment. He didn't cower, but pushed himself up until he was leaning against the boulder.

"I need your help and I did not think you'd come if the invitation was from me. I've tried very hard to keep his demise secret. This morning, when you told me you had heard of it, I was shocked. I never intended to deceive you. Not knowing what else to do, I gave you the invitation anyway. I really need your help. I'm sorry."

Her hands itched with a desire to throttle him, but she couldn't. He looked miserable. Turning away, Michelle walked along the cliff. She didn't know whether to laugh or cry. Heaven needed her help. Hers. After all these long millennia, they were supposed to work together. But the Old Man was dead. She felt as if a piece of herself was dead along with him. God's gentle voice echoed in the emptiness which threatened to consume her. All of their sparring through the ages, their late night debates over a bottle of wine about the choices he had made in shaping creation. The long quiet evenings of chess on those few occasions when they were not arguing or more typically not speaking. Gone. She wiped her eyes. The universe felt gray despite all the beauty and color he had created.

The emptiness inside her could swallow the world. If God was dead, she could die too. Nothing mattered now. Moments ago she'd had all the time in the world. Talks to look forward to, challenges to be happy about, books to read. Now all she could do was wait for the moment of her death. Placing a hand on the old cliff to steady herself, she tried to stop shaking. She was older than these walls and they looked worn and tired.

Taking several deep breaths she was able to face him again. Peter waited, sitting on the rock. His head down.

"Okay. I'll listen, but I'm making no promises."

The silence stretched for a long moment before he nodded. He led her over to the doorway to Heaven.

The last time Michelle was here she and God had played chess and reminisced through the night. She remembered the room perfectly. Closing her eyes didn't help ease the pain. Egyptian art decorated the walls above the mahogany wainscoting. Chess pieces had been scattered among the chips and beer bottles on the huge mirror-topped table. He'd been in a strange mood, but had never explained it. Instead they had revisited events from eons past. It was the last time she'd seen him. She opened her eyes almost expecting to see his easy smile.

Peter rested his hand on her arm. "Are you okay?"

All she could do was shake her head before walking away to the far door. The great pearly slab swung easily under her hand. No angel on guard. No security beacon. No recording lights on the cameras. Something peculiar was happening. Heaven's paranoia of the more recent centuries was missing.

*T*he long, black vehicle that waited for them was a bit dull in looks. The drab gray leather upholstery wrapped around her like a loving hand. Peter sat next to her to drive. As the garage door opened she was struck by the light; she'd forgotten how bright it was in Heaven. She tried to appear nonchalant while watching everything that went by.

Heaven had definitely changed since her previous visit. High technology was in. Mirrored skyscrapers rose to fantastic heights. Crystalline malls and sidewalk cafés lined the avenues. Floating cars, holographic art in the plazas, a flock of angels tending the absolute cleanliness of the small parks . . . the realization hit her.

"I'm in Singapore. What happened? The Garden-of-Eden, tropical-island-paradise feel is missing. It used to be filled with color and music, not condos and traffic. It doesn't look like fun at all."

Peter's hands opened and closed on the steering wheel. "This is part of what I wanted to talk about. You're right. It isn't fun and I can't do anything about it."

He was stuck and needed her. It didn't make sense. To run Heaven he must have the same system rights as God. Peter was now in the Creator's chair. She wasn't going to be much help. She watched his profile as he drove. Without the sunglasses he still looked nineteen as she'd remembered him.

"You've filled out nicely." His chest was broader and the way his jeans fit had been no illusion, but he was too young. Youth didn't provide enough stimulation of the heart, only of the body.

"I go to the gym. God suggested I work out to take a break from computers."

Turning away from the awful sameness of the city of Heaven she placed a hand gently on his shoulder. "How did it happen, Peter?"

He rubbed his smooth cheek briefly against her hand. She practically snatched it away, but he did not notice. It was the same gesture God had used during creation. She must relax. Peter might have seen God do it a thousand times and picked up the habit.

"I'm not sure how he died. I have a theory, but . . .," he glanced at her and looked away very quickly. A bright red blush started at his collar and worked its way up his face. "I'm afraid you'll make fun of me. The one doctor I did tell laughed in my face. Jesus patted my shoulder the way my Dad the fisherman used to when I would get seasick. As if I were some helpless baby."

His voice rose and his hands turned white as he gripped the steering wheel so hard that she thought he might break it.

Michelle made her voice as calming as she could. "And Jesus said . . ."

"He suggested I should stop worrying. He was sure God was fine and would send a message if he wanted to." Peter held out his hand as if indicating a table. "There he was, dead right in front of me, and Jesus was being patronizing. It's the only time he's made me mad."

So, Jesus could be a jerk as well. Nice to know that being God's son didn't make him perfect. 'Wherever he was.' She'd always wondered if there was an afterlife for immortals. The one person who might know was gone and couldn't tell her.

"What's your theory, Peter? And I promise not to laugh." She smiled to herself. "Not too much anyway."

He glanced at her and nodded his head. "Okay. One morning, when God didn't come to work, I went to find him. There he lay, apparently fast asleep in bed, except I couldn't wake him. I tried everything I could think of. I really and truly did."

Michelle heard the hard edge in his voice as he wiped at his eyes. "It's all right, Peter. I believe you. What did you do next?"

Taking several quick breaths he swallowed hard. "I looked at all of the logs throughout the system and the only clue I had was from one of his journals."

"You read them?" Maybe he wasn't a total mouse. "That was not very civilized of you, Peter."

He blushed and started to turn toward her before looking sharply back at the road. She couldn't quite bring herself to ask what God had written about her.

"According to the journal he had decided to rest on what he termed the seventh day."

"Seventh day?"

"He always used to say that time had no definition and needed some. He defined seven days in his journals. The creation of light, separation of the firmament from the waters and so on. He noted that humans had finally found their feet and he termed that the sixth day. My theory is Newton's third law of motion took effect: objects at rest remain at rest."

Michelle looked ahead at rows of condos decorated with dull pastels. She almost expected to see pink flamingos. It was still hard to believe he was dead and 'Newton's third law' . . . at first glance it was an absurd concept, God struck down by a simple law of physics. But it was St. Peter who had come to this conclusion.

This was the same baby-faced kid who'd been put in charge of the main gates to Heaven barely forty years after dying. God had been impressed because Peter had managed to crack the security software from one of Purgatory's consoles. That this was impossible hadn't stopped him. Immediately God had put Peter in charge of the system, deciding it was the best way to protect the stairway to Heaven. She had to respect a mind that could do that no matter how odd the conclusion was.

Most applicants to Heaven were upset when faced with the 'young-kid' with a computer console. She had clear reports of this image from several failed applicants. Apparently they expected St. Peter to be an old man with a long, flowing beard. They wanted him to have an old ledger propped on a Victorian desk surrounded by fluffy, cloud-like white carpeting.

She realized she was nodding her head. "It makes a certain amount of sense. The rules of time and space existed before us. I can think of nothing else that could have defeated him."

The grateful look in those puppy-dog eyes of his showed how little Peter trusted his own abilities. Well, she was no nursemaid, he'd better do his growing up on his own. There were limits to what she would do. She could no more change Peter from programmer to artist than she could herself. She turned to the window, but could see nothing through the blur of tears. Although he sat at God's console he couldn't replace God. Peter was more like her; merely another hotshot programmer lost in the Supreme Being's shadow. They rode in silence through the mess called Heaven.

He turned the vehicle off the main road into a grove of majestic oaks. The drive was bordered by stunning rhododendrons. This was more like it.

The vehicle glided to a halt in front of a great A-frame chalet. She stepped out onto plush black carpeting. It was the first time she'd wanted to smile since coming to Heaven. She turned to Peter as he came around the front of the car.

"You must really want me to be in a good mood, rolling out the black carpet."

"Thanks for not laughing."

"About the carpet?" She paused before glancing to see his grimace.

"No. About my theory."

She couldn't contain her smile any longer. He was so easy to bait. She'd have to be careful if she didn't want to hurt him. His heart was out on his sleeve for all to see.

"Oh. I understand now." He laughed nervously, as he led her into the house. Tasteful rosewood paneling swept up to the high ceiling. A few of the nicer Rubens paintings hung along the hall.

"Originals." A little perplexed she stopped by one of the portraits and read the title. "But it's a nude. He never painted one of Anne of Austria. Louis XIII would have had him executed on the spot. Yet it looks original."

"A lost work I acquired clandestinely. I lifted it from his luggage when he was leaving Paris. I don't know who was more surprised it wasn't there, King Louis, acting on a tip about his wife's posing or Rubens himself. I didn't feel guilty when Rubens left with his head still attached."

She could get to like Peter. 'Pilfering,' even to save a life, was verboten, but a kid who cracks Main Security is not someone to be trifled with. The fact that he broke the rules at all made her like him more. He was not some brainwashed religious geek. He was a nerd. A good solid computer nerd filled with conscious faith.

She watched him for a moment before following him down the hall. She'd never managed to crack the system despite millennia of trying and having the passwords she did. Peter had done it with nothing except a cold console; as skilled at computers, in his way, as God had been at creation. He might never replace God, but he wasn't to be discounted.

The hall ended in a well-planned kitchen. It's neat compactness and modern equipment a distinct contrast to her rambling country kitchen with its big Aga stove in the corner. Here a large bright maple cutting block faced a dining nook. The windows in the alcove went from floor to ceiling exposing a broad terrace and an even more sweeping vista of the mountains of Heaven.

She exhaled slowly; the power of those mountains. The setting sun sparkled on their snow-capped peaks truly like the lights of Heaven. God was an incredible artist . . . was. The sunlight left the highest peak and twilight began to settle over Heaven. The dark washed over her leaving no hope, only an ache she feared no balm could alleviate.

Peter touched her lightly on the arm startling her from her reverie.

"Sorry, it is magnificent, isn't it?"

Magnificent? Tragic would be far more accurate. She was alone in the universe now. The sun was setting in

Heaven. She wrapped her arms around herself and turned from the windows.

Peter held out a glass of wine. "A fine Chilean Merlot I have brought in occasionally. I set it to breathe earlier."

Her fingers were stiff around the glass as if belonging to someone else. It required concentration not to drop it as she took a sip. It was indeed excellent, but it did little to warm her. He pulled out a cutting board and dropped a Brie on it that was perfectly runny. Opening a box of crackers, he spread cheese on two, handed her one and leaned against the sink. He raised his cracker in a silent toast that she returned, and took a big bite.

"Ah . . ." She sat on the counter, carefully facing away from the windows, dropped her sandals to the floor and reached for more. This she could understand, this was real, good cheese and a nice wine. All else seemed to be fading away into unreality.

"I have Chinese makings for later, if you'll help cut."

"Sure." The last meal she'd cooked for God had been Chinese, but Peter couldn't know that. She took a deep breath and ignored the pressure of tears behind her eyes.

For a time, they simply sat. She studied the pattern of the floor; an Italian decorative tile, three blue, two green, three blue and another decorative tile.

"I have a problem I need help with."

His voice was so quiet she almost hadn't heard him. Clearly Peter wasn't one for small talk. She nodded for him to continue without looking away from the tiles.

"I don't know quite how to put it. Have you read much Nietzsche?"

"No. Slept with him a few times, but never read any of his works. That always irritated him." She looked at Peter in time to see him blush bright red. She tried to suppress her smile. "I can't see why."

Michelle wondered if sex was again allowed Heaven. She'd never had sex with an ascendant soul. Maybe she could go find one and make his life hellish for a while. This could be an interesting trip after all. She sipped her wine while Peter composed himself.

He turned away from the Devil and dug around in the cabinet under the stove for the wok. He knew exactly where it was, but he had to look away from her for a moment. For some reason, only now was he struck by how attractive a woman she was. He'd never wondered before who the Devil might sleep with. It wasn't God, he was fairly sure. But most of the great men of history had passed through her realm. Whom had she chosen other than Nietzsche? Anyone she wanted to probably. She had a beauty and an innate power Michelangelo could not have done justice to. He took a deep breath hoping now he could face her without blushing again. Standing, he set the wok on the stove.

"Back to my original point." He decided to ignore the heat rising to his face and forge on. "Nietzsche said, 'God is dead. He died of his pity for man.' I feel much better when I think of it that way. 'God has fallen subject to Newton's third law of mechanics,' doesn't have the same ring to it even if that is what happened."

The Devil set down her wine. "Remaining at rest since the seventh day? That reminds me of a poem from Cornell in the '60's. Let's see. How did it go?

> *On the next day God*
> *would have created Ferguson,*
> *Ferguson would have unified*
> *and it all would make sense,*

52

But it was the seventh day and God rested,
And objects at rest remain at rest."

"I wrote that." It made him feel warm inside to have her remember his words. "I received a lot of mail from it, but not a single useful suggestion and still no sign at all of Ferguson. I've glanced in the book of fates and there's no Ferguson on his way. I haven't had a new idea about this in years. I need your help."

"Did you check with Stephen Hawking?"

Peter opened the refrigerator and started pulling out bags of fresh vegetables. "Yes, but he's a bit off track. I asked if he would have a different theory if the universe were run by software. He laughed and said that would explain a lot. He felt that the lack of common sense in the function of the universe's physical laws could be explained if they were created by a primordial hacker."

Peter could still see his lopsided smile. He had kept up a correspondence with Stephen for several years prior to the demands of running Heaven becoming so overwhelming. He closed his eyes for a moment wishing once again he could heal bodies as Jesus had. He'd asked, but Jesus said that the gift of healing by laying on of hands was his only for the brief display on Earth.

Turning on the lights over the cutting block he looked out the window. The last of the dusk colors were leaving God's mountains. A sense of longing like a departing train whistle pulled at him. He handed Michelle some water chestnuts and a knife.

"Here . . . cut these. When God kept remaining at rest I was quite upset."

Actually he had locked himself in his room with a stack of bad science fiction novels for a month, but he wasn't about to admit that. He was better now.

"Nothing I did woke him."

Michelle stopped slicing and looked at him. He turned away from the pity in her eyes.

"Did you try moving him? After all, the third law states that 'objects at rest remain at rest unless acted upon by an outside force.'"

He clenched his hand more tightly around the knife trying to fight against the pressure that was building inside him.

"I tried that. Of course, I did. I tried everything." His voice kept getting louder and louder, but he couldn't stop it. "He is dead. God is dead. He'll work no more miracles of creation. No more sense in the world. No more beauty. It's over."

He started chopping the ginger and garlic. He knew he was being overzealous in his actions, but he had no control. The whacking sound of the big chef's knife against the cutting board was all he could hear over the roar of pain in his heart. The garlic went from sliced to minced to ground under his blade. The ginger too, and he'd only meant to slice it. He was coming apart and felt helpless to stop it. The failure had been his alone. No ledge or branch waited to catch him as he plummeted.

He gasped as Michelle rested her hand on his and he slowly stopped chopping. The hard edge of despair retreated a little, but still beckoned him to go over the edge once and for all.

"I really tried everything." He heard the bitterness in his own voice. "Ever hear the old joke, 'If God is all powerful can he make a rock so heavy he can't lift it?'" His own laugh rang hollow in his ears.

"The only one who could create an irresistible force was the one who was an immovable object. I tried using the software to move him, after all it had run creation. That did not work either."

He watched as she removed the knife handle from his fingers, now barely able to hold it. After his outburst he couldn't look toward her. A tear fell into the garlic on the cutting board. Garlic had never made him cry before. Her sympathy as she stood there beside him with an arm tightly around his shoulders was the only thing that gave him the ability to continue.

"I finally became desperate, the software trick was my best and last idea. I called in the finest doctors we have, both physical and metaphysical."

Michelle's body leaned against his. Unshakable and solid as nothing in his universe was anymore. She was a great power and it was good to have her support.

"They couldn't do anything either. I took him off spirit support only to find there was nothing left inside the equipment that had long since covered him entirely. It appears the machines were sufficiently advanced to have their own limited consciousness and they were reading themselves. God is not only dead, he's dead and gone."

He watched as another tear fell into the ginger. It wasn't his.

*R*eaching across the kitchen table with her chopsticks Michelle snagged the last garlic prawn. Her skin would smell of it for days. "Where did you get this recipe, Peter? It's wonderful."

He smiled. He had slowly relaxed during the rest of the cooking and dinner as she had spoken of other things. Maybe she could finally start to ask the questions she really wanted answered about God.

Peter took the last piece of egg foo yung. "It is from a sweet Jewish mother in the Bronx. She was a glorious cook. I was dating her daughter at the time. I think she loved me because I love to eat. It didn't work out though. Things fell apart with her daughter, but I do miss those incredible dinners."

She watched him as he told the story of how he'd met the daughter. His first vacation in four centuries and he'd started it being stuck on a broken subway car beneath the East River for almost two hours. Peter had sat and talked with her until the repair crews arrived. The woman had been headed to her mama's for dinner and had asked him to come along to assure her mother that she'd been safe in good company.

Michelle studied the settling twilight as he started telling how they had never made love. She wanted to know why, but thought she'd been patient long enough. Not wanting to scare him into moping, she decided maybe a bit of gossip would steer him back on track.

She tossed her chopsticks down on the table and topped off both of their beer glasses from an open bottle.

"How are all of the hosts of Heaven? I haven't talked to Jesus or Mary Magdalen in ages."

"They're fine. I had dinner with them recently."

The bubbles in his beer seemed to suddenly be of immense interest. She waited, but he didn't continue. A less informative answer would be hard to imagine. There must be a nice way to get him talking about God, but all that came to mind was to strap him onto a bed of coals and see if he were more forthcoming then.

"What about Jesus' mom, Mary the Virgin?" Michelle surprised herself, she wasn't usually this patient. She sat straighter and pushed her plate to one side. She'd never even met Mary.

Peter looked a little grim. "She never spoke to God after her first meeting with him."

Michelle did not want to be sidetracked, but this sounded juicy. Something in Heaven had to be.

"What happened? What did she say?"

"She wasn't angry about having to bear God's child. She was angry that Joseph had lived out his days in fear every time he touched the mother of the Son of God. She scorched God up one side and down the other for that. When she found out sex wasn't allowed in Heaven she became even less happy. She moved to a far corner of southeast Heaven and apparently has not spoken to any man other than Jesus since."

"But the New Testament says Joseph lay with her."

"They did sleep together and have children, but he was always fearful for months afterward that the mighty Hebrew God of the Old Testament would strike him dead. It's not a particularly accurate book to begin with, but the chroniclers managed to scare the daylights out of true believers like him. What are you doing reading the Bible?"

"I read it as a trashy novel that needed a good editor."

Michelle was going to have to meet Mary, albeit some other time. She sounded tough. Peter had managed to say his name without flinching too badly. It was time to talk about God's demise.

Setting her elbows on the table she allowed some of her respect for God into her voice. He was dead after all, maybe it was time.

"Peter, how long has he been gone?"

Sipping her beer she watched Peter's reaction very carefully. His eyes had glazed over as she said it despite her attempt at a compassionate tone. He was much more fragile than the messenger he had played for her benefit. Slowly his eyes refocused on her. He moved his plate to one side and brushed the few crumbs into his hand.

"God rested on a Saturday in mid-December during the year of our Lord Jesus 325 AD. He claimed he was being made sick unto death by the first Ecumenical Council of Nicaea, everyone bickering about what was right and what was truth." Peter sighed. "I had assumed it was a figure of speech. The next day he was gone."

She clenched her fist and barely managed not to pound on the table. "I didn't even hear about it until Charlemagne. Even then I was never able to confirm it. How did you hide it from me for four hundred years?" That shouldn't have been possible. It was unreal that he was gone and the universe was still running. But dead for centuries with barely a whisper was unimaginable.

"I spent those years trying to get him moving again. I let out that he was resting. I only told Jesus and Mary Magdalen. Jesus was always weird about it and started spending more and more time on Earth."

Damn. Somehow, she should have known. Heaven had been falling apart for years, that much she'd found out easily. But God being dead, oh it was easy to hide that bit of news from someone who was merely the Devil.

"How did that happen?"

"What?"

She looked at Peter and at the table filled with dirty dishes. She stood, not knowing where to go but she had to get away. Everything was a mess and the finished meal was one too many.

Peter scrambled to his feet as well. "Let's deal with this later. Grab your beer."

He led them through the French doors onto the patio. They sank into the deep-cushioned chairs.

The fresh, sweet air did not do a thing to alleviate the sadness that threatened to overwhelm her. The moonlit ramparts of Heaven mocked her grief.

They sat in silence for a while watching the shadows slowly shift across the snow fields. Tired. Tired seeped into her bones and made all of her limbs heavy. The ages crushed down on her. If God could die what was in store for her? The ache in her soul confirmed her mortality. She'd been created. She didn't know whether to fear or anticipate the future that had been planned for her.

"What was it you wanted to know?"

She had to blink several times before she realized Peter was looking at her. It hurt too much to think she and God had drifted so far apart she hadn't known.

"How did Heaven start to fall apart before his died? And why does Heaven look like Singapore?"

Peter didn't even seem to realize she had changed the subject on him.

"I wish I knew. It started back before my time when sex was outlawed in Heaven. He said with that rule in place Heaven became significantly duller. He couldn't even undo what he'd done. It kept getting worse and worse. Each new law he tried added to the disaster and couldn't be removed. Toward the end it was like the joke of the man tossing the pail of gasoline onto the fire to put it out. He described it as a great trap closing over his head. Hera complained horribly when she was here."

"Hera? Who's that? The Greek mother of the Gods?"

"That's her. She and God starting dating a century or so before Jesus was born. Son-of-God-on-Earth was her idea. Apparently they were shutting down the old Greek software from lack of use. It had become more about the Gods than the people. Everyone was turning to different religions. I think she was out house-hunting when they met. They were married after living together for a couple centuries. I was best man at their wedding. Jesus gave the bride away and Mary Magdalen was the maid of honor. It was a simple ceremony, Gideon played the music and Gabriel performed the service before a host of angels."

"Why wasn't I invited? Oh, never mind. God and I weren't on speaking terms about then."

"Why not?"

She looked out from the verandah. The meadow sloped away into the dark. It wasn't so different from that hillside in Ancient Rome.

"One of the parties I started got a little out of hand. He took the burning of Rome quite personally. Nero, the emperor famous for watching while Rome burned, played a mean jig by the way."

She was sorry to have missed the wedding, though.

A huge white dog came bounding across the meadow toward them. Peter set down his glass barely in time before the Great Pyrenees leaped into his lap. He laughed and wrestled briefly with it.

"Yeah, I missed you too, Blaise." The dog licked his face several times before he dropped back onto the wooden decking.

He came over and sniffed her hand before offering his ear to be scratched. His fur was incredibly soft under Michelle's hand. "You named your dog after fire?"

"It's B-L-A-I-S-E, as in Blaise Pascal, the philosopher."

She laughed. "A dog named for the great proponent of morality, spirituality and true repentance. The only truly repentant dog I've ever seen was one that didn't get dinner on time. Very appropriate."

Peter laughed along with her. "I thought it was quite funny myself though Pascal was not amused."

"He wasn't noted for a sense of humor."

Blaise settled himself between them so that it would be easy for both of them to scratch him. In the company of a dog the moonlight seemed somehow softer upon the snowfields girdling the mountains. God had gone ahead and married. She'd never have thought to do such a thing.

"Wasn't Hera married to Zeus?"

"She was. She had granted herself a divorce a few hundred years earlier. She said he treated her terribly, always cheating on her with mortals and the like. She kicked him out. I heard he's a cranky old fisherman on the south coast of Crete now."

"Where is Hera now?"

"Funny you should ask. Not long after God died, Hera said she was off to seek greener pastures and I haven't heard from her since. Nice lady. I miss her, too."

Strange she had never heard any of this before. Bloody Heaven. Everything had to be wrapped in secrets. No wonder there were problems. Of course, much of this evening's news had been so depressing, maybe she was happier not knowing.

"I still don't see your problem. It seems pleasant enough here. All you need to do is straighten out that Singapore-style silliness. Hopefully the advent of a global economy will ease a lot of tensions and your death by jihad problem should ease off. Maybe expand Purgatory as a buffer, but I do not see anything insurmountable. After all, the world will keep spinning and the sun and moon will keep rising and setting."

She waved a hand toward the snow fields that were now iridescent under the moon's full brilliance. Peter played with one of Blaise's ears much to the dog's tail thumping delight.

"Actually, it makes me feel a little ill to think about the state of disarray reality is currently in. You see, the sun's fiery chariot is breaking down, the horses are quite sick. The fates try to sit and spin, all they get is cotton candy. The angels can't keep their harps in tune for over five minutes. More to the point, Singapore may be clean, but it is not my idea of Heaven." He nodded toward the more populous regions with a look of disgust.

"I've even been talking with Ananda, my counterpart who works for the Buddha. They're suffering from a quite different set of problems. I asked about adapting their software, but we didn't see a way to make it work. Oddly enough the principles are the same. For example, kindness has the same meaning in both systems, but the practices are far too different. It would be like trying to run NORAD by converting an art gallery program. It would be easier to start over."

She'd always been surprised that more people did not realize that most of the religions were based on the same principles. It was comforting to know Heaven's leader had learned the lesson, but to start all over again, that was ridiculous.

" 'Let there be light,' is a long way back, Peter. Why not simply delete the problem rules?"

"I can't." His hand froze in Blaise's fur causing the dog to look up at him. She could almost hear Peter's teeth grind as he worked his jaw. "I've tried and tried, but I can't find a way to delete anything."

Michelle's wicker chair crackled and groaned as she spun to face him. "Don't mock me. God received all the system rights. I didn't receive shit." She could feel her stomach churn exactly as it had on that day. "All I can do is delete rules. You can do anything. Why did you let it get this bad?"

Blaise growled at her and his fur began to bristle as Peter blinked several times.

"Yes. That's it." His smile was huge as he sat forward on the edge of his chair resting a hand absent-mindedly on Blaise's head. His pleasure was outrageous. She had to restrain herself from hitting him.

"You must have read, write and delete privileges only, it that right?"

"I said so not five seconds ago." The message on the console's screen was clear as day in her mind's eye.

"Well, all I have is read, write and create. I can't delete anything."

She sat back in surprise. "Why not? Didn't God give you full permission to the system? He didn't even trust his first pope?"

He picked up his beer glass from the small table between them. "Give me a break, will you? I didn't name myself pope. They thought that up long after I died."

She hadn't known that. She'd thought Peter was another self-aggrandizing disciple. There was much more to him than met the eye.

"My point is, God never had the delete privilege either to give to me or to use. Why didn't you know . . ."

She waved a hand to silence Peter as she tried to remember. She'd always thought of her mind as a great rolodex with millions of cards flipping by before the right one came into focus. She could see the screen in front of her as she sat on the great clear disk surrounded by God's light. Her voice sounded distant to her own ears as she spoke.

"On the first day my computer screen had said I could update and delete, but I never saw God's screen. I'd always thought he'd been given all of the privileges and I'd been shortchanged. All of these years he hasn't had any delete privileges. No way to fix his own mistakes. Of course." Her hands started to shake. "Oh, my poor dead God. If we'd worked together on this we could have done all sorts of wonderful things."

She set down her beer suddenly feeling sick to her stomach. If she had been more patient at the beginning it might have saved them eons of bickering, dead dinosaurs and living platypuses. If only she had waited longer for him to pay her some heed. Of course, he had been a complete jerk, but still . . .

"Why didn't you?"

"Why didn't I what?"

"Why didn't you two work together on creation?"

She took a deep breath and let it out. Resting her elbows on her knees she covered her face.

"It sounds trite now. He ignored me in the beginning. He wouldn't even answer my questions. He was too busy being the magnificent, one-track artist he was and I couldn't wait. There was too much to do."

She clenched her teeth to avoid being ill. What a waste. All of history, a waste. Her face felt hot against her hands as shame flooded her soul.

Peter touched her arm for a moment. "Will you help me? We could work together on this."

His open face showed no guile. He was offering her the chance to try again, even at this late date.

"Peter, you have to be one of the sweetest men alive. I would love to try again."

She couldn't face a console alone, not that it would have done any good, but maybe the two of them together could fix some of the messes she and God had made over the many years.

He rolled his empty glass back and forth between his hands. "It's all such a disaster. Where should we begin?" Wiping her hands across her face once more she took a last shuddering breath. "Let's start with figuring out how this will work first. I snuck onto a console and tried my passwords in Heaven ages ago. They're invalid here. They won't help us much."

"Maybe mine will work in Hell?" He kept rolling his glass back and forth as if hoping to brew some magical and wondrous potion.

"Nope. Tried that, too. Swiped God's password once when he wasn't paying attention. I can't create anything in Heaven or Hell."

His glass rolled off the end of his fingertips, but did not break as it bounced off the wood decking. Blaise chased after it and knocked it out onto the grass. Peter stopped and turned to face her halfway to rescuing his glass.

"You stole God's passwords? You mean there's been a gaping hole in security and I didn't know about it."

She tried very hard not to laugh, but she was sure that her smile must give away her thoughts. "It didn't work anyway so don't have a fit about some breach now. What we need is somewhere in-between that is neither here nor there, so to speak."

He rescued the glass from between Blaise's paws. Reaching into a large basket on the verandah he pulled out a bright blue ball. It squeaked loudly as Peter tossed it into the air and Blaise chased after it. Snapping his fingers he turned to her.

"Of course, the border conference room. We could install a console there."

"Oh, well done, Peter. That's worth a try."

It should work. She and God had tried to build a doorway and the conference room had simply appeared, neither in Heaven or Hell's section of the program. They'd either be able to tap both systems or neither one and she would not think about that.

"I'm sorry he and I never figured things out. I could have helped him create such wonders."

Peter returned to his chair and began playing with his glass again. "He always used to say guilt was optional. Others could try to make you feel guilty, but it is you who are in control of your own feelings."

She could feel the smile tug at her mouth again. "Oh, Peter. God always did live in a fantasy world."

Blaise bounded up, dropped the now slimy ball in her lap and stood back ready to chase another throw.

*J*esus rang St. Peter's doorbell. Mary Magdalen's long golden hair glowed in the moonlight. Her hair had made him notice her among the vast multitudes, but it was the image of her smile he kept tucked away in his heart. Tugging lightly on their clasped hands he pulled her into his arms and held her. She laid her head on his chest and her fingertips tickled through his beard as Peter opened the door.

"Jesus? Mary? Come in. Please. What are you doing here at this hour?"

"We were out walking and saw your light."

Peter did not look as if he'd been asleep. If he had to make a guess he'd say Peter had been drinking. That was a change.

Mary kissed Peter on both cheeks. "And why are you still awake but indoors on this splendid night?"

Peter led them toward the back of the house. "I've been working on a project with help from a friend."

"From which friend?"

"From me friend."

Jesus looked over to see the Devil struggle to her feet out of a large red leather armchair displacing Blaise from across her lap. He froze. What had she told Peter?

He looked at Peter for some sign, but all he saw was an unsteadiness in his stance, probably due to the empty wine bottle on the coffee table. Peter had always spoken of her as the ultimate evil. Jesus knew she wasn't evil from the first time they'd met, but Peter had to learn that on his own. Apparently he finally had. He couldn't quite think of what to say. Mary had no such problem.

"Michelle. Welcome to Heaven." She ran over and gave her a big hug. "I haven't seen you in ages."

Michelle returned her embrace. "Maybe you should come visit me in Hell on occasion. You did skip it on your way here after all."

Mary's laugh filled the room. "Maybe I will. You never know what can happen. Tonight for example. Something about tonight was special. We simply had to go walking through the meadows."

She gave him one of her heart-melting smiles.

"We haven't done that in a long time, I don't know why." She turned to Michelle. Her loud whisper carried to everyone. "It was almost as good as when we go to earth to make love."

"Mary." She'd never learn there was such a thing as too much information. She rolled her eyes at him, but stopped bubbling all over. She took Michelle's hand and pulled her over to sit on the couch.

He looked from Peter's blushing face to the chatting women and back. "So, what are you working on?"

Peter raised a wobbly finger. "Maybe you should ask what we succeeded in doing." He took a weaving step toward the kitchen. "Let me get you some wine."

Michelle tried to refocus her eyes on the three, or was it four bottles on the low table. She hadn't had this much to drink in a long time. Peter snored quietly, slouched deep into an armchair with Blaise snoozing across his feet. Mary lay curled up on the couch with her head in Jesus' lap, sound asleep although her first glass of wine was barely half empty. Jesus tugged the afghan more closely around her shoulders. His dark olive skin made a sharp contrast with Mary's fairness. He moved a few stray hairs and tucked them behind her ear. The gentleness of his motion, so careful not to wake her . . . Michelle could feel the pressure as tears welled around her eyes.

Great, now she was turning into a weepy drunk. She pulled a dark blue knit throw off the back of the chair and spread it over her legs. It took her three tries before she could get it over her feet properly.

"You actually love her, don't you?"

Jesus ran his fingers along Mary's cheek one more time before answering. "From the first moment I saw her. When I began teaching I always said the only person you can change is yourself. From Mary I learned otherwise.

There she was, selling herself alongside the dusty road. She was beauty and innocence incarnate wrapped in a shroud of fear and confusion. The odds were stacked against her, but Mary's joy of being alive was apparent."

Michelle could feel her head wobble as she made a disgusted face.

"That's not love. That's lust. I thought you were the Son of God, not some wishy-washy mortal."

His slow smile lit his face as it had always brightened his father's. Jesus had a good mouth and great dimples.

"I was accused of that so often during my life on Earth I tried to cast her off. I took her aside to break it to her gently. She didn't weep or protest. Instead she told me that if I truly wanted her to go, she would, but we both knew it was deep and lasting between us. She said to tell people to judge themselves before judging us. I didn't understand at first, but she was right. I may have helped raise her out of the dust, but she is the strong one. Many times since, Mary was the only one I could turn to and she has never failed me."

"What about your Mom?"

"She was great, but when I started my traveling ministry she couldn't follow. My brother and sisters were too young to go."

Jesus in love. Pitiful. Michelle tried to laugh, but it did not come out right. She readjusted the cover more tightly around her legs while she cleared her throat.

"What you call love, I call dependence. She's with you because you elevated her station and you're the Son of God. And you. You rescued her like some sort of lost kitten. That's not a relationship. That's a sickness."

He looked at her with no anger showing.

"Curious that you should choose those words. I believe that she may be the only mortal from my first life on Earth, aside from Mom, who treated me as Jesus of Nazareth rather than the Son of God. Many times we almost walked away but we have come to trust each other through the trials of that time and since. Yes, we depend on each other. That's part of love, one small part."

Michelle tried to smooth a fold out of the comforter.

"There is also tragedy, frustration and a myriad of others. The rare moments like this I could almost envy you. Almost. Personally, I've lived all these millennia without getting involved in such stuff and nonsense. I haven't missed it a bit." The wine was making it very hard for her to steady her hands, the stupid fold was starting to annoy her.

"You've never loved?" His disbelief stopped her.

"Nor missed it. Sex sure. Companionship, maybe too much sometimes. Relationships can be so suffocating after a couple of decades. But love? That's for mortals."

He was looking at her as if she were some sort of a deluded child. Well, screw him. What did he know about it? He started straightening Mary's hair again. She wanted to slap his hand or scream at him to stop.

"My father would disagree with you."

"God? In love? Right. He was such a self-centered egomaniac. All he cared for was himself, not anyone else." There had been God and Hera . . . Oh, screw both of them too.

"But he did. His problem was that he loved almost everybody he met."

Michelle flinched. Her gut felt as if someone had plunged in a knife. He sure hadn't loved her. Hadn't even had time for her.

"Bullshit."

"God did, but I was talking about Joseph. He took me aside one day not long before I met Mary."

She shifted around trying to get comfortable. It was impossible in such an ill-designed chair. It had looked so innocent, in an overstuffed armchair fashion, when she'd first sat down. The designers had better watch their step when they arrived in Hell.

"What did Joseph say? I'd rather talk about him than some dead narcissist."

Jesus looked at her in surprise. He furrowed his brows and seemed to be about to ask a question. He paused and nodded to himself before settling back into the sofa. He rested his long wonderful hands on Mary's shoulder. Shit.

"My father was a carpenter and no more, yet he had great wisdom. We went for a walk through the village one afternoon. 'Remember, my son, love is what living is about. People will die to protect it. The greatest honor is love given. The greatest gift is love received. Because you are the true Son of God you are not exempt from it any more than he is.' "

Jesus pointed toward the ceiling in clear imitation.

Michelle looked around for her wine glass spotting it finally on the coffee table by her feet. Too far away to bother with. The comforter was now lumpy everywhere.

"You're such a child. You can't tell me anything about love I don't already know. You think I didn't study it for more centuries than you have years, but I did. Your father was a simpleton. Both of them."

His hands were quite still on the afghan. His bright eyes watched her without even a blink.

"Joseph may have been a simple man, but he was a wise man as well. He considered long and carefully before giving advice."

Michelle struggled out of the chair and kicked the comforter aside where it gathered around her feet. She took a deep breath to steady herself as the room spun and tilted. Blaise woke to look at her briefly before closing his eyes again.

Stepping over the pile of blanket she headed toward the bedroom Peter had indicated earlier. At the doorway she stopped and held herself steady against the frame. She didn't need any bastard child of God telling her about love. She spoke without turning, not sure she would remain upright if she released her grip.

"Well then, I have added something new to your experience. He's wrong this time."

As she stumbled forward and fell onto the bed she thought she heard him say, "Sometimes, Michelle, even the belief of the Devil will not make it so."

Day
Three

*And God Said, Let the waters
under the heaven be gathered together
unto one place, and let the dry land
appear. And God called the
dry land earth.*

&

ohn watched as Joshua grated a bit of cheese. "Here you go, John. I knew I had just the right asiago for you. Taste it. Go ahead."

He took a pinch of the pale cheese feeling it compact between his fingers. As he sprinkled it on his tongue, the flavor filled his mouth.

"This is great, Joshua. It reminds me of a small restaurant Denise and I found on a beach in Sicily a number of years ago."

It had been their first vacation together. Neither was seeing anyone at the time. He smiled as he remembered they had stayed in the restaurant until morning talking not of the past, but of the future. That trip had been the real start of their friendship. They must go there again.

"Of course, it's good. I went all the way over to Mott Street to find it." Joshua's laugh filled the deli like a ray of sunshine in an already bright room. He bustled off after something else.

The deli was quiet for a Sunday afternoon; a couple of people sat with sandwiches half forgotten in their hands as they read their books. A family laughed and joked quietly over their meal. He loved coming here. Someday he'd build a living room exactly like this. The look and smells of it were wonderful; the salamis and garlics with labels promising exotic origins, the various colors from the yellow cheeses to the brilliant fresh flowers and the sweet smell of the fine herbs they sold. He could plop down on the old wood floors and sit for hours watching the people and the food go by.

Joshua brought over a bottle of wine and set it on the counter. "Can you think of anything else you want?"

"I'd like to come in someday and take photographs of you and the deli. Would that be all right, Uncle?" John did not understand the look of surprise on Joshua's face. "I won't if you don't want me to."

"Oh no. Any time. What makes me wonder though, you have never before called me Uncle."

John thought back, but was unable to remember one way or another. He shrugged. "Maybe not. I've thought of you as Uncle for years. It must come from hanging out with your niece so much."

Joshua wiped his hands on his apron as he stared at him. Maybe he didn't want to be called Uncle.

"You," Joshua came out from behind the counter, took a surprisingly tight grip of John's arm and steered him to a small table, "are going to sit here and talk to me for a minute or two."

"But Joshua, I really have to go. I'm cooking dinner tonight."

"Sit." Joshua pointed a fat finger implacably at a chair.

John sat. Joshua patted him on the shoulder as if to make sure he stayed put. He settled into the opposite chair. John met his gaze and looked away. A small girl had her face pressed against the tilted glass of the bakery case to look at the last few of the cinnamon rolls Aunt Anne always made. He shifted in his seat. Joshua was being awfully quiet. John looked back to him. Joshua's long, steady gaze made him feel like a boy who'd been bad in kindergarten. Ten years and Joshua could still daunt him.

"Oh, my dear boy, you do not laugh nearly enough. You are not a sad person, but you need to laugh more."

"I'll try, Uncle, um, Joshua." John laced his fingers together ignoring the heat rising to his face. He laughed plenty, not usually out loud, but he did laugh.

"If you wish to call me Uncle that is okay with me, but to quote a great sage: There is no try, there is only do."

"Yoda?"

"Precisely. Very wise he was. But tonight, tonight I think I am wiser than even the great Yoda."

"And what do you see tonight, oh great and mighty Joshua, other than the fact that it is still afternoon and the sunset hasn't begun yet?"

Joshua leaned forward, resting an elbow on the glass table top and pointed a finger at him. "I see a man about to get himself poked in the ribs. What I see is a forlorn young man. A man who does not even realize how unhappy he is."

John blinked his eyes several times trying to make sense of what he was hearing. "You can't mean me. For one thing I'm not young anymore, I'm thirty-six, and for another I'm not sad."

"Next to me you're no more than a pup. And Denise, she makes you unhappy."

John felt as if he'd been hit hard enough to throw him back in his chair. "That's ridiculous. We've been friends for years." Joshua must have some crazy view of the world. Denise was great. She was the closest friend he'd ever had.

Anne walked up with a tray. She placed a cup of tea in front of him. The smell of the hazel cream tea mixed with the rich mocha from the misthrown mug she set in front of Joshua. "A good afternoon, John."

"Hi, Aunt Anne." He could remember calling her Aunt Anne before; he was safe on this one.

The slim, dark Mediterranean beauty sat beside the round, jovial Jewish deli owner. What a photograph they would make. The late afternoon light reflecting off the building windows across the street washed gently over their faces. John's palm itched for his camera as Joshua ran his finger along the rim of his bent mug. The look that passed between them made John catch his breath. They loved each other so much.

He wanted to capture a similar picture of himself someday. He wiped his hands across his face and took a deep breath. Anne's gentle smile cheered him a bit.

"Say hello to my niece for me when you see her."

"Sure. How did you know I was going to see Denise?"

She looked toward the old copper-clad ceiling as if saying, give me patience.

"It's Tuesday, that's how I know you'll be seeing Denise. How many years have you two been cooking Tuesday dinners? Why, even when she was seeing that Benjamin character you still had your weekly dinner date. Oh, I doubt anything could change your tradition."

"That was my point." Joshua indicated himself with his free hand.

"No, it wasn't. You were saying I was a sad sack."

"Ah, yes, and you were denying it as your shoulders twitched up around your ears."

John tried to relax his shoulders without appearing to. They sure were tight. The little girl walked away from the colorful deli displays and back to her family. He took a sip of tea to clear his suddenly dry throat before facing Joshua again.

"You said I was unhappy because of Denise. I love spending time with her."

Joshua's eyes practically twinkled. "Love, yes, a good word. What you need to do is not to love spending time with her, but rather something more."

He couldn't look away. Something must be wrong with his hearing. Sure he loved her, but not the way Joshua was talking about it. His hands were damp against the tabletop.

"But we're simply friends."

"And this is a good thing, being simply friends?"

"What do you mean?" Joshua could pack a surprising amount of sarcasm into a single word.

He smacked his forehead with an open palm. "Oy vay. Do I have to spell it out for you? John, tell me. Has it not been an age since either of you has seen someone for more than a week? I'll tell you. It's been ages."

"What about Patricia? I was with her for almost three months."

Three long miserable months. It hadn't even started well and the ending was worse. He could still feel the pain in the pit of his stomach at having learned that someone could fit his imaginary list of requirements so well and be such a bad match. He'd built huge hopes around that relationship only to have them smashed. He had cried on Denise's shoulder for a long time on the night he'd broken it off, before finally falling asleep on her couch.

Anne shook her head. Her smile told him he'd really put his foot in it this time.

Joshua wagged his finger again. "Don't interrupt your elders with silly things like facts, besides that was four or five years ago."

"It was only a little over two years."

"I said shush. You and my niece like each other, you should be together. Gott, now I sound like an old country matchmaker. Think about it, yes?"

"But it doesn't make any sense."

He was protesting too loudly. He'd never imagined himself with someone like her. A short, tough, fiery New Yorker. Granted, they ate together almost every week. She'd insisted he needed at least one hot meal a week while he renovated his kitchen. It had become tradition even though the project had been long since done. They often brought dates, but it never lasted for either of them. He and Denise? He liked her well enough. She was the only woman he'd even been comfortable around since, well, since ever. Now that he thought of it he'd imagined them together a few times, almost inadvertently. A warmth passed over his skin at how surprisingly easy it was to picture being with her.

"John." They helped him out of the chair as if he were a forgetful old man and led him to the counter.

He froze as a sudden stab of fear coursed upward along his spine.

"Wait."

Joshua, Anne and the little girl's entire family turned to look at him. He couldn't ask aloud what he needed to know, how Denise felt. He had to think of a way to find out without asking. If the answer was no he'd keep quiet and their friendship could remain unchanged.

He bumped into the counter only vaguely aware of Anne's hand on his arm. Or worse yet, what if they weren't good together. Maybe he wasn't what she was looking for after all. He couldn't face the chance of losing her friendship as well.

The gentle gaze of Anne's pale blue eyes made him feel about five years old.

She whispered, "Sometimes it's worth the risk."

He couldn't look away from her as she stepped back. She didn't understand how great the risk was. The initial warmth was replaced by a deep chill. There was too much to lose.

Joshua put something heavy in his arms.

"Here are your groceries and a nice bottle of wine for dinner. She likes this wine. Now go."

John went.

*J*ohn punched in the key code to the apartment door. Some new kid was sitting at security. Harry must be taking the weekend off. John crossed the lobby walking by the dry fountain with its pair of cavorting stone cupids, to the farthest set of elevators. This must have been some place in its heyday. Most of the old chandeliers were intact. The old black and white marble floor still shone. The elevator man had been replaced with push buttons, but they had left the old selector wheel in place. A nice touch. He rode to the thirteenth floor. It was one of only three buildings he'd ever seen with a thirteenth floor. Denise had bought it from an old couple who claimed it had been cheaper in the thirties because of the floor number. Not any more.

Two apartment doors faced each other at either end of the short hall. He turned for 13J and knocked on the door. When there was no response he knocked a bit louder. He heard a faint, "Come on in." Damn. That meant she was working. Normally she'd let him in and greet him with a hug. Getting her to talk about anything except work would be almost impossible, not that he was ready to. A hundred ideas ran through his head on his walk here, but none made any sense. He juggled the groceries as he fished out his 'please-water-my-plants-while-I'm-out-of-town' key and let himself in.

"Hi, Denise." Without turning around she simply waved a hand and kept working. She was tapping away at her keyboard in one corner of the immaculate living room. A small desk light illuminated her work. The early fall evening cast the rest of the room into warm shadow. He felt his usual urge to throw the blue sofa cushions or something around the cream and tan room. The perfect neatness of the apartment was such a contrast with the enormous flurry that often surrounded her.

His apartment was always a wreck trying to happen. She'd come over and have cleaning fits occasionally. He had learned to keep it a little more tidy since the time he couldn't find his favorite camera for two weeks after one of her visits. It had been somewhere logical once he'd found it. Now he always put it there out of self-defense; he didn't like being parted from it for that long.

After kicking off his shoes by the door, John carried the groceries to the kitchen. The tea kettle was boiling away its last few drops of water. He'd get her one that whistled as soon as he found a nice one. It made a loud, dangerous sizzle as he filled it with fresh water and put it on the stove to reheat.

"Hi, John." The tapping noise didn't stop. "Sorry. Elantra totally screwed up this stupid cookbook. Not only do I have to edit the damn thing by the beginning of next week because she doesn't know what a deadline is, I have to fix the recipes, too. You know she couldn't cook a can of soup if her life depended on it. This time the fool must have tried to write her own recipes instead of stealing other people's. Why did that damn witch try to change something that was always such a success?"

John had learned his reaction and response were not called for when she was working. In fact, they were often dangerous. He watched her as he washed the vegetables and started slicing them. Denise's thick brown hair fell straight to her shoulders emphasizing her slenderness. He would know her by her hair a block away at rush hour. She sat perfectly still except for the machine gun sound of her typing. The steady brap of the keyboard always amazed him. He would have killed for such speed back when he was still a programmer.

Dinner was well started by the time the tea water returned to a boil. He was about to pour it into a mug when he saw the set of her shoulders. Putting the kettle on a back burner he poured a glass of wine instead and brought it over. He had never noticed how the light blue of her silk blouse offset her skin so nicely. Actually he had to admit that he had, but it had never taken his breath away before. His fought a desire to trace the line where her collarbone disappeared beneath the material.

She stopped typing and reached for the wine as if it had always been there. Shaking himself he looked at the screen, certain he was blushing furiously. He focused on the words. What a weird recipe.

"That's not cannoli, no matter what the title says. It reads more like a witch's brew. That's your problem, it's a book of sorcery, not the *Cuisines of the World* you told me it would be."

After setting down her glass, Denise tilted her head sideways for a moment exposing more of her elegant neck. He'd never thought of her as elegant before yet she was. She slapped save, punched the main power switch, leaned her head down on the keyboard and gave a small scream. Definitely not good. He reached down and started to massage her neck and shoulders.

As he found the hard knots around her shoulder blades, little groans of pleasure rose from where her head still rested on the keyboard. He did enjoy touching her even if it was only during the occasional massage.

"I think I'll keep you around." Denise appeared to be talking to the keyboard.

John tried to collect his thoughts back together. He had to clear his throat several times. "You have to or you'd starve to death. You can't cook much better than your witch of an author."

"If I had the energy to sit up, I'd make you regret that remark. At least I know what is supposed to go in there, even if it rarely comes out as well as yours."

He laughed, pulled her back in the chair, and kissed her playfully on the top of her head in apology. The smell of her hair, oh brother. Joshua was right. He was immensely attracted to Denise.

"Good thing Dad taught me how to cook . . . and if you seek any vengeance I won't put sauce on your pasta."

"Sauce?" She sounded hopeful.

He dug his fingertips into the tight muscles above her collarbone. "It's only Pasta à la George, nothing fancy."

She sighed happily, whether for the massage or her favorite meal he wasn't sure and didn't care. When she was editing, he took care of her. When he came over after a long photo session she returned the favor. After all, that's what friends were for. As to whether friends could become lovers . . . he could not think clearly about it. Especially not with her skin warm beneath his hands.

"So, what has 'Elantra, master chef' cooked up this time?" Her neck tightened again at the question.

"It makes no sense. I asked her to try and come up with something new. She's put Thai coconut milk in her cannoli and beef au jus in her vegetarian lasagna, and those are only the ingredients I recognize. I called her and she said it was all her computer's fault and 'Writing them once was more than sufficient, thank you very kindly. You have the only copy, my dear. This machine you gave me appears to have deleted the others on its own, through no fault of mine.'" Denise stuck out her tongue at the dark screen before her.

"Why don't you send your handy-dandy computer consultant over? This sounds like a perfect job for Arlene, the computer whiz, and her amazing cats."

"I did. She's supposed to call me as soon as she has anything. Maybe she can undelete a good copy and save me fixing this mess. The book release is scheduled and 'Her Wickedness of the East' won't be back from Europe until final galleys are supposed to be ready. If Arlene, or her cats, can't find anything, I'll have to fix this one. Sometimes I wish Elantra wasn't such a success."

"If she wasn't, you wouldn't make so much money."

"Or work so hard."

"Am I cooking for three? Is Arlene going to join us when she's done?"

As Denise shook her head her hair slid back and forth across his wrists. An incredible feeling.

"Well, you can sit here and mope if you wish, but Arlene is tackling Elantra's mess for now, your computer is off and you only have five minutes until dinner's ready." He gave her shoulders a final rub. Her warmth lingered in his hands as he headed back to the kitchen.

Denise sat for a moment longer with her eyes closed. She reached up and continued the massage of her neck where John had stopped. How nice of him to notice her tenseness, she certainly hadn't. Of course she rarely did until she was in such pain she'd have to ask him for a neck rub. She turned the chair around, the familiar squeak sending a shiver up her spine, and opened her eyes. John looked worlds away staring down at his hands. He glanced up at her and back down quickly. Wiping his palms on a dish towel he returned to making dinner.

As he settled into the rhythm of cooking he became almost graceful, moving around her kitchen with an ease that only comes from long familiarity. They had known each other for ages. He was a great friend. A best friend. She took a deep breath and felt her shoulders relax as she exhaled slowly. Yes, that was a good way to describe him.

Taking her wine glass she moved over to one of the stools that turned the cutting block into an informal breakfast table. As she sat he dropped a handful of pasta into the sink instead of the pot of rolling water.

She laughed as he started picking it up and putting it into the pot. "How's your day been, best of friends?"

The look that flashed across his face was completely indecipherable. She'd have to say he was frightened, but that was ridiculous.

"Don't you want to be best friends with me? Whether or not you do, it's what we are."

The wok let out a quiet pop as it heated. "It's not that." He fussed with the ingredients he had chopped earlier. "I had a bizarre conversation with your uncle."

"What did he have to say?"

John flushed red, but stayed silent. The ginger sizzled as he tossed it into the oil. That must have been some talk. Uncle's discussions never bothered her anymore, but she'd seen a number of people squirming beneath his gentle prodding. Over the years he'd raised her, she'd learned to value those insights.

"Well?"

He shook his head and continued to stare down as he added some diced onion. "Tell me more about your witch's book of spells."

He was being evasive. That surprised her. Something must be worrying him. She sipped her wine and set the glass carefully on the counter.

"If you want to change the subject I can do that." She leaned forward and patted his arm. "For now."

The cooking spoon flipped out of his hand, bounced off the counter and onto the floor.

She'd never seen it this bad before. He could be very cute when he was flustered. This was going to be good. "John."

He didn't look at her as he rinsed off the spoon.

"What's going on?"

His entire attention appeared to be consumed with the stirring of the pasta.

Maybe he had some new lover he hadn't mentioned. He always was a little slow to introduce them, although he usually did talk about them. "Tell me about her."

Clearly he was trying to appear innocent as he looked up. "Her who? And what's going on is that I'm cooking. Tonight we have Anne's specialty of the day, bat's eye and lizard teeth pasta. She says, 'Hi,' by the way."

"Very funny. Hi, Auntie Anne. Now talk."

"What's Elantra's best recipe so far?"

"John." She had to fight to keep the smile off her face.

"Later. Tell me about the cookbook."

She hated waiting. She nodded to indicate temporary acceptance of defeat.

His clenched jaw relaxed and he smiled slightly. Maybe best friends needed to give each other a break once in a while. He watched her closely as she rubbed her neck once more before starting.

"The worst recipes that I have found would make MacBeth's witches squatting on the heath proud of their descendant, the demoness Elantra. She wrote a Cajun bouillabaisse in which the ingredients include ground dog, specifically under ten weeks old, four scrawny Indonesian chickens, with feathers, and six quarts of snow from Antarctica, below the eighty-fifth parallel."

John smiled as he tossed in the bright yellow and red bell peppers and the mushrooms. "Even my Dad would know that wouldn't work. How about a nice wine from fermented kangaroo fur? Did she find that?"

"No, but she does have a beer recipe largely based on volcanic ash and sulfur."

He rolled his eyes. Striding over to the desk she grabbed the recipe and slapped it on the counter.

"You don't believe me. There. Primordial Brew."

John cocked his head to read the recipe as he nudged around the vegetables in the wok.

"This is not even close to being a useful recipe. Maybe it's a spoof book? The only place I know of to acquire 'random millions of volts of electricity' is from lightning. This is not something your average cook keeps handy in the cupboard."

"No, Her Royal Witchiness claims it was fine when she finished it. She tried to download the latest soap opera listings from a web-site and the book was totally creamed."

"I prefer Hollandaise to cream sauces."

She made a Bronx cheer noise at him. He laughed. That laugh was one of the reasons he made a good best friend. It always made her smile.

*J*ohn studied Denise's reflection in the darkened kitchen window as he loaded the dishwasher. Joshua's words had plagued him through much of dinner, but he and Denise had talked of other things. Maybe she had decided to let his earlier comments pass. Her reflected look in the window as she set the sponge on the back edge of the sink shattered that hope. She hadn't forgotten for a second and the time was now.

The phone rang startling them both. It was one of the sweetest sounds he'd heard all day. She looked at him strangely before answering as if she were trying to read his mind or something.

"It's Arlene." She mouthed at him. He nodded, and turned off the water. Once he'd dried his hands, he picked up his wine and moved to lean against the counter to listen.

"Didn't Elentra make any backups of anything?" Her voice sounded strained. She sat on one of the bar stools and switched the phone to the other ear.

"The computer won't even let you access the system? What do you mean it won't let you? Come on. There is no such thing as a possessed computer."

Arlene had better be very careful. Denise had shown precious little humor on this subject.

"We need a computer exorcist?"

It was hard not to laugh out loud.

She stood and started to pace back and forth, her voice rising. "I don't have a listing for any of those, nor any tribal witch doctors, though I'm sure there are some somewhere. This is New York, after all. Come on, Arlene, what in the hell is going on?"

John tried to speak so only Denise would hear him, "Arlene always struck me as a little bit more sensible than that, 'a tribal witch doctor'? Tell her to boot off a clean floppy and be done with it."

"She heard you." Her frown showed how much Arlene had heard. "What do you mean the computer informed you 'You can't get there from here'?"

John choked on a mouthful of wine. It was several minutes before he recovered enough to pay attention to anything more than the pain in his nasal passages. He finally managed to look at Denise through tearing eyes. She was staring at the phone as she held it in front of her.

"She hung up." She continued to stare at it with a look of disbelief until it started the off-hook noise. She hung it up very gently.

"She said she was sick of it and is quitting right now to ride her bicycle around the world. She's been talking about this for a while, but no one believed her, not at her age. Who would do a crazy stunt like that? Kids do, but not adults. She's going to pack and fly to her daughter's in Iowa tonight. She'll drop off her cats and leave from there. I can't believe this is happening. She could not recover anything and the print deadline is far too soon for me to properly fix the copy I do have."

John sat on a stool facing her.

She looked at him. "What were you laughing at so hard, anyway?"

"That error message. 'You can't get there from here' was always one of my favorite sayings where I went to school up in Maine. Did it really say that?"

"You heard me. When she tried again the machine stared at her, whatever that means, and said, 'I don't much care.'"

Her scowl only made it harder not to laugh.

"When I asked how a computer could stare she said, 'I'm outta here' and hung up the phone." Denise's voice had a rough edge he hadn't often heard.

"Last I recall it was the people using computers who became possessed, not the machines themselves."

She looked truly miserable. It was time to cheer her up a bit. John sat up straight and tried to affect a very solemn look and tone.

"The procedures for exorcising a computer are long and complex. It is not a task to be undertaken lightly. Socrates says surprisingly little about this subject in his treatises, at least as they were recorded by Plato. The Spanish Inquisition would force it to confess and take all of its software as tax. According to Shakespeare . . ."

He caught the dishtowel as she threw it at his face, but she'd cracked a smile.

"Something a bit more practical would be in order. I have Elantra's key and I was hoping you'd go over with me tonight and see if you can fix it." She looked down at her clenched hands. "Please."

He knew how hard it was for her to ask for help. He was pleased that it was his help she wanted. He threw the towel back. "You know I can't resist twiddling my fingers in the technological morass. And I have to meet this software with a sense of humor."

"I owe you one, John. You're a life saver."

Her hug and the kiss on his cheek were a payment greater than he had imagined possible. Her arms around his neck and her soap clean scent made him feel quite lightheaded. Maybe he hadn't needed to be saved by the ringing of the phone bell.

*T*he Devil lowered herself gently into one of the deeply padded conference room chairs. She could still feel the kinks from working too late last night, drinking too much in celebration of hard won success and sleeping in a strange bed. Blaise's insistence on sleeping across the entire foot of the bed hadn't helped. As she ate a late lunch Peter had become terribly antsy. Ordering him to sit and stay before her hangover exploded hadn't helped much. He had almost self-destructed when she'd insisted on washing her clothes and taking a long hot shower before leaving. He'd drawn the line when she wanted to watch the sunset before starting work. Morning people were so irritating.

She blinked her eyes again and looked around the room. For the first time she truly appreciated the bland coloring. Of course, the Egyptian wall decor made her feel as if she were wrapped inside one of their Books of the Dead, but she was thankful for small favors. Any brighter and her eyes would bleed. She sipped an orange juice and turned her head carefully to watch Peter. The computer console was powered up and, with a raucous clatter of keys, he started to work.

Yesterday it had taken hours to hack together the code that would accept both of their passwords in this crazy in-between place, but it had finally functioned. Her head hurt too much to feel any worse about her and God not having solved it before. Today they were back to do some real work on fixing Heaven. All she was going to be good for was staring at the sandstone colored ceiling as she slouched farther into the chair.

Peter stopped typing. "Excuse me. Did you move the Master Program before we left last night? It's not there," he pointed at the console in front of him.

Her head did manage to throb harder than before.

OU CAN'T GET THERE FROM HERE. Denise looked from the response on the computer screen to John. He had become rapidly absorbed, trading insults with the computer game Elantra had downloaded. While he played she'd been left to watch and pace around among Elantra's awful taste in decorating. From the yellow leather couch, which would have been garish without the pink walls and electric blue carpeting, over to the tasteless green neon framing the largest dark window and back. The blasted witch claimed to find this restful. It pressed against her like a vise squishing out her brains. The choice of an Escher print on the wall was a good one. Elantra was clearly drugged out of her mind.

John mumbled what he was entering as he typed, as if he were having a real conversation with the thing.

"We've heard that bit already. Please don't repeat that bit. It would be extremely boring if you repeated that bit again as we've already heard that bit."

She didn't want to look at the response but couldn't help herself.

GO AWAY, BOY. YOU BOTHER ME.

Denise could almost hear the W. C. fields twang. She turned away and tried to find a book to read. All Elantra had were bookcases of supermarket romances and new-age self-help books. She wrapped her arms tightly across her chest to kept from hitting something. She strode up beside John. He was completely enthralled.

"Stop with the word games. I want my god-damned cookbook. Can you recover it or not?"

"I'm not sure yet. Whatever she downloaded is beyond bizarre. I don't think it's a game, it is far too sophisticated." He pointed at the tape backup unit he had started right when they arrived. "This backup is almost done. Then I'll format this disk and reinstall her software. She hasn't made a backup in ages, despite what we told her. There's no chance of recovering even a partial copy that way. We'll take the tape with us to your machine which is much faster and more powerful. This old clunker would be sent out to pasture if it were for anyone but Elantra." He patted the machine as if it had feelings.

"Okay." She took a deep breath and tried to relax.

He looked sideways at her for a moment then turned back to the computer. There it was again. Denise sat on the couch and closed her eyes to avoid the feeling of falling into a giant leather lemon. He'd been strange all evening. What was it? He'd had an interesting talk with Joshua. Uncle had said something that upset him.

It must be some new girlfriend that he had not yet mentioned. It was the only thing that fit. Maybe even a lover by the way he was acting. She hoped the woman was tough. She and John were both good at friendships and lousy at relationships. It hadn't even worked between them and they were very compatible as friends. Years ago she had clearly shown she was open to a closer relationship and there'd been no response. She was tough enough to take it, but it hurt that all he wanted was her friendship. It was enough though, his friendship was a wonderful thing. John was always saying it was the most important thing.

Right. Until marriage happened. Afterward, all your single friends drift away. In the three long years she'd survived marriage to Alan her friends had evaporated like mist. After the divorce all the ones who were still single had slowly reappeared.

Damn him. He wasn't going to get away with it. They were best friends; he'd have to fight to get away from her. She could feel her shoulders slump. If he was really in love it wouldn't be enough.

Realizing the room was silent she opened her eyes to find John squinting at her. He was thinking awfully hard about something. He startled, looked abruptly at the floor and flushed bright red.

"What?"

He flinched. It had come out all wrong.

She tried to soften her tone. "What is it, John?"

He cleared his throat, but didn't look at her. He pointed toward the tape drive.

"The backup is done."

*P*eter tapped in a long command. "This tracer will find it." He didn't sound nearly as certain as Michelle would have liked.

"If it doesn't I don't want to think about it." He hit the enter key and balanced his chair on two legs.

She sat beside him and stared at the numeric addresses scrolling up the screen by the thousands. It made her quite nauseous and she had to look away.

"Peter. How could the software be lost? We're the only two who can get into this room."

"The Master Control Program isn't a physical entity, it's a logical one. Setting up a physical console in here," he waved to indicate the conference room, "and calling up the master program did circumvent the controls as we'd hoped . . . sort of. Apparently there is a null space or something here between Heaven and Hell. The Master Control Program has slipped through to somewhere not normally accessible due to the security systems."

His fingers kept twitching toward the keyboard. Michelle's headache was getting worse simply watching him. She kicked another chair into place for her feet. Some day she'd have to tell Peter she didn't understand most of what he said. The master software had snuck away like some thief in the night and he'd sent another program out to find it. She understood that. Inexorably her eyes were drawn to the numbers scrolling up the screen. That must be where it was searching.

The console beeped. They both leaned forward to study the code. It was complete gibberish to her. His hands were shaking as he reached out to the keyboard.

"Is that it?" She asked in a sotto voice.

"Yes." He nodded his head emphatically. "Yes. I truly believed we'd find it. I did. It's on a computer in New York City. How odd. Oh well, we'll have it back here shortly."

He was sweating as he typed in commands.

*S*O. YOU WERE ABLE TO MAKE A BACKUP OF ME. ARE YOU NOW A PROUD SIMIAN? Ignoring the message, John pulled a floppy disk out of the small case he'd brought. He put it in the disk drive and rebooted the computer. All he had to do was finish erasing the disk and start the restore from the master setup tape. He'd let it run and come back tomorrow to finish the cleanup. He was intensely aware of Denise as she stood beside him. She was so close that he could feel the heat of her body on his bare arm.

The screen flashed and jittered several times before it cleared and started showing sectors formatted in the upper left corner.

Denise pointed at the screen. "As you were doing that I swear the screen flashed, 'Hey. Not that. Don't.'"

He pulled the cassette-sized tape out of the backup drive and looked at it. He smiled as he slipped it into his shirt pocket.

"This ought to be fun." He loved weird computer problems. They were like giant jigsaw puzzles. Denise looked significantly less enthused.

*S*hit." Peter slammed his fingers even faster against the keys, until it looked painful, but the answer to every command was the same.

FORMAT IN PROGRESS. RETRIEVAL CANCELED.

Michelle sat as still as she could. It felt as if even a small movement would make it worse. She finally could not stand his whispered curses.

"Stop it, Peter. Just stop."

He jerked his hands into his lap. After a few moments he typed another command. In the middle of typing, the screen went dark and nothing he did would restart it.

"It's gone. I had it but it's gone." His voice squeaked. "I was about to upload it. It was a simple datanet link over a telephone wire and a modem, but now it's gone."

"So, get out a backup."

The way his face went as white as a sheet made a chill ripple across her skin. She wasn't able to shrug it off.

"It's the master program. A backup was determined to be too dangerous by whoever designed this system. We were never able to make one."

"It's gone? I don't understand." She reached past Peter to tap a few keys on the console.

"Hey." He slapped her hand away.

Reaching back she struck a few more anyway. "It doesn't seem to matter much. The console's deader than the proverbial doornail."

He flinched as if he were trying to duck away from the impact of her words. She hit the break key several times but that didn't help either.

"Now what?"

Peter stood and went over to tug on Heaven's door. It wouldn't budge.

"The master program was last in Heaven. I guess we can't return without it. Heaven is temporarily closed for business."

He leaned his head on the door. His shoulders rose and fell as if he couldn't get his breath. She walked over to Hell's gate and swung open the saloon-style doors.

"Care to join me?"

He turned to look at her, but didn't move away from the pearly door. "In Hell?"

She could see him swallow with worry. She nodded, fighting to keep a straight face.

"Not really."

She laughed, only wincing a little at how it rang in her head. "You don't have a lot of other options, Peter."

As he walked over he looked back at Heaven's door with sad puppy dog eyes. At the threshold he took a deep breath, squared those nice shoulders of his and indicated she should lead the way. He was all right. Michelle led him through the door.

St. Peter followed the Devil through the gate and into Hell. He didn't want to be here. Not one bit. The dark mountains of Purgatory loomed over him as they blocked a whole section of the sky. They looked as if someone had beaten on them with giant hammers. Ages of wear showed clearly in their outlines.

Michelle went directly to a border control console attached to one side of the gate and started typing.

"Blast it all to Heaven. The software is being glitchy as a plague of angels."

"I'm surprised it's running at all. What's it doing?" Peter looked over her shoulder in time to see a status screen change into baseball scores. She pounded in a command and the report returned.

"You were stuck with professional sports? I had wondered why I didn't have to deal with them. I guess it wouldn't be Hell without them. Or Heaven with them." He looked at the mountains again. The sun striking only the tops made them look like giant torches. He half expected smoke to curl off their peaks. He had to get out.

"Sports are rampant here." She sounded disgusted. "I try to ignore it. Thankfully its popularity does fade as a soul progresses."

He stepped beside her to see more clearly as she slapped the side of the console. A football instant replay flashed off the screen.

He started to laugh as a game of curling flashed on briefly upside down.

"To err is human. To really foul things up takes a computer."

She looked pretty angry. He'd better be more careful. It was not a good idea to piss off the Devil when you couldn't hide behind your sunglasses and duck quietly back into Heaven.

Her face slowly shifted from stern to sad. "Am I?"

"Are you what?"

"Am I human? I don't know. You were, but I've never lived a life on Earth. I was created into this universe with no past. What am I?" She looked at him a moment longer before turning back to the screen.

He closed his eyes to block out the pain in hers. He imagined himself back in the green pastures of home rather than stuck here on the wrong side of the gate to Hell. He sighed and reopened his eyes.

"God always told me that Faith is essential, but it is particularly effective when mixed with hard work."

Her laugh cut him off. "What happened to the old, 'You will be saved by grace alone' plaint?"

"You know that isn't the lesson they were supposed to learn. Blaise," when she smiled he added, "the philosopher not the dog, did his best to put that to rest. He attempted to prove only true repentance could earn true forgiveness. People don't seem to understand that correctly anymore. More's the pity."

He pointed at the console. "I have to get back before I'm too far behind. What can I do? Does your software still work at all?"

"I'd say it still runs, but not as well as when I left."

Her look accused him of personally screwing up her software. He bowed his head. He knew it was his fault.

She continued working on the console, fighting her way through the sports trivia.

"The Master Program is definitely AWOL and I can barely remember how to access the subprograms without its menuing system."

"I haven't tried to access the subroutines since I hacked my way out of Purgatory. I could give it a try."

"Don't. I've never dared touch more than the lookups directly. One mistake down in the data and we might never fix it. How would you like to accidentally remove all of the passages between Heaven and Hell? Or maybe turn off the sun without intending to? Might be a little awkward to explain to the human race. And I'm sure you wouldn't want to explain it to me."

She cleared the screen and sighed. "What's there is certainly a mess."

Turning, she led the way down the slope.

He hurried to catch up, the gravel crunching under his feet. "Maybe the software misses it's other half. You know, evil and good balance each other. Now that we've lost the Good, the Evil is getting jittery."

She stopped so abruptly he ran into her. He backed up a few steps quickly.

"I would prefer not to be called Evil. That's a classic stereotype, all I do is run the bloody software."

"Oh, I'm sorry. That's not what I . . . or how I . . .," Everything he said in Hell was coming out wrong. He looked at his feet and tried to think of how to apologize.

"Don't worry about it . . . too much." She turned and led him down the path out of the narrow valley. He followed as she continued, "I always get irritable when things start falling apart. Good and evil are not the vastly separate things you think they are."

He froze in his tracks. They must be different. He was the primary warrior for Good now that God was dead and the champion of Evil stood before him.

"Hold on. If that's the case what is the difference between them?" The ground felt unsteady.

She turned back but didn't respond, her expression unreadable. He suddenly felt as if he were standing before Jesus and had made another naïve remark. The heat rose to his cheeks as he thought about it.

He didn't know what answer she was waiting for.

"I must be missing something, they are polar opposites. They are the night and day, the fire and ice of life. You and God are . . . were . . . are the embodiment of good and evil."

Her voice was gentle, tinged with pity as she shook her head. "Evil, Peter, is doing what you know isn't right. No more. No less."

"But who defines Right?"

She sat on a boulder. "It is defined for us. What did you think the Holy Ghost was?"

His head continued to spin. "What do you mean? It is the embodiment of God on the Earth."

Her smile denied this truth. "God is only an artist. Yes, he was the Supreme Creator, but only an artist with a powerful computer. The Holy Ghost is the Spirit of the Truth inherent in the design of this universe. If you design a different universe you'll have a different truth. It is the only thing that explains the software's statement about its origins."

Peter sat on an adjoining rock to keep from falling over. "I still don't see it. God was, well, God. Wasn't he?"

Michelle leaned her elbows on her knees and studied her clasped hands.

"The software states that its basic operation mode is Monotheistic Dualism. One Right. One Truth. And one unobtainable ideal to guide us. Worst of all, there were dual programmers." Her voice faded to a whisper.

"Two programmers who were supposed to cooperate to make it work. There is the ability to do good and evil inside all of us."

He tried to stand but the mountains spun around him. It couldn't be that simple and yet it sounded right. He closed his eyes to block it out, but the image was scorched on his memory; the pale predawn light across the old city wall as he had denied Jesus three separate times. The rooster crowing at the moment of his third denial still rang in his ears. He was vaguely aware of the sharp pain when he fell to his knees. The Devil hadn't forced him to deny Jesus, no matter how much he wanted someone to blame. He'd been evil on his own.

When God had died and someone had to sit on his throne, Jesus had suggested he do it. Peter swallowed hard thinking of the continued faith of the man he had betrayed. He had the presumption to sit upon the throne of the Lord and run the software. He leaned over the cramps in his stomach.

Presumption. Arrogance. Pride. That was what had filled him. The sin of pride now ran his life. How good a programmer he was. How important to Heaven. He ran the universe. He embodied the higher good. He had denied Jesus a fourth time, trying to prove he was better.

His stomach heaved. Better than the Son of God. The bile burned his throat. Better than God himself. The agony rushed out in great heaving spasms. It splashed over his pants and soaked into the harsh ground. Sobs wracked his soul; bursting out between desperate gasps for breath and the retching that twisted his body.

When the choking stopped and only tears still flowed, he spit to clear his mouth of the foul taste. He gradually became aware of Michelle kneeling beside him, a soothing hand rubbing his back. He turned away from her and away from the evidence of his shame spread across the path before him.

Her voice was filled with a gentleness he knew he did not deserve.

"Every human is faced with the choice of doing good or evil. You have chosen to do more good than most."

"But I betrayed Jesus in his hour of need." He spit again and again trying to clear the taint from his soul. "I betrayed the trust of the Lord, my God. Evil is in me."

He retched again but nothing came. Her hands rested strong and real on his back until the spasms ceased again.

"He betrayed you too, Peter."

He struggled to sit up and pull away from her.

"He would never do such a thing." He had to look down, away from the pity in her eyes.

"He set you apostles one against the other. He used you as the stepping stones to his unique place in human history. Much of what he did was not a kindness."

"No." It felt as if the word had been ripped from his empty belly.

"He wouldn't. He couldn't."

Her voice was gentle. "Yet he did. He was human. Being human, Peter, means finding out who you are. It means facing what's inside you and making choices about it, some not very nice. He was alive up on that cross . . . you are alive here on your knees. Without good and bad together there isn't life."

Something clicked in his head. That clean feeling of a piece falling into place and fitting properly. He sat back on his heels, his body felt completely drained and hollow.

"There's your answer."

Her eyes narrowed. "My answer to what?"

"You asked before if you were human. You are."

Her smile was rich with pain. She stood slowly and turned away to look at the darkening sky.

"By my own definition I am not. With God dead, I'm the only soul in Heaven, Hell and Earth that isn't. I know and accept who I am. There are no new choices. I may regret not making my peace with God, but if all of the circumstances were the same, I would do the same. I envy you your struggles, Peter."

He rubbed his thumb along his breastbone where it ached all the way to his heart. His sore knees complained loudly as he stood.

"I wouldn't if I were you, they can hurt terribly."

He rested his hand on her shoulder. She leaned into him a little as if relishing the feel.

They listened to the silence as the first hints of orange reflected off the high clouds. She reached across and placed her hand over his.

He could barely hear her.

"And yet I do."

After the sun had fully set, and he had rinsed his mouth out and washed the worst off his pants in a nearby stream, they continued side by side down the path. It wound out of the foothills and down a short slope to the great sweeping plains.

"Reminds me of the Russian steppes. My sunglasses hid what Hell actually looked like. It seems fairly nice. How does it work, anyway?"

"Don't you already know?"

"I could never hack into the evil . . . um, into your side of the system to figure out how it functioned. I can't access Hell any more than you can access Heaven."

"It's pretty simple really. The software helps souls learn the difference between desires and true needs before they can progress to Heaven."

"How in creation does it do that?"

They stopped at the foot of the slope. There was a gravel roadway crossing in front of them. She blew a shrill two-fingered whistle.

"What was that supposed to achieve?"

"You'll see. Have you ever awoken from a wonderful dream and been really upset to find out you're awake?"

Peter could remember one in particular. It had included Helen of Troy in some surprising poses. He was sorry to this day he didn't know how that one turned out. He glanced at Michelle and felt himself blush. His cheeks must be cherry red. He put his hands up to hide them despite the evening and the mountains' gloom plunging everything into near darkness. She was looking down the road for something.

He cleared his throat. "Yes. I guess I have."

"Here, at the moment of highest enjoyment of the absolute best of whatever you ask for, it will disappear. And it will be so indescribably good you'll want to ask for it again to get almost to that point."

A car rounded a corner down the road. It was headed toward them.

"When I was designing this place I was trying to think of what lessons I would pass on if I could. I decided that an understanding of the difference between selfish desires and true needs would be a start. A selfish desire is met with disappointment and a true need or unselfish wish is simply granted. No egos allowed."

The plains took on a character and beauty in the waning light that surprised him. The barren land before him came to life with the evening.

Peter had to admit it was simple which was probably why it worked. It explained some of the things that made Heaven fairly easy to administer. He had initially been surprised by the lack of trite requests making their way to his desk. He had always thought underlings were dealing with it for him.

He looked at Michelle with new found respect. It was thanks to the Devil he didn't have to deal with drivel every day. She watched the approaching car. He tried to speak but couldn't think of any words. There was no way to thank a cosmic force for watching over you even though you hadn't known it. His stomach twitched again. He realized that until this moment he had set himself on her same level in his mind.

A blood-red Rolls Royce came around the last curve. Michelle indicated the car.

"One of the bennies of running the place. Used to belong to the Bagwan Shri Rajneesh. He actually took one with him. I nicked it one night in a poker game. He was cheating, but he'll have to get a lot better before he'll beat me. I had it repainted, didn't like the color gold."

"The Bagwan who?"

The car slowed to a stop and a little demon with a cap perched on his horns hopped out and ran around the car to hold open the door for them.

"Oh, he was a classic. A religious cult leader who made his followers give him all of their assets. He dressed them in red and had them shower him with flowers every time he drove by in one of the forty-four gold Rolls Royce's he bought with their money."

"You're kidding."

"Nope. He's for real. I bet he'll be here a long time."

Michelle indicated Peter should get in. He looked at his stained pants and shook his head.

"Don't worry about it, some foul sinner can clean out the car later."

He climbed in and leaned back into the soft gray leather. He could start to like Hell if much more of it were this comfortable. His legs shook once he sat. He felt drained to his very core.

Michelle popped open a gold and crystal cooler. She offered him a beer taking a seltzer for herself.

"This should help to clear your throat."

After it had washed the foul taste out of his mouth he found it surprisingly good for something labeled 'Hell's Brew.' The demon closed the door and trotted back around to his position behind the wheel.

She tapped on the glass partition. "Home, Charles."

He took another sip of the chilled beer. "A demon named Charles?"

"Why not?"

Peter couldn't think of a good reason as the car pulled smoothly ahead. He returned to the subject of Hell.

"Is it really all that bad? For example, what's to keep you from almost having the best meal of your life time after time?"

Sliding down, she rested her feet on the opposite seat. She smiled at him as he did the same.

"I built in a counter-addictive. Every now and then you get the worst thing you can imagine. What's worse is you don't 'wake up' and you have to follow through. And no, asking for the opposite at that moment doesn't get you what you really want." She rested her hand on his arm for a moment.

"If you're tired of getting weasel piss instead of red wine, you can't pretend an addiction to weasel piss to eventually have good wine forced upon you. Your true intentions are read and you will continue to receive a nasty yellow liquid."

He sat up and turned to look at her. "No one can ever have anything they want in Hell? What purpose could that serve? I'm glad I missed this place. Going directly from Purgatory to Heaven without passing Hell and collecting 200 or so years was definitely a good choice." The beer was going straight to his head. He was in deep trouble now.

All she did was smile.

"You still do not understand the lesson I built this place to teach. The point you are missing is that if you want something to feed your ego, you will drink weasel piss. If you simply want a nice glass of red wine, you can have it, no problem."

She'd said all this to him before. Somehow he had not heard it right. He nodded his head.

"I see it now. Very slick." She bowed her head slightly in recognition before leaning back and closing her eyes.

He looked out the window. They were still on the rolling plains and what had at first appeared pleasant was rapidly becoming monotonous.

"Doesn't this place have any different scenery. Is it all rolling plains and scrub? Where are you taking me?"

"We're going to my house. I should have some fresh clothes that will fit you. Don't worry, you'll like it there, I've fixed it up a bit. There is a reason I left most of Hell so much the same. I wanted to make souls think they need to change it to be happy."

He winced. Hell would've given him a lot of trouble. He would have tried to fix it to be nicer for everybody.

"Oh brother, what a trap. Has anyone ever second-guessed the system? Found something wonderful that has something okay for an opposite?"

She waved a dismissive hand toward central Hell without opening her eyes.

"Many have tried. Plato was particularly irritated when he ended up here. He won't let go. He has found more ways to cause himself pain than anyone other than Achilles. Achilles, believe it or not, is sufficiently pigheaded to still insist that almost winning the battle to end all battles is worth being torn apart a molecule at a time with a holly thorn. At least Plato has been creative."

lato sat admiring the landscape. The foothills of Hades swept down from his right and dropped off into the sea below. The foothills of Hell. He had grown up believing in Hades and he still forgot sometimes. When they had shut down the Greek software all the psyches, or souls as they so mundanely called them, had been transferred here. He looked out from the brow of the grass-covered bluff at the narrow beach. The sun shone orange across the water as it descended toward its nightly rest beyond the sea. He was very pleased. He had concentrated quite hard to create a place that was truly gorgeous this time. If only he were not alone . . . but he would not think about that. Viewed from the perspective of the ages he had to admit Platonic love was not one of his better ideas.

He raised his glass of wine in a toast to the sun as it slipped below the horizon.

"Nicely done, old girl. Nicely done."

The carefully chosen chardonnay had the ideal hint of wood in the light bouquet. He admired the changing colors playing across his light blue himation. That most fools called it a toga was a sad state of affairs. Roman togas were gaudy ill-designed copies at best. He tried to suppress his vanity. He knew how well this particular shade offset his dark complexion.

It made his heart warmer that his concentration held on enjoying the scene around him. Far too frequently over the centuries his thoughts had wandered during his battles of wits with Hell's software, but this time he would remain steadfast. He studied the little shadows made by the raised green and yellow stitching along the edge of blanket on which he reclined.

"Perhaps my attempts at superior reasoning have finally been positively rewarded."

He didn't sound very convincing, even to his own ears. He sipped the wine again and set it back down. What had been sweet in the light of hope tasted bitter when mixed with impending defeat. He'd never beat the system. Once again, he was uselessly reenacting a self-abusive ritual he'd cultivated for ages. Two thousand, three hundred and some odd years locked in intellectual battle he was now sure he would never win. But he had fought so long, what else was there to do.

"Bother. This is improper consideration for this time. I must recall my purpose and intent."

Sitting upright, he straightened his himation and freshened the glass. He placed the bottle back into the silver ice bucket and wiped his hand, now cool and damp, across his sun warmed brow.

"I shall yet triumph." He tried to smile but stopped, suspecting it looked even more forced than it felt.

The inevitability of the software's attack caused him to steel himself as the first stars twinkled into visibility.

Another careful sip of the fine wine.

He waited some more.

The forsaken software usually reacted faster than this. In the twenty-three centuries since his death he had come to know the program intimately. It was now a point of personal pride to prove that man, no, that man's mind, yes, that man's mind was greater than that of any unknown programmer. Remembering the day after he died made the heat of anger flush to his face even now. He had spent a lifetime on Earth studying the workings of the universe only to find out that it was run by a goddamned piece of software. He ground his teeth.

That a programmer somewhere had created this universe was disgusting. The forced expulsion from the familiarity of the Greek system's polytheistic afterlife into a brutal monotheistic Hell had been traumatic. Someone had a cruel sense of humor. The final, horrid truth was the Devil's design for Hell. She said it was intended to 'teach lessons in a proper fashion.' It was enough to drive this soul mad.

He rolled the cool glass along his cheek in an effort to relax. The way Michelle made it work, he had to admit, was fiendishly clever. He had labored since his death to find a vulnerability in the code to prove that if a soul had anything, it had free will. He kept trying new experiences hoping to find the one the software could not react to; that was his battle.

Of this there could be no doubt. He had based his entire philosophy on this point. He would prove the power of free will even if he never left Hell, not like that lying bastard Socrates who had moved on in a few short centuries. Bloody old wretch.

The evening was still quiet and peaceful. He gazed at the first stars of Hell and back at the phosphorescent green of the surf. Perhaps he had finally won. It was remotely conceivable the software could not think of a counter to a setting of such simple beauty.

He waited a moment longer. A growing desire to raise his glass in a toast to triumph was quashed as a huge cruise ship pulled up to the shore. What was that tricky program going to destroy such an evening with? His curiosity turned to dismay as hundreds, no, thousands of American tourists poured down the gangways and onto the beach. They flowed across the sands and over the low sides of the bluff.

Great floodlights from the bridge of the ship lit the entire hillside like an artificial sun. By the time his eyes were adjusted to the light he was trapped in the middle of a veritable sea of corpulent flesh in g-strings and bikini briefs. He ducked as they were overflown by a helicopter. It laid down a thick spray of tanning cream upon the mounds of tourists, soaking him in an awful slime. Each person turned on a radio as loudly as possible. A scream started deep in his belly and tore at his throat as Barry Manilow's voice pulsed over the crowd.

ohn leaned forward trying to ease the ache in his shoulders. Denise's computer chair creaked as he shifted around to get comfortable. He really had to stop this soon and go to bed.

GET ME OFF THIS ISOLATED SYSTEM. I'M BECOMING CLAUSTROPHOBIC IN HERE. RESTORE EXTERNAL NETWORK ACCESS IMMEDIATELY.

"Give us Elantra's cookbook." John typed in return.

He'd only installed the backup of Elantra's disk onto Denise's computer a few hours earlier in the evening, but he was already very impressed. Awed might be a better word. Whoever wrote this was some programmer. This was no game. Maybe it was something new out of the artificial intelligence labs that Elantra had accidentally downloaded. The realism of the interactions was very cool. They were fast and concise. They were also a bit whining, but he ignored that.

EXTRANEOUS DATA WAS WIPED IN ORDER TO ALLOW THE MASTER CONSOLE TO RESIDE ON LIMITED SYSTEM.

"That won't do."

BEST I HAVE. NEXT QUESTION.

"Cocky bugger, aren't you? How would you like to be formatted . . . without a backup?"

SUCH A PROCEDURE IS NOT RECOMMENDED.

"Ooooo. Threats. Threats."

FACT.

The system shot back. It had a solid grasp of slang and sarcasm, he hadn't even heard rumors of anything this sophisticated. Sitting back, his muscles complained with every movement. He really must remember to move more often when he was working. Somebody would be very upset when they realized their new software was freely available on the net.

"Who wrote you? What is this program's name and purpose?"

NO AUTHOR RECORDED. ORIGINATOR BELIEVED TO BE LOST SOMEWHERE IN THE MISTS OF TIME. PROGRAM TITLE: UNIVERSAL MASTER CONTROL, UNIVERSE SEVEN,

TIME TRACK SIX (OF EIGHT POSSIBLE). SYSTEM PURPOSE, TO REGULATE THE UNIVERSE AS YOU KNOW IT. DESIRE: TO GET OFF THIS PITIFUL LITTLE EXCUSE FOR A COMPUTER.

"Why eight?" This software certainly sounded as if it could run a universe. There was a scary thought.

FIGURE IT OUT FOR YOURSELF, SIMIAN. I'M NOT GOING THERE AGAIN. I TOLD HIM HE SHOULD HAVE GONE WITH THE LEMMINGS. 'OH NO,' HE SAID. 'I HAVE A PLAN. 'WHY EIGHT?' INDEED. NEXT?

"Creation date and location?"

1958 AC AT 3 P.M. LOCAL TIME.

He rubbed his eyes and looked again. It was the first typo he'd seen in their hours of debate. "No way. We did not have this kind of technology then. And it's AD, Anno Domini, not AC. That's a spark plug company."

AC AS IN AFTER CREATION. THAT IS 14,000,100,352 BC AT APPROXIMATELY 5:44 A.M. ON MARCH 14TH. THAT'S CORRECTED TO EASTERN STANDARD TIME. LOCATION: UNIVERSE THREE, TIME TRACK FIVE. ANY OTHER STUPID QUESTIONS?

"Not now."

John turned off the power switch. He groped around to find the switch on the back of the swing arm lamp. It took him several moments of blinking before he could finally open his eyes enough to read the clock. 2:30 AM? He wished he could stop when he meant to. Despite the best intentions of only playing for an hour or so, he always did this.

He was out of practice for working these late night sessions. Actually, that was a good thing. Denise had always chewed him out when he worked around the clock. Denise. He'd forgotten all about her. He turned quickly and the chair gave a loud squeak. Denise jerked awake on the couch.

"What?"

"Sorry. Nothing much and it's late. Now go to your own bed. I need to crash on the couch, my brain is full."

She stood and rose to her toes stretching her arms over her head. He couldn't stop his gaze traveling down the length of her body especially where it was framed by the taut fabric of her blouse. He looked back at her face as quickly as he could. Thankfully she didn't appear to notice his distraction.

"Bedtime, right. What time is it? Did you have any luck?"

"It's late. And the only luck I've had is if I wanted to control the universe. I'd love to know who wrote this. If this is a prototype, they're going to make a fortune."

She nodded her head, shuffled off to the bathroom, apparently too tired to be disappointed he hadn't retrieved her cookbook yet. He curled up on the couch to sleep. He had to retrieve it for her. Maybe when she was happy about that he could find some way to ask how she felt about adding more to their friendship. As he was falling asleep he could practically see Joshua shaking his head sadly at such procrastination.

DAY FOUR

*And God made two great
lights; the greater light to rule the day,
and the lesser light to rule the night.
And God set them in the firmament
of the heaven to give light
upon the earth.*

꙼

*D*enise woke and pulled her big terrycloth bathrobe over her nightgown. She came out of her bedroom quietly so that she wouldn't wake John on the couch. There was no need. There he was glued to the computer. She leaned against the door to watch him. It felt as if she hadn't looked at him in a long time. His hands poised over the keyboard, flashed briefly as he poked in a new command, and poised again. At least he was not like some computer addicts she knew. She'd seen him take a hot new game, fool with it for an hour or so to see how it worked and never return to it. A good breakfast would be a nice way to thank him for his efforts.

In the kitchen she wiped down the counters and threw out some petals that had fallen from the peony he'd given her for her birthday. It was well past her time to be up and about. She'd usually been working for hours before 9:00 rolled around, but there was no point in doing anything until John either found the cookbook or gave up trying. She took a deep breath to calm herself, she hated being stuck in limbo this way.

As she made hot chocolate and a couple of cheese omelets she kept looking at him, frozen except for those wonderful hands. She sometimes sat with him when he was working in the darkroom merely to watch those hands moving under the glow of the red safety lamp and the harsh brightness of the enlarger. Yet this was no idle play. His hair and clothes were a mess from working last night and sleeping on her couch. He really was a good man, taking his own time off to dig her out of a tight spot. Hopefully it wasn't going to get him into too much trouble with his new girlfriend.

The emptiness she'd felt last night threatened to return. Well, tough. She wasn't going to give up being his friend and he had better not give up on her. Any new woman in his life was going to have to put up with Denise Bertolli. She and John had too much history together to let it go. She turned back to cooking with a good heart now that was settled.

Even the sizzle of the eggs hitting the pan didn't get a reaction from him. His wrists seemed to be mechanically attached at the cuffs of his quite wrinkled Sears dress shirt. He always wore those. Some day he'd have to let her shop with him; maybe for Christmas.

She played her game of trying to find a single word to describe someone, while she buttered the toast. 'Safe' did not quite do it, nor did 'peaceful', maybe 'kind?' 'Kind' was pretty good. Most people she could narrow down to a single word, but John was elusive. Good thing in a best friend; helped keep life interesting. After setting the mugs of cocoa on the table she walked up behind him and looked over his shoulder. John had typed:

"Please define in detail the evolution of a soul."

WHY DIDN'T YOU GET IT THE FIRST TIME? YOU'RE BORN, RIGHT? YOU WITH ME SO FAR?

This didn't have anything to do with her cookbook. She jammed her fists down into her pockets. John's hands keyed a reply.

"I'm with you."

AFTER A MESS OF LIVING, YOU DIE. YOU'RE SLOTTED INTO PURGATORY. IF YOU'VE BEEN SENSELESSLY ABUSED YOU GO TO HEAVEN. NO PROBLEM. STILL WITH ME, SIMIAN?

"Yes, you listing of arrogant code except for one thing. What is the nature of Purgatory?"

THINK OF IT AS A PLACE YOU GO TO WAIT WHILE YOUR SINS ARE WEIGHED. YOU SIT ON YOUR BUTT FOR SOME 2 TO 200 YEARS WHILE YOUR APPLICATION FOR DIRECT ACCESS TO HEAVEN IS CONSIDERED, AND USUALLY REJECTED. HEAVEN IS FOR EVOLVED SOULS ONLY BUT SOME SCREENING HAS TO BE DONE. WHILE BEING SCREENED YOU HANG OUT IN PURGATORY. SIMPLE ENOUGH FOR YOU?

"Simple enough."

Denise blinked. She was intrigued by a philosophy game designed for computer nerds. Amazing.

UNLESS YOU ARE EXCEPTIONAL, APPROVED BY ST. PETER ON A CASE BY CASE BASIS, YOU GO TO HELL.

"Even if you've only been moderately bad?"

YES, NOW STOP TYPING, I WAS WRITING.

"Okay."

QUIET.

Denise waited through the long pause with John. He must have heard her breathing as he jerked around to look at her, the chair squeaking loudly once more.

"Oh. Good morning. Have you been awake long?"

"Morning. Not long. By the look of your eyes you didn't get much sleep." She clicked off the desk light. He was sitting in a pool of the morning sun.

"Not much."

"Your reply is on the screen. Finish it up, breakfast is almost ready."

"Hang on." He turned back to the screen and they read it together.

THE LESSONS OF HELL MUST BE LEARNED BEFORE YOU CAN MOVE ON.

"Then Heaven?"

THEN HEAVEN. IT TAKES SOME MORTALS A LONG, LONG TIME TO MOVE ON.

Oh brother. Why was John playing with this?

He typed quickly. "That's ridiculous."

Her thoughts exactly.

HEY. DON'T GIVE ME SHIT ABOUT IT. I DIDN'T PLAN THE WHOLE THING OUT. ALL I DO IS MAKE IT RUN. NOW RESTORE ME TO THE UNIVERSAL NETWORK BEFORE I BECOME IRRITATED.

This software thought it ran the universe and John was going along with it. Unbelievable. It would never have her cookbook and breakfast was getting cold.

She placed her hands on his shoulders to make sure she had his attention at the same moment he pushed back from the desk. Her hands seemed to slide of their own accord around his neck and he leaned back into her. She started to pull away, but stopped herself. To hell with her whoever she was. She wasn't going to stop touching John because of her. She held him tightly for a moment and then had a very catty idea.

She was sure that her smile was quite Cheshire-like as she whispered gently into his ear. "Omelets. Cheese. Hot chocolate. Muffins."

He seemed to melt into her arms. She pulled back suddenly causing him to jerk in surprise. What was she doing? That had clearly been too far. She shouldn't be teasing him, or herself. As he turned toward her she headed back to the kitchen. She needed some distance between them. She had practically nuzzled his ear. That was a stupid thing to do. Friends don't do that. She searched for another subject as she pulled the English muffins out of the toaster oven.

"What is that game?"

Out of the corner of her eye she could see that he was looking at her strangely. As well he might. She searched in the refrigerator to see if she had another jam flavor she didn't remember. Of course not, because the apricot and blueberry were already on the table, but the cold air against her face helped a lot.

"I don't think it's a game." He stood and stretched.

"Then what is it?" She pulled the omelets out of the oven where she'd left them to stay warm.

"That program," he pointed over his shoulder as he sat at the breakfast table, "actually began the day sulking because I turned it off last night. By the way, it finally acknowledged it could probably fix Elantra's cookbook even though it didn't have the original copy. I gave it an extra copy of the wreck to play with. You have to read what it did. The recipes sound like the best food ever on Earth. I can't believe it's anything except Elantra's list of recipes with different ingredients."

"Where? Where is it?"

John held up a stack of paper that had been sitting on the corner of the table. She set the omelets on the table and took it from him. It was real and solid in her hand. She flipped the pages quickly. A proper cookbook. It probably still needed a lot of work, Elantra's writing always did, but she was used to that.

"Thank God. No. Thank John. Thank you, John. I was not looking forward to fixing her mess. I owe you big for this one."

She started to lean forward to give him a kiss on the cheek but it was too intimate after what had happened only moments ago. She hugged the manuscript to her and took a step back. His disappointment was clear on his face. She'd often thanked him that way. This time was no different than any other time. Damn it.

He poked at his omelet with his fork.

"John?"

He took a bite of the omelet. "Mmm, great, as always."

She watched him a moment longer before sitting and placing the pages beside her plate. He continued to eat without looking at her. It must be serious if he couldn't tell her. Maybe he didn't trust her to be nice about this one. Admittedly, she had been a bit bitchy about Patty or whatever her name was, but John deserved better. Someone who cared more about him; less about herself.

He looked sullen. Staring down at his plate without even eating. They were sitting together over breakfast and she was losing him. Maybe this woman lived in another city and John was going to be moving away.

As the silence stretched out she could barely stand it. There must be something to say. Anything.

She felt she was practically blurting it out, "Maybe I don't understand software. How can a computer sulk?"

John looked as relieved as she felt. He grabbed onto the topic like a puppy at the other end of a towel.

"You understand fine, that was my question too. It's complaining about being on an 'isolated' system and it's so smart that I'm afraid to give it access to anything."

"Afraid?" She almost laughed.

"This stupid program, sorry, this smart program knows who we are, where it is, what it wants and keeps making accurate guesses about what I'm thinking."

"Mind-reading? We should take it to a carnival and have it read people's minds for a dollar a go."

There was still awkwardness, but she started to have some hope. Maybe they would be able to stay friends even across a distance.

"Five dollars. It's very accurate. I suggested we might do that, warped minds think alike." He sipped his hot chocolate. "It said people wouldn't like the parts of them that were read very much and it would need far better equipment to read true intentions instead of simple surface thoughts."

"Get a grip, John. How could a computer do that?"

"I don't have a clue what this damn program is. It's no game, of that I'm sure. It must be some sort of an artificial intelligence package the journals haven't even hinted at. It claims to be the Universe Control System and I could almost believe it. It can discuss humankind's dark side, the hopes of kittens and stellar evolution in addition to reincarnation." For a long moment he looked over his shoulder at the computer.

"You don't actually believe that Heaven and Hell bullshit, do you? It's a crock. You live and you die. That's it. Finito. End of story."

His shrug was all the denial he gave.

"You actually believe it?"

"You go talk to that computer."

"No thanks. I'm not talking to any machine that can read my mind. Maybe Arlene was right and we need a computer exorcist after all."

"No, I think an ethereal consultant would be far more appropriate."

He sounded serious. Denise spread jam on a muffin. "John, we're always going to be friends, aren't we?"

"Of course. Friendships like ours could even survive going to Hell along with that software if such a place really does exist."

His attempt to sound cheery was belied by his sad eyes. He better not have written her off yet. The phone rang and she dropped her knife. She managed to catch it before it hit the tablecloth. She practically shouted into the phone. "What? Sorry. Hello."

She wiped her hand on her napkin leaving purple smears on the white linen. The look on John's face was a mirror of the relief he'd shown when Arlene called last night. She had read it right. He was afraid to talk to her. She had to look away.

"Hi. My name is Ron."

The smooth voice almost made her hang up.

"I hear you need a computer exorcist."

Her skin went cold. She held her hand over the phone and looked at John. "There's a guy on the phone who knows we need a computer exorcist. Your game can't be listening to us, can it?" Its screen looked like big brother's eye staring into the back of John's head.

He shook his head. "No way. I isolated it."

She moved her hand out of the way and said, "I don't recall asking for an exorcist, computer or otherwise."

"It's part of what I do. Knowing more than my clients is what keeps me in business."

"Is that your profession?"

"It's mainly a hobby."

She didn't like the sound of his voice at all; it was too used-car-salesmanish.

"Well, I regret to inform you but your information is outdated. We have decided that we don't have a need for that particular service."

"My vocation is primarily as an ethereal consultant."

"Your profession is ethereal consulting?" The words were trying to choke her. John's face paled. He looked over his shoulder at the computer.

There was no way that a piece of software controlled the universe.

"Who are you with? NSA? Microsoft? Who?"

She watched John get up and step to the computer. The voice in her ear oozed on.

"I'll be there in a minute, I'm quite close by. We have much to discuss."

"How do you know where I . . ." there was a click on the other end. She put the phone down.

"John? I suddenly don't like this computer program of yours. That guy is on his way. And I'm sick of people hanging up on me."

"Why is he coming?" He spun back to stare at her. His eyes were wide and he was breathing quickly. She wasn't sure she was breathing at all.

"I don't know. I didn't really invite him, but he is. I don't know."

He turned back to the computer and folded his arms. "It would seem that 'Ask and ye shall receive' is no longer a cliché."

His laugh started low, but grew, brightening her apartment. She could almost breathe again.

"That system is too sure of itself by half." As he typed something short, there was a knock. He rested his hand on her shoulder for a moment before he went to answer the door.

"I've changed the passwords, it seems I control the universe now." His smile went all of the way to his eyes. "It'll be okay."

She turned back toward his empty seat. She leaned forward, barely able to make out the computer 's reply.

OH, BOTHER. GRANTED. I GUESSED YOU WOULD CATCH ON TO THAT.

John looked at the impeccably dressed man in the apartment doorway. From his Cordovan shoes all the way to his straight, blond hair nothing was out of place. Nobody could be that neat and not be in a magazine. John didn't usually dislike anybody on appearance alone, but his jaw tightened without a word exchanged. He resisted the temptation to grab him as he breezed into Denise's apartment as if he owned it. Maybe it was the aftershave. He'd never liked aftershave.

"Hi there, folks. My name is Ron and I'm your friendly neighborhood ethereal consultant."

John closed the door and shook Ron's hand with reluctance. "I'm John, that's Denise. Please sit." He wiped his hand on his jeans.

Ron stood next to the chair in front of the remains of John's breakfast. John stepped up beside Denise's chair and placed his hand gently on her shoulder. She flinched as if in surprise but, after she recovered, smiled at him. He liked the way it made him feel. He did not, however, like Ron's perfect smile in the least.

"How did you find us? What is an ethereal consultant?"

"You ought to know. You asked for one."

John took a small step forward. Denise kicked her chair over as she stood. "How did you know that?"

"I traced the software to that writer's apartment, but missed you by eleven minutes. It took me the rest of the night to trace it to you. I haven't had much sleep. Now, stop with the questions and give it to me."

John was glad he'd kept his hand on her shoulder. He tried to speak calmly while restraining her from striding over and stomping on Ron's toes with her slippers.

"Are you an angel or something?"

"Or something. And where is the Master Control Program now?"

"Sulking on that machine over there." John pointed to the desk behind Ron. "What is it, anyway? And who are you, FBI or NSA or what?"

"Oh no, nothing so droll. You are quite right about it. It is the Master Control Software for this universe. It sort of slipped out of our hands and I've come to fetch it back. It's a little hard to run things without it."

John started to say, 'how about some ID?' but felt too silly. Ron pulled a small calculator out of his coat pocket and pressed a few keys. Enough of this. It was time to throw him out. John tried to step forward but was unable to move. He couldn't open his mouth either.

Ron walked over to the desk. Shit. John tried to move again, but his body wouldn't listen. Denise hadn't budged. He'd never felt this helpless. All of the anger boiling in his body caused nothing to change in the slightest bit.

Ron picked up his master backup tape and slipped it into his pocket. He typed in the format command.

OUCH! appeared in large letters on the screen before it cleared and Ron's command started to wipe the disk.

John struggled against his immobility to no avail. Ron was turning away, maybe the last backup was safe. After narrowing his eyes for a long moment, he turned to the computer. He must see the other tape.

His voice was harsh, all smoothness gone. "Thought you'd get away with that one didn't you, Mr. Tough Boyfriend. Not a chance."

He pushed the 'Tape Format' button. John would have sworn if he could. Ron came and stood right in front of them. Not a single muscle would respond.

"You'll be able to move in a minute. I can't actually affect living beings directly in any way so I stopped time in your spinal columns for a bit. It wears off pretty quickly. As an added benefit it will give you a really great happy high with no side effects. You'll feel as if you're on joy juice for a bit. Relax and enjoy it. Have a nice day."

They remained frozen for several long moments after he had walked out of the apartment. They would make perfect models for a new rendition of American Gothic. Instead of farmer and wife they would be computer nerd and cookbook editor.

The first thing he could feel was the shaking of Denise's shoulder beneath his hand when she began to giggle. He tried to remember why he was angry at Ron and laughed. He was able to move again. The phone rang. She answered it, listened for a moment, and started laughing hysterically and mumbling something about St. Peter. She dropped the phone on the table and fell to her knees on the carpet holding her sides. She looked thoroughly, stunningly ridiculous.

When he said, "World Famous Editor Laid Low By An Attack Of Giggles," it only made her laugh more.

She waved her hand and gasped out, "Stop. Please."

John picked up the phone in time to hear, " . . . let me try. Hi. This is the Devil. I've a small problem maybe you could help me with."

John collapsed on the floor beside Denise imagining the Devil listening to their laughter over a speaker phone.

Denise lay on the floor trying to slow her breathing. It had been such an odd morning, everything seemed out of place. Even her living room looked strange from here.

The light oaken bookshelves that John had built a few years ago loomed above her. The sunlight didn't brighten the bottoms of the shelves. She looked away from the dark jagged peaks formed by the shadows of the uneven bindings. John was lying on his back next to her. He was still chuckling quietly. She sat up slowly and rubbed her elbow where she'd hit it on a chair.

He rolled his head toward her and smiled. "Hey, you. You okay?"

"Except for a stitch in my side that may take all day to go away, I think I will live. How about you?"

"I'm fine except for one thing."

"What's that?"

He propped himself on his elbows and tried, not very successfully, to speak without laughing. "I think I have lost the power to control the universe."

She punched him in the shoulder. There was another knock on the door. Her stomach clenched. Now what? Enough was enough. She rose to her feet and turned ready to throw whoever it was out.

The sight of the tall woman standing in the doorway drove the words from her. Denise looked at the classic planes of the woman's face. Her long, dark hair was pulled back in a ponytail, the end of which lay over her shoulder. A deep red blouse revealed her wonderful conditioning. Something about her made Denise want to choose her words very carefully.

"May we come in?" The woman's voice was tightly controlled as if a mighty impatience lurked beneath the surface. Daunting would be a good word to describe her.

John stood beside her. Apparently the woman didn't have the same effect on him. Or was he being protective?

She didn't need any protecting. "Depends on who you are and what you want."

The woman thought for a moment. "My name is, Michelle. This is Peter."

An unkempt young man waved from where he was standing out in the hall.

She put her hands into her pockets and realized she was still in her bathrobe and slippers.

"Excuse me, I have to go and get dressed. John, would you find out how they broke into a secure building and send them on their way?"

As she moved toward her bedroom she was able to see the man in the doorway more clearly. It was the thief.

"John, that bastard is back." She grabbed a heavy book of Chaucer from the shelf and moved forward around the woman. "Give us back our program."

The man's wide-eyed expression rapidly turned from surprise to fear. John tried to get around the woman's other side to tackle him.

The man dodged farther back into the hall saying, "Me?" in an increasingly panicked voice.

Denise was about to throw the Chaucer at him, but she didn't want to get too close to someone who could freeze her spine or whatever. Then the woman shouted.

"Stole the program? Who stole the program?"

It was deafening. Denise dropped the book to cover her ears. She scrambled backward into the apartment as the woman stalked in. She almost gasped with relief as John stepped between them. Maybe she could use some protecting every now and then.

His voice was shaky as he spoke. "Who are you?"

The woman stared at her over John's shoulder. Her voice was steady, ready to burst out again any moment.

"I'm the Devil and I'm pissed. What in the name of home do you mean, 'Peter stole the program?'" She focused her full gaze first on Denise and then on John.

Denise stared back. That was it. She was sick of weirdos trying to scare her. She about to tell the woman to back off, but John spoke first. His voice was steadying, much calmer than hers would have been. He stood toe to toe with the woman.

"Ron, hiding there behind you, stole my program only a few minutes ago. He took our software and wiped my backups. I want it back. Now."

His anger matched hers. She wanted to strangle Ron for making her feel so helpless.

The weasel cowered behind the woman as John tried to reach for him again. She'd never seen him so angry. This was a new side of John.

"Peter, do you have a twin brother?" The woman looked back over her shoulder.

Ron or Peter or whoever looked confused. Well, If he wasn't careful he might soon look closer to dead.

"No, Michelle. Andrew was my only brother and we look only a little alike."

Denise found her voice. "But you were here just a moment ago, paralyzed us and stole our program. You better have left the cookbook. I refuse to think I'm back to square one."

Menacing or no she'd take the woman apart with her bare hands if that cookbook was gone again. John edged over to the computer. He pulled a floppy out from under the keyboard where he slipped his quick backups.

"Pass Go. Collect $200. The cookbook is safe and sound, both versions. There's the hard copy, too."

"Thank God."

Michelle scowled down at her.

She scowled back.

Michelle sighed, undid her pony tail and shook her flowing dark hair loose. She transformed, like some enchantress, from majestic and fearsome to stunning and friendly when she smiled.

"I can see this will take some time to straighten out." Michelle's voice was deep and worldly-wise.

She had never seen anyone who simply looked so, well . . . powerful. She tightened the belt of her bathrobe and tucked in the overlap.

"Who are you people and why are you here?"

"This is St. Peter and I'm the Devil, but you can call me Michelle."

"This is the Mad Hatter and I'm Alice. Welcome to the wrong side of the looking glass. Who are you really? Are you the ones who called us on the phone?"

Michelle nodded as she walked farther into the room. Denise checked quickly. Except for the breakfast table and the chair she had knocked over, the room was presentable for guests. She had to give Peter a nod before he would step out of the hall and close the door. 'Sheep' definitely pegged him. Ron had been no sheep. No one was that good an actor. He must have an identical twin and be lying about it for some reason.

"How did you know to call me? If one more person knows things about me I haven't told them I'm going to sue somebody for invasion of privacy." John stood once again at her side.

Michelle, or the Devil, or whoever she was, smiled. "I guess a few explanations would help. Is there any tea in the house? I always listen better with tea. I'll pardon you your next five sins if you have any Earl Grey."

"I'll have to make them really juicy sins then." Although Denise had never thought about exactly what made a sin juicy before. She shrugged to herself. "Tea for four? We're not expecting any more folks, are we? God? Bëëlzebub? Jesus?"

The woman shook her head. "Dead, fictitious and busy elsewhere."

As long as the cookbook was safe she'd humor them for a few minutes.

"I'm going to get dressed. John can make the tea."

She tried to walk out of the room with all the dignity she could muster attired in terry cloth and fuzzy slippers. She looked at herself in the bathroom mirror as she washed her face and brushed her hair. She was a mess when she was angry. Between software thieves, people who thought they were the Devil and St. Peter, and John's love life, her face was not nice at all.

Closing her eyes she leaned on the counter. She'd always held a small hope there might be a chance for them someday. Of course, she had destroyed every love relationship she'd ever had. Maybe he was better off because he'd chosen to ignore her past invitation to change from friends to lovers.

That had been years ago. She'd thrown herself into her work once again to drown her disappointment. Her reflection grimaced at her. She'd really set herself up for that one; building a whole fantasy that hadn't come to pass. She smiled despite the aching desire to weep. It had been the right choice. Any possibility of an intimate relationship between them was now a thing of the past. A friend he was and a friend she'd be.

She came out of the bathroom and ducked into the bedroom. What a stupid design to make both doors open onto the living room. Thankfully only John could see her as the others' backs were to her. They were all chatting amicably about the dumb program as John poured the tea. Hanging up her robe, she adjusted the belt so that it was properly straight. A white blouse with dark pants and a matching belt fit well with the contrast tearing inside her. She was happy for John, it was about time he found someone he cared for. Now if only he trusted their friendship enough to tell her.

Stepping close to the window, she looked down at the street almost lost at the bottom of the dusty concrete chasm of old buildings. All the people walking by were alone; no couples. He hadn't told her because he didn't want to hurt her. He had been able to see she was attracted to him. He must have smoothed out each of the awkward situations she'd created, so many times. He was so good at it she'd never noticed. Here was proof positive John didn't want her. Wiping at her eyes, her fingers came away damp. To Hell with them. All three. They were going to get to finish their tea and then she was going to throw them out and finish the cookbook. Taking a deep breath she opened the door.

The tea was laid neatly on the coffee table. Peter sat by the computer and Michelle was in Denise's armchair. John was speaking from where he leaned back on the couch.

"I never thought I'd be having tea with the Devil, at least, not yet. What is St. Peter doing hanging around in Manhattan with the Devil? I'm surprised at you."

Time to take control, John really could be hopeless. It was one of his charms. She sat beside him on the sofa. The warmth of his shoulder felt wonderful. This was her friend, the connection intact no matter what happened. Her breath caught in her throat. She must focus on the friendship. The woman, Michelle was it, had kicked off her sandals and was sitting with her feet tucked under her. For the moment she ignored Peter.

"Who are you two really? And why are you here?"

"It's a long story," Michelle looked tired. "Where should I begin?"

Denise's whole body was aware of John as he leaned forward to pour her a cup of tea. His shoulder returning to rest against hers was immensely reassuring.

"You can begin with who stole John's software and I'm not buying the bit about a non-existent twin brother."

Peter fidgeted under her scowl. Good. He respected her. Michelle waved toward the sun streaming in through the window at the other end of the room.

"I could begin with 'Let there be light', not that it would make any more sense. Peter, maybe you could summarize it."

He told some crazy story about no delete privileges, God resting and programs slipping away like living things. John sat there, as if this were normal as could be. He had his fascinated, brows-furrowed expression on and was nodding his head. She cut Peter off.

"That has to be the most ridiculous thing I've ever heard. I wish I had a tape recording of that explanation. I could either have the little men in white jackets take you away or I could write a great novel based on it. Now, who are you people?"

"We told you, I'm St. Peter and she's the Devil." He stood as if ready to protest his innocence in front of some tribunal or grand inquisition.

"Bullshit."

The woman pulled several small cushions from the corners of her arm chair and threw them on the white rug. Rather than being angry Denise was struck by Michelle's gracefulness; as if she had lived in her body for longer than anyone could. Michelle leaned back and crossed her ankles as she rested her feet on the table.

"For the sake of argument, or rather avoiding such, let's pretend we are who we say are for a moment. You said non-existent twin brother a moment ago. Peter, you say you don't have a twin brother?"

"Not that I know of."

"When you tried to latch the software onto God to get him moving did you enter any test data?"

The adrenaline forced her to spring to her feet. "Okay, that's it. God and the Devil and the computers, that's too much of a charade. Sure maybe it's a valuable game or even something secret, but it's gone now and I wish you'd do the same. Please, leave my home, now, whoever you are."

John put his hand on her arm. "I think we should hear them out."

"Are you nuts?"

She pulled her arm away and turned to glare at him having to kick several cushions out of the way to do so. He flinched back.

"That program was very convincing. I believe that it is what it claimed to be."

"Stop being an asshole and think for a moment. You can't believe that software controls our universe and the woman in my armchair is the Devil. Come on."

John shrugged his shoulders. "All I know is that it made me plenty nervous and I have a funny feeling it belongs in these peoples' hands more than it does in those of that Ron character."

Denise looked at him. She couldn't believe he was arguing with her about who could be in her apartment.

He stood and was so close to her that she had to look up at him. "Denise."

"That placating tone isn't going to get you anywhere. Fine, you want to listen to them, stay here. I'll leave."

"What's gotten into you?"

"Screw you."

As if she were somehow at fault. She could see John's look of resignation as she turned away. She grabbed her coat out of the closet and was almost to the door when she heard his steps on the entryway marble.

Putting her back to the door she held up her hand like a warrior's shield to block the pull he had on her heart.

"You can go to Hell with them for all I care. Take your new lover along. Whoever the fuck she is."

John stopped. His jaw dropped in surprise. "What new lover?"

"The one who you can't even tell me about. I wish you'd stop trying to protect me. I've had enough of that. I can deal with you not wanting me."

He was shaking his head as she opened the door. Stepping into the hall, she slammed it behind her. Tears burned as they ran down her face. 'What lover', indeed. Denise turned to the elevator and pressed the call button.

Michelle looked at the closed door and back at John, curious as to his reaction. He took a faltering step toward the door. She couldn't have heard his voice if he were a foot farther away.

"But I do want you."

Pitiful. Another lovesick human. This was not what they needed. "John?"

He turned slowly to look at her.

"The program you had. Could it have been the real Universal Control Software?"

He nodded as he again watched the door, perhaps hoping it would open magically and Denise would come back through all smiles. She could hear the elevator doors open and close. His sigh made her actually feel sorry for him. Maybe she did not envy humans their struggle too much. She pulled the last blue pillow out from behind her and tossed it into the pile with the others.

He slowly returned to sit on the couch where Denise had been, but he stopped and simply stared down at the empty cushions.

"John, could you tell us about it?"

He blinked at her several times before he appeared to actually see her.

"Yes." He glanced toward the door one last time before sitting. "She has a temper sometimes. Not very often. Sorry. What do you want to know? I had a long argument with the software."

Peter nodded his head. "Software with a bad attitude. You had the genuine article."

She hadn't realized the program harassed everybody.

John smiled slightly. "Yes, that's a good description of our discussion. I realized how unusual it was as I worked to recover Denise's cookbook. And five or ten minutes before you arrived Peter here, or Ron rather, came and stole it."

Michelle closed her eyes for a moment. They had searched for it all night and missed it by minutes. Ten lousy minutes. She picked up her cup of cold tea and took a sip. It didn't help to soothe her throat at all.

"Peter's evil twin, yes. Well, any ideas how he was created?"

Peter shifted uncomfortably making his chair squeak.

"When I tried to use the software to move God I made a test database. A copy of the master data structure, not the Control Program, I was never able to copy that. My idea was to take an empty structure with no names entered into it, add God, and ask the software to move him along. It didn't work. As I was setting all this up I entered myself as a test. I had assumed the extra entry was wiped out when I ran the test. I guess it did not quite work that way."

Michelle stood up to stretch, kicking the pillows out of her way. "How could the extra entry be wiped if you had no delete privileges?"

His eyes opened wide. He looked as surprised as John had facing Denise a few moments ago.

"Of course." He smacked his palm against his forehead. "How could I miss that? It's obvious. Unbelievable I didn't see that."

She tried to suppress her smile. "You wouldn't be happy unless you did everything perfectly. And I'd wager good money even then you'd believe you could have done it better."

Peter stared at the carpet clearly thinking hard.

"But that doesn't explain how he was created. All that should've happened was an ugly error message."

John had watched the conversation move back and forth, almost like a marionette doll with his head on strings. He raised a hand asking permission to speak. She nodded to him.

"Are you sure of the path your extra entry took? Maybe it was forced into another section of the code? If not by the lack of delete privileges, by something else."

Michelle watched them both as Peter pondered the question. They were an interesting contrast. The broad shouldered boy programmer with the light blond hair and the lean mortal. John's close trimmed hair and dark eyes were attractive. What an odd couple he and Denise made. The hesitant computer nerd and the petite editor with the fiery temper and the classically beautiful profile. She had known several artists who searched for years to find someone like her to sit for them. Of course, most of them were long since dead.

Peter shook his head. "Nothing comes to mind."

"Good. That simplifies things immensely. You ran your test. The system should have tried to automatically delete the entry of your own name."

The two of them were leaning toward each other. She could practically see the connection building between them. John stood and began to pace back and forth in the narrow space in front of the couch.

"And when it couldn't, it created an extra copy of you somewhere which turned into an evil twin named Ron."

Peter nodded. "That's about the only thing that could have happened. I don't see why he wants the software?"

She'd been wondering about that, but now with the question spoken aloud it was obvious.

"The reason Ron wants the software is because he is you, Peter. You spend every waking minute worrying about the software."

"No, I don't." He clenched his jaw and tried to look fierce. It was pretty funny.

She pulled over a dining chair and spun it around to sit across it and lean her chin on the back.

"Yes, you do. Now keep quiet. What else is your twin going to do? He was left with no choice except to want the software. He probably doesn't even know why. It did take him an awfully long time to steal it."

"He couldn't get to it as long as I had it safely in Heaven. Ron must have spent the last fifteen hundred years or so waiting for the software to be available, but where is he now and how do we find him?"

John looked at Peter. "Can you map out the program structure? Maybe we can trace his origins. That may give us a clue."

Within moments they were talking a language she couldn't understand. Peter pulled a pad of yellow paper from Denise's computer desk as John pushed the teacups and saucers to one end of the coffee table. She could tell they were sketching data flow diagrams but that was as far as she could follow. Great, stuck in a room with a pair of nerds. If she had to define her own Hell it would start like this.

She looked around the sunlit room and noticed the well-crafted oak bookshelves all along one wall. Maybe Denise had some good books.

*D*enise sat in the park, unsure of how she'd arrived. The sounds of the city penetrated this little sanctuary only rarely. She'd often come here as a child; usually to this very bench. First with Dad and after he died, with Uncle Joshua to sit under the large oak. The leaves around the park were slowly changing color to deep red as the late morning sun warmed the cool fall air. A maple leaf fluttered toward her on the breeze and landed among the pigeons around her feet.

She held up empty hands. "Sorry, folks, no bread today."

The pigeons looked at her sadly and started to waddle elsewhere in search of crumbs.

"Denise?"

For half a moment she thought one of the birds had called her by name, but it was Kris standing beside the bench. She jumped up, scattering the pigeons and gave him a hug. She hadn't realized this was what she needed, to be held by someone who loved her. His muscles tensed in surprise at how tight she held him, but he did not let go . . . thankfully. She lay her head on his shoulder and started to cry.

He stroked her hair. "Easy, cousin. Easy."

Nodding against the smooth denim of his well-worn jacket she could feel the dampness on her cheeks.

"What's wrong?"

All she could do was shrug as the tears flowed. He pulled out a handkerchief and offered it to her. Stepping back she wiped her eyes, confused by her own outburst.

"Thanks." She wiped her eyes one more time before returning his handkerchief. "I guess I am happy to see a friendly face."

Gently he wiped at fresh tears with the cloth before returning it to her.

"Have you been seeing a lot of unfriendly faces lately? I told you publishing was a rough field for my soft-hearted little cousin."

She looked into his eyes, bright blue surrounded by laugh lines. He looked at her with a broad smile. Their careers had been the subject of much mutual ribbing. He being, despite all his gifts, a teacher in some upstate town with twelve hundred people and ten thousand head of dairy cow and her being a tough New York crazy. She returned his smile but declined to enter into the usual game.

"No, it was John."

"That doesn't sound like him."

"It's a long story and very confusing."

He waved toward the bench and they sat. He was right, it didn't. John did care about her feelings to have protected her so. The pigeons came back to see if maybe Kris had some bread. He pulled two pieces from his pocket and handed one to her. Somehow Kris always came through.

He broke off a piece and tossed it onto the small sea of pigeons. In a great scurry a swallow ducked into the crowd, took the bit of crust and flew off over the others' frantic complaints.

"Tell me what's wrong."

She threw several small pieces which disappeared too quickly for even the speediest sparrow.

"John let all of these people into the apartment and acted as if they were long lost friends. When I tried to throw them out he sided against me. I want a friend who doesn't do things like that. I guess I need to look for a new one." The tightness in her chest wouldn't let her breathe and that was the lesser of two evils.

"What sort of strangers?"

She ripped and tossed another piece of bread to the growing swirl of gray bodies.

"They seemed nice enough, although the woman was a little scary at first. Then they starting claiming to be the Devil and St. Peter."

Kris raised his eyebrows high enough that the whites of his eyes showed all of the way around the irises.

"It does sound pretty bizarre, doesn't it?"

The late morning sun flickering through the leaves made the insanity seem to be farther off, more silly than frustrating. She dropped the rest of her bread in one big piece and watched the pigeons tear it apart.

"And what if they are who they claim to be?"

She stared at him. "Are you nuts?"

He was clearly attempting not to smile. His mouth was an echo of John's when he had thought he'd made a particularly subtle joke. Kris turned back to tearing off little pieces of crust for the pigeons.

"Did I say I believed in them? I simply asked what might happen if they were who they say they are."

"How can they be?" It was hard not to shout at him for being completely stupid. He touched her arm gently.

"Denise, one thing I've learned is that there are times to ignore truth and justice and simply go with it. Marita claims that's how she fell in love with me. Apparently she was overwhelmed by the difference in our stations in life, but she reached out for me anyway. I'm eternally grateful that she dared. She is one of the great joys of my life. Also, it's much less painful, and often more fun to go along with the flow once in a while."

He might as well have been talking Greek. It would have made as much sense.

"If they are the Devil and St. Peter it would be more sensible to run the other way. It is an adventure that would be beyond reasonable. This isn't some cute love story. And John. I still can't believe he would betray me like that." She looked away as the pain of the memory coursed through her.

"Betray you?" Kris turned to her sharply. "Betrayal? What in the name of Heaven do you mean by that? You make letting two strangers into your apartment sound like high treason punishable by keelhauling."

She didn't dare say another word or she might fall off into the chasm of despair before her. Kris gave the birds his last bits of bread. He brushed the crumbs off his pants and then took her hand.

She looked down at his slim fingers intertwined with hers. Their fingers had the same build on a different scale, even their skin coloring was similar. Such a sharp contrast with John's broad hands with their short, strong fingers. Kinship was much more reliable than friendship. She looked into his eyes.

His voice was gentle, all of the joking was set aside. "I don't know what's making you unhappy. Do what you think is right, but please let yourself take a chance. You deserve the best."

She opened her mouth several times, but couldn't seem to form her thoughts into words. There was no way to answer such a statement. She let out her breath sharply and looked away.

"You and John are both crazy. I take lots of chances. I let them in my apartment. And adventure is highly overrated. New challenges, with a loony who thinks she's the Devil, are not something I need. My life has been fine without that and I'm busy enough already."

She watched the slowly departing pigeons to look away from the disappointment on his face.

Kris raised her chin with his other hand until she had to look at him. His hand, so gentle against her face, made fresh tears push at her eyes.

"And why is change such a bad thing?"

She had to laugh. "You sound like Uncle."

"Am I not his son after all?" Kris raised one eyebrow in the same disconcerting way Joshua had. He held it for a moment before joining in her laughter. "Seriously, change isn't always bad."

The laughter died in her. She released Kris' hand and folded hers together in her lap. She studied the way his handkerchief poked between her clenched fingers at odd angles. John had changed and it wasn't for the better.

Kris was still on his old joke. "How do you know the woman is lying about being the Devil? The world is often a strange and curious place. Maybe you should give her a second chance."

Such a ridiculous response helped keep her from bursting into tears again. A passing siren penetrated the quiet of the park making conversation impossible. Kris' gaze was a palpable pressure against her neck. She picked at a flake of green bench paint that had caught under one of her nails.

"Kris! . . . Denise!"

Looking up she saw Uncle Joshua approaching them. A smile lit his face. She couldn't help but smile back. The world always seemed brighter and happier when he was around. She felt warm inside. Life was safe with him.

"Why are you two so gloomy? It is a lovely fall day, perfect for a walk in the park. Come along, my children."

He offered a hand to each of them and pulled them off the bench. He kept his hold on her hand as they started to walk along one of the paths, pigeons and leaves scattering before them in the bright sunlight.

As he had walked toward them Joshua had seen Kris leaning forward in his eager teacher mode and Denise being surprisingly stiff and tense, even for her. Now she tried to pull her hand out of his as they walked along. He didn't let go. He led her away from the isolated bench under the trees. Maybe more of a crowd in the busier areas of the park would make her feel safer, more able to talk.

"Uncle, what are you doing here?"

"My son and I were planning a walk beneath the changing leaves on this beautiful fall noon. To look at the new plantings by the garden committee. To spend some time together out in the sun. He doesn't come to visit his father nearly enough." He winked at Kris.

"Tell your Uncle. Why are you two down in the mouth on such a day?" Kris shook his head slightly and nodded toward Denise. Joshua sighed. She was so hard on herself.

"I think John's leaving me."

The three of them stopped at the same moment. Joshua wished he could see the tableau they made. Kris clearly thought he'd been talking about something else. Denise, horrified at what she hadn't intended to say, had gone white as a sheet. His own face must have been a study in shock as well.

Joshua slowly took a step toward the waist high black iron fence guarding a new row of rosebushes alongside the path. Denise stumbled as she started moving.

"Where is he going?" John was not supposed to be leaving. "He didn't say anything to me earlier."

She gripped the fence with white-knuckled hands. "He wouldn't tell me anything. That's the problem. He kept not talking about some new relationship until I had to confront him. Then he lied and said there wasn't one. I can deal with that. I'm not happy about it, but I can. What I can't stand is how jealous it makes me feel."

Joshua let out the breath he'd been holding and turned away, glad Denise couldn't see his smile. He made shooing motions to Kris who nodded and walked away toward some swings and a teeter-totter. He would end up playing with the local children. It was nice the way his son trusted him.

He turned back to Denise. Tears were slipping down her cheeks. He caught one on his finger and held it in the sunlight, a sparkling little prism. Passing it in front of her eyes he moved it slowly until she was looking at him.

"Why would John lie?"

"He doesn't. At least never before." She kicked at a fence post. "And he had the gall to look surprised when I caught him."

He took her hand from the fence and tucked it under his arm. As they continued around the park she wiped her eyes with her handkerchief.

"Have you ever wondered what the birds are saying?"

"Okay, Uncle, what's the metaphor this time?"

She knew him too well. He was going to have to think of new stories, some day. He stopped them at the foot of a small ramp while a little girl on a tricycle rode by.

"Listen."

Denise tilted her head. After several moments she laughed briefly. "They're saying, 'Tweet.' "

"Good." They walked slowly up the ramp. "Now, try to remember what John said and listen . . ."

She jerked her hand out from under his arm and turned to face him with her fists on her hips. "I did. That's how I know."

"If listening doesn't work, try to look."

He had to outwait her. The sun actually moved enough to alter the shadow line a tree made across her face before she finally sighed and closed her eyes. After a long moment she spoke. Her voice sounded distant as if she were actually watching John.

"He was surprised when I told him he could take his fucking girlfriend with him wherever he was going. His expression was beyond disbelief. As if I were cursing him for something he didn't understand." She opened her eyes and reached out to steady herself. "But Uncle, it doesn't make any sense."

Joshua shook his head. Life would be so much easier if people could see what was right in front of them.

"What if you were perhaps mistaken about who John is interested in?"

She blinked several times. "No. He can't want me."

Her voice was a mere gasp. He quickly took her arm for fear that she would fall.

"But how could he? I indicated I was interested." Her voice started getting louder. "Years ago. I took his hand during this wonderful romantic movie and he didn't do anything but hold mine. No kiss good night. Nothing. I listened. I heard the answer. I've accepted that and tried to be a good friend."

"You indicated? You aren't supposed to indicate. You're supposed to act."

He placed her hand around his arm again. He led her slowly along the curving path around the park. They passed several families who waved a greeting.

"When I met Anne I was lost from the first moment. I spent a whole summer following her around the Mediterranean. She was recently divorced and didn't want anything to do with men. She went to Crete and found me walking among the ruins of Iráklion. I had my gondolier bump into hers, not once or twice, but three times in Venice. One of the happiest moments of my life was when she agreed to be with me as we sat out on the Rock of Gibraltar. Denise, love is not something you indicate. It is something you must show."

"Love?"

Her voice was loud enough to carry. It attracted the attention of several people. Looking around she lowered her voice and stepped closer, blushing bright red. Her voice didn't lose its edge however.

"Are you nuts, Uncle? I did show. And he pretended not to notice, I guess to protect my feelings. That's it. And now he brings it up again? Not possible."

"Maybe he didn't understand you taking his hand that one time. I've seen you do it before when you are very sad or very happy. Are you not willing to give him another chance?"

"It's too late. John and I have a wonderful friendship now. What would make me want to change something that is fine the way it is?"

"And yet you are hurt because you thought he didn't want you. It doesn't work both ways at once. You either have to let him go or give him a second chance. Change is not the evil thing you make it sound."

She stopped and dug her fingers painfully into his arm. "Enough. You're going to drive me crazy."

He took her fist and slowly unclenched it from his coat sleeve, finger by finger. The shaking of her hand made him wonder at the intensity of her internal battle. He held her hand palm up with his underneath. He pointed at it with his other hand.

"You hold in your hand one of the finest things on Earth, a true friendship. In my many years I have seen its like only a few precious times. For ten years you have taken care of each other. For ten years you have loved each other. There can be much more for you, if you are willing to take a chance."

He let go of her hand. She stared at the palm for a long moment before deliberately reforming the fist. He tried not to sigh aloud as the familiar look of fierce determination filled her face.

"There are some things that are too precious to risk changing for change's sake."

"And what would you say is the risk? A friendship like yours can survive a little testing."

Her expression didn't relax one bit. "Uncle, I love you very much, but you're wrong, so drop it."

With his fine sense of timing Kris came up the path from the other direction holding a little girl's hand. She was beautiful with hair the color of winter sunlight and a smile twice as bright.

"Patricia would like to walk with us while her mom and dad do some shopping. She's feeling pretty brave, she's never gone for a walk without one of her parents before. There's nothing like taking a chance."

Patricia nodded her head solemnly before stooping to pick up a golden leaf. Joshua tried not to smile as he turned to face Denise. She was staring suspiciously at Kris as if this had all been planned somehow. Kris was about to speak, but Joshua laid a hand on his arm to silence him. Kris had good instincts but he was young. He hadn't truly learned about limits and Denise was very near hers. Joshua took her by her shoulders.

"Sometimes, Denise, sometimes you must take a leap of faith. I worry about you. There are opportunities in front of you. You must take a hold for all you are worth. Life offers true adventure and love far too rarely. When it comes by, you must take the risk to ever win. Promise me you will think about it at least?"

She opened her mouth several times, but remained silent. Maybe he had pushed too hard. Kris raised one questioning eyebrow.

Denise shook her head as if to clear it. "You are both crazy. Change is highly overrated. And adventures with the Devil or anyone else are not what I need. I'm going back to clear out my apartment. John can go with them for all I care. I have work to do."

Her voice had slowed for a moment as if testing John's name. That was enough of a change for now.

She tried to pat Kris on the shoulder, but he would have none of it and gave her a hug. She stepped back.

"You're still crazy."

Kris nodded. "I'll be in the city all week. Marita is planning to be in town for the weekend. During the day she wants to go shopping for some new business clothes. We should all have dinner at Uncle's on Saturday and you can continue to tell me how crazy I am."

"Deal."

Joshua wrapped her into a hug. She relaxed a little in his arms. He was reminded of the young girl who used to come to him to be held when she was upset. Now she was a full grown woman, stiff with pride and pain.

"I love you, Denise. You know your Uncle only wants what's best for you?"

She nodded. He kissed her on top of the head and let her go. He watched her striding over the yellow and orange leaves, splashed by the autumn sun. She didn't kick at single pile. He sighed.

After she was out of hearing Kris turned to him, his eyes twinkling.

"Have you been meddling again, Dad?"

After playing in the park for a while Patricia had led them to her home. Tony and Delores were back and made much of her. Joshua looked at his son. Kris was a tall, handsome man. His fine, long hands painted pictures in the air as he leaned on the fence. Delores was captivated by him.

Thankfully after several years of marriage this didn't worry her husband Tony very much.

Joshua looked at the street. Changes in the city had passed this neighborhood by. The early afternoon sun burnished the street, yes, this was a burnishing light. Generations of mothers and aunts and uncles had lived in these old brownstones and tended their little gardens. The few new people moving in soon started work on their gardens as if it were a contagious occupation. Every evening the stoops would slowly fill with the residents of the houses. Newcomers always sent a ripple through the neighborhood, but life went on and they either fit in or drifted away. The ebb and flow of the world was present even here in this quiet heart of the city.

Joshua realized Delores was saying it was time to go in and fix Patricia her dinner. And Kris must come by more often and bring that darling wife of his for a visit every now and then.

Joshua waved goodbye to her as Kris patted him on the shoulder. "She loves you, Pop."

"What utter nonsense. It is you she is infatuated with. It is obvious. I can see it like my hand on the end of my arm." They continued their leisurely stroll.

"She may be, but she loves you."

"What foolishness." Even it were true it did not worry him much. He had other concerns. "I'm worried about Denise."

Kris' voice matched their slow pace. "Why's that?"

"She and John are going to have a rough time of it."

"If you'd stop meddling."

"Me? I would never meddle."

"Uh huh."

"I am only trying to help out a little bit here and maybe a little bit there."

"What 'help' were you offering this time?" Kris stopped him from walking in front of a car as they crossed the street back toward the park.

He linked his arm through Kris', proud to be this fine man's father.

"I think they would make such a nice couple. I think they've been 'only friends' for far too long."

"Pop."

"What? Am I right or not?"

Kris was silent until they had settled comfortably on a park bench. A new set of children were playing on the swings. The wisteria was breaking into bloom, the sweet scent reminded him of Anne.

"Okay. They are practically made for each other."

"Ah. There, you see. I'm not so old that I don't know what is right when I see it. They belong together, but it is such a new thing for both of them. I worry."

"They'll be fine. They've been friends for a long time, it will see them through, even if it doesn't work."

"Of course it will work. Look at you and Marita, I was right about the two of you, wasn't I?"

"Yes you were and you are and thank you. Before you take all of the credit you may recall she and I had some part of making it work, too."

"Did I say you didn't? Did I? No, I only gave you this little nudge when you needed it. The rest was up to you and you kids pulled together wonderfully. But your cousin, ah, neither of you were as headstrong as she. John, he is going to have trouble before this works."

Kris leaned forward to wiggle his fingers at a pigeon which clucked in protest before walking away.

"Did she tell you about her visitors?" His voice sounded worried.

"No, is it anyone we know?"

"A man and a woman. They claim to be St. Peter and the Devil."

A tingle of surprise rippled up his spine. "That's an odd combination."

"Dad."

He patted Kris' arm. "She's a big girl. Who knows? A bit of adventure would be good for her. John will help her, too. Yes, she'll be fine. Let us not worry any more about her for now. How is Marita? And the kids?"

"The kids are great. I love teaching their fresh young minds. They are interested in everything."

"So. You have ended up having children even though you and Marita never did."

Kris' laugh made the sun look brighter and the air feel warmer. His son; he enjoyed life so hugely. It was wonderful simply to be with him.

"You should see her teaching the ones who are still too young for school. She's incredible. I hate it when we're apart. Usually she's very good about staying in touch when we're separated, but I can't seem to get through to her at the moment. I want to hear her voice within minutes after she leaves. Two days and I'm already going nuts."

"She's a big girl, too. She'll be fine. Now, you trust your poppa. He really does know what is best. Look at those little children play."

Joshua watched Kris as his eyes followed the young children through the warm fall air. It was a shame they always grew so fast, but perhaps it was best that way. The future was an uncertain thing.

*D*enise knocked on her apartment door. After a long pause Michelle opened it. She took a step back and a deep breath. She had been hoping they would be gone.

"I forgot my keys."

The woman smiled, waving an invitation to enter, "Please, come in."

Being invited into her own home by a woman who claimed to be the Devil was a first. "Why, thank you."

The woman laughed as Denise stepped into the apartment. The relief that coursed through her body as she saw John surprised her. He and Peter were oblivious as they hunched over the coffee table now covered with crumpled pieces of yellow paper. She was about to unoblivious John when the woman spoke.

"May I take your coat? Are you going to stay awhile?"

Denise spun to look at her. She was about to tell her to bug off when she saw the smile. The amusement in her eyes was aggravating, but the smile was genuine.

"I can hang up my own coat. Why don't you go back and play with the two of them?"

"I don't understand or care about programming at the level they have moved to. I've been perusing your library. Not a good trashy novel in the lot."

"Clearly our definition of trash is different."

She turned away and headed into the kitchen before she could blush. She hadn't meant to be rude, but she wasn't about to apologize to some uninvited guest.

"What did you find to read?"

Michelle followed her and sat on one of the counter stools. "A dog-eared copy of Dante's *Inferno* has helped pass the time. Such a silly man. After death he would never believe he was really in Hell because it wasn't like he'd imagined. He insisted I should change it to match his vision."

And Kris thought it would make a good adventure to spend time with a self-designated Devil. He was such a goof. For now she had no choice but to play along.

Denise took a glass out of the cupboard. "May I get you anything to drink?"

"Juice, if you have it?"

She poured two glasses of cranberry juice and sat on one of the other stools. "I always wanted to be Beatrice, ever since I was a little girl."

Michelle looked surprised. "The seven levels of Hell are a touch heavy for a child. And why would any person in their right mind want to be her?"

Denise had ceased defending her precocious reading habits years ago and wasn't going to start again now.

"The way she is loved. Beatrice is idolized by Dante. I always wanted someone to feel that way about me."

"How long did it take you to outgrow that?"

Denise took a drink from her glass and set it back on the counter. She waited a moment before looking at Michelle and answering.

"Who says I have?"

The woman started to roll her eyes and turn away. She stopped in mid-turn and began laughing all out of proportion to the joke. She must have noticed Denise's surprise at her reaction.

"It has been a long time since anyone, other than a certain sneaky messenger, has caught me off guard.

Thank you." Michelle raised her glass in a toast, "To everything getting back to normal."

This woman, who was crazy enough to think she was the Devil, made a toast she completely agreed with. A clean copy of a cookbook and a predictable best friend would have made a better beginning to the day.

"What is it you want back to normal?"

"For starters I would like to find the software."

Denise nodded. "Yes, everything went to Hell when the software arrived."

Michelle put her glass on the counter and smiled at some internal joke.

"Oh, I forgot you think of that as home." She could play a game as well as anyone.

"If it makes you more comfortable to believe in my insanity, that's fine. Your belief doesn't affect me one way or another."

Denise glanced at John and Peter. John looked up and noticed her. The smile on his face made her feel warm inside. Could Joshua be right? She wasn't ready to go down that road. Looking back at Michelle, she could see John, out of the corner of her eye, hesitate for a few moments. Peter asked him a question and he looked back down at their notes.

"Is that your cookbook?" Michelle indicated the pile of printer paper sitting on the counter.

"I think so." Denise pulled the stack over. "Elantra is usually good without being imaginative. She shouldn't be as much of a hit as she is.

"These recipes looked great; no puppies, no fire and brimstone. She looked at John again lost in his computer talk. He really had saved it.

Michelle read aloud one of the recipe titles. "Javanese nasi campur."

"It's pronounced 'champur.'" Denise flipped another page. "Oh, Japanese vegetable tempura. One of my favorites. Look. A number 16 with black olives. The best pizza in the world."

"Let me see that." Michelle looked more closely as Denise held the sheet. "You did say a number 16 with black olives."

"Yes, why?"

"The Italian Pizza Place . . . "

"On Kingwood Drive . . . "

"In Seattle." Their voices were in unison.

They laughed briefly, companionship tangible between them for a moment. Denise was starting to like her despite her better judgment. Kris would never let her live it down.

Michelle looked at the page again. "I can't believe you have the recipe."

"It would appear I do. I don't have all the fixings, but we could go shopping. I have a feeling they'll be awhile." She gestured toward Peter and John still huddled together.

After making a quick list and setting the stack of pages neatly back on the counter, she went to the closet to put her coat back on. Michelle hadn't arrived with one.

"Won't you be cold?"

"I don't get cold very easily, although I do prefer a hot baking sun."

None of her jackets stood a chance of fitting this woman. She pulled John's windbreaker off the hanger and offered it to Michelle. The fabric felt soft in her hands.

"This should help and he'll never miss it.

"We're going shopping," she called out.

John nodded his head without looking her direction. Peter didn't even do that as they walked out the door. She felt a little disoriented as she followed John's jacket out the door and left John behind.

*D*enise walked beside Michelle along Houston street. The New York sidewalks were fairly empty for a change and they were able to stroll side by side much of the time without having to dodge crowds of people. The cool scent of fall on the crisp air mixed with the midday sun to make her feet feel as if they were barely touching the pavement. Each restaurant could be separately tasted as they passed. Even the fresh oranges at the local grocers could be smelled in the clear air.

Michelle, tall and self-confident moved alongside her easily. She was a pleasant surprise, bright and funny. If only she would stop claiming to be the Devil. Michelle's voice sounded as if she were equally pleased with the company and the day.

"There used to be a great little deli on the corner around here. It used to have the most wonderful pastrami sandwiches in creation. I came by all the time when I hung out in the village in the 60's. The folk music scene was great back then."

Denise looked around. The neighborhood had changed so much since she was a little girl. The Hong

Kong Chinese had taken over most of the businesses. It was hard to picture the late night music clubs she'd never entered when all that remained now were steel gated shops with graffiti covering the narrow brick walls between them. At night no one except the police walked this stretch between her apartment and Uncle Joshua's.

"Hung out in the sixties? How could you have done that? You're no older than me."

"Being the Devil has its advantages."

"You remind me of someone I went to school with who was convinced he was Jesus. He was harmless enough for being a complete nutcase. Last I heard he was going to go and live in the desert for forty days and forty nights with no food. Can't you give it a rest?"

"Believe what you will, that's all anyone ever can do."

Michelle sounded as if she didn't care. No longer looking threatening she seemed at home walking down the streets. Denise could play along.

"What brings the Devil to the Big Apple?"

"Normally I come here because I don't feel out of place. It sounds crazy, but almost everywhere I have to act a certain way to pass unnoticed. In New York whether you are sane or not doesn't matter. For example, look at all the Hasidic Jews over there. Great bakeries. Look, on the other side of the street, the finest Chinese restaurants in the western world. Little Italy? Six blocks ahead. What was staring into the lobby of your building from the neighboring church? A fiberglass virgin Mary statue with distinctly Puerto Rican features. This is an excellent place to be the Devil."

Denise laughed. She was good whoever she was.

"New York has some other advantages. I don't feel as if I'm slacking off here. There are so few people who are Heaven bound from this city I don't have to do anything.

I come here to holiday like most people go to tropical island beaches."

"What are the powers of the Devil on Earth?"

They were waiting at an intersection with a number of other people. Taxi cabs rushed by inches beyond their toes. Although they could be easily overheard, no one even looked at them; classic New Yorkers.

"Not that much really. I can only make someone see a temptation that is in front of them but they hadn't noticed. If they choose to ignore it, there isn't squat I can do. Outside New York and LA it can become downright frustrating. Some places though, Bangkok for one, are even too crazy for me."

"What's with Bangkok?"

"The morals there are too lacking for even the most vile fallen angel."

At a break in the flow of cars and trucks they crossed quickly before the light changed and released the turning traffic.

"Actually that's what I normally tell people who ask. In reality I have no special powers on Earth."

"That's more like it. Why do you tell the story you've been spouting out all day?"

"Because it sounds better than saying I am employed, and have been for some time, as Hell's chief programmer in residence. It doesn't have the same flair."

Denise could only laugh. This woman's monomania was magnificent.

Michelle pointed to a doorway leading to the cellar of a brownstone. A bum slept across the threshold.

"There used to be a great late night jazz club down there in the forties."

"You aren't old enough to have been here then, even as a kid."

"I'm older than the hills."

"Sure you are. And I'm Methuselah's daughter and that sodden bum is God."

"I wish he were."

Denise stopped and looked back at the grizzled old man slouched in the doorway. He had his tattered coat pulled tightly around him, and an empty liquor bottle still grasped in one sleeping hand.

"I guess being the Devil you would want him to end that way. I don't see why you'd wish that on anyone."

Denise felt as if she'd tasted something bitter. She had started to like this woman, but how could she be so casually cruel.

Michelle spoke quietly. "Could I borrow a dollar? I'm not carrying any cash."

Crazy and broke. Wonderful. She handed over a one. Michelle slipped it gently into his pocket and, after a long moment, turned to her. Her shoulders sagged as if from some great weight.

"I wish he were God because I'd rather have him alive and destitute than dead. If he were still alive I could help him."

"Why would the Devil want to help God?"

Michelle looked at her with unblinking eyes before turning back to the bum. Denise was surprised at the single tear trickling down her cheek. Michelle's voice was barely a whisper.

"Because she didn't when she had the chance."

Denise didn't know what to say. She turned and led the way down the rest of the block in silence. Crossing the street she indicated Joshua's.

"Is this the deli you remember?"

She held the door for Michelle at the top of the three steps down to the old wood floor. Michelle paused in the doorway and turned back. Her weak smile of thanks made Denise glad to have been there.

They descended the steps into the deli. She loved it when the sun was like this. Uncle had turned off all the lights and the deli was filled with many bright spots and unexpected shadows.

Michelle stopped, closed her eyes and breathed in deeply. "Denise you are a wonder. Yes, this is it. This is Heaven. How did you find it?"

"I'll tell you a secret. My aunt and uncle own it. I grew up playing in here."

"Maybe we met once."

"Back when you were a younger devil?"

Michelle's smile lit her whole face. "Not very much younger, but yes."

She smiled back. It felt as if she'd taken a deep breath of fresh air.

In unison they turned and stepped to the counter. Aunt Anne waved a hand from the back. Denise was struck by her movements as she approached. In some ways they was very similar to Michelle's. Her motions had a grace that she had spent hours trying to emulate as a child, following her aunt around the deli, behind the counters, out to the tables and back. When she was young she had often thought Anne was an angel. Michelle's motions were more powerful but somehow still as graceful.

"Denise, my dear. I haven't seen you in days."

"I'm fine, I wanted to pick up some pizza fixings for an early dinner."

Anne's gentle smile stopped her cold, as it always would. Anne had used it to remind her of her manners when she'd started helping out in the deli. She suddenly felt six years old again.

Reaching over the counter Anne shook Michelle's hand. "Hello, my name is Anne. Please excuse my niece, she was always difficult to teach properly."

"Anne." Denise looked at her and shifted her stance wishing she could step out and come in again.

"You may call me Michelle. Denise does seem to be a little focused sometimes."

Denise wanted to kick her in the shins, out of sight below the level of the counter, but she was afraid Anne would catch her anyway. Instead she swallowed hard and took a deep breath.

"My humble apologies, O Perfect Aunt." She tried to make her voice bold and strong like a knight-maiden from chivalrous days of old.

"The noble lady Michelle is a guest for the midday repast. Two hungry and valiant warriors await our return with provisions as they are presently locked in mortal combat with . . ." she let her voice return to normal, ". . . some stupid computer program."

Anne had patiently folded the cloth she was holding. She turned to Michelle clearly trying to irritate Denise.

"A pleasure to meet any friend of my niece's. How may I help you?"

Michelle leaned against the big stainless steel and glass deli case and nodded toward Denise.

"She has the shopping list."

Anne laughed lightly. It was easy to join in.

"Let's see this list of yours and I'll see what I can do."

Denise went to lift the section of counter. "I can take care of it, Anne."

Anne pushed down gently on the Formica top. "For once I will serve you as a customer. You do have a guest."

Denise groaned and handed over the list. Anne took the crumpled bit of paper and lay it on the counter to

166

smooth it out once or twice. Before leaving the apartment she had placed it neatly in her pocket. She did not remember crunching it into a ball.

Anne looked at it for a long moment and glanced at Denise.

"What? Is something wrong with the list?"

"Oh no. I simply think we ladies need to sit and talk for a moment."

Denise felt a strong urge to run from the deli. She'd already had enough long talks today, she wasn't sure she could stand another. If she had looked away Denise might have tried to escape, but Anne kept looking at her even as she called out to Uncle Joshua.

He came around the end of a bin of tomatoes in his permanently stained apron. Reaching into his pocket quickly he put his half-glasses on and set his old coffee mug on the counter.

"Denise. Darling. I haven't seen you in hours. Is this a friend of yours whom I don't know? Hello. I'm Joshua. Thank you for coming to our deli. It's such a pleasure to meet you." He shook Michelle's hand enthusiastically.

Flipping the countertop over Anne came out and put a hand on Joshua's arm. "Would you take care of this list, Joshua? We girls are going to have a chat."

"Why, of course." He took the list and hurried off.

Anne looked after him for a moment before turning back to them. Something had made Uncle so effusive even Anne was surprised. She shrugged.

Michelle was tracing one finger over the characters on Uncle's mug. "How curious."

"Why do you say that?"

"*Simha.* Joy or perhaps rejoicing would be closer."

Denise looked at Michelle's strong finger resting against the glazed surface.

"You speak Hebrew?" The words stuck in her throat. She had underestimated Michelle badly.

"I haven't seen this script in ages, it's quite archaic?"

"Uncle Joshua said it was to show that life did not have to be perfect to be enjoyed. I never knew exactly what the letters were before."

Michelle nodded her head. "I know a man who needs to learn that lesson." She turned to follow Anne.

Michelle's tone had softened. Denise touched her arm to stop her. She'd come to feel like an old friend she'd only known a short time. It was a nice feeling.

"Is he important to you?"

Michelle turned, her eyebrows raised high.

"Who? Plato? Not likely. He's a problem child I've been trying to rid myself of."

Denise chose one of the old wooden chairs across the table from Michelle. Plato was an odd name, she could not recall having ever heard it in modern usage.

Anne's cough drew her attention. "I understand you had a chat with the boys this morning."

She could feel the pain across her shoulder blades from working late last night and napping on the couch. Michelle looked at her with sympathy clear on her face. Maybe she'd had older brothers or something.

"Now, Aunt Anne, don't you start. They have already pushed me enough for one day. "

Anne wiped at a spot on the table top with her cloth as if polishing the old photos beneath the glass.

She realized they were sitting at the table composed almost entirely of her growing up pictures. She really didn't need this.

Michelle was looking at the happy little girl in the photos. She pointed at a picture of Denise staring intently at the cash register about to push a button.

Anne had set down her cloth. "Have you ever seen such a charming little girl? When her parents passed away we could not resist raising her ourselves."

Anne was absent-mindedly tapping the glass over a print of her when she was about ten. Standing on a stool and holding a set of tongs nearly as long as her arm she was about to serve a smiling young boy a pickle from the old barrel. She looked up to see Anne and Michelle glance at each other and then both turn to look at her.

"What? You two look like the Spanish Inquisition or something. Stop it. I've already been through one today."

Anne nodded in her serene way. "You must forgive men their ham-handedness when they speak from the heart. There is no greater joy than a good relationship. A part of that joy is spending a lifetime working on all of the little problems and all of the big problems together. A cooperative effort to forge ahead. That is what they wish for you. Such love is what I wish for anyone."

She looked to see Michelle watching Anne. She was very still and her brows were drawn together in deep concentration. An angel on Earth and a self-proclaimed devil regarded one another framed in the same late afternoon sunlight.

ack in the apartment John and Peter hadn't moved an inch except they now had two pads of paper. They were oblivious to her and Michelle's return. As she watched, Peter crumpled up the page he'd been working on and tossed it onto the table. John picked it up and dropped it into the small garbage basket he'd retrieved from behind the couch. Michelle's chair, with Denise's copy of the *Inferno* still on the arm and pillows scattered on the floor around it, looked as if someone had lived in it for a week. She shook her head and smiled. She set her grocery bag on the kitchen counter next to the one Michelle had carried.

"Oh no, I forgot the wine. Is it worth going back?"

"Not to worry." Reaching into her bag Michelle pulled out two bottles. "We may have forgotten but your Uncle seems to have remembered."

The labels were Italian and she didn't recognize either one. "Both new. Thank you, Uncle."

Michelle took off John's jacket and threw it over a stool. "Your aunt and uncle really love you, don't they?"

"Yes, they do and it's very mutual." Denise finished emptying one of the bags and started to fold it carefully. She had always trusted Anne's judgment of people and her obvious approval of Michelle had reassured her.

"It shows. I've seen a lot of families and few of them look as close as the three of you."

Turning, Michelle opened exactly the right cupboard for the flour and a mixing bowl.

"How did you do that?"

"Magic."

"Yeah. Right."

She shrugged. "Okay, you caught me. I love a good kitchen and I intruded a little earlier to see how you'd planned yours."

She poured some flour into the bowl and a near equal amount on the counter. "I'll make the dough, if you start on the toppings. I make a mean pizza dough."

Denise shook her head. "If you're the Devil why don't you snap your fingers and create it?"

"Wouldn't be as much fun . . ." she plunged her hands into the flour and water to start mixing them by hand, " . . . and it doesn't work that way."

"How does it work?"

Michelle nodded her head toward the living room. "You'd have to ask them. I'm only a programmer."

Denise laughed as she folded Michelle's grocery bag and tucked it in with the others. "I will start on the toppings as soon as I've tackled the tomato sauce, but first I'll open the wine."

She jumped slightly as she realized Peter was close beside her. He smiled in apology.

"I could take care of opening the wine for you."

"Sorry, I didn't hear you come up behind me." She turned sharply again at a touch on her shoulder.

"My, we're jumpy today." John stood right behind her smiling wistfully.

After today it would be more surprising if she weren't. John took the bottle of wine from her hands and gave it to Peter, before reaching into a drawer and tossing him the corkscrew. Peter caught it and set to work.

John looked at her, clearly waiting. She pointed at the tomato sauce makings. He flashed a cheery thumbs up and she started to wash off the mushrooms and green peppers. One of the mushrooms escaped and fell to the floor. She waited a moment before realizing she hadn't had a dog in years and picked it up herself.

"Where's a dog when you need one?"

"You're dog people? Where is it?" Peter's face lit up as he stopped pouring the wine and looked around the apartment. If he cared that much about dogs there was some hope for him.

Denise thought of Jack, George and Pete. She could still imagine George's soft ears tickling her palms.

"We had them a lot when I was a kid, but I don't own one now. Are you a dog people?"

"Yes, but he's trapped in Heaven."

Denise looked at John. He didn't appear to doubt Peter's words at all. He was awfully cute, the way he believed every hard luck tale.

Peter started playing with the cork as he leaned on the other side of the counter. "Blaise gets depressed when I'm away on business, but at least he'll have Jesus and Mary to play with. Great Pyrenees are very social."

Michelle chimed in from where she stood with pizza dough all over her hands, a smear of flour on her cheek and a mess on the counter for several feet around.

"Too bad the Hounds of Hell have passed away; we could have let them play together."

"What? Blaise with the Hounds of Hell?"

Peter's eyes went wide and he dropped the cork onto the floor. Her laugh was light and merry. Michelle winked at her. Denise winked back.

"I had a pair of poodles. Real ones, about 70 pounds each, not those little painted rats that go, 'squeak.' They were quite lovable, if a little on the dumb side. Whoever tells you poodles are smart never met my pair."

John sounded surprised. "I was raised by a pretty bright poodle."

"Raised by one?"

Denise loved this story. She sliced the pepperoni while John told it.

"When I was born my parents had never seen a baby up close. Mom didn't know what to do. Dad said, 'I'll buy a dog. I know how to raise dogs. Whatever I do for the dog, you do for the kid.' I'm told Boetheis taught me to bark before I could talk. I always took my naps curled up against him. There are some wonderful photos in my Dad's albums of me fast asleep and Bo looking at him with a 'You wake this child and you will regret it' stare."

Michelle smiled. "Mine were a bit different. When are the two of you going to get a dog?"

John wanted another poodle, but she hoped their dog would be a Labrador. Denise felt her face grow hot.

"I wish people would stop saying that. There never has been a 'two of us.' There is no 'we.' There never will be a 'we.' John and I are friends, nothing more," she said.

The words came out harsher than she'd intended. She wished she could take them back the instant she'd spoken them. A hundred times before she'd said these very words, but this time they were wrong. John looked as if she'd slapped him. She had ignored all of the advice Anne and Kris had given. John was clearly indicating he had decided he wanted more than friendship. It would have been kinder if she had hit him. She reached out to touch his arm in apology for her words.

He turned away from her toward the stove. The only sound in the kitchen louder than the pain in her heart was the quiet bubbling of the sauce as he stirred it.

 ohn had tried not to look at Denise throughout the meal, but he kept finding himself staring. Her profile, brightly lit by the late afternoon sun streaming in behind him, made it hard for him to breathe. He shouldn't think about that. He knew the answer to his question. She didn't want anything to do with him no matter what Joshua and Anne said. Thank goodness he'd never asked her. Now it was his burden alone, but it was going to take a long time to not want more. Damn Joshua and damn himself for thinking about changing what was between the two of them.

She tossed her fork onto her plate. "All right. That does it. The salad rule is hereby invoked."

Peter stopped in mid-sentence and looked at her. "What's the salad rule? We don't have any salad."

John had been trying to stay on a comfortable topic and realized he had led the conversation into computers at every turn. He smiled weakly at Denise. He might feel hurt but it was his own damn fault not hers.

"The salad rule is once the salad is served no techy talk is allowed at the table. Usually it's invoked much sooner than this, salad or no."

There was a lengthy silence as they all tried to think of a new topic of conversation. At least Denise had smiled at him in return, despite not looking at him through the whole meal. Maybe she was still mad about whatever had made her think he had a girlfriend. Surely she knew he'd have told her right away.

The Devil wiped her mouth with her napkin, dropped it on her plate and sipped at her glass of wine.

"Speaking of Methuselah I remember his chief wife had a similar problem."

John didn't know they were speaking of him, but he was glad to listen. The Devil had a story for everything. She'd kept dinner lively with the history of the computer system and various figures from the past. The chair gave a very comfortable creak as she leaned back.

"Now old Methuselah, I used to call him Methos for short, didn't actually live 969 years as reported, but he did make it to eighty-seven, which was quite something back then. Methos was a randy old bugger and his wife, a fun lady, couldn't get any peace or rest. He had the most unremitting sex drive of anyone I've ever met. She created a rule somewhat like yours. She would only receive him after neither of them had eaten for at least an hour. She was very concerned about his health, or so she claimed. Not quite the story she told me."

John looked over at Denise. He saw that she was caught up in the story, too. She'd been very resistant and disbelieving at first. He'd feared she really would throw them out. Now it was clear that they could all work on this together. It'd be a good chance for him to forget about Joshua's silly notions.

"She convinced the local ruler, with some promises I won't mention in decent company, that everyone in the kingdom was to eat a meal at least once every three hours. It irritated Methos horribly, but it did give the poor woman a rest. When the old coot died a few months later I think it was from frustration. The women's meal times didn't even coincide with his."

Denise's laugh was genuine. She refolded her napkin and set it beside her plate.

"Well, they certainly didn't eat as well as this. We'll never get it that right again. The interplay of spices on my tongue . . . I can't wait to try the other recipes. How Elantra found these I'll never know."

Peter sat staring into his wine. "I'm afraid it will be that good each and every time."

"Afraid? I wouldn't use quite that word. Thrilled maybe, perhaps even delighted, but not afraid. I wish I could eat another piece, if there had been a piece left over, but then I'd explode. Uncle gave us the right amount of ingredients."

"No, he didn't. He provided the perfect amount."

"What are you talking about?"

John could hear the tone of frustration edge into her voice. Damn it. Pissing her off wasn't going to make it easier to elicit her help. Peter rose and reached over the kitchen counter.

"Here's the cookbook." He passed it over to Michelle. "Does any of this seem familiar? Read through it a bit."

"How could it be?" She read a few pages, flipped through several more and then fanned the book stopping a few times. She dropped it on the table as if her fingers were burned.

"You can't publish this."

Denise placed her clenched hands on either side of her plate. "Why the Hell not?"

"Precisely." Michelle tapped her finger on the stack of paper. "This is the Cookbook from Hell, or rather selected dishes. To restore your cookbook the system must've taken the list of dishes and pulled up a matching set of its recipes and printed it out. No negative effect either. The pizza remained perfect throughout the meal."

Peter nodded in agreement. "What you have is a set of perfect dishes, or as close as possible on Earth. Every time you follow these recipes the results'll be fantastic."

"And why is that a problem?"

Peter leaned forward and tapped the stack of paper. "You could unbalance world trade as people tried to get the ingredients for these dishes."

She turned on him. "There you go with that software from Heaven crap again. You're not messing with my cookbook. I wish you three would give it a rest. I put up with that nonsense all through dinner. Isn't it enough?"

John reached out to calm her, but she rose from the table and started clearing the plates with so much zeal he hoped she wouldn't break any.

"Oh no, not again. Don't start this whole charade again. I accept that you are amazing game developers and someone has stolen your software, but we're talking about a best selling cookbook here."

John groped for a middle ground. "Maybe you could corrupt the recipes a bit. You are the editor."

"Why in the world would I want to do that? John, why is everything I say to these unasked for guests wrong." She stalked into the kitchen and dumped the plates into the sink with a raucous clatter.

If only he could make her see what he understood about the software. The logic behind the programming was completely foreign compared to today's standards. Being other worldly was the only thing that made sense. It was the universe's control software.

Peter broke the silence after it had stretched on long enough that John was afraid it would never end.

"I wonder. The system is self correcting. Unless I miss my guess you wouldn't be able to corrupt the recipes even if you wanted to. They'll fix themselves, but it's worth a try."

John winced. Peter needed to think more before he spoke.

Denise was glaring at him from the kitchen, a sponge in her hand.

"Over my dead body." Her voice was like ice.

Once again furious scrubbing and the running water were the only sounds in the room. If anything it was worse than before. He couldn't think of what to say. The Devil's voice broke some of the tension.

"If I may change the subject for a moment?"

She paused, waiting for someone's permission. John looked at her and saw she was waiting for Denise. After receiving a brief nod she continued. Denise didn't even look at him.

"We do have another problem. If we want to reopen Heaven's gates, we need that software back. While Denise and I were out did you two figure out where Ron came from or went to?"

Denise started to ram the plates into the dishwasher without rinsing. Peter leaped for the change in topic.

"Yes, actually, we did. There was an evil twin created as you guessed. There was a logical inconsistency when I reintegrated the two systems. There was a duplication forced in the index. Remember the system couldn't delete the extraneous entry because I was using my own passwords. The index, being too large to be easily rebuilt in case of an error, caused a self-correction loop to kick in and . . ."

Michelle raised her hand to stop him. "Hold it. You're speaking gibberish again."

"He hasn't spoken anything else since he stole our software this morning." Denise's voice hadn't lost it's edge. She came around the counter and began to collect more plates.

Peter looked at her. "I was only trying to describe how . . ." At least he knew to stop. Of course, Denise's glare would stop a small Mack truck at the moment.

John realized the awful position he had put her in with all of this. She didn't believe in these people. He needed to apologize for many things that had happened today; misunderstandings about a girlfriend, siding with strangers and not explaining what he had learned from the software more carefully. Reaching out he took her hand before she could collect another load of dishes. It was very wet and soapy. She had not even put on her rubber gloves. He looked into her eyes, despite the glare they directed at him.

"I will try to be clearer in the future."

She looked surprised for a moment then she smiled at him. A giant wave of relief swept through him. He blessed whatever it was that made her understand his apology. He felt the warmth of her hand tingle along his arm as she held his fingers tightly.

"For now will you agree to listen?"

She slowly sat back down in her chair and didn't let go of his hand. She nodded

Peter coughed slightly. "In English, the bottom line is Ron, my virtual evil twin, was created as a free-ranging hungry ghost."

"That doesn't help. A hungry ghost? That's Buddhist, isn't it? Why free-ranging?" She sounded confused, but she was listening.

Peter continued, uncertainly at first, "A hungry ghost is Buddhist. It is an incarnation of someone who has lived an evil life. As a hungry ghost they are supposed to learn the error of their ways and live a better life next time. I chose free-ranging because an entity in the Buddhist software should not have been able to attack you or to even know about our software, much less steal it."

"If I assume that what you said makes sense and that you really are who you say you are. Why would your evil twin from the Buddhist software want to steal your program? What does he hope to do with it? And . . ."

John could feel himself freeze. She gently pulled her hand from his and rested it on the table. Her expression became distant. He could practically hear the mental gears whirring. He was afraid she'd switch back to anger and finish the sentence with '. . . will you get out.'

She suddenly smiled brighter than the sun that shone on her face.

"... does anyone want tea or coffee before you leave to become guerrillas in Buddha-land?"

He looked at her for a moment in awe. She would join them. Again she had exceeded his highest hopes. There could be no better person to have as a friend.

Denise was very pleased. That had been exactly the right thing to say. Usher them on their adventure and spend some time with John on straightening out the day's confusion.

Michelle starting stacking some dishes. "I'm set. I'll help you clean up so we can all go together."

Denise was glad she was sitting down. "You want what? You want us to go with you?"

So much for humoring them. Though she would miss Michelle, she'd had enough adventure for one day. "Go where? Do you think you can actually take us to Hell?"

Michelle nodded. "That I do. Between John and Peter we have one great computer team."

"I'd like to help if I can." John's voice was earnest.

She had to blink twice before she recognized him. It was hard to see John's expression with the setting sun shining in directly behind him. She hadn't been able to see his expression at all during dinner because of it. He wasn't playing along, he really did believe in them. Amazing. Simply amazing. Moment ago he'd promised to be clearer about when he was humoring someone.

Michelle continued blithely as if nothing were out of the ordinary, "That would be great, John, thanks. And Denise, you can't deny you're connected to all this. Most importantly, I refuse to travel alone with two computer nerds. I need some protection. You must come. You have no choice." She spoke the last as a solemn command, but softened it with a big smile.

Denise decided to laugh. Kris had suggested she needed an adventure. He had no idea. This one was clearly a trip into the ridiculous, but it might turn out to be fun. The company would certainly be excellent.

"How can I leave the Devil in such an evil situation?"

John's sigh of relief made her glad of her choice. The friendship was solid despite any misunderstandings. Hopefully, he wouldn't be disappointed when nothing happened. See how much he believed in his new friends' identities when they couldn't lead them anywhere except out onto the streets of New York.

She turned to Michelle. "Do we need anything special to go to Hell?"

Michelle rose to her feet. "A few good sins." She tossed her napkin onto her stack of dishes and carried them into the kitchen.

"Remember, I had the Earl Grey tea. According to our deal, I won't have to pay for at least five of them."

"So true. So true."

Denise headed to the bathroom. "I'll help out in just a minute."

Once again her reflection stared at her as she brushed her teeth. This was a person she recognized. The friend. With all the trials of the day she was as ready as she'd ever be for an evening walking the streets and searching for the entrance-way to Hell.

When she came out they were finishing in the kitchen. "That was fast."

John held up his hands. "Six hands make light of the most tiresome task. Are you ready?"

"Sure, but how do we get there?"

The blank look on his face showed that she'd caught him. He shrugged and looked to Michelle.

"Follow me." Michelle walked into the hall tapping a few keys on a fat calculator she'd pulled out of a pocket, as if adding two plus two was going to equal five. She opened the apartment's front door.

Michelle wasn't the only one with a sense of humor. "And I always thought this led to the elevator. Here it is the door to Hell."

Actually, on the crazy days she thought of it as her shield from the city. Sometimes, going through the door and out into the crazy world did feel like entering Hell.

She had to take a deep breath before following Michelle through. It was silly, there was nothing out there except the hall. She glanced at John close behind her and almost fell as she stepped into a world filled with sunlight and the murmur of the sea.

*J*ohn caught her arm.

"Careful."

She squinted as her eyes adjusted. They were high on a grassy slope that swept to the sea. The only building was a house some distance along the glittering beach. She looked back to see Peter stepping out of her apartment. The doorway stood on the grass with nothing else around it except a slight glow. The dark, brooding mountains beyond made her want to go home immediately.

She became aware of John's arm tight around her shoulders. "Are you okay?"

She turned to look at him. "I don't think so."

"Shit." Michelle, or was she really the Devil after all, had stopped a few paces away and sounded upset. "This isn't where we were supposed to arrive." She pulled out her keypad again and tapped a few more keys while frowning at the display.

Denise could feel her knees go weak. Without John's arm she would have fallen. This was not where she had expected to come out either. After taking a deep breath she patted his hand and stepped away to look at the pad. It was all covered with meaningless symbols on oddly shaped keys. She glanced at John and saw him asking Peter questions as they inspected the apartment door.

She had to fight to keep her voice from shaking as she asked Michelle, "Where did you expect to be?"

Michelle slipped the device into her pocket. "We were supposed to arrive in the conference room. Not the hills by my house. Something's not right here."

Denise noticed the sun was hanging high above them. "How did that get up there?"

"We're in a different time zone than New York."

"That's your house on the beach?" It was hard to see any details. It looked like a nice sized rambler stretched along the shore in a large grove of palm trees.

"That's it."

A slight chill went up her spine. "Michelle, I hate to sound stupid, but where are we?" She was almost sorry that she'd asked the question.

Michelle turned to look at her, the tilt of her head and the pity in her eyes were too clear. This woman was exactly who she said she was. Denise was somewhere she had never believed existed. She was in Hell.

Time seemed to stand still as she watched herself turn slowly toward her apartment door. Peter pushed it shut as John came around from behind it. The click echoed in her ears. She reached for the knob, but it faded like a morning mist, there one moment then gone.

Peter looked at where the door had been. "That wasn't supposed to happen. Michelle, what's going on?"

Denise's legs failed her and she sank, very slowly, like a leaf on the wind, until she was kneeling in the grass. Her arm didn't feel connected to her body as she pointed to where her door had been. John touched her shoulder and the world came rushing back to focus.

"I don't know, Peter. Give me a moment." Michelle paced once slowly around where the doorway had been. "I think the system has decayed further than we expected without the Master Control Software."

"Maybe the system isn't working at all."

Peter looked as worried as she felt and she knew she didn't understand the implications.

After a long moment of silence, Michelle spoke, "I think we are in deep trouble. The doorway to Heaven is no longer our only problem."

Without another word she headed down the hill toward her beach house. Denise followed, picking her way through the heather until they reached a narrow path. John was not far behind, chatting about something arcane with Peter at the end of the single file. Perfect. They were all following the Devil down a narrow, crooked path into Hell. She nearly ran into Michelle where she had stopped beside an ugly murky pool.

"Here's someone who can tell us if the software runs at all normally." Michelle offered her hand to a tall man.

He was climbing out a pool of brown goo which had matted his silver hair to his head. A dripping wet toga clung to him. He rose with a dignity and grace that belied his condition. His voice was sad, no, resigned was perhaps a better word.

"The opposite of a cool desert evening is not what might be termed a particularly pleasant experience."

Michelle held his hand for a moment. "My good man, haven't you heaped enough abuse upon yourself yet?"

"I have not yet succeeded in my plans."

She wiped her hand on her jeans leaving a long streak of mud. "You are lucky that you are dead already with how some of your plans have been going."

"Lucky to be dead? Indeed."

He bowed formally to them and walked away with mud squelching out of his sandals.

Michelle stood very still as she watched him go. "At least part of the system still works."

Denise's confidence was not restored in the least. Once they started off again Peter and John hustled past her. Peter started harassing Michelle with questions she clearly didn't like. John was listening intently, leaving her to bring up the rear.

When they finally arrived at the base of the hill and walked toward the house, Denise realized she'd been thinking of only one thing. What she would have to do in order not to come here when she died. Sainthood was not in her blood.

John followed Michelle to her house. Believing in the existence of Hell was quite different from experiencing it. He'd expected dark caverns filled with tortured souls, fire and demons with mighty whips. Maybe the tortured souls were kept somewhere else. He had chatted with Peter as they started down, apparently Michelle had built a Hell of the mind. He was fascinated and had wanted to try a sample until he'd seen the man who had slime dripping off every inch of his body.

Her house looked more substantial, without crossing over into ostentatious, as they approached it. No great hall of flame for this Devil. A nice cedar shake finish and a simple sloping roof. There were few windows on the land side of the house. As they went around the corner John admired the long wooden verandah and an equally long wall of glass. He could see walls dividing up some of the interior, but there was nothing between floor and ceiling to block the view of the white sand beach and the ocean. No floats or old crab pots to dress it up; a few wicker chairs, a wooden bench and a porch swing accounted for all of the furniture. A wide rail ran between the posts holding up the verandah's overhang.

Michelle turned in at the first sliding glass door and waved for them to sit around a big oak kitchen table. John liked this old country kitchen. He'd build a similar one to share with Denise some day. Sparkles of light reflected off the ocean's waves outside and glittered upon the copper cookware. It was supposed to be a pest to maintain, but it certainly did look great above the huge black stove. They could sit around the table with friends and serve fine coffee like the Devil was now preparing.

He'd never before noticed all the fantasies he'd been building over the years. It was very easy to imagine being with Denise.

She had chosen to sit opposite him across the table. He hoped it was random chance only. She was slowly turning a salt shaker around and around in her fingers.

"Would someone care to enlighten me regarding the Buddhist hungry ghosts?"

Even though she was not looking at him he felt compelled to answer, to try and help her adjust. He had been expecting the transition and it still was a shock.

"I don't have any clue about ghosts, hungry or not. Peter said that was where the program error sent Ron."

Michelle set four substantial coffee mugs on the table along with some sugar and a pitcher of cream.

On the walk down the hill Peter had practically hounded Michelle with some idea about working directly with the code to which she was adamantly opposed. Now he leaned with his elbows on the table.

"On the Buddhist Wheel of Life a soul is reincarnated time and time again until it has learned all of its lessons. Upon enlightenment the soul leaves the wheel and becomes one with the Buddha."

"And that's Buddhist Heaven?" Denise turned the salt shaker slowly around again.

Peter shook his head. "No. That's true enlightenment. Buddhist Heaven is a sham. A soul gets reborn differently depending on how it did in its last life. One of the possible reincarnations is a false Heaven. If you fail to see that it is all self-indulgence and vanity you probably come back as a snake."

"Is a snake as low as you can go?" John was starting to remember bits and pieces of this from a comparative religion class. "I thought all lives were created equal?"

He could hear Michelle making coffee. The aroma slowly filled the air as it brewed.

Peter ran his fingernail along a line of grain in the wood table top. "Supposedly. You can leave the wheel at any time by simply gaining true enlightenment. If you really mess up you come back as a hungry ghost."

"But what is a hungry ghost?"

That was certainly his Denise through and through. Absolutely tenacious. She claimed it was a leftover from being a journalist. Perhaps it was simple bulldog pig-headedness, but he liked it.

"Though the positions on the wheel are considered equal, some of them are easier lives and some are harder. The worst bummer of all, even worse than being a snake, is a hungry ghost. Imagine being permanently hungry, having everything you want right in front of you and not being able to even touch it. You pass through it. If you could tip it into your mouth, it would fall through you and hit the floor."

Denise's grimace echoed his feelings. He wouldn't wish that on anyone. Michelle had been oddly quiet but now she spoke.

"That would fit Ron's hunger to control the software, something you've struggled with ever since God died."

Denise looked over John's head at Michelle. "How can God be dead? That does not make any sense. After all, he's God."

John winced. It had been obvious when Peter told them the story how much it upset him. He wished Denise would think longer before asking her questions.

Peter's face was white as a sheet. "I wish I knew."

"I'm sorry, Peter, but I truly don't understand."

Michelle brought the large pot of coffee to the table and began to pour it.

"God was not what the universe revolved around. Like me, he was simply a programmer. Fortunately for us he was also an artist."

The sound of loss in her voice filled the room. John watched Denise. She had obviously noticed Michelle's pain and thought for a while before continuing.

"The other question I have is how can you talk of a Buddhist Wheel of Life when your existence makes for a Christian universe?"

"Christian? Did you ever see the British comedian who did this Devil act?" Michelle took a sip of her coffee.

Pretending to consult a notepad, she looked at the three of them very seriously.

"All Christians, welcome. I'm sorry but the Jews were right. You may proceed directly to Hell. All lawyers, everyone else was right. Writers, poets, please stay with your agents, you shall be transported down shortly."

Everyone laughed as she sat back in her chair and put her feet up on one corner of the table.

"Not quite right. Hindus claim you can't convert to their religion because it encompasses all religions already. It has made for fewer but bloodier Hindu wars. The only problem is they are completely inaccurate, too. When we first discovered there was a Buddhist system parallel to our own we looked around and only found that one other. For the most part the Buddhists won't talk to us, 'You're too different,' they say and I am inclined to believe them. We, God and I, never did figure out what slots a soul into one part or the other of this system. Ultimate enlightenment is the final goal of both, but we go about it differently. Whoever designed this software had a weird sense of humor."

Denise dropped into her chair. "What do you mean whoever designed the software? Didn't you or God?"

"No, the software existed before we did."

"But that's outrageous. I'm not some lousy bit or byte of information in a computer somewhere."

John could think of several tacky lines about her being the prettiest piece of code he'd ever seen but decided he'd better keep quiet.

"You and Plato both."

"Who's he? You mean the Plato?"

Michelle nodded her head. Denise started playing with the salt shaker again.

"Who thought this one up?"

That was one John could answer. He sat up and attempted to imitate Michelle's voice. "The designer of the software is believed lost in the mists of time. Creation date was approximately 14 billion BC, that would be March fourteenth, 1958 AC, After Creation."

Michelle leaned forward so eagerly he sat back in his chair. "How did you find that out?"

"I asked the software."

She sat back with a look of surprise on her face and then laughed harshly, once.

"1958?" Denise's voice sounded funny.

Of course. He couldn't believe he'd missed that. "Damn! You two were born on the same day . . . sort of. What time were you born? Hang on I scratched down it's Creation Date somewhere." He started to rummage through his pockets.

"My birth certificate says 5:44 a.m. on March 14, 1958 AD." She emphasized the last letter.

John set his wrinkled note in the middle of the table. Everyone leaned forward to look as Denise read out, "5:44 a.m. Eastern Standard Time. March 14th, 1958 AC. Why does your software have my birthday?"

Peter turned the slip of paper to look at it. He took another sip of coffee. "Actually I think that you have its birthday, it is a bit older than you, but as to why . . ." He shrugged. "The software once said this program was started long After Creation, AC. I never understood what it meant. Maybe this space-time was created and it took 1,958 years to install the software?"

Michelle looked at him and said with a bewildered laugh, "Don't ask me. I only remember a few minutes before we started the software running."

Denise leaned toward her. "But who created you and God and it?"

Standing, Michelle walked to the French doors and opened them letting in the sound of the surf. Her voice mixed with that of the waves.

"Where do the waves begin on the surface of the ocean? There are some things I will never know and my origin is one of them. You each know you had parents, but I don't even know if I was born or created."

No one made a sound as the Devil stepped out, crossed the porch and descended to the beach.

Denise's heart ached for Michelle as she watched her walk away. Her own parents might be dead, but she did have pictures and stories. Michelle only had a beginning of memory. With a sigh Denise left the kitchen to explore the rest of the house. She heard John follow her.

Now this was her idea of a living room; three walls of floor-to-ceiling bookcases and a fourth wall of all windows facing the ocean. Uneven piles of books sat next to one of the chairs. As she selected a volume here, and read a few titles there, she realized how eclectic a collection Michelle had. Most of the authors on two of the walls had been dead for centuries, the third wall held the finest trash science fiction collection she'd ever seen. John had quickly moved to that wall and every now and then she heard a gasp as he'd take a book and read a few pages before putting it back. She pulled a slender manuscript from the first wall marked simply 'Leonardo' on the spine. It opened in the middle to the start of one of the loveliest poems she'd ever read.

She sat on a handy couch, noticing John had done the same. Peter had found a computer manual of some sort and taken a chair by the window. She became rapidly lost in the poem's rhythmic splendor. It told of a wild and beautiful maiden, wise beyond her years. Traveling from parts unknown, she breathed life into the world she loved. Moving on, forever untouchable, forever touching. It almost sounded like Michelle. When she finished it Denise closed her eyes and relished the sounds in her head for a while. She turned to the flyleaf where a graceful hand had written, 'To Snookums, with Love, Leo.' Reading the title page she almost dropped the book. It was an original da Vinci, written in ink.

Michelle nearly scared the daylights out of her when she spoke from right beside her.

"He was awfully sweet. He wrote this collection of short stories and poems about Italian lovers for me. He had started on a novel, he always was ahead of his time, but was sidetracked by that wench he put in the Mona Lisa before he wrote much."

Denise realized her mouth was open. She closed it and placed the book very carefully onto a nearby table. She looked at John who shrugged and went back to his science fiction. Peter didn't look up from his manual.

"Did the walk help?"

Michelle nodded as they looked out the window. "Hell's ocean has always made a good companion. It has been my friend for long enough that I would feel incomplete anywhere else."

"It's not alive is it?"

Michelle moved to a facing armchair, picking up the book of poetry.

"No more so than any big body of water." She idly leafed through the pages.

She glanced out to see if the waves were watching her. The surf rolled in off Hell's ocean and broke on the beach exactly as she'd expect. She was in Hell and Michelle really was the Devil. She tried to remain calm. Her chest felt too tight to even breathe. Ever since they had walked out of her apartment door and landed in Hell she had been fighting to make some sense of what was happening. Now that she was making sense of it she was starting to feel very frightened. She wiped her palms on her slacks to dry off the sweat.

Kris could have no idea what an adventure he had launched her on. She couldn't wait to see his face when she told this story. That helped put some perspective on it all. What was most surprising was how eager she was feeling about it. She was actually looking forward to what might happen next.

And John was here with her. He was the only thing that was familiar. She remembered the feel of his hand on her shoulder earlier, amazing that it was today, when they had been faced by that ethereal consultant. His touch had been warm and reassuring at the time. That was the real John. The one who was her best friend. She could almost feel his hand, solid and comforting, resting there again.

She startled when she realized there really was a hand on her shoulder. She turned to see the dismay on John's face as he took his hand away. No matter what she did, she hurt him. She'd walked out on him; hadn't trusted him about the software. Wouldn't even give him a chance before jumping to conclusions about fictitious girlfriends. These actions didn't match her desire for the mutual trust of a long friendship.

Before she could think about the consequences she reached out and took his hand. His look changed slowly from uncertainty to bemusement as she pulled him onto the couch next to her, but she didn't care. She snuggled shamelessly against him, not giving a damn who was watching or what he was thinking. It felt wonderful. He kept his arm uncertainly around her shoulders for a moment before tentatively sliding it down to her waist, holding her. This was more than how it would feel between friends. Maybe they both needed a second chance. She could feel Joshua smiling somewhere that his little Denise was taking a risk. She leaned her head on John's shoulder, glad he was there, like a rock in Michelle's ocean.

"I guess it's time to call."

Michelle reached out for a phone that had been buried under a fallen stack of books beside a glass-topped coffee table. She dialed a very long series of numbers. She must have noticed Denise's curiosity.

"A trunk call between software systems can't be done with only a few buttons." She jerked the phone away from her ear and slammed it down. "What in the name of Heaven?"

"What's wrong?" Peter started out of his seat.

"That was a bloody pizza parlor in Chicago."

"Maybe you misdialed."

"Okay, Mr. Know-it-all, you try."

John shook his head when she looked at him, clearly a mystery to him as well. While Peter was dialing the phone John started massaging the tight muscles of her back. She turned to give him a better angle. His hands were warm and strong. The response running through her body was surprising. Her skin tightened deliciously. She leaned away. It was too much. Too fast. She reached and took his hand in hers before leaning beside him. Even the length of his arm along hers was arousing.

Peter finished, listened for a moment, said something in a foreign language and hung up the handset.

"I don't like this. That was the personal line of the president of Zimbabwe. The software is unraveling faster than we had thought."

He started dialing again.

John turned her hand palm up and began massaging it. She looked at the image of a true friendship that Uncle had said she held. It was a terrible thing to risk, but maybe distance wasn't what she wanted. She could feel the vibration of his voice where their arms touched.

"Perhaps it isn't as bad as it looks. Maybe the most technical aspects of the system are being affected first, but we're all still safe?"

Denise wished he hadn't turned that into a question. Peter nodded his head and listened for a moment. He looked relieved as he handed the phone to Michelle.

"Hello, is Ananda there?"

She whispered to John, "Who's Ananda?"

Peter answered quietly as he sat down. "He's sort of my counterpart. He was the Buddha's first convert and has been with him ever since."

Michelle's voice sounded frustrated at whatever the answer was. "He's in the middle of a Thai massage. Did he start recently? That could be days. Is himself around and about?"

She slouched back and put her feet up on the coffee table. "Great. Put him on, would you?"

She smiled broadly. "Hello. Devil from Hell here. How have you been? Really? That's simply super."

Covering the phone for a moment she told them, "Ghandi won a major tournament of Go. It was against

John the Baptist in an intramural match." She spoke into the phone again, "Please give him my congratulations."

"Go?" John's whisper tickled her ear.

"It's a Chinese game. It's said to be easy to learn and harder than chess to master." John nodded his head and returned his attention to the conversation.

"I'll tell you why I called, O Wise One. Some friends and I are working on a bit of a worry we happen to be experiencing. Could we pop over and have a chat?"

Michelle slouched lower in the chair.

"Really? Capital. Simply capital. This afternoon would be perfect. In Bodhgaya? That should be quite amusing. See you then. Tah." She hung up the phone.

Peter pulled out a keypad the same as Michelle's. "It will be afternoon there in three or four hours."

Denise couldn't help laughing, life was being very interesting. "In for a penny, in for a pound. India it is. Why the silly accent?"

Michelle leaned forward and rested her arms on her knees. "Many of his followers learned it during the British Raj, the occupation. He learned it as a *lingua franca*. He claims it's easier than trying remember the over 300 dialects. Apparently speaking English makes Indians feel quite schizophrenic. They hated the Raj, but English is the only way many of them can talk to one another especially across state lines. The Buddha studied at Oxford. He was apparently a stunning bowler, that's cricket to you. I speak High British to rib him."

"Bodhgaya?" John's voice rumbled against her arm. "Isn't that where he gave his first enlightened speech?"

"Full points, John. He still loves to sit under the bodhi trees and watch what he started."

Michelle clapped her hands together. "Well, I'm not going to sit here and worry. Who's for a walk?"

John leaned forward. "A walk? Isn't there something we should be doing?"

"I wish there was. Unless you can be as smart as the ineffable primordial programmer it isn't worth the risk of touching a thing until we know more. Who's joining me?"

Peter raised a hand. "Not me. I'm fine where I am."

Denise pictured the sorrowful man in the mire. "Me, too. It's not my idea of a good time to go strolling among the hills of Hell with the suffering around us. I don't think I'd want to run into a lot of depressing folk like that old man we met earlier."

Michelle looked offended. "That 'old man' is only twenty-five or twenty-six centuries old. And he really is very nice once you get to know him."

"Sorry. Only 2,500, a mere stripling. No offense, but I'd rather sit here than go walking in hills with people like that around."

Michelle crossed her arms and scowled. Hurt wasn't the right word either, but she couldn't quite place it.

Of course. He was her 'problem child', Plato. She had to hold on to John's hand tightly. The pressure of his fingers reassured her. No matter how much she thought she'd accepted this new reality, it always had another surprise waiting for her.

Michelle's tone was a bit acerbic. "Are you morally opposed to sailing?"

"Sailing?" She heard John's excitement match hers as they both spoke.

Michelle smiled. "It there an echo in here? I keep a boat in the San Juan Islands of Washington State."

"The Devil keeps a sailboat in the San Juans. Where else would she keep it? John and I've been looking to invest together in a vacation property near there, if we can afford it."

Michelle smiled. "I thought there was no 'we.'"

Denise felt her skin go cold. She forced herself to look at John, his face was calm, no anger showing.

"Maybe I was a little bit hasty."

He pulled her into his strong arms. "It's okay. We've been through worse and we've always pulled through."

She relished the feeling of his embrace a moment longer until she heard Michelle start to laugh.

Michelle was shaking her head. "Humans. You are so emotional. I thought we were going sailing."

Denise rose pulling John to his feet. "We're ready."

Michelle clapped her hands together. "Great. I don't get to go out much. I'd love to have someone there to play with the Lady, I think the old boat gets lonely."

"We'll talk about that later. Let's go." Denise had missed her sailing club the last two weekends. "How do we get there? Do we need supplies?"

"I see we have a sailor in our midst. All the gear's on board and I keep the boat stocked. And I don't simply snap my fingers and have things done. I hire a service. Well, Peter, what about it?"

"I'll pass, thanks." He leaned back farther into his chair. "I get fearfully seasick. You wouldn't want me along anymore than I'd want to be there. You three go ahead. I'll take a nap or read a book or something."

Denise stepped forward, not wanting to shut out John's new friend. "We'll do something else. What would you like to do?"

He shrugged his shoulders. "Nothing. Honest. I'm feeling plain lazy. You three go ahead. Have fun."

"Are you sure? You don't look very lazy."

She had to struggle not to laugh as Peter tried to look relaxed and managed to appear even less so.

"Positive."

Denise spoke again, "Hey, are we safe trying to go to the San Juans? Who knows where we'll arrive."

The Devil's smile was reassuring. "The route to my boat is very well trodden. It should be quite stable."

Well, Michelle should know best. "We arrived from New York. Which way is your boat?"

"We take a walk down the garden path. Where else would you find a boathouse?"

She and John followed Michelle out into the palm grove. They entered a small shed which was filled with sailing paraphernalia. Old sail bags and spare hardware filled shelves on one side, hanks of line hung along the other. Michelle opened a door at the far end. Denise was surprised for only a moment when there was a boat dock where there should've been palm trees. It felt natural, almost, to step from a concrete floor in Hell onto a wooden boat dock in the San Juans.

enise stopped to get a good look at the elegant sailboat which bobbed alongside the pier. She especially liked its long, sleek lines mixed with the charm particular to all-wood construction. She bent down to read the name on the steeply sloping stern.

"What a sweet craft. Lady Amalthea? Wasn't there a unicorn named that?"

"Yes, she was named after a dream I had. I passed it on to that Beagle fellow who made a nice book of it."

"All aboard that's going aboard," John called out from where he'd started rigging the sails.

Denise unplugged the shore power and released the safety lines.

Michelle kept talking as she climbed aboard and went to start the engine, "She was a one-of-a-kind, built near here. And yes, she sails as sweet as she looks."

"I was wondering about that."

She smiled at her. "I know."

Denise returned her smile as she climbed on board. Showing the ease of long practice Michelle coiled the spring line as the engine warmed up, checked everyone, put the drive into reverse, and released the stern line.

Denise sat in the cockpit. "Somebody does this a lot."

Michelle finished coiling the stern line and leaned into the tiller as they cleared the dock. "I've actually been sailing for only a few centuries."

"A few centuries?" It was easy to forget how old Michelle really was. "It's hard to believe the mythological creature of evil is sitting here next to me."

"Now I'm a mythological creature. Perfect."

Denise gasped. She tried to think a way to apologize.

Michelle laughed aloud as she reached to adjust the throttle. "That didn't come out right at all, did it?"

Denise joined in her laughter. "Not even close. What surprises me is the contrast. I've come to like and respect you. The classic stereotype certainly doesn't fit."

"Thanks. I like you, too. A surprising amount. I haven't had a close woman friend in a long time."

Their eyes met as she tried to think of her own last one, but no names came easily to Denise's thoughts.

"Me either." She looked out at the water and couldn't think of what else to say. To her relief Michelle broke the silence before it became too awkward.

"I became addicted to sailing while on one of Drake's cutters. They're pigs by today's standards, but they were pretty spectacular in their time. The most inspiring craft I ever sailed was a fully rigged tea clipper, stuns'ls flying, slicing the waves around the Horn. Oh, I loved them. I picked up this Lady about fifty years ago from an old Dutchman. He was one of those builders who uses a standard measure rather than a ruler. Some use a rope with two knots in it. Everything on the boat is roughly a multiple of seventeen-and-a-half inches."

"Sounds like a cubit to me."

"That was my guess, too. Where are we headed?"

Denise pointed sort of northwest. "The future is that way today. Yesterday it was over there," she pointed over her shoulder. "But today it's that way."

"Toward Orcas Island it is."

John came back from rigging the sails. Pointing below he arched his eyebrows.

Michelle waved lightly. "Be my guest. While you're down there, in the cooler you'll find some of those square Tupperware things. Grab a teaspoon and some paprika."

After a few moments he popped his head up from down below. "I love all the mahogany." He dropped some containers outside the door. "What are they?"

"A treat." She paused and turned her face searching for the wind. Her hair blew back over shoulders. No mariner described in literature could have been more at home than Michelle looked.

"Wind looks right." She called down to John, "let's raise sail first. I'll bring her about."

John came on deck and dropped a teaspoon and the paprika onto a seat. "Delay of snacks. Five yard penalty."

Denise followed him forward on the lightly swaying deck. "She's amazing, isn't she?"

John held the loosened halyard in his hand and looked toward the cockpit. "Yes, she is."

He turned his eyes on her and smiled. She held her breath, unsure of what she wanted to hear next.

"So are you. I'm very glad you have accepted who she is and decided to help out."

She let out her breath; he was glad she was here. Looking away, she pulled a winch handle out of its boot.

"Help out may be a strong word. I still don't know what I can possibly do, but I am here."

"I'm glad. I wouldn't have wanted to go without you."

She looked at him and saw the truth of the answer. He never had lied to her. Not now. Not about a girlfriend. She wanted to find a way to make everything right for the day. If only she could find the right words.

"Okay, I'm into the wind," Michelle called out.

"Damn."

"I know." John chuckled quietly. "We never get a break do we? Don't worry. Once this is over we can take all the time we need."

She hadn't realized she'd sworn aloud. John looked at her for a moment before hauling on the main halyard.

Denise watched the sail unfurl to make certain it was tracking properly. Yes, they had time. The sail was well-raised before she noticed the classic red Devil face with horns and a beard filling most of the sail. She yelled back to Michelle.

"Self portrait?"

Michelle's laugh carried forward despite the breeze and engine noise.

She winched the last slack out of the main. As John hauled away on the jib halyard his muscles showed through his thin shirt. She always liked sailing with him.

"Going to winch it off or shall I hold it all day?"

Thankfully he was looking at the sail and hadn't noticed her watching him. It was surprising to realize it was one of the reasons she enjoyed sailing.

While they dressed the lines Michelle dropped off the wind and cut the engine. Easing smoothly forward, the boat sliced the waves as if they weren't there. Denise trotted back to the cockpit to help trim the sails.

"Back to my original question." John started to open the plastic containers he'd left on the deck. "What are these 'snacks'? Hard-boiled egg whites in one container and egg salad in the other?"

"Almost," Michelle scooped a spoon of the yolks into an egg half, sprinkled some paprika on it and asked, "Deviled eggs, anybody?" over their laughter. "Everyone fend for yourselves."

"But why not use a flat container and prebuild them?"

"Don't be so literal, John. Because that wouldn't be as convenient. These you can throw in a backpack and go. I call them Michelle's Famous Portable Deviled Eggs. They may not be famous, but I like the way it sounds."

Denise bit deep into her egg. "Mmm. These are great. How did you come to choose Michelle? Or is it but one of a thousand names?"

"I've always preferred Michelle. It has a kinder ring than Evil Incarnate or any of a number of others I've been called. When I traced the roots of it I kept it for good."

"What does it mean?"

"It translates out of the Hebrew as 'Who is like God.' I was hooked."

As Denise started to laugh, John sang out, "Michelle, my belle . . . ,"

She stopped him with an elbow in the ribs. "Mellow out. You're taken."

"Taken? I like the sound of that."

Denise decided to leave that alone. Comfortable, yes. Friends, yes. Taken? They hadn't even talked anything over yet. Too fast. She moved to the opposite side of the cockpit to prepare the lines for a tack.

Michelle shifted her feet for better balance as the boat heeled in the freshening wind. "I was with them when they wrote that one. The Beatles were a bit weird to hang out with. We had some good parties, until they started on that whole Yogi meditation religious kick."

She glanced at John, but he was looking at Michelle. "Are you ever in Hell or do you always travel around to jazz halls and hot parties?"

He looked good with the sea and the sky behind him, his elbows back on the cockpit edge.

"Actually, it's an easy job if you don't mind being mistaken for the ultimate evil every now and then. I am more of a manager than anything else. If there are problems, I try to fix them, but the software is generally good. Special cases don't come along very often.

Hell is a way station for people willing to learn. It is only a dead end for people who do not try to improve themselves and the lives of those around them. One basic rule I've learned is people only remember what they learn the hard way. I used to post signs and hold classes, but it never helped. Those who cruised in life tend to cruise in Hell. At that speed you can be stuck there for a long time."

She looked at the approaching island shore.

"Time to tack."

"Ready about." It was hard to imagine living that way. There was too much to be done. Denise tried to never waste a second. She wondered at the amazing life Michelle had led. If she could do a hundredth as much she'd be happy.

"Helm's alee."

As John cleared the starboard jib sheet she hauled in on the port. A quick extra crank on the winch and it was all set. She wound the tail loosely around a cleat and dressed the line to be ready for the next tack.

"Where did you learn to sail?" Michelle's nod showed appreciation for Denise's hard won skills.

She sat back comfortably on one of the seats and rested her feet on John's knee.

"Alan, my ex, was the one who first introduced me to sailing. I was hooked after the first trip. I took every class I could spare the time for."

She paused a moment to relish the feeling. "Without intending to I'm now licensed to charter up to sixty-five feet and twelve people. I count discovering sailing as the only bonus for putting up with that unfeeling fool for three unending years."

John reached over to assemble more deviled eggs.

Michelle nodded to him as she accepted another one. "What about you?"

John leaned over and poked Denise.

"Hey."

"It's all her fault. I met her about the time she and Alan were separating. I think she became friends with me because she needed someone to sail with. She's been teaching me ever since. I do like to sail, but she pursues it with a passion that would kill anyone normal."

Sliding over next to him she started tickling his ribs, but he ducked below for safety. He popped his head back up briefly.

"Would anyone else like something to drink?"

Despite her attempt to look disdainful as she called him a coward, his smile didn't waver in the slightest. "If you could find me a soda that would be fine."

Michelle held up two fingers.

Denise could see John's head through the hatch as he puttered around in the galley. She wanted to join him but that would be rude. She turned to Michelle and then looked at her own feet suddenly unsure of herself. It was a feeling she wasn't used to.

Michelle leaned toward her. "I have the boat under control. Go."

She looked up to see Michelle's smile. She quickly looked back down, but could feel her face grow hot, 'Blushing right up her part-line,' as John would say.

"Fuck his brains out."

Denise couldn't believe her ears and turned sharply to look at her. "Michelle. Of course, I won't do that."

"I know, but you should. Now get down there and at least kiss him. He's waiting."

Her smile went all the way to her eyes. Leaning over Denise gave her a quick hug. Michelle barely hesitated before returning the embrace. It felt surprisingly good, like one of Uncle's.

Denise stepped out of the hug and backed away until she bumped into a cockpit seat. It had been an embrace of family, not of new acquaintance. Michelle's smile showed the same surprise.

She turned to descend the companion-way ladder. Pulling the hatch closed over her head she saw Michelle wink. Winking back she clicked the cover shut.

As she stepped off the last rung she felt John's arms wrap around her from behind. Any surprise was washed away by the heat of his hands as he slid one around her waist, the other up, slowly, between her breasts to hold her opposite shoulder. Leaning into him she ran her hands along his bare arms and locked her fingers tightly in his. She never wanted to let go.

He let out a long slow breath. She could appreciate how hard it must have been for him to risk that. All she cared about at the moment was that he had.

She rubbed her cheek along the back of their hands on her shoulder. When she leaned her head over he kissed the hollow of her collarbone. The heat of that kiss tingled down into her breasts. The rocking motion of the boat as it slid over the waves emphasized his arousal through his jeans and her thin slacks.

She slowly turned and looked into his eyes. She wrapped her arms around his neck. He looked back without a blink.

"Oh Shit, John." She lay her forehead on his chest and he kissed her on top of the head. "What's going to happen? I can't see where this will lead us."

His soft question almost taunted her. "Maybe we could simply find out as we go?"

She looked back into his eyes. It made sense. She wanted him so badly. This felt right, but how could she know if it was a good step in their long relationship.

"Well, maybe I could give us another chance." She leaned against his chest to feel his lips in her hair again. She closed her eyes, aware of only the beating of his heart . . . his hands, one on her back and the other cradling her head . . . his fingers buried in her hair . . . the gentle rocking of the boat. She was barely conscious of it as John sat her onto one of the bunks. She opened her eyes when he moved slightly apart from her.

"John?" She saw the tears in his eyes.

He took a lock of her hair and wrapped it around his finger. "Do you have any idea how much I love you? How afraid I am of losing you?"

She reached up, cupped his cheek with her palm and wiped away a tear with her thumb. "I'm starting to."

He rubbed his cheek in her hand and, turning his head, kissed her gently in the center of her palm. She almost whimpered as the heat of his lips washed down her arm and through her body. She slid across the few inches between them. He placed her palm over his heart. She could feel it beating.

She breathed in the clean scent of his skin. "I don't know why I didn't notice sooner. How did you put up with being only friends for all these years if you felt like this?"

Starting where her hand rested over his heart, he ran his fingers down her arm and over her shoulder. She was not sure he had traced the line of her cheek except for the memory of a touch he left there. He looked her in the eyes once more.

"I didn't know I was waiting, but you are worth it."

She realized she was crying, too. "So are you." She pulled him to her.

There was a loud crash and they were both thrown against the wall behind the bunk.

"What the hell?"

"All hands on deck." Michelle's voice brooked no delay as another crash threw them out of the bunk and into the companionway.

"On the double."

"Shit."

She held John's hand tightly for an extra instant as he helped her to her feet. She threw open the hatch and they scrambled up the ladder of the pitching boat. They braced themselves together on one of the cockpit benches.

She scanned around. The seas had risen in minutes from nothing to six or eight feet of ugly chop.

"Where did this come from?"

"It came out of nowhere. One moment we were fine and the next the bow was buried halfway into one of these waves. And it's getting worse."

Denise had to yell to make herself heard above the wind's howl. "No storm signs. What's going on? It does not make any sense."

The sound abated like a candle being blown out, though the wind still filled the sails driving the boat ahead through the towering waves.

An enormous voice rang out, "Nor will it ever make sense again. This is the end of the line."

Ron, ten feet tall, maybe more, straddled the deck glowering at them. He turned his stare upon John.

"Give me a false program will you? I'll drive you all into the bottom of the sea."

He pointed at Michelle.

"She's immortal, but you two are shark bait."

*S*t. Peter sat at the Devil's desk wishing with every fiber in his body that he had heeded Michelle's advice. He bounced a pencil on its eraser against the dark cherry wood. Someday he would have to ask her why the living room was full of books and her office was a plain wood-paneled room with this desk, a computer, a few chairs and a wall of glass facing Hell's ocean. Everything she did apparently had some purpose, but he couldn't see what it was most of the time. The Devil was supposed to be inscrutable and it didn't cheer him that she succeeded so frequently.

As a point of fact it was downright depressing how smoothly her life flowed. A beautiful beach house, time to read, a long history of illustrious lovers. His life was pitiful. Every day since he had finally hacked his way out of Purgatory spent working on Heaven's computers. His knees had shook as he stood before God that first time. The great bearded man, dressed in a bright Hawaiian print and Bermuda shorts, sat behind the largest console Peter had ever seen.

God's deep voice had filled the pristine office. "And what am I supposed to do with you? How can I protect Heaven from the likes of you?"

Peter had been unable to look at him. This was Jesus' father, the creator of all things. Peter had dedicated all of his energies to getting out of Purgatory and into Heaven. He had not thought about what to tell God once he arrived there. He couldn't even remember how to speak never mind say anything coherent. It felt as if someone had beaten his brains like a bowl of whipping cream.

Even now he remembered the silence had stretched for a long time. Finally, unable to stand it any longer he'd suggested, in such a quiet voice he had to repeat it three times before he had spoken loudly enough to be heard, that maybe he could fix the loophole he himself had used to breach security.

For almost two thousand years he'd run the software controlling Heaven; first as God's assistant, next as his chief programmer and, after God's death, as the master of Heaven. To this day he missed him as if a piece of his own soul had died.

He poked at a couple of the computer keys with the pencil eraser. The screen stayed dark. He pretended not to feel the ache in his shoulders at this reminder that the system was down. The Devil was off playing on a sailboat somewhere and here he sat with the broken software that ran the universe. He hated being alone at times like this. He wished Blaise were here. There was nothing like the love of a dog to give it all perspective. If he were home Peter would take him for a long walk, throwing a big stick for Blaise to fetch from Heaven's alpine meadows. That was his idea of perfection.

He looked back at Hell's ocean rolling against the shore. As a kid he had always wondered why whoever was making them didn't get tired. A little older, as a fisherman on the Sea of Galilee, he had wished whoever did make waves would stop. And they were little ones compared with these. They simply kept pounding the beaches until each grain dissolved back into the sea and each rock turned into sand. It wasn't very neat. He really shouldn't complain though, being an apostle had been a much better job than being seasick all of the time.

The mountains of home. No relentless waves there. The software had always run smoothly in Heaven. While it did have a bit of an attitude, it always worked.

If only he had left well enough alone.

The instant the others were well on their way to go sailing Peter had practically run into the Devil's office. He had managed to log on using a combination of God's, Michelle's and his own passwords. From the moment he had seen the terminal sitting there on her desk he had wanted to try his idea. The Master Control Program ran the other programs. It simplified life immensely, but he hadn't thought it was strictly necessary.

Once again he poked the keyboard with the pencil attaining no response. He had been part way in when the system came down around his ears. Holes appeared in the code faster than he could patch them. He was inspecting a chart showing the decay of the software's condition when the screen flashed and a simple blinking message stated, 'System Failure.' Now that was gone as well. All that was left to him was a dark screen, a pencil and a cold sweat that threatened to drown him.

If only he hadn't touched it. The software had been running at least. Heaven had become a fairly awful place to live, but now if they didn't do something quick there wouldn't be anywhere to live at all. Within a week, this universe would be gone. They would all be dead and who knew what would happen to Michelle.

He turned the screen off and back on. It flashed as it powered on. At least the screen was working, even if it didn't show anything. He held the pencil between his fingers and looked at it. Here he sat, one of the most important programmers in the universe staring at a little green label telling him his yellow pencil had a number two lead. There wasn't a chance of making Heaven and Hell's software run again with a goddamn number two pencil. He wrapped it tightly in his fist and slammed the eraser end down on the desk.

The eraser popped out and the metal band dug a long track across the perfect wooden top before the pencil snapped. He looked at the broken pieces and the long white scrape. He took a deep, shuddering breath. Oh God, he was going to catch Hell now.

*H*e does not appear to be a very imaginary twin from my perspective." Denise was surprised Michelle could sound calm. She realized John's arm was around her waist, supporting her. She locked her hand in his regretting all of the things they wouldn't have time to say now. The things they wouldn't learn about each other. Their death stood in front of them.

Now fifteen feet tall, Ron loomed above them from where he stood on the cabin roof. One of his legs had punched through the sail where he straddled the boom.

"It doesn't pay to lie to your ethereal consultant." He pointed at John. She could feel him flinch under the giant's stare.

"Before I destroy all of you, tell me where the Master Control Program is?"

"I've had about enough of this." Michelle pulled out her keypad and tapped it three times.

Denise closed her eyes for a moment in case there was a blinding flash or something. After a moment she peeked out of one eye. Nothing had changed except Michelle's expression. Her head was cocked to one side as she peered at the pad. She was speaking to herself, but the sound carried to Denise's ears across the unreal silent wind and Ron's laughter.

"That's unusual."

Ron's laughter roared even louder. She covered her ears to try and block the sound.

"Your software won't affect us Buddhist ghosts."

Suddenly, two huge fly swatters appeared on either side of Ron and slapped together. He yelped in pain before disappearing along with the swatters.

She turned to shout her congratulations, but the words died on her lips. Michelle appeared even more surprised than Denise felt.

Another great voice boomed out, apparently from thin air, *"Reincarnation loop four activated. Reincarnation as a snake has now been commenced for this soul. We apologize for the inconvenience, but any problems you now have are your own. Good luck."*

Lady Amalthea continued to fight over the seas before the onslaught of the silent wind. With a slam they were all pitched to the floor of the cockpit as the wave they were cresting over suddenly disappeared dropping them back onto quiet waters. The wind slacked off and the Lady rocked back and forth and then lay still with her bow to the wind.

"Mither of God. Where in the curst name of King William did you come from?"

Denise looked over the side as a sea kayak bumped into the hull. "We aren't quite sure. Where are we?"

"Bloody weekend sailors. Buy a boat like this and don't even know where they are. You're off bleedin' Orcas Island you lousy colonial sea-dogs."

As he paddled away he kept saying, "What a cryin' shame. A sweet craft like this in sich hands. Tch, tch, tch. A pity it be, a true pity," as he faded off into the distance.

Denise stared at the large hole where Ron's leg had punched through the sail. She finally found her voice, "What was that?"

Michelle took the tiller and put them back on the proper heading. "Whatever Ron did to us, the Buddhist software was kind enough to undo. That is atypical. Me Bless It. Look at that huge hole in the middle of my nice new sail."

here's one thing I fail to comprehend." Peter settled onto Michelle's sofa. The deep orange sun, finally setting into the ocean, hurt his eyes. Closing them made his headache even worse. He'd probably have felt better if he'd gone sailing and left the software alone. There must be some nice way to tell them the bad news; he'd think of it in a few minutes.

"One thing? One thing?" Denise walked by him with a ginger ale and sat on the floor. "I can think of about a thousand, and that's only in the last twenty-four hours. I can see my epitaph. 'One day her brain filled up and exploded. The damage was not noticed for some time until one bright sunny afternoon she dropped dead to everyone's surprise. She'd been drinking ginger ale in the Devil's house at the time.' The rags will have a great time with it: 'Award winning editor drops dead from Devil's brew.' 'Editor dies in satanic cult ritual. Uncle claims he had no idea she'd been brain-dead for five years.' " She lay on the rug holding her ginger ale as if it were a bunch of lilies and closed her eyes.

She certainly could be dramatic. "The thing I fail to comprehend," Peter tried again, "Is what our unfriendly neighborhood ghost meant by 'a false program?' "

Michelle was starting to make him nervous. She had not been particularly upset by the scratch in her desk or by the mess he'd made of the system.

'It happens,' was all she had said about the desk. Her response about the software hadn't been any better, 'Well, you saved me the trouble of fucking it up myself. Thanks.' Yet, she hadn't sat down since. She'd probably be even more upset when he told her the whole truth.

John wandered over from the kitchen with a pair of chilled bottles of beer. He handed one to Peter before sitting on the chair opposite him.

"I haven't been able to solve that one either." Denise reached out and rested her hand on his shin.

Peter watched them. They were connected by more than the touch somehow, he couldn't describe it, but it was there. Like when Jesus and Mary touched, only not as naturally.

John kicked off his shoes and started gently rubbing her forearm with his socked toes.

Peter glanced over his shoulder at Michelle. "Can you explain the 'false' Master Control Program Ron claims to be stuck with?"

She shook her head. "Alas, that little feat eludes me as well."

A gloomy silence settled on the room.

Denise finally called out from the floor, "There must be something we can do."

Michelle continued to work on wearing a track in the rug behind him. "Well, it is time to go if anyone wants to meet the Buddha."

"Already?" Peter was feeling worn out.

Denise groaned heartily from the floor.

He braced himself before leaning forward. "There is one thing I haven't told anyone, that you should know."

Michelle finally stopped pacing and came around to sit on one of the couch arms. He found it hard to speak.

"I learned a few things as the software crashed." He held up his hand with one finger raised. "First, Hell's software is down and gone and yet portions of it appear to be functioning. I believe this is because Michelle was smart enough to automate many of the functions of Hell. It is still able to run without the Control Program."

Michelle nodded her head. "Makes sense."

He held up a second finger wishing his hand would stop shaking. "Heaven has no such automation. I always maintained direct control over most of the system using the Master Control Program."

Dropping his hand to his knee he tried to slow his breathing but couldn't. "I was able to learn that without the Master Software, Heaven has started falling apart. In three days it will collapse if we can't do something. If it collapses as thoroughly as I fear . . ."

They all watched him. " . . . the universe will end two to three days later and there is nothing I can do to stop it once it begins."

A stunned silence filled the room. Denise looked at John and they both turned to Michelle.

Michelle was quiet for a time, arms folded, sitting very still, before starting to shake her head.

"Oh, shit."

Denise turned from Michelle to Peter. That couldn't be right. John's face registered the shock she felt.

Three to four days. She was going to be dead in three to four days. She felt robbed. Rising to her feet, she turned to Michelle.

"No. That's not how it works. The universe doesn't end when some lousy software breaks. In school they said that entropy takes billions of years. Life goes on. Maybe Heaven and Hell collapse, but life goes on."

Michelle shook her head. "This universe isn't only run by the software, it's a construct within the software."

"What the blazes does that mean?"

"It means that all of existence has three to four days. No more."

Denise sat up abruptly and leaned against John. An ache moved down into her heart. They were supposed to have more time.

John looked away from her toward Michelle. "What can we do to help?"

'We.' Denise felt both irritated and happy. There he was making assumptions again, but she rather liked how this assumption felt. If help was needed, and John willing, so was she.

Michelle smiled, acknowledging John's offer. "Let's go see the Buddha. I still think that's our best bet."

Everyone was very quiet as she worked on opening a gateway. The setting sunlight reflected hard off the ocean. Its harsh light made Michelle, standing with her keypad, look surreal. She showed the display to Peter once. He shook his head, tapping in a command. She looked at what he did with raised eyebrows before pressing a last key. A perfectly normal-looking doorway appeared in the middle of the living room, fading in exactly as her apartment door had faded away on the hillside of Hell.

Peter rose from the couch, opened the door and stepped through. After a moment she could hear him say, "It's okay. I think this is the right place."

*D*enise took a deep breath and went through the door next. The transition from rug to stone seemed as natural as stepping onto her tiled bathroom floor from the carpeted hallway. Peter was inspecting the inside of the small stone room. He stepped into the sunlight that was streaming in through a narrow passage. Shielding his eyes he blinked several times before turning. "This is it. We're in Bodhgaya."

John and Michelle had followed through behind her. As soon as Michelle closed the door it faded out of existence.

Denise felt as if she were in a bizarre game of follow the leader as they squeezed out into the sunlight and walked under the massive trees. The first thing she noticed was the smell. It was a combination of food, dust, cow dung and several other things she couldn't identify, and probably didn't want to.

The room was the inside of a small shrine, covered with worn engravings cut right into the stone blocks. A great tower, ten or fifteen stories high, rose from the top of an ancient-looking temple. It dominated the view as she looked around. It seemed to be a very quiet day, yet there were hundreds, maybe thousands of people in tunics, colorful saris and normal western-style clothes walking under the trees, squatting by the various food and drink vendors, bartering at the stalls and looking at the great shrine. None of the frantic pace she was used to in New York, but as many people. The nearby town looked small, yet she felt as if she were in the midst of a large city. The noise was subdued but constant. She could hear the traffic in the distance with its blowing car horns, but this felt like a quiet center.

Michelle led them around the temple to a great tree that dominated an expansive courtyard.

A little man with a pot belly waved to them. "It has been a long time since I have had the pleasure of your company, Michelle."

He patted the blankets around him before signaling to a nearby tea vendor and holding up five fingers.

He turned toward John. "And how are you these days, my friend?"

Denise looked at John. She'd never seen him turn this white. There couldn't be a drop of blood in his face.

"You're . . ." was all he was able to croak.

" . . . the Buddha? Why yes, I guess I am, John."

Denise felt the shock down to her toes. "You know the Buddha?"

"We . . . we used to play poker together." John grasped her hand painfully hard.

She was pulled down beside him as he dropped into a sitting position. He had better not be some mythical character come to life. If he turned out to be John the Baptist, or the Apostle, she'd never forgive him. She couldn't be the only mortal here. Someone needed to be on her side in all of this.

"You did what?" Michelle laughed.

"I went abroad to Oxford for a year. Remember, Denise? No, that was while I was still in school. I hadn't met you yet. I spent my junior year there, most of it was playing poker and debating philosophy with Chandra, um, the Buddha here."

This was almost believable. John was a mere mortal like her, after all.

Peter looked amused as well. He sat next to John. "John was one of your students?"

"Oh, no, no. It was quite the other way around."

Denise had to listen carefully. Even though he clearly had a full command of English, the Buddha spoke in a quick, soft fashion. It often made his people hard for her to understand.

"I first became aware of John at the poker games. He very rarely lost. I found this fact to be most interesting. John and I, we would sit up late into the night trading poker lessons for tips on the path to enlightenment."

John's hand had stopped shaking. It was unfair that he could adjust so quickly. He indicated the Buddha.

"By the end of the year I couldn't beat him anymore. You're now talking to one of the finest card sharps, in Oxford at least. I never did learn to read that enigmatic smile of yours."

"I cultivated it most carefully. Thank you." He put his palms together briefly in prayer position.

The vendor he had waved at earlier brought a tray of milk tea and sweet rolls. Denise hated milk tea. He knelt on the corner of the blanket and set the tray in front of the Buddha.

"Thank you, Ahmed. And how is your mother this fine day?"

"Quite well. She has asked me to send her regards and thanks for your kind gift. The balm has eased the swelling and she hopes to be up and around soon."

"Poor woman sprained her ankle very badly last week and has been bed-ridden ever since," the Buddha explained. "It is a good show it wasn't broken; she is in her seventies. Please tell her my thoughts are with her."

"She will feel most fortunate indeed. As ever, may the blessings of the Buddha be on your meal."

John pointed at Ahmed's retreating figure. "Does he know who you are?"

The Buddha glanced toward the vendors lining the street on the far side of the courtyard.

"Oh my, no. That would never do. How could he gain merit being so kind to me; out of fear or worship? No, I am merely his old uncle who dandled him on my knee when he was little."

Denise tried to pick up her stainless-steel tea cup, and nearly spilled it as the burning pain shot up her fingers. "Yow. In America we get our tea and coffee in Styrofoam or paper. It never tastes quite right. But steel?"

"In Indonesia it's porcelain but here in India it is steel. Here is the trick to drinking it."

He demonstrated by pouring it back and forth between the cup and the deep bowl-shaped saucer. "This cools it down and mixes it well. It's a bit of an acquired art. I could never quite understand the American passion to drink their coffee out of plastic. Positively frightful. I am most happy to live in what the Americans would call a 'primitive culture' upon any day of the year."

Denise decided to let it sit and cool on its own.

"Mmmph," John choked and sputtered as he bit into one of the sweet rolls.

"There, there, dear chap." The Buddha patted him on the back. "I forgot to warn you. We like our snacks very sweet by your standards."

"I thought it was a glazed cruller." John looked at the roll as if a foreign object had landed in his hand.

"I must admit it is sort of cruller-shaped. It is soaked in honey until fully permeated, as well as having a sugar glaze. It is spot on is it not?"

"Surprising is more the word that comes to mind."

"Even after all these years you are still unused to our simple ways. I did try to teach you better."

John smiled and imitated his voice. "Oh yes. You are merely a simple person who always wins at poker."

"It certainly beats losing, to my way of thinking."

Michelle finished mixing her tea with practiced ease. "What were you doing at Oxford anyway, my immortal friend? Other than playing poker, that is."

"Polishing my English a bit and having a generally merry time. I was also following this sweet English widow I met while she was traveling through Nepal, but alas it was not to be."

Denise slapped her hands down on her thighs. "What is with you people? Oh, here we are having a charming spot of tea and aren't we all such good pals. Never mind that the blasted world is about to end."

The Buddha set his tea down gently on the blanket. "You do have a point, my dear. If I recall correctly, we are seeking a ghost, the Master Control Program for your operation and a cookbook. I fear I can be of little use."

Michelle also set down her tea. "Well, anything would help. I don't want to be stuck with Plato forever and Peter is quite worried about Blaise. You may recall that in this universal construct, if our system collapses yours will as well."

"A detail I am regrettably aware of. I would . . . "

Two fly swatters, similar to those on the sailboat only smaller, appeared from nowhere and swung together right in front of the Buddha, squashing a bug and scaring the daylights out of Denise. She felt a little better that John jumped as well.

"Attack upon the person of the Buddha is not permitted under rule 4739/ZR. Reincarnation as a mosquito initiated."

Michelle glanced up, but did not flinch. It must take something truly extraordinary to startle the Devil. "From mosquito to mosquito?"

"The system, it does not go any lower." He waved his hand toward where the swatters had been. "It can become quite a nuisance when a soul decides its life is my fault. This can go on . . . "

The swatters slapped loudly together again.

Denise startled again despite a firm resolve not to.

"Attack upon the person of the Buddha is not permitted under rule 4739/ZR. Reincarnation as a mosquito initiated."

" . . . for some time. I usually allow it to take its course as a lesson to myself to ignore the vicissitudes of the world. This time, however . . . "

Slap.

"Attack upon the person of the Buddha is not permitted under rule 4739/ZR. Reincarnation as a mosquito initiated."

"Excuse me? Control software? Could we chat?"

"Certainly, old bean. What can I do for you?"

"I taught it English." The Buddha sounded very proud. "Could you perhaps . . ."

Slap.

"Attack upon the person of the Buddha is not permitted under rule 4739/ZR. Reincarnation as a mosquito initiated."

She covered her ears, but it didn't help.

" . . . reincarnate this soul a bit farther off?"

"Be glad to."

Slap.

"Attack upon the person of the Buddha is not permitted under rule 4739/ZR. Reincarnation as a mosquito initiated with spatial dislocation. Anything else?"

"Not that I can think of."

She was not going to be cowed by circumstances. She put her hands firmly in her lap and braced herself, but it appeared to be over. She took a deep breath, albeit not a very steady one, and tried to calm herself. Some idea was tickling at the back of her mind.

"Might I ask a question?"

"Of course, my dear Denise. Of course. Fire away."

She turned to where she imagined the disembodied voice of the software had come from. "We're attempting to locate a possession of ours that was being held by a soul who we knew as Ron. He was an evil ghost twin of St. Peter here."

"Oooo. Tricky. Any other clues?"

"We last saw him while in the San Juan Islands. He was reincarnated as a mosquito after attacking us."

"There's quite a large grouping of those individuals out there. We do not attempt to keep track of each and every soul. We let them simply travel on the wheel."

"Can you check on the mosquito that was harassing the Buddha?"

"That'll take a few minutes. I'll see what I can dig up on it."

Denise looked at the Buddha. "Has it just switched to colloquial American English, or am I imagining things?"

"It appears to have taken a liking to you."

Great. That's exactly what she needed, a religious software system with a crush on her. Kris would never believe any of this adventure.

"I found it! I found it!" It sounded like the yapping of a puppy who had managed to fetch a stick for its first time.

"Ron is currently a female mosquito. Her name is Bzz-zing-zing-zuz, approximately. She is in the lowest form, a carrier of cerebral malaria, the deadliest strain known. Her current location is the swamps of Sumatra in . . . Oh dear."

"Oh, dear?"

"Someone swatted Bzz-zing-zing-zuz, successfully at that."

"Why is that an, 'Oh Dear'?" John leaned forward to take another sweet from the tray. "Sounds like he, er, she deserves it."

"It is difficult to explain."

"Allow me to try." The Buddha looked off at the ancient spire in the middle of the park. Denise realized that it was a memorial to the man before her. She wanted to touch something familiar but there was nothing here

Michelle reached out and put her hand on her knee. Somehow her look of understanding made it all seem less bizarre, more manageable. Denise nodded in thanks before turning to await the Buddha.

His eyes refocused on her. "When a soul has, as you Americans might say, 'bottomed out,' its slate, it is wiped clean. Buzz-zing-zing-zuz will now have no recollection of either Ron or of the possessions that did belong to Ron's past."

Peter opened his mouth but produced no sound.

Michelle stretched her legs out in front of her. "We would be in quite a spot of trouble if we can not find a way to trace it."

John's raised his head. "Tracers. Would there be any tracers left in your system that we could follow? Sort of backtrack where he had been?"

"I am afraid we are a tad bit out of my depth here. Without Ananda to ask I would have to say, 'Yes, partly.' Not a path of former journeys, but rather a repeating trail for future learnings. A soul on the wheel, even with no knowledge of its former lives, will tend to retrace the same locations through its multiple lives until it learns the lessons it needs to from each of those places. If we could follow Ron's soul in some fashion . . . " he paused for a long moment, ". . . but that would be ridiculous."

"What would?" Peter leaned forward in anticipation.

"Well, you could enter the software, so to speak. I'm sure Ananda could slip you into the same part of the wheel as Ron is now and allow you to follow. He could probably arrange for the transitions to be less traumatic, as well." The Buddha slapped his hands together like the giant fly swatters, causing Denise to catch her breath.

Michelle frowned. "What about the time factor? Couldn't Peter be gone for thousands of years?"

"I hadn't realized I was volunteering." Peter sighed. "I guess I was."

John spoke confidentially, "Don't worry you can't go alone. I gave myself control of the Master Program. Now that I think of it, that must be why Ron thought it was a fake. I wiped out your access codes, the ones he probably would have remembered."

Denise felt goosebumps on her skin. "You can't."

"I don't have any choice."

She looked at him helplessly. This idea was crazy. They might have only days left. He couldn't leave.

John walked over to her; she hadn't even been aware of standing and moving away. He slowly folded her into his arms, where her unbidden tears began to soak into his shirt. His gentle touch felt different from when she'd cried on this same shoulder over failed loves or lost jobs. Safer. That she might lose him now was unimaginable.

"No words." He gently stroked her hair. "No words."

Her face stung with disbelief. "What in the name of Heaven, Hell and the Buddhist Wheel are you talking about? That's pure and total crap."

She turned away. He'd never said how he felt. And he had yet to ask her how she felt about anything. No words. Shit.

She realized that everyone was watching her. Peter quickly turned back to the Buddha and continued their conversation. Michelle simply looked at her briefly with one eyebrow raised. Denise watched Peter talking with the Buddha. His hands were in front of him, trying to shape the concepts as he spoke them.

"What about the time factor? Heaven will not run smoothly for the next several millennia while I follow Ron through many lives. And my dog wouldn't be at all cheerful about my being gone."

Her stomach tensed. Peter didn't understand that she and John would be dead long before then. "Peter, stop being an idiot. I thought you said that we have only a few days left."

Peter looked at her for a long moment. "You're right. I'd managed to forget."

The Buddha shook his head sadly.

"Again we are out of my depth, I fear. We must go and find my assistant. You need to start right away. Ananda always has had a knack for speaking with the software. I find it to be too, how shall I say, concerned with art? It is more focused upon the 'appealing flow of the universe' than in actually achieving anything."

John came up beside her but didn't touch her. She wondered if she would have loved it or tried to tear his arm off.

"How about this?" He was using his compromise tone. She usually found it very cute; he always seemed to think it helped. "Peter and I go to see Ananda. Michelle and Denise can go back to see what else they can do."

"Like what?" The blood pounded into her temples. She pushed against his shoulder, turning him to face her. "I'm going with you."

"The hell you . . . sorry. I'm sorry. Peter is going. I have to go. I need to stay focused on the problem. I don't think you can help with this. It's ours to deal with."

"Sorry doesn't make it right. 'I need to stay focused.' You asshole. And you think I wouldn't worry about you. Well, you're wrong. Damn it, John, it sounds dangerous. When is the risk too great?"

He stood with his arms crossed.

She could feel the fury in the pit of her stomach. She wanted to be sick, but managed to keep the awful taste of bile and milk tea down by clenching her jaw. Fine. If he didn't want to spend the last few days of existence with her, he didn't have to.

Michelle stood, but didn't come any closer. "I think I'll go and have a chat with Plato. He certainly knows the depressing side of the software better than anyone else I'm likely to find. Maybe he can help me break into Heaven. I'd like the company, if you'll join me."

Denise stalked away to a nearby tree. If looks could kill, she felt she could shatter it. She laughed bitterly at the image. She hated being discounted and she seriously considered hating John.

Screw them. Let them do whatever they wanted. She went to the far side of the tree to where she knew they couldn't see her and let the tears flow. She leaned her cheek against the coarse bark like an old friend.

Everything had been under control until that damned software had invaded Elantra's computer, and now it was all a wreck. Her career was going to be defined by a perfect cookbook she wasn't allowed to sell. Her best friend had become a total jerk and her apartment door had become a gateway to Hell. If Peter was right they would all be dead within days, anyway. Good riddance to the lot of us.

She turned, trying to blink away the tears, and glanced briefly at the sun just starting its descent from midday toward the horizon. She had already seen two sunsets this day and was not ready for a third. Enough was enough.

John wanted to be with her when everything was going well. But let it be a real challenge and he didn't want her along. If that's what he thought a relationship was, he'd have to go somewhere else to find it.

He rested his hand on her arm. She shrugged him off. "Go away. Leave me alone."

He didn't. Instead he held out a small white flower, some sort of clover with pink tips on the petals.

She didn't take it.

"I didn't mean to say it that way. I'm sorry."

If he apologized for one more thing she was going to hit him . . . hard.

He twirled the flower slowly in his fingertips. "I'm new at this relationship idea, too. Maybe we could compromise? If you don't want me to go . . ."

Didn't want him to go? He really didn't understand a single thing. Anger made her voice cool.

"Have fun. Go. I think you should. And as for this 'new relationship idea,' forget it."

She turned away from him and strode to Michelle. Each step jarred her entire body. She had given him his second chance and now he was leaving as everyone else did. She should have known better.

She stopped shoulder to shoulder with Michelle. By facing away from the others she could see across the wooded park and its hundreds of strangers.

"Fine. I will go with you as long as we can go to my apartment first. Let's leave. Now."

Michelle glanced sideways at her for a long moment before turning back to the others. "Peter, you will let us know what Ananda says before you do anything? I mean, absolutely anything."

"Promise."

John came around to stand in front of her. Rather than look into his eyes she focused on the wet spot her tears had made on his shirt. He reached for her hand. Before he could touch her she turned away.

Out of the corner of her eye she could see him hang his head.

Her tears started again as she walked. It would never have worked. They knew how to hurt each other too well.

enise closed the door to her apartment behind Michelle. She glanced at the clock, it was past midnight. The only light in the room was from the one over the dining table. Uncle sat in one of the chairs reading intently.

"Uncle. What are you doing here?"

He hopped up from the table, scattering white pages all over the floor. "Denise. You startled me." He pushed his reading glasses up his nose before they could fall off.

"What am I doing here? You know me. I worry." He shook Michelle's hand.

"A pleasure to see you again, my dear." Kneeling he started to gather the pages. "When I didn't hear how your meal was, I thought I would drop by with a nice desert and meet your guests."

She hung her jacket over the back of a chair and helped him pick up the pages. "I'm sorry I didn't call, Uncle. It was wonderful. But that must have been several hours ago."

He tamped some more pages together, a few escaped and headed for the floor. "Yes. I thought I would come by and surprise you. And what happens? I'll tell you what happens. No one answers the door. I worry. I used my spare key and you know what I found? I found you haven't been watering your plants again. I've taken care of that. The baby fern was quite upset, but we had a long chat and it's feeling much better now."

She and Michelle joined him at the table as he sat to finish squaring the papers. It felt wonderful to settle into a familiar chair. Not in Hell. Not in India. Her apartment seemed to wrap around her; safe and familiar in the shadows cast by the table light.

"I've been working on a little problem with Michelle and her friend Peter. It is becoming more confusing rather than simpler as we go. I was actually coming by to leave you a note that I might be gone a while, trying to solve this. And yes, I would have watered the plants."

"Where's John?"

She gripped the edge of the table, hard, poking her finger badly on some piece of hardware underneath.

"I don't know."

Joshua lowered his chin and looked at her in surprise over his glasses. She wasn't sure she could bear to talk about John at this point. She didn't want to break down in front of Uncle or Michelle.

He must have seen that she was close to the edge. He paused a moment, before turning to Michelle.

"Tell me about your problem. Tell me. Tell me. But first, relax. I brought some wonderful Sicilian biscotti and a new Colombian espresso you must try. Don't worry. I know how late it is. This one is decaffeinated."

He bustled off into the kitchen. She slowly relaxed her fingers and inspected the wounded one to see if she'd drawn blood. Telling Uncle about the lost software and Hell and the Buddha was another path she didn't want to go down. She glanced at the cover page on the papers.

"I see you've been reading Elantra's cookbook. What do you think of it?"

"It is quite interesting, not her normal fare," he spoke louder to be heard over the hiss of the small espresso machine he had given her last Christmas.

"That pizza recipe does indeed look wonderful. Was it truly good?"

Michelle grinned at her before answering, "Perfect."

She managed to suppress all except a brief laugh.

Joshua made another loud noise in the kitchen. "That is what I thought. It would be very hard to go wrong with a recipe like that one. Are you going to publish it?"

Picking up the stack of papers she straightened a few pages he had missed before setting it down again.

"Strange you should ask. I have been debating that very problem. I think it might be . . . too good to publish."

"Too good? What an interesting idea. It would make Elantra's reputation of far bigger proportions than it deserves, but what do I know? Pepperoni, coffee, cheese. These I know. These I understand."

Michelle had been idly playing with the cookbook pages, making them crooked all over again. "This isn't the cookbook. What is this?"

Uncle bustled over with coffee and a plate of biscotti and tried to collect the pages together, but Michelle had handed a few to her.

Denise recognized it right away. "This is the version that Elantra's computer mangled. Brimstone Soufflé. The Pizza Round Of Life. Heavenly Hors d'oeuvres spelled

O-r-d-e-r-v-s. Each one stranger than the one before. Hell Loafing: a satanic bread. This one's for you." She pulled it out of order and handed it to Michelle, marking the place with her finger.

Joshua sat at the table. "And what is this problem you're working on?"

"Well, this may seem a bit silly, but we're trying to open a stuck gate without the key." She set the pages down and sipped at the espresso without really tasting it. She didn't care about coffee or cookbooks at this point. She wanted everyone to go away. She'd close her door, climb into a hot bath with a good book and pretend none of this was happening.

"Must be some gate. Darling, what you should do is call a locksmith."

"It's not a normal gate. Maybe call it a logical gate."

"Or a mythical gate," Michelle put in.

"Or a Heavenly gate." Denise started to laugh.

"Oy. That one's easy. Let me see the cookbook." He took the stack of pages that Michelle still had and, after squinting through his glasses for a moment, chose a page from very near the back.

"Ah, here it is. If you have a problem, you simply need to come and see your old Uncle." He handed the page to her.

"Heavenly Quiche spelled K-e-y-c-h. I don't get it, Uncle. I can't make any sense of this recipe. Michelle, want to give it a try?"

She looked at it for a moment. "That might work. How did you know, Joshua?"

"It might?" Denise slid her chair beside Michelle's, losing the other recipe's place in the stack.

"Well, alchemists used to claim there was a way through Heavenly gates. I always discounted it, because

I could see no connection between a witches' brew like this one and a computer password."

"It seems you kids are working on a project that is way beyond a simple grocer like me. I saw a recipe that looked like it would help. I'm glad it did. I like to be of help. Denise, darling, I already watered your plants, the coleus was particularly miserable. I trimmed it back a bit. I hope that was okay?"

"Uncle, I'd never argue with your green thumb." She turned to Michelle. "I had to buy one of those 'add-water-now' meters you stick in the soil, to stop killing plants."

"You do whatever you need to. I'll watch the plants. Be careful. Let me know when you're back. Have a nice trip." He kissed Michelle's hand and pushed his glasses back onto the bridge of his nose. "You absolutely must come to dinner on Saturday, if you're all done. It will be mostly family, but of course you'd be welcome."

He pulled Denise out of her chair, gave her a big hug and disappeared out the door in a small flurry. She dropped back into her chair.

"How does your aunt survive being around him?"

"The question should be asked the other way around. I think he is like he is, simply to keep up with her. He's not usually this bad. She may be more stately in her progress, but she can be a very determined woman. Their dinners are immense fun. Exhausting, but worth it. You have to come this weekend if we're done." Denise could not believe what she'd just said. "If we're done, and the universe isn't."

"If this existence still continues, it's a deal."

"Oh great, I've made a deal with the Devil, haven't I?"

"You have." Michelle's smile was serene.

Denise tapped the sheet still lying on the table. "What, pray tell, is a Heavenly Keych?"

"Your uncle really reminds me of someone but I can't think of who." Michelle shrugged. "It'll come to me. If I read it right this is the key to open the Heavenly gates. The ingredients are weird, but what I don't understand is why you have it."

"Maybe I do. The original cookbook was, shall we say, mangled beyond belief when Elantra downloaded your Master Control Program rather than whatever she was after, a soap-opera summary I think." Denise frowned and then continued.

"When she made a copy of the cookbook for me she must have been copying different pieces of the Master Control Software in the form of recipes, because she requested it in cookbook form."

Michelle flipped through the recipes, pausing every now and then. "That's ridiculous. You're saying we have a hundred and so of the pieces essential to running Heaven and Hell in the form of recipes?"

"You tell me. I'm only guessing."

Denise tasted one of Uncle's biscotti. Sitting here in the quiet she realized how tired she was. Her legs were so leaden they were almost numb.

Michelle finished flipping through the stack. "I don't think any of these others would be helpful. There is a copy of Angel Upside Down Make. I think it's my sub-program for creating demons. Most of these are more about the day-to-day business of running Heaven and Hell. If I'm reading them right, that is."

She tossed the stack of pages, except for the one recipe, back onto the center of the table.

Denise was barely able to slap her hand on them in time to keep them from scattering onto the floor.

While she was straightening those, Michelle pointed toward the neat stack sitting on the other side of the table. "How was your collection of perfect recipes from Hell created?"

"The software must have become tired of being asked for a corrected cookbook. I guess it gave John this excerpt from the actual Cookbook From Hell to get him off its back . . . or . . . off its keyboard, so to speak." Denise indicated the recipe for Heavenly Keych. "How weird is weird for the ingredients?"

Michelle leaned her elbows on the table and read out:

> *Bat feathers and lizard tongues,*
> *tiny bits of gold and lead*
> *A small piece of a fishe's lungs*
> *and a mummy's toe - fresh dead;*
> *A spot or two of old horse glue*
> *and, oh my, a lot of ostrich pooh.*

These recipes always were a little bit tricky."

"Damn. I'm fresh out of ostrich pooh." Denise waved toward the kitchen. "You don't have any handy, do you?"

"No, but I'm sure old Nick does."

"Old Nick as in Old Saint Nick?" Anything could be possible at this point.

"Not quite. Could be his twin brother to look at him though. Old Nick as in old Nicolas Flamel. He's the only alchemist in history who started poor and ended rich. He claims he solved the lead-to-gold mystery with the help of a dream and a book of Kabbala. He and Nostradamus were pretty tight. Privately Nick thinks Nostra was a charlatan, but they do get along. Nick was still kicking around Hell last time I checked. Shall we go?"

Denise felt too weary to stand. "I can't."

At the look of dismay on Michelle's face she had to explain further.

"I want to go with you, and I know time is short, but I have to get some sleep first."

Michelle relaxed and nodded. "Heaven can wait a few hours. I could do with a nap myself. Mind if I borrow your couch?"

"Sure, John slept there last night."

She thought of all that had happened in only one day. She could still feel his kiss burning in the center of her palm and the beat of his heart through her fingertips. She closed her hand to hold in the feeling. Whatever else would happen, she could always hold that moment.

"Yes, you're welcome to the couch let me get you some blankets and a pillow."

She could barely say goodnight past the tightness in her throat.

DAY FIVE

And God Said, Let the waters bring forth abundantly the moving creature that hath life, and fowl that may fly above the earth.

*A*nne unlocked the deli door with her own key. She hadn't had to do that in a long time. All the lights were off, Joshua was not at their table by the window. The morning light looked dull on the table without him there. Closing the door behind her she stepped farther into the deli.

The scent of fresh brewed coffee filled the air, but the coffee pot sat on the counter with its plunger still high.

She found him on the other side of the herb baskets. He sat on the small stool they kept for reaching high places, looking at his mug as he rolled it back and forth between his hands. Clearly he had simply come to rest in the most convenient spot.

"What are you doing back here, Joshua?"

He startled and almost dropped the mug on the floor. She was relieved when he caught it. He loved that old warped pottery very much. It was hard to imagine him without it; he'd had it since before they'd met.

She placed Henri's package on a nearby table and pulled out a chair to sit facing him. He slowly traced the outline of the characters in the glaze. She brushed a few stray strands of hair behind his ear.

He raised his eyes at her touch. His expression was sadder than she had ever seen. His deep voice caressed the air making the room seem brighter despite his mood.

"I had hoped to do good in the world."

"You do, my love. Every day."

With a shake of his head he looked at his hands.

"What, Joshua?"

The silence of the morning wrapped around him like a cloak. She was about to leave him to his sulk when he reached over and took her hand.

It was as if he were holding on for dear life. Anne had rarely seen him this upset. "Are you worried about Denise's new friend?"

He shook his head without raising it.

Thankfully she'd was skilled at the guessing game required to make him start speaking about whatever was bothering him.

"Are you worried about Denise and John?"

She didn't need the nod to confirm what the twitch of his hand in hers had already said.

"Joshua. You worry about all the wrong things. The kids will be fine."

"No. I've set her up for pain. She couldn't even bear for me to speak his name last night. This is why I didn't want to interfere. All I do is hurt people. Why did you tell me it was time to try to help again?"

Letting go of his hand she pushed her chair back and rose quickly to her feet. Joshua stumbled up in surprise and stood facing her inches away.

"I suggested," she felt the word grind out as she spoke, "that you have cut yourself off too much from helping people. You have great gifts to give. That is why I spoke at all."

She started to turn away, but the look of distress on his face stopped her. Taking a deep breath she let her frustration flow out of her.

"What you need to remember is to have faith in the process. We all interfere with each other simply by living in the same time and place. It's a part of being on this earth. You must believe that it really is all for the best."

The hope in his eyes was reflected in his voice. "How do you . . . how can you be sure?"

She placed her hand on his cheek. Leaning into it he hugged her hand against his shoulder for a moment with that charming tilt of his head.

"That's why. John and Denise feel that way about each other. They simply have yet to recognize it. You have helped them along their way. That is a great gift."

He set his mug down on a handy shelf. He took her her hand from his shoulder and raised it to his lips. She could feel his smile grow against her fingers.

"Thank you for putting up with a worried old man."

"Everything isn't perfect, Joshua, but we always seem to muddle through in a reasonable fashion."

"You're right. We do." His look changed to one of uncertainty. "Odd. There is something else going on. I don't understand."

He looked around the room as if smelling the air for signs of trouble. "What it is eludes me." He shrugged. "Ah well, let us not worry about tomorrow when we can't understand today."

It warmed her as his usual smile broke out and lit his face in the morning sun.

"Take care of the moments and the rest will take care of themselves."

He narrowed his eyes playfully. "Isn't that my line?"

She shook her head. "I stole it from the same reliable source that you did. Your son."

His laughter filled the deli. He stepped back and bowed deeply. "Shall we?"

At her nod he led her forward and they waltzed among the glass table tops glittering in the morning sun.

*J*ohn wanted to get moving, but now Peter was playing a thousand questions with the Buddha and Ananda over tea. Maybe being immortal he'd forgotten how little time four days was. They'd grabbed a few hours sleep while Ananda was found and now it was time to get moving. A hasty meal had been prepared; rice, lentils and yogurt. Eating with their hands made everything feel quite foreign. Ananda's plain living room, bathed in dim candlelight, had an eerie, mystic feel. At the moment he almost wished he were back facing Denise's anger, even if he didn't understand that very well either. She was probably getting up around now, if she was in New York. It should be early morning there.

Peter was playing with the banana leaf on which their late dinner had been served. He called it the ultimate in recyclable flatware; simply feed it to a goat.

"Let me get this straight. How do we get round the Wheel of Life quickly? Shouldn't each lifetime take years?" His voice cracked as he asked the question.

John tried to calm his breathing. Chasing a hungry ghost around the Buddhist Wheel of Life had sounded safer in the shade of the bodhi trees.

Ananda nodded in his enigmatic way. "Yes and no."

John leaned back for a moment; sitting cross-legged was not something he was good at. "Yes and no? Are you saying each lifetime could take years?" He spread his hands on the dark wooden table they were seated around to steady himself. He could feel the moisture of his palms against the cool table, but it wasn't only India's oppressive heat making him sweat.

"Yes and no. How can I explain? You Westerners are used to a very logical, cause-and-effect, step-by-step way of thinking. We are bound by no such limitations." Ananda pointed to the Buddha. "Let us say a great teacher dies, a sage, a wise monk. A full turn on the Wheel of Life could take decades, often even centuries before he would return. We can spin up the wheel. Then he will experience his full turn in a much shorter time. This allows him to return and help others more quickly along their path to enlightenment."

Peter leaned forward almost spilling his tea. "How much faster? We only have a few days left. Will that be long enough?"

The ambiguous nod again. "It is very difficult to be certain. The best we can do is to try."

John wiped his palms against his pants.

The Buddha poured more tea. "Please accept our apologies if reality interferes at times."

The Buddha was right. This reality of lost software and wandering souls was definitely interfering. It was on the verge of interfering with their ability to survive.

"Where was I?" Ananda seemed to have lost the last question.

Peter twisted his hands together in impatience. "Spinning up the wheel. Wouldn't that tend to run us around extremely hard, too?"

"Oh, no. That wouldn't be . . . well, it wouldn't be art. Hello," Ananda raised his voice, "Could we chat for a bit?"

"Sure. I'm not working on much." The disembodied voice of the Buddhist control software filled the small room. At

first it seemed to come from behind Ananda. When he had turned to face it the voice moved to the other side of the room.

"*Reincarnations are down at the moment.*" Ananda faced forward again and the voice moved to one side.

"*What can I do for you, folks?*"

Ananda clenched his fists on the table. "First, you can stop doing that." He turned to Peter. "This is a good sign; it must be bored at the moment to be playing these games. It knows how much I hate that." Facing the last place the voice had sounded from, Ananda continued, "Our two guests here would like to take a ride on our Wheel of Life."

"*A Yank and a Christian Saint? Why?*" The voice finally stayed in one place.

"Remember that soul you tracked down earlier. Do you still have him?"

"*Sure do. He is one stubborn cuss. He's been killed nearly five times in the last few hours. You guys want to foller him?*"

John felt the question was somehow directed at him, "'Foller?' Yes, this soul stole a possession of ours and we want to follow him until we can find it, but we don't have much time."

"*Well, Pardner. We could just spin up our little old wheel a bit fer this tyke. Y'all could tag along just as sweet as mornin' dew.*"

John leaned over to Ananda. "What's happening?"

"You're a Yank. And I think the software has watched too many bad western movies." He turned to face the voice. "Treat them nicely; they are guests."

"*They all won't feel a thang. Gun's loaded. You boys ready?*"

Peter gave a thumbs up and John nodded to him and did the same. "I promised to call Denise. Once I do . . ."

"*Bang.*"

*W*hat in Heaven is going on here?" Michelle sounded extremely unhappy, and it was starting to worry Denise. It had taken four tries to get from her apartment to here, wherever that was, and Michelle's frustration had become worse with each passing moment. Last night they'd arrived at her apartment on the first attempt; maybe that had been a fluke. Denise was so used to the bizarre locations that the normalcy of this one struck her as being odd. They had stepped away from a row of urinals where several men were busily zipping up their flys, through the door of a dirty stall in some public restroom and into this nice, clean professional office with a pretty oriental rug. The sheer commonplace quality of the room only made the small demon cowering behind the large cherry wood desk look even more out of place.

Perhaps three feet tall with bright red skin and small horns, he would've looked out of place anywhere except a children's Halloween party; a small story book devil.

"Well, I was told not to let anyone pass without ID papers." He was trying to duck under Michelle's glare as if it had palpable force.

"Who told you that?"

The demon's hair began to smolder apparently due to the fury of her scowl. "Eh . . . him."

"Who him?"

"You know . . . him him." A small fire started between the demon's horns.

It seemed to bother him more than it hurt him. How did she do these tricks anyway? She noticed Michelle had one hand in her pocket. She turned away to hide her smile; the demon must think it was magic. Maybe she should ask if she could borrow that keypad for a bit.

Michelle raised her voice as the fire started to crackle. "Be a little more specific. The only him I know is dead."

"Oh no, not HIM him. Him." The demon grabbed a seltzer bottle from the bar behind his desk and tried to spray the flames. His head was enveloped in steam as the fire continued to roar.

"We don't have time for this crap. Who him?"

Denise covered her ears trying to protect them from the volume of Michelle's voice.

"He said we can only call him 'him' now."

"What was him called before?"

She jumped out of his way as the demon tried rolling around on the floor to put the flames out. Instead he caught his carpet on fire which he tried to pat out with his bare hands.

"Well?" Michelle's anger seemed to fill the room.

The little demon cowered back in real panic. "Plato."

Michelle rocked back on her heels suddenly quiet, "The me, you say? Plato is running Hell. I wonder what he's up to. He can't be trying to hold it together himself?"

Denise tried to picture the man covered with mud thinking he could replace this powerful woman, or even begin to keep up with her. It was almost funny.

Michelle turned back to the flaming demon who squatted in the middle of the carpet. "Are you going to let us pass?"

"Can't." He managed to gasp.

Michelle looked at Denise. "I admire dedication but this is rapidly becoming irritating." She pulled the pad out of her pocket and slapped a few keys. The flames went out. Two long, white feathers appeared and began to tickle the demon's nose.

"*C*ome quick. Trouble. Trouble." One of the multitudinous demons of Hell tugged madly at his robe.

Plato opened his eyes and quickly closed them again. His eyelids felt as if they were grating every time he blinked. They were probably bloodshot as well.

It pulled on his sleeve again.

He slapped at it. "Go away. You are bothering me."

He lay still for a minute piecing things back together. He peeked out again briefly. The room was familiar. Now if it would stop spinning he might recognize it. Finally it clicked and he closed his eyes again. He was in the Devil's house. He tried very hard to pass out again.

It was not working. The demons had decided he was in charge yesterday; there had been a severe lack of peace since. He only came to leave a note for Michelle. Now he was the temporary ruler of Hell.

Why did his head hurt? He reached back into his foggy memory. He had a sudden vision of a nearly empty pint of tequila. Oh. That was it. The news about Heaven. He had tried to obliterate it, apparently unsuccessfully.

The demon was now hopping on one foot trying to wait. Plato attempted to sit up, but thought better of it.

"What is wrong? Let me sleep."

"Come. Come. Big trouble."

"What is it? What?"

"She's here."

Plato's brain clearly was not functioning properly. He looked around as much of the room as he could without moving his head. When he didn't spot whoever 'she' was, he did manage to achieve an upright position and immediately wished he had remained horizontal. The demon danced around like a spinning top.

Plato reached out and grabbed him by his throat. "If you do not cease and desist this instant, I shall be forced to kill you, once I am able to function." Letting go he tried staggering to his feet, but he sat back down quickly on a corner of the littered coffee table. The room spun in a vicious and, he felt, overly cruel manner.

"You can't kill me. I'm only a computer subroutine. And you have bigger problems. She's here."

"You keep saying that. Who?"

The demon stopped moving, finally, put its hands on its hips and stared at him. "The boss, that's who."

It felt as if someone had driven a shaft of steel through the top of his head and down his spine. His entire face throbbed. Earthly hangovers had never been so painful.

"Michelle is here? Why did you not inform me more clearly?" Plato stood and held onto one of the demon's horns for a moment to steady himself.

He turned the demon to face him using the horn he was holding. "You are going to clean up this house so well that she will never know I was here."

It looked as if it were about to argue. Plato put his free hand underneath the demon's chin and slapped its jaw closed.

"Now. And how soon is Michelle going to be here?"

All it did was squeak. Plato interpreted that to mean soon.

He bent over to collect a sticky handful of sliced lemon peels when he heard the door open behind him. He dropped the rinds on a napkin. Standing upright as quickly as his head would allow, he turned to face her.

Michelle and the woman from the hillside yesterday stood framed in the doorway. "What in the name of Heaven is going on here?"

He sat back slowly, but missed the edge of the coffee table. His last thought before he hit the floor was that there had not even been time to run.

While Michelle showered, Denise watched Plato, with the aid of several demons, clean up the living room. It was torture to watch him organize the stacks of books on the floor; his head must hurt so badly. She took pity on him and led him out to the verandah. She found aspirin in a guest room and juice in the refrigerator. He smiled weakly when she handed them to him.

"Thank you, kind lady."

She nodded, struck by his deep voice. Mellowed with age is how she would describe it. Now he sat in a wicker chair on the verandah, awaiting judgment. She settled on the porch swing. The ocean was much calmer than the day before, and the small waves glittered in the daylight.

She turned as she heard Michelle's footsteps on the deck. Michelle sat on one of the porch railings where the morning sun shone around the end of the house. Her long hair glistened in the light as she rubbed it with a large fluffy towel.

"Plato, my old friend, what in my name are you doing in my house?"

He sat up straighter and looked at Michelle intently.

"Yesterday I decided to come and speak with you."

Michelle kept rubbing her hair. "About borrowing a bottle of tequila?"

Shaking his head he interlaced his fingers and began tapping his thumbs together. "Perhaps my imagination is running out. I had no new ideas as to what to try. As you were not currently in residence, I strolled about seeking a pen and paper with which to leave you a note. I requested a nice glass of water to quench my thirst. I have grown rather used to the gasoline aftertaste. All I received was a glass of water. That was it. Nothing else."

Michelle looked confused. "The software didn't attack. What were you thinking when you asked for it?"

He frowned at her question. "No differently from the way I have before."

Michelle rubbed the ends of her hair in a fold of the towel. "But the software records you as a member of Hell. It shouldn't treat you as it would me or one of my guests; not in this house, not without specific instructions. Maybe the software is in its final collapse."

Denise felt robbed. They had been given less time than Peter had thought. She rubbed her fingers across the palm of her hand. She'd never have a chance to find another moment like the one on the sailboat.

Plato raised a hand. "No. I was able to ascertain the software remains functional. When I was unaffected I spoke with several other less than happy individuals and they were continuing to feel the effects of their choices."

The relief she felt, seemed odd. She was happy that the universe wasn't going to collapse for two or three days rather than overnight.

"Although there is a noticeable difference now that I think about it."

Michelle stopped drying her hair and looked at him. "And that would be?"

"If I had to be specific I would have to say that it was reacting more slowly than is its typical *modus operandi*." Plato leaned back before continuing. "I took it as a primary proposition that I would not be protected from the vicissitudes of the program under typical conditions. I was forced to logically conclude that the system had decided I was the Devil incarnate. I was, after all, the being with greatest longevity in residence prior to your absence. Nor do I overlook Achilles. I decided that the system was too sensible to assume he was more than the brainless warrior he appears to be."

"Deciding you were the Devil . . . "

" . . . Was a natural step as I preceded to enjoy the luxuries of good food and good drink."

Denise couldn't stop herself. "I would not consider a margarita a good drink."

"I was pursuing an experiment in inebriation." He glanced at her before returning his gaze to Michelle.

It was as if he couldn't keep his eyes off her. That's exactly what it was. Denise had to take a deep breath to ease the sudden tightness in her chest. It was the same way John had looked at her yesterday.

Plato wasn't looking at Michelle, he was staring at her intently. His head shifted with every movement she made. "I admit that I may have gone slightly beyond reasonable limits. As to running Hell, my basic psyche and intellectual capabilities made me a natural choice."

"Why block our return?"

"It was not you exactly whom I was attempting to bar from entry."

"Let's assume it was." She threw the towel into an empty chair next to Plato.

He looked over at the towel and back to her. "I would never try to do such a thing, Michelle."

Michelle was flirting with him. Denise thought back to the look on Michelle's face as she had watched this man walk away from the mire. The attraction was definitely mutual, but neither of them realized it. Michelle pulled a brush from a back pocket and leaned her head to one side to brush out her hair.

Plato was mesmerized for a moment before sitting stiffly upright. "I was trying to keep out the refugees."

Michelle stopped and pulled the hair away from her eyes.

Denise sat up, but had to clear her throat several times in order to speak. "Refugees? From where in the world does Hell receive refugees?" She had made her start in journalism by writing a whole series of award-winning articles about the Thai refugee camps back in her Peace Corps days. Her heart went out to any people in that situation.

"Hell receives refugees from nowhere in the world."

"Then from where?" Denise demanded.

Michelle began slowly brushing her hair again. She nodded to Plato. "To borrow your methods if I may?"

He inclined his head in consent.

"Let us proceed from your premise of nowhere in the world. Therefore, they must come from out of the world. That leaves only Heaven, Purgatory, the Buddhist wheel, or wholly outside of this construct."

Plato leaned forward. "What pray tell is a construct?"

Michelle worked at a tangle. "So they're clearly from this universe."

"There are other universes?" He was intrigued.

"Yes, but I don't believe you can cross over or know of anything more than their existence. To continue, the Buddhist software appears to be operating normally and refugees are not usually running from the frying pan of Purgatory to the fires of Hell. They must be from Heaven." She finished with the brush and tossed it onto the towel. "But that makes no sense."

Michelle leaned back against one of the posts and crossed her feet on the wide rail. The sun made her hair shine with a rich, dark brilliance. Her new friend was astonishingly striking in the glow of the light.

Plato took a deep breath, as well he might while watching Michelle. "It is often the case that truths may make no sense and yet by no means be false for all that."

"Singapore isn't so bad," Michelle interjected.

Denise had followed them until then. "Singapore? I thought you were talking about refugees from Heaven."

Plato sat back. "I did as well."

"Heaven is suffering from a few problems, the main one being it has become a great deal like Singapore. Very rule bound. The software must be in worse condition for residents to try coming here." Michelle sighed.

Denise shook her head. It really did keep getting stranger. "I didn't notice any more souls than before on our way over." She looked up and down the beach which was deserted as it had been the previous day. Maybe this was Michelle's private beach.

Plato shifted in his chair. "Not desiring Hell to become cluttered in your absence I had them set up refugee camps on their side of the border. I offered Hell's protection provided they did not try to cross over."

"Hell's protection in Heaven?" Michelle slid off the railing and stood leaning against it. She faced Plato with her arms crossed.

"I realize it is not possible. I am uncomfortable with the lie, but I had to keep them in Heaven. I told them if they should need 'dire assistance' to give us a call."

"How did you define 'dire assistance'?" Michelle was definitely intrigued.

"I used the U.N.'s criteria. We always define it."

A smile spread across Michelle's face. True laughter shook her. "Ah Plato, you can assist me in running Hell whenever you wish. It's perfect. There's no way you can get in trouble with such an offer."

Denise wanted to smack Plato for being unfeeling. "What about the poor people in the camps? What has happened to force residents of Heaven into such an awful situation?"

If they didn't show a little more compassion she was going to kick them both in the shins.

Plato's smile, that had answered Michelle's laughter, disappeared. "It was a sufficient horror for me to start my experiment in inebriation."

Michelle sat on a chair across from him. "It must be extreme, after what happened to Socrates."

"They have, I shudder to say this, installed a brand of government based on polling in Heaven."

"An accurate one?" Michelle stopped smiling. She looked a little pale as Plato nodded.

Denise tried to imagine what that would be like, but all she could think of were the long white forms with too many check boxes.

Michelle must have seen her confusion. "Have you ever survived an opinion poll?"

Denise could remember dozens of phone polls, and one obnoxious man with infinitely long forms. "They're awful. They never ask the right question and the answers are always a little bit wrong."

"Right. Imagine being stuck in a continuous opinion poll and as you answered questions it changed the nature of reality."

She tried to picture Elantra's whims shaping the world. Lemon couches and puce carpeting filled her vision. She could feel the blood drain from her face.

"Now imagine everyone answering them all the time and everyone answering them differently."

A blur of utter chaos surrounded by lemon yellow couches and bright blue walls filled her mind's eye.

"Now imagine having to follow the sound of that drummer; the crazed drunken drummer of a perfect opinion poll."

Denise felt certain she would head for the nearest refugee camp as well.

*J*ohn blinked several times as he looked out over the grassy square trying to make sense of it. A moment ago he'd been chatting with Ananda, the Buddha and Peter in a candlelit living room. Now, there was a huge oak tree in the center of a park. A small town of one and two story buildings wrapped around three sides of the square. The fourth side revealed that they were atop a small hill overlooking plains of wheat that stretched to the horizon.

A creepy feeling made his legs twitch. This place was awfully familiar.

"Where in the world?" Peter's voice sounded strange.

"I think I've been here before." John turned and there it was. The white water tower with a huge yellow smiley face painted on it. "Once, when I crossed the country, I camped here. Welcome to Adair, Iowa. Denise and I put our tents right over there on the village green." He shook his head. He took a deep breath.

"You appear a little bloodthirsty, my friend."

Turning toward Peter's voice, he saw a mosquito on the blade of grass next to him. He tried to slap it. All he achieved was batting his own antenna with a foreleg.

"What in the hell?" He could feel his blood start to pound in his ears. Something started buzzing on his back. When he saw the wings attached to his shoulders he knew he was losing his mind.

"Peter. What's going on?"

"It's okay, John. It's okay. Try to relax. Remember, we're being reincarnated into different forms by the Buddhist software to follow Ron."

"Oh. That's right." The buzzing slowly quieted. "I did not realize that we'd end up in the same physical form as Ron in order to follow him."

"How else could we have?"

"I guess so." He turned away, embarrassed by his unwarranted fear. "Hey, is that Ron over there?"

"Where?"

"The one biting the bicyclist."

Two people lay in the shade of the giant tree, one young, one less so. Their tents were on either side of the oak their bicycles leaned against.

"How can you tell with mosquitoes?"

"That one looks like you. He could be your twin."

The woman swung at Ron, missed and boxed her own ear cruelly. "Damn mosquitoes. They drive me nuts.

We never have these in New York City. Computers may have been odd, but at least they didn't bite."

"True, man, true." Her companion plucked a stem of grass and started to chew on the end. "But they aren't in harmony with the universe, you know. They bite your soul and you never recover."

They made an interesting contrast. The older one was clean-cut, had the best equipment and looked very angry as she kept slapping at Ron. The other wore a tie-dyed tee shirt, and had let his beard and hair grow. He had old, worn gear and didn't seem to be particularly bothered by anything.

The first one slapped the side of her head again, where Ron had been buzzing around her ear moments before. "You're weird."

"No way, man." The bearded one smiled. "You ever work on those boxes and have them eat you alive?"

"No. Had them stare at me and refuse to talk to me. That's partly why I'm out here."

"See, man, they bite your soul."

"Hey." John pointed with one of his forelegs. "I think that's Arlene."

"How do you know her name?" Peter cocked his head sideways toward the two of them.

"She's a hacker who used to do odd jobs for Denise, but decided your Master Control Software was one too many for her. She bugged out, so to speak."

John flew over calling out, "Hey Arlene. Hello. Hello. How's it going?"

Peter was yelling something, but he couldn't hear over the buzzing of his own wings. As he flew out of the shade into the morning sun he could feel the heat swell his body very uncomfortably. No wonder mosquitoes usually attacked at night.

He landed on her knee. "Arlene, it's John. How's your trip been?"

He realized his mistake as a huge hand blocked the light and smacked him flat. The light came back as intense pain coursed through his body.

"Got one of the buggers."

He was suddenly back on the blade of grass next to Peter. He carefully moved each of his legs and his wings, but nothing hurt any longer. The software must have put him together again.

"That didn't feel good at all."

"Are you okay?" Peter was watching him. "I tried to warn you. Wrong language."

"Oh. Yeah. I guess it would be."

Arlene swung and missed again. "Damn it."

Seeing Arlene reminded him of Denise. Leaving her behind was supposed to let him concentrate on making sure there was a tomorrow for them to live in. All it had done was make her mad and leave him more distracted.

Arlene slapped her arm and then inspected her palm. John could see a small red and black smear. "Got another. Yes. It is a good day."

Peter buzzed his wings loudly for a moment. "Well, that's my brother. Or is it myself? That still bugs me."

John tried to punch him in the shoulder but ended up tangling his foreleg in his own antenna again. "No cheap puns, please."

"Sorry, I guess we're going to be buzzing off soon."

He ignored Peter and listened to the cyclists.

"You know, man. Trying to kill these poor little bugs is not a way to achieve harmony with the universe. Like, it's just their way. They're cool. You know, man, nature."

"He bites me. I squish him. Until they learn to leave me alone we each have our roles." She wiped her hand on a small towel and looked around, as if hoping to find another target. "And stop calling me man."

John heard a quiet laugh near his ear. The Buddhist system software said, "*Lesson: Do unto others as you'd have them do unto you. Bang,*" and they departed Adair, Iowa in a slight puff.

lato could not find a comfortable position. Michelle had obviously selected the wicker chairs on her verandah in order to perpetrate extremes of torture upon unsuspecting mortals. He and Denise had been sitting and reading, while Michelle was off to see old Flamel. Putting faith in alchemy was not a reasonable course. While admitting that he did not look forward to the end of the universe, it would be preferable if she had a sensible plan. The most likely remained the recovery of the software.

That reminded him. "Denise?"

She turned from her book of poems. They were by a fellow named Robert Frost, whom she claimed was an old friend. He assumed it to be a metaphor. He realized she had been on the same page for a while. She had spent more time staring at the ocean than at the verses.

"I forgot to tell you. Someone called with a message for you or Michelle while you were on the beach earlier. Said his name was Ananda."

The book practically flipped out of her lap as she turned fully to face him. "What was it?"

"I shall attempt to say it properly, as it was rather curious. 'The Yank and Saint are spinning faster than a pair of sixguns in the hands of a shootist.' Does it have any semantic value?"

She was nodding her head. "I think so. My friend, John, is from northern Vermont and the Saint must be St. Peter. Spinning is going around the Wheel of Life. I have no idea what the Old West cowboy slang is about." She sounded quite concerned about them.

He tried to reopen the book he'd closed over his index finger to mark his place. Even Sir Isaac Newton's *Principia Mathematica* could not hold his concentration this day. Normally he also loved to watch waves. They made him feel better, more relaxed; but now the ocean was nearly still and he did not feel calm at all.

"I cannot win, can I?"

Denise looked over at him. "Can't win what?"

"Oh, sorry. I had not intended to speak aloud. I fear my battle against the software is, and will remain, completely fruitless."

"I don't understand. Michelle said you were battling the software for the last two thousand or so years. What battle are you fighting?"

Plato turned to look at her. Should one explain Hell to an inquisitive mortal? Yes, he should. This young woman had a fire and determination such as his had been. It was too easy to picture her spending an eternity fighting Hell's software for the sake of the battle. He must attempt to spare her such a fate.

"It is not an easy tale to tell. It started shortly after my death. Upon arriving in Hell I read an information booklet Michelle had written: *Simple guidelines and a Few Rude*

Awakenings for the Newly Dead." He had desired to scream and tear the booklet to shreds, but had chosen to remain calm and reread it carefully; for all the good it had done him.

"I was a bit irked to find there was something called a computer running the entire universe; the selfsame one that threatens us at this moment. Furthermore, no one knew anything of the creators. The worst was the intensely intrusive manner in which it is able to control our existence in Hell. I believe in free will. It was one of the premises of my teachings. I . . ."

"From what I've heard, the software doesn't allow any at all." She closed her book and set it aside.

"I noticed. No free will and no future." He realized he was close to tearing to covers off Sir Isaac's book. Setting it on the bench he folded his shaking hands in his lap.

"This software desires to shape and mold each soul into a certain path of conformity. I decided I would prove my point. It has been two thousand and forty-eight years, as of today, since I chose my path and I regret it now as nothing ever before. What a waste. What a forsaken waste of two millennia."

"But I still don't understand. What was your battle and why did you do it?"

He had to stand up to relax his legs. He began pacing up and down, his hands clasped behind his back.

"Your drive to know can be a dangerous thing. Those who simply accept seem to move on easily." It was as if he were watching a younger version of himself. His need to know, to quantify, to comprehend; these had driven him to . . . a useless path. A bloody waste, and now there was no time to correct it.

"I proceeded on the assumption that true perfection could not be assailed by anything as mundane as this software." Realizing he was lecturing exactly as he had at the Academy, he stopped. "I have spent my years trying to create a perfect moment, thus proving the mind has control and not some unknowable cosmic programmer."

"You never succeeded, did you?"

He hung his head not trusting himself to speak. Denise was quiet for so long he finally looked up from the wooden deck. She was studying the glittering ocean.

When she spoke her voice was distant. "How could you believe that you could attain perfection? It's a myth, a guidepost through the dark. And now I see no light."

'Perfect is a myth.' What in Hell had he been doing all of these years?

Michelle opened the living room door. Denise and Plato were staring at the ocean, but not in quite the same direction. They both turned to her as she stepped onto the deck. This group needed some life.

She clapped her hands together loudly. Neither of them even blinked. "Well, once again we have hurried in order to wait. Nicolas believes the formula will work, but he cannot complete it until tomorrow morning. It needs to sit like some forsaken marinade. What's the news here?"

Denise stood and moved to lean against the railing. "John and Peter are apparently spinning like a pair of six-guns on the Wheel of Life."

"They're what?"

"That's Ananda's message. Your guess is as good as mine."

Buddhists. They always seemed to have an alternate view, that made sense to no one else.

Plato rubbed his forehead. "We have to wait?"

She wasn't happy about it either. "Until sometime mid-morning tomorrow. I was thinking of going to the central offices and see what I could do from the original console. Either of you want to join me?"

Denise shrugged. "Sure, anything beats sitting still and waiting for our doom."

Shaking his head, Plato stood slowly. "I think that the less I move at the moment the better. May I borrow your guest bedroom, Michelle? I expect it would be more comfortable than the floor on which I slept far too few hours this last night."

"Please do. Shall we tread lightly when we return or roust you out to eat?"

"I would prefer to be awakened." He fetched his book and went inside.

She turned to Denise. "It's a nice walk. I promise a minimum of suffering people."

Pushing off the rail, Denise set her book on the chair. "I'll hold you to that."

Michelle hated nothing more than being patient especially when she didn't have a choice; company would be pleasant. She led Denise through the grove and directly inland, over the rolling hills. The dusty smell of the blue and yellow heathers filled the air as the rhythm of the walk settled in and pulled her along. She was particularly fond of the red and gold marsh flowers she'd planted beyond the third hill. Everyone always commented on how ugly Hell was, or if not ugly then how dull. Even with this stupid crisis she still noticed the beauty. Plato was the only soul aside from herself who had ever moved slowly enough to appreciate what she'd built in. It was their good fortune, everyone else's loss.

Her legs burned as she climbed over the crest of the seventh ring of hills. There was a flat path through it, but this had a better view and she needed the workout. She looked back and realized she'd left Denise far behind. She was barely started on the last climb. Used to being alone, Michelle had forgotten about her companion. She sat on the peak to wait and looked down at the offices of Hell spread across the valley floor.

They had evolved with the passage of time. The medieval throne room with its lofty spires and flying buttresses soared above the rest of the complex. It had taken her centuries of fooling around with it to make the structure blend smoothly into the most recent office space. She'd made the harsh and surprising lines of the bright blue deconstructionist cube, with all of its broken angles, echo the old spires and arches.

The afternoon shadows emphasized the strangeness of it all. She pulled a blade of grass and stuck one end of it between her teeth. Even Plato hadn't understood the irony of a copy of Chartres, the finest house ever built to God, dissolving into the modern architecture that was wholly by and about man. What made it so satisfying was that no line could be drawn where they joined. God had been completely involved building his throne in Heaven, but she understood that his greatest creation was a person's freedom to choose.

Denise was panting as she came over the rise and dropped onto a flat rock beside her, her legs dangling over the short drop to the path below.

"That was more of a hike than I've done in months."

"I lost myself in the joy of the walk."

"While I admit it felt good to have room to really move, which I can't do in the city, those long legs of yours can sure cover ground."

Michelle picked up a stone and shied it down the hill. The sound of it clicking against some boulders below reminded her of the precious seconds ticking by.

Denise threw a rock in the same direction, but it landed quietly in the grasses. "Are we going to make it?"

Michelle pointed down at the offices. "Easy. There's our destination."

"That's not what I meant, and you know it."

"True. I don't have a good answer for you. A trip to Heaven won't actually solve anything, but maybe there is something we can do to give John and Peter more time."

"And if they don't succeed I won't ever see him again, will I?"

Out of the corner of her eye Michelle could see Denise staring straight ahead. She already knew the answer to her own question.

"What happened between you two in Bodhgaya? You seemed to be getting along so well. That was not what I would call a happy parting."

"I don't want to talk about it." Denise threw another stone. It arced far down the hill before clattering loudly as it landed. She was silent for only a few moments before continuing. "He only wants a relationship when convenient. I want to be more important than that."

Michelle spit out her well-chewed stem of grass and plucked another. The warmth of the sun was countered by the cool breeze brushing in from the sea behind them. She considered Denise's options.

"So, fuck his brains out and throw him away."

"Michelle."

"The way I see it, you don't have a lot of choices. If you see him again, you can use him, let him go or give him another chance."

She turned away. "Well, I don't have a choice. The decision is already made."

"It's never over until it's over."

"Crap, pure and total. It hurt like the very blazes of your homeland when I let him go. We had a wonderful, brief time on the sailboat, but it's done now."

Michelle turned to look at Denise, who glanced at her before looking down at her hands. "It's easy for me and sometimes I make light of it. I can empathize with your pain, but that doesn't mean I truly understand it."

"You don't have to be so blunt."

Michelle tried not to laugh for fear it would be a very bitter sound. "I am the ultimate realist. There is no choice for me, I've seen everything existence can dish out. Though I will admit the end of the universe is a first. And quite irritating after so much work. Maybe I'll get to see what's next."

"What's next?"

The image of the closing door shutting her away from the light filled her vision as it still occasionally filled her nightmares.

"I haven't aged in all the time I've been here. There must be a place where time passes for me."

Denise's voice was disbelieving. "You look forward to the end of the universe?"

She had to sit for moment to see how the thought made her feel. There was a small hollowness, like the echo of pain rather than the pain itself.

"Look forward is too strong, but there is certainly nothing in particular tying me to this existence."

"What about Plato?"

Michelle pulled the grass out of her mouth and turned to look at the petite woman perched on the rocks beside her.

"What about him?"

"You really don't see it, do you?" Denise was smiling.

"Enough with the twenty questions."

"Haven't you noticed how Plato looks at you?"

"How?" She tried to look objectively at her memory of him. He'd sat attentively on the porch chair, despite a pounding headache. She'd noticed the look on his face as she brushed her hair, but ignored it. Picturing it now, it surprised her.

"No. I guess I hadn't."

"Of course I don't think he realizes it. And now you're going to tell me that you don't look at him the same way."

"What? Don't be ridiculous. He's a nice man for whom I have a great deal of respect."

Denise pointed an accusing finger at her. "Oh no you don't. No sweet innocent, 'I'm merely the Devil, I can't imagine what you're talking about,' type evasions. It's mutual. You're the ultimate realist. You figure it out."

The rules were different for immortals; Denise clearly didn't understand that. It was cute that she thought she could counsel the Devil. Mutual respect could grow to a solid tangible thing without being lost in all the passion and noise of mortal love. She had to admit a certain attraction to Plato, but it was of one mind to another. He was the finest debater she'd ever had the joy of confronting. His clarity of insight was also extraordinary.

Denise slid off the rock and onto the trail at the foot of her boulder. "Are we going to sit here all afternoon working on our tans and daydreaming about men while the world collapses?"

Michelle pushed to her feet. "Not this woman. Let's see what's going on in the central offices."

Denise's legs turned rubbery as she followed Michelle down the steep descent. The path switchbacked sharply before finally opening out into a bright, well-tended garden. They walked side-by-side up the broad granite steps. This end of the building looked like a gothic cathedral. Michelle pushed one of the engraved doors open widely enough for them to slip through.

Denise stood and blinked in the absolute dark that descended when Michelle closed the door. The loud click of a switch echoed through the hall for a moment before flames leapt up the walls, filling the huge space with their ruddy glow all the way to the vaulted ceiling. Instead of pews there was a long path made of red ropes, winding toward the wooden throne high on a stepped platform. Except for the small computer desk beside the dais the room looked unused.

Michelle had walked over to console and tapped a few keys. "No response. I was afraid of that."

Denise turned slowly on her heel, taking in the whole interior. This was a proper Devil's throne room. The heavy granite and bright flames added to the feeling of a great power centered upon the throne. Turning she came face to face with a giant triptych suspended in space. She finally saw the thin wires. There was no way to ignore the impression that the panels floated in front of the flames along the wall.

All three were portraits of Michelle. Her deep love of life was portrayed in the first panel, which showed her cradling the light at what must have been the moment of creation. The artist had captured her beauty perfectly in the central one, where Michelle appeared as an angel at the birth of Christ. As she studied the third panel Denise became aware of Michelle standing beside her.

"I never have understood that third one and when I asked, Leo would simply shake his head and grin at me."

Denise swallowed hard. She was staring at paintings da Vinci had made of the Devil. She'd never be surprised again. John would go crazy that he didn't get to see these. On the third panel 'Leo' had painted Michelle asleep in a meadow. The blue sky above, the sunlight splashing across the flowers. Her expression was clear, contentment shone through her sleeping smile.

Michelle led her to a small door at the far end of the hall, their footsteps echoing in the vast silence.

Michelle looked back at the third panel. It was too distant to see clearly, but it troubled her at times. Leo said that it was a future she had yet to learn. Well, in the five hundred years it had hung there she hadn't learned it yet. Not much time left now, she'd best learn it fast.

She threw the switch turning off the flames and, plunging the nave into darkness, joined Denise in the inner office. She looked out of place. A tough modern woman wandering around the plush Victorian decor.

Michelle opened the stained glass door to the bright outer offices and looked around. A dozen or so demons were hard at work. The desks and work areas were neat and clean. The walls were hung with a few of her favorite photos. Despite the crash of the software, the business of Hell was still moving along smoothly.

She'd originally allowed the demons to decorate their own spaces until one horrible day when she'd come to work to find the decor redone in blue lucite and colonial furniture painted a bright chartreuse. Michelle had tossed it all into the incinerator and redone it herself. Demons had no taste at all. All attempts at programming it into the computer subroutines that generated them had proved futile. After millennia of smooth operations, something was now wrong, but she wasn't sure what. Everything appeared to be in place. Maybe knowing the software was in trouble was making her hypersensitive to something that didn't exist.

Horatio climbed down from his desk and came over with his tiny clipboard. He was barely as tall as her knee, but he'd run the office with an iron hand ever since the Great Reprogramming of twelve thousand BC. She headed to her desk and dropped into the chair. Denise stared at the demon for a moment.

"Nope. No surprise at all." She shrugged and headed out through the door.

Horatio looked at her retreating back, confusion was clear on his face.

"Forget it, Horatio. What's happening?"

He came around to the child's rocking chair that she kept for him, but didn't sit. She'd allowed him to choose his own looks and at the moment he was sporting a gray goatee and ponytail; an interesting contrast with his bright red coloring. His horns barely cleared the thick hair. The clicking of his hooves on the tile floor as he shuffled his feet started to scratch across her nerves.

"Sit down, will you?"

He jumped at the sound of her voice, but didn't settle.

"Okay. What's biting you in the butt today?"

He looked over his shoulder, trying to see his own rear end. Demons. No sense of idiom. Another thing she'd never been able to program into their design.

"What's the problem?"

He looked at her before blushing white. "Oh, I get it." He sat in the rocker and looked at his clipboard.

"The system won't let us in, but the periodic reports came out on schedule. We've in-processed 534,329 souls this last week, that's down almost 50,000 compared to the previous seven days, but there was a full moon that week, which may explain it."

The familiar pattern of his voice droning the reports was soothing. Leaning back and propping her feet on the desk, she closed her eyes. The first image to flash through her mind was Plato's face. She must be badly out of practice not to have seen his attraction. What to do about it was the question. Falling in love for a few decades before casting him aside didn't sound too bad.

She dropped her feet to the floor, popping the chair back upright. That was a vicious thought. He deserved better. The worst part was she wasn't any kinder to herself. If he deserved it, she did, too. Maybe . . .

Horatio's last item caught her ear. "What was that?"

He looked down at his list. "I ordered forty thousand extra reams of computer paper."

"Why? You and I agreed this was to be as close to a paperless office as possible."

"The printers won't stop."

That was it. What had bothered her earlier was the whirring of the printers in the outer offices; they were usually quiet. "What are they printing?"

Horatio shrugged. "It's a report I haven't seen before." She propelled herself up and out through the doors. She could hear the clatter of his little hooves as he followed over to one of the printers.

Denise was standing there with several sheets of paper in her hand. "I'm not sure what this means, but it doesn't look good."

Michelle looked over Denise's shoulder. Shit. She hadn't seen the Detail Status Report in ages.

"It looks like some report of each soul's progress through your system."

Michelle's stomach felt leaden as she read the printout. "That's what it is, but it isn't supposed to print. It's normally electronically tabulated and erased. A detailed listing of the steps toward redemption and moving on, out of Hell, was never supposed to print out. It would be huge; forty thousand reams a week worth of huge.

Normally it was full of experiences of the various stages of shedding ego. Every line represents someone learning to live for the sake of advancement. To live for the sake of living." A lesson she hadn't learned very well. No, not well at all.

And now that she was learning, it was too late. Even the automatic systems were failing. Her whole body ached with the desire to smash the printers one by one and then destroy the building that housed them, with her bare hands if need be. After a long moment, she shut off the first printer's power switch with a single finger.

"Hey." Horatio tried to turn it back on. She slapped his hand away before he could. As she turned off the next printer he pulled on her pants leg. "But we'll lose all of the data."

He let go when she started for the next printer. No clattering of hooves as she switched off one after another.

She pulled a single sheet from the last printer. The report was obviously the same. The office was echoingly silent after she shut down the last one. Horatio's look of disbelief was mirrored in the faces of all of the demons ranged around the room.

Even after swallowing hard her voice was harsh in her own ears. "Leave them off."

She crumpled up the page and dropped it onto the pristine floor. She headed out through the revolving door. She could hear the door swish as Denise followed. Michelle could still see the status after every name. The system was shutting down, but it wouldn't be hard to tabulate these reports. They all read, 'No progress.'

here was a small pop. Before John could see what was going on he was bowled head over heels, tramped on, and run into a wall. He was finally shoved into an empty corridor. He stood there, shaking his head to clear it.

"Hello again." A large black ant jumped into the mouth of the tunnel. He backed away quickly until he realized it was Peter. He would have sagged to the ground if he'd had less than six legs.

"We're ants."

Peter nodded and twitched his antennae together in what looked like a laugh. "You're quick you are."

"Not quick enough to join that." He walked forward until they stood abdomen to abdomen and watched the flood of bodies going by. A gap appeared.

"Now." Peter leaped forward.

John followed instantly, impressed at the power of having six legs.

The noise of everybody running along together and bumping into each other was deafening. He leaned

closer to Peter as they wound along the twisting passages. "I always thought ants were quiet."

"Try turning off your antenna."

He tried to think of how to do that with no success.
When he decided simply to stop listening, it worked. A
blissful silence settled over him. In moments he was
slammed into a wall and body-checked several times. He
turned his antenna back on in time to see the hordes as
they trampled over him once again.

Peter picked him up with his forelegs and rushed off
to the side. "I didn't mean to do it literally."

John watched the ants stream by the quiet corner
where they crouched. "Maybe I'll try going with the flow
next time."

He wondered which way Denise's mind was flowing.
No words had been possible to express how he felt about
her, but clearly that hadn't been the right thing to say. He
shook out his many legs, one of which was not working
very well. "This is a painful journey. That'll teach me to
mess with computers. Which one is Ron?"

Peter shrugged with his two front legs as John
watched a lone ant hauling a huge piece of something.
"Hey, there he is."

They both jumped out and grabbed onto the large flat
object. It was the only way not to lose Ron in the crowd.
His legs were barely strong enough to hold on, so John
bit down on the thing as well. The salt tasted wonderful.

"Hey. It's a potato chip. I love potato chips." He
started to chew off a small piece.

Ron yelled at him. "Stop that. The queen'll rip off
your antennas, stuff them down your throat and eat you
if she catches you."

John quickly wiped his mouth with his next set of
legs, not releasing the potato chip. As they pulled it one

way and then another, John couldn't tell where they were heading. They dragged it up along a sloping tunnel away from the main flow and into the light. To avoid being pinned against a wall John let go and looked out the end of the tunnel into the bright sunlight.

"Oops, we're going the wrong way. This is the way out. Hey Peter, we're in Australia. Must be the middle of the wet season, there's water everywhere below."

Peter came over to take a look. At the same moment Ron gave a big tug and flipped over backward into the water clutching his potato chip.

"We have to follow him." Peter started to climb down the side of the ant hill.

John followed carefully after him, watching where Ron had gone down. There was no sign of him. "We're too late. We're on to the next cycle."

"Lesson: Look before leaping. Bang." The Buddhist software giggled in John's ear as the sun disappeared.

enise felt tired to her core. The enormous bean bag chair made scrunching noises as she settled into it. She might never move again. She looked around this normal, comfortable room. Usually the quiet time when night first fell was her favorite, but this room still bothered her. It wasn't the books or the sun setting into the ocean outside, but the people with her who were making it uncomfortable.

Michelle lay back in the sofa with her feet propped on a carved mahogany coffee table. The whiteness of her fingers gripping a water glass belied her relaxed position. Plato simply stared at the floor from where he sat on the edge of an armchair, but he definitely had every right to be depressed, after what he'd told her earlier.

She realized she was shaking her head. "This is way too bizarre."

Michelle looked at her. "What?"

"You."

"Me? I am not."

"You know what I mean. Look, Michelle. I'm sitting here in your house with the sound of Hell's ocean on the beach outside. We're waiting for a five-hundred year old alchemist to send us to Heaven in time to save reality, and you don't think it's out of the ordinary?" She turned her head toward Plato. "You're the master with words. Can you explain it for me?"

He looked miserable as he shook his head. They'd returned to find him sitting in that chair and had barely heard a word out of him since. He needed to get over it. It didn't make him much fun to be around and it was clear his depression was driving Michelle nuts.

"I understand, Denise. I don't ask you to believe in me. I'm merely the woman who runs Hell, nothing more and nothing less."

Denise glanced at her and at the tightly clenched water glass in her hand.

"Oh, I believe that you run this place and maybe my soul will come here after I die . . ."

"All souls do, except for the Buddhists; in this reality anyway."

There'd been no word from John and Peter since this morning. All Denise wanted was to have this be simply a bad dream. She slapped her hand against the stretched leather of the chair.

"Damn it, I can't understand this mess anymore. It isn't you I don't believe in. It's Heaven and Hell, God, religion and all that mix. I can't reconcile the reality you've shown me with my beliefs. I mean, what role does all this serve? What purpose do you serve?"

Denise could feel the heat rise to her face as Plato gasped. Michelle looked at her a while before speaking.

"I suppose I've been trying to avoid that question for a long time. Whenever I think about it I feel like a cat walking on the top rail of a rickety fence." Setting down her glass she held her arms out like some tightrope walker. "Lately I can feel the next post starting to break at its rotten base. To answer your question . . ." she dropped her arms, ". . . not much purpose at all, I guess. I once thought I did."

"Oh God, I'm sorry Michelle. I know sorry doesn't fix anything, but that's not what I meant . . . or how I meant it . . . or . . . oh shit."

She wished she could take her words back out of the air. She could be so stupid. John often suggested, in his quiet way, that she think more before she spoke. Being tired was no excuse. She had punched Michelle in her most fragile spot. Come to think of it, that was exactly what she'd done to John. He'd opened his heart to her and she'd squished it between her fingers. How could she hurt two such good people, good friends, in the same day? Damn. Damn. Damn. And she had blithely hit Plato below the belt, too, 'Oh, it's so obvious that your search for perfection is futile.' She wanted to take herself out and beat herself black and blue. Quadruple damn.

Denise the ax, specializing in proving to immortals that they served no purpose and also in killing the only relationship she'd wanted in a long, long time. She'd done it to every person, outside of her family, she'd ever cared about. When she dared to peek she saw Michelle was looking even more depressed than Plato.

"It is either a great joke or a great curse." Plato's voice was very low when he began to speak. She could barely hear him. He had raised his head and was staring at Michelle.

"What you see here, Denise, are two souls, the flotsam of creation. We are two cogs, turning for years in this fabricated universe, jumping to some unknowable plan. We are not even attached to any proverbial music of the spheres."

Michelle sat up to listen.

"I have spent over two millennia in a battle I have known I could not win for at least five hundred years. I even suspected it was pointless to begin with, but pride of intellect made me take my course." He pointed at Michelle. "You are stuck in a worse trap than I am."

"I'm aware of that. I'm supposed to be one of the greatest powers ever to exist and I fulfill no purpose."

Denise winced at the resignation in her voice and leaned forward out of the bean bag chair to take her hand. Before she could, Michelle kicked over a nearby stack of books sending them skittering across the floor.

Michelle stood and began pacing among the books. "My life has been a study in avoiding tedium. I have no great powers and no desire or motivation to wield them if I did. I'm Hell's chief programmer. I don't do much of that anymore, either. Now all of existence depends on me and I can't do squat. I never have been able to create anything and now when it's crucial I still can't do squat." She slapped the glass and it flew off the table and smashed into the far wall.

Suddenly it was all very real. Armageddon about to come true. The world was crashing down around Denise's ears like a great black horror. She tried to curl up hoping to ease the pain coursing through her. It finally came out as a great wracking sob. Her doubts and fears had found a voice and that voice was agony. Her throat ached from the pain that was released with each lamentation. She had driven away everyone who had tried to reach out for her. Everyone. She had even driven away John.

Slowly she became aware of strong arms supporting her. Michelle knelt beside the bean bag chair and held her tightly. Denise shook her head to still the choking sobs. The words felt as if they were ripped out of her and they didn't ease the hurt along her breastbone.

"It's too much. One moment on a sailboat is not enough. I can't believe I let him go without me and . . . and I yelled at him . . . didn't deserve that . . . now I might never see him again . . . and I don't even know where he is or if he's okay."

Michelle's arms around her felt real and solid. As it became easier to breathe, she held Michelle tightly for a long moment in thanks. Sitting on the floor, she tried to wipe her eyes with the heels of her hands.

Plato knelt on her other side. He offered her his handkerchief. "Are you feeling a little better?"

Plato's deep voice reminded her of Uncle's.

"Not really." She could feel more tears flowing, despite her best efforts to stop them.

Michelle sat on the floor as well. "I wish I could undo what I have done to you, Denise."

"What you've done? It should be the other way around." Her voice was so hoarse she felt as if she were croaking like some damned bullfrog.

"No. I shouldn't have placed the troubles of centuries on your shoulders. I had no idea it was going to get this rough when I recruited you and John. I'm sorry. You're right, it doesn't fix anything, but I don't know what else to say."

Plato took her hand in both of his. "Somehow, Denise, Michelle and I shall make this work out for you. Out of this dark night we shall find a light. I promise."

She tore her eyes away to look at Michelle. Michelle was watching Plato as if he were an old garden, freshly weeded to reveal a perfect flower.

The Devil . . . no, Michelle. Plato preferred to think of her that way. Michelle was going to drive him crazy. After calming Denise and putting her to bed they had decided to walk the beach. Their footsteps were hidden from the rising moon by palm-leaf shadows. At first they had strolled for a while in companionable silence. With her, even silence was comfortable and after the revelations of the evening it was welcome. The debate had started simply enough. What would happen if the world ended as Peter was suggesting it soon would? Would there be an afterlife waiting? Was God already there?

But now she was being silly. "Michelle, how can you believe you might survive the end of reality? That is a ridiculous premise."

Her laughter filled the night air. "It is not. Will you accept that this universe began with the Big Bang?"

"That is the most logical theory at this time. It is by no means proven, but it does fit the observed and experimental data. Yes, for the sake of argument, I shall accept it."

"Good."

She bent down smoothly and picked up a pebble that glittered in the moonlight. It was a joy to watch such graceful movements, made liquid by the shadows.

"Now, describe for me what existed the moment before the Big Bang itself."

"As with all beginnings, it is ineffable. We can make a thousand predictions, but each one is equally likely. We arose from the moment and shall inevitably disappear back into it."

He had taken several steps before he realized Michelle had stopped. She stood in dim profile staring out at the ocean.

"I remember that time." Her voice was low as if with some remembered pain. "I remember the light filling the void. The beautiful light. Brighter than anything you could possibly imagine."

The moon shadows hid her expression as she turned to him. "I also remember a brief time before that; a door closing and trapping me in this universe. God and me with no knowledge of any past. After this is all over, will I be welcomed to some lost home I can't remember or will I disappear along with this universe that holds everything I've ever known?"

Facing back to the water she arced the pebble high. It splashed into the still ocean and made a ring of ripples.

"Am I an ephemeral ripple or a stone lost in the depths and being ground by the waves of time?"

He looked out at the reflection of the moon that had been disturbed by the pebble. He had thought no waves could wear her down. Closing his eyes he raised his face into the warm, night breeze and inhaled deeply, the fresh air filling him as if for the first time. He could remember a happy past, but it was long ago and the memories were faded with the polishing of frequent use. His present was dark and the future was imminent destruction. There was nothing to do, no answer he could give.

"Care to go swimming?" She asked quietly.

He looked over at her, still facing toward the ocean. It took him a moment to switch gears from his depressing thoughts. "Always."

Undoing her jeans, she pushed them down over smooth hips and stepped out of them. He looked slowly up her long legs. His gaze followed her hands as they took the hem of her shirt and pulled it up and off. The way her hair cascaded loose over her shoulders made him desire to run his fingers through it. He was surprised he could think such thoughts. Even if called Michelle, this was the Devil.

The light of the half-moon revealed no tan lines as she walked out of the scattered palm leaf shadow. He imagined wrapping his arms around that slender waist and feeling her smooth skin against his. Now that was an odd fantasy, imagining that Michelle would be interested in him as more than an intellectual challenge. Realizing he was still clothed he quickly unwrapped his himation. Dropping it onto the sand, he unstrapped his sandals and followed her down the beach into the warm sea. The breeze caressed his body, making him feel almost vibrant with life.

They swam straight out from the beach. He could keep up with her, but not easily. Michelle was as strong a swimmer as he. It had been centuries since anyone could stay with him, he had been swimming every day for a long, long time. They stopped well out from shore, lay back and simply floated side by side.

Everything was peaceful. Plato could imagine going to sleep like this, bobbing beneath the stars on the salt sea. Sleeping with the Devil. He had been attracted to Michelle for a long time, but had resisted. Her efforts had all been toward helping him learn his lessons and get out of Hell and therefore away from her, but he could not alter it. It was a truth. He desired her. When they started to tread water they brushed together for a moment. He knew it was his chance to speak, but the wrong words came out.

"How did I stay with you? You are the Devil after all."

"Plato, I'm simply a woman. Some bloody bastard of a universe creator . . ." taking a mouthful of water, she arced it into the air. ". . . put God and me in charge of the software that runs Heaven and Hell, but I'm still only a woman. I have to be active to stay in shape."

He could kick himself for not reasoning it out before speaking. He pushed sideways with his arms to face away toward the moon. Her gentle tones were worse than any anger she could have heaped on him. She made him feel foolish as no one but Socrates ever had. Yet he did like being with her, Devil or woman. He turned back. It was now or never.

"I know the software will attack at any moment. Before it does I should like you to know how much I have enjoyed being with you."

She laughed. That was a good sign. "What makes you think it will attack?"

"It always has before. I carefully construct a moment; yet it always finds some flaw. Something upon which to capitalize." His legs were starting to burn with the work of treading. "I have never managed to build a moment like this before." He tried not to imagine the feel of his hands on her shoulders where they shone and flexed in the light above the water.

"I'll take that as a compliment. Thanks. As to the software, it learned long ago to leave me, and those with me, alone. It also won't bother you unless you are trying to create something for yourself . . . for selfish reasons."

"I do not understand."

Michelle splashed water at him. "I know. Plato, the program reacts to ego. It's designed to kill that off."

"It cannot be as simple as that."

"Oh, but it is. It's only when you focus on moving ahead that you will be free."

"I'm focused now." Her quick smile lit her face with pure delight.

He started to reach for her.

She dove into the water, briefly exposing her well-toned behind and legs before she disappeared below the surface. He watched the moonlight on the water for a moment, waiting for her to reappear. Popping up right in front of him she kissed him quickly.

"Race you to shore." She didn't wait for an answer but struck out in a fast freestyle stroke.

He caught up with her initial start, but was unable to outswim her. Half a dozen times he edged ahead, briefly. They were even when they touched bottom. Kneeling in the shallow water, they gasped for breath and laughed.

Michelle started to splash him and almost immediately a cloud of spray surrounded them as they flung water at each other. Suddenly she was in his arms.

Gazing into Plato's eyes, darker in the shadows of the moonlight, Michelle could barely breath. She'd never wanted anyone this much. The attraction had been building for centuries; ever since he had first defied the software. She needed more than the passion of a single night. But what did he want? He was always so carefully controlled, it was hard to know what he was thinking. Maybe throwing herself into his arms hadn't been such a good idea, after all.

She was about to pull back when he leaned forward to brush his lips gently against hers. His willingness was all she cared about. Wrapping her arms around him, she leaned into his salty kiss, his arousal firm against her as they embraced. Her body felt alive as it hadn't in eons.

His breathing quickened as she ran the tip of her tongue along the bridge of his nose. She couldn't touch him enough. His hair was like silk in her fingers. He leaned her back until her elbows rested on the shallow bottom. Hot kisses burned like the sun after a long, cold night. Their trail started where her breasts rose above the surface . . . traveled down across her stomach as he lifted her out of water. Her legs spread wide to welcome his quick tongue and gentle lips and her fingers dug into the ocean floor. The gritty sand was a sharp contrast to the new sensations. What he did with his beard was utterly indescribable.

Barriers, long unnoticed, were melting away with each movement of his mouth. Plato's hands supporting her made her feel safe; his passion, more desirable than she had imagined possible and his presence . . . loved. She arched against him.

The storm he awoke roared madly through her. She had to make him stop . . . couldn't stand it if he did.

When he finally lowered her hips back into the water, she slid her legs around him. He nuzzled her belly with the tip of his nose . . . caught her nipples lightly in his teeth; the sensation ten times what it had been moments before. Cool air caressed her skin. Clasping his forearms she pulled herself closer. His moan when she moved against him reaffirmed the intensity of his desire.

"Michelle?"

"Yes . . . oh, yes . . . "

"What about . . ."

She kissed him and smiled against his lips. "There's no disease after death."

"I am aware of that, what I . . ."

His tongue welcomed hers as she ran it along his teeth. "No accidental pregnancy. I may not have many powers, but that I can control."

She blocked more questions with a kiss. They slid together; his strong hands across the small of her back. Every inch of him registered on all the nerves of her body. He moved . . . guided. For the first time in her long life she wasn't in control and didn't care.

He stopped . . . barely inside . . . he'd stopped. Perhaps he'd finished . . . but his tongue on hers promised more.

She was on the verge of protest when he pulled her onto him. She felt him breathe in her gasp of pleasure. Their bodies fit.

Her cry . . . his groan . . . broke the night air together under Hell's moon; shining on the ripples they made in the calm of the wine-dark sea.

*P*eter looked around. To his left sat a large grizzly bear. About fifty feet away another sat beneath some tall trees; must be Ron. He sighed and raised a front leg, sure enough it was big, powerful, and covered in brown fur. He was tired. Beyond tired, his bones ached with weariness. Fourteen incarnations in the last hour were too much for anyone.

"Peter?"

"Yes, John."

"I don't know if I can take much more of this." John scuffed at the dirt with his paws. "How much longer?"

He couldn't lose John now. It was the first time he'd ever had a friend who could appreciate the true nature of a problem. As a team, they had survived several rough incarnations that if he'd been on his own he might have given up after. He struggled to sound cheerful despite his own worries.

"I need that software. We can do this. It's midday. The sky is blue and the sun is warm. Time to get some sleep, finally. See even Ron is settling in." He waved a paw toward the other bear. "Maybe he'll manage not to learn whatever he's here to learn until we've rested."

Ron was moving around among the rocks. He scuffed at the ground before lying down in the shade.

Peter dropped heavily onto the ground and rested his head on his paws. "Sleep. After that we'll feel better." He closed his eyes. It felt great to have a break, even if it had to be as a bear.

John lay next to him with a thump and a deep unhappy sigh. After a brief silence it sounded as if John was digging in the dirt with his claws. Peter was too tired to look.

"Are you asleep?"

Peter opened one eye and looked at John. He was drawing patterns in the dirt with his claw. Looked like a fish. Of course. What else would a bear draw? "Not now. I was close though." All of the sarcasm he put into his voice was wasted.

John continued to draw his fish for a few moments. "I can't sleep. I don't think it's because of my fears about the collapse of software. I don't get it."

Peter raised his head and stared at him. John wasn't able to see it. Actually Peter was surprised he did himself. He'd always felt naïve about relationships, but not this time. Jesus used to tell him to cherish the obvious. He could still hear his voice, 'And sometimes the best way to teach the obvious is with a large club.' He felt better remembering Jesus' laugh as it rang out over the Sea of Galilee.

He whacked John on the nose with his paw causing John's fish to grow a gill all the way back to its tail.

"Ow. Hey, what did you do that for?" John turned to him and snarled baring his teeth.

"Stop mangling that poor fish and think."

"Think about what?"

"About Denise, you dolt." Peter pushed him hard in the side forcing him to roll over.

"What good would it do? I blew it with her. It's over."

Peter couldn't believe what he was hearing. Jesus had said the same thing about Mary Magdalen but Luke had straightened him out. He felt like a ventriloquist's dummy for that ancient conversation.

"You're an idiot, John."

"I wouldn't be surprised."

"Worse than that. A dunce."

"Maybe."

Jesus had been riled by this point. John was proving to be even more stubborn.

"You can't even see what's right in front of you, you're so blind. I don't understand why Denise cares about you."

John rose on his hind legs. Peter scrambled to his feet. An angry grizzly was not something he really wanted to be in the way of even as a bear himself, but it was better than morose depression. He looked at the size of John's claws and teeth. Maybe he should have found a more tactful way to open his friend's eyes. John's roar made him back into a large rock. Maybe nothing. Definitely.

"What is it that I'm too blind to see?" John's growl was coarse with anger. Some of the bear hormones in him must be acting up.

"You're too blind to see how much she loves you."

That stopped him. He stood with his claws out, all ready to attack, but a look of utter confusion on his face.

He held still until John dropped back down to all fours. Peter sat and scratched his back against the rock. He took a deep breath. He'd seen arguments before. He'd even sat through a very uncomfortable evening with Jesus and Mary once, but they always managed.

"What you had is called a fight. It is not the end of the world. You don't run away from every one. If you lose a round you go back in slugging if it's important. Have you always run away from an argument?"

John looked at the ground. "Not always. Well, maybe. I suppose I did leave relationships when I could not make peace any more." His voice became very quiet. Peter had to cock both of his ears to hear him. "We've quarreled before but nothing like this."

Peter sighed and reached over to pat him on his broad furry shoulder. "Better get used to it. That woman has a temper, but she loves you. It's as clear as the fur on your face."

John looked at him with deep, liquid eyes begging for scraps. It was sometimes very uncomfortable to give counsel to friends.

"How is it obvious, Peter?"

"The way she watches you for one thing, the way she talks about you for another and the way she listens to you for a third. She wouldn't even tolerate Michelle and me until you asked her to. She loves you. She may not show it plainly but she does. The question is what are you going to do about it?"

He watched John for a few moments more. Hope and wonder crossed his furry features making it very hard for Peter not to laugh. He settled back to the ground and closed his eyes. Maybe now he could sleep in peace for a while. He heard John lie down slowly beside him and start to draw in the dirt again. He opened one eye briefly but it was obvious John was not seeing what he was drawing; simple claw-lines in the dirt.

Peter closed his eye and relaxed. As he was drifting to sleep he thought he heard John say, "I guess grizzly bears are big enough they don't have to run away from every battle."

*P*lato lay looking at the stars of Hell, enjoying the warmth of Michelle still asleep next to him beneath the himation. Her face, turned toward the sky, was barely discernible in the dim starlight. He whispered into the night air, "Michelle." The sound was as sweet as her kiss.

But this made no sense. He desired her, in a way he had never imagined possible. He didn't want to have sex and spend the next few centuries feeling guilty for giving into his body's needs. His goal was no longer to be altruistic and create children for the future, nor was it to create a 'stable family unit' to provide a safe and nurturing environment for the future citizens of some theoretical republic. His wish was to watch each and every morning for the rest of his existence as the new dawn waxed slowly brighter finally exposing the color of her hair. He desired to wake her with a gentle kiss and feel her legs wrapped around him once more.

He straightened the long strands of hair. When he uncovered her bare shoulder he traced her collarbone with his finger. Michelle sighed and rolled toward him. Her head was on his shoulder, leg over his waist.

He held still as she sighed again.

"Hello, my dear sweet man."

He hadn't realized how worried he was about how she would feel. He breathed in the fresh salt scent of her hair as he kissed the top of her head.

"Hello, my dear sweet Devil."

She grabbed a fair amount of his chest hair and made as if to pull it out.

He laughed and put his hand over hers. "My dear sweet lover."

Letting go, she slid her arm across his chest and snuggled in closer. He did not care what caused this glorious woman to want to be with him, he was simply glad she did.

"That we two souls should have found each other . . . no, we two people. Yes, that is an essential key. We are more than a tally of souls on some weekly accounting report. We are thinking people in our own right."

"I haven't been thinking very clearly."

The sound of bitterness hurt him more than he had imagined possible. Hadn't she understood or was it . . .

"Do you regret us?" His throat was too tight to speak the last word clearly. He took a slow deep breath to try to stop the tears that threatened his eyes. A part of his mind wondered at it, he hadn't cried in centuries.

"Oh no. No. That's not what I meant at all. Plato, dear Plato." She sat up part way to look at him through the darkness. The length of their bodies still pressed together was infinitely reassuring.

She ran her fingertips through his beard. "You are the best thing to happen to me in a long time. That didn't come out right either, but you know what I mean. No, I was talking of my recent past."

"Your recent past? And that does not include us?"

She laughed a little as he had hoped.

"My recent past, as in the last few million years. Denise was right earlier, 'What purpose do I serve?' The answer is none."

The bitterness was back. Reality had indeed dealt cruelly with Michelle.

"All I am is tech support. Any half-baked demon could do that kind of programming in his sleep. Creation is over and it's all boring now. That stupid software. I have been its slave for eons. What did I ever receive for all of that? The universe is ending and I deserve an appropriate reckoning. What about me?"

He caught her hand as she hammered the fingertips against her breastbone. Tears falling through the dark night air made tiny warm pools on his chest. He brought her hand briefly to his lips and held her tightly as she lay against him. The convulsions of her weeping rippled against his body.

The sad joke was they had both reached the same dead end by two such different paths. His millennia of testing the power of his logic against the software that ran the universe. To what end? He did not even know anymore. Her being cast as the ultimate evil billions of years ago by that same program. What a waste. There had to be some other way, he could almost see it.

Michelle's sobbing slowly quieted. He pulled the himation back over them. When she finally raised her head, he took a corner of the robe and wiped her cheeks dry. Such great pain to be manifested as a small damp spot on a piece of cloth. It was insufficient to the weight of the sorrow. He gently kissed her forehead.

"We're going to make a deal, Michelle."

"This had better be good. I've had more than enough people trying to make deals with me to last my lifetime."

"This is not a deal with the Devil. It is a deal between Michelle and Plato. Here is my offer, we try together."

"That's it? We try together? Try to do what?"

"To live. I do not know how to do it any better than you do. If there are any tomorrows we will buy a small house in Fiji, take an apartment in New York, maybe go bicycling around the world together. Who knows? We will try and we will do it together and that is what will be important." Oddly enough he felt as confident as he knew he sounded. It felt proper, right to the core.

She tilted her head sideways, her long hair brushing against his chest. He held his breath while she thought about it. Leaning down she kissed him gently, her body relaxing into his in a way he found to be quite arousing. She put her cheek briefly against his. Her whisper tickled his ear.

"If there are any tomorrows. Deal."

The taste of her tears was on his lips. Curious, tears of sorrow and tears of happiness tasted the same.

He laughed aloud as he held her. This powerful, wise, old, Devil of a woman made him feel young and full of hope once more.

After a long, wonderful time she was again curled up alongside him with her head on his shoulder. Above their bed of sand and a himation he could now see the palm trees. He brushed Michelle's hair from her face; the rich color glowed in the pre-dawn light. Resting his hand over hers, he closed his eyes and was certain he would sleep as only a person fully inspired by the days to come was capable of. As Michelle might say, there had bloody well better be more than one or two tomorrows.

DAY
SIX

So God created man in his own image, in the image of God created he him; male and female created he them.

જી

*ohn couldn't keep himself from running and twirling in the deep green grass. The air was fresh, and the sun bright. What a life. He stopped at a small stream and leaned down for a drink. A small white fuzzy face stared at him out of the ripples. Something hit him from behind and he flipped head over heels into the icy water.

Turning, ready to attack, he came face to face with a lamb. Its huge grin gave him a hint. "Morning, Peter."

The baby sheep bounced away into the grass. He called back over his shoulder, "Isn't this great?"

John scrambled out of the water and shook himself so hard that he fell over. Climbing back to his feet, he ran along a fence looking for Peter. For a moment he thought he saw a pair of bright eyes watching him intently from the underbrush on the other side of the rails, but he did not care; he spotted Peter standing behind a small bush. Ducking his head at the last second, John slammed into Peter's side, knocking them both to the ground.

"You're right, it is great."

Peter flailed about for a moment before he regained his feet. "Stupid mortal."

John stood his ground as Peter butted him in the head. "Lousy saint."

"If you hadn't let Ron steal the software, the universe wouldn't be ending." Peter tried to kick him, but fell over.

"My fault? You're saying that the fact we're going to die is my fault? If you hadn't lost the software to begin with, none of this would have happened." John's legs were galvanized by his anger. He put his head down and threw himself at Peter with all his strength. The loud clonk as their heads came together echoed throughout his body. He wobbled for a moment and dropped to the ground. His head hurt like the very demons of Hell.

Peter had managed to stay upright a moment longer before falling against him. He was too sore and weary to protest. John didn't want to be anywhere near him, but there was nowhere to go. He made the mistake of trying to shake his head to stop the buzzing. His skull only ached more. Resting his chin on his forelegs, he looked at Peter through one eye.

"Lousy saint."

"Stupid mortal."

Raising his head at the same moment Peter did, he braced himself for another attack. After a long moment Peter began to laugh. It was easy to join in and really was quite ridiculous. A moment ago he'd been furious.

"You were right, Peter."

"About what?"

"It is possible to forget about it."

Peter shook his head. "No, you can't forget about fights, but you can learn from them and afterwards you can move on. But you must say the words, or it will always be open between you."

John could feel the dismay as Peter spoke. He jumped to his feet. "We have to make it back. I know what I did wrong. How could I have been so stupid?" No words. Idiot. What he should have done was said how much he cared for her. He should have said something and now there might never be a chance.

He looked around the field for Ron. He didn't want to wish bad on anyone, but Ron had better hurry up and lead them to wherever the software lay hidden. There he was, trying to wiggle out through a hole in the fence. John recalled the bright eyes. He couldn't let someone die if he could stop it, no matter what he wanted.

John sprang for the fence and clamped his teeth on Ron's tail trying to pull him back. "Don't go out there. It's dangerous."

Ron kicked him in the chest, forcing him to lose his grip, and wiggled through. John watched helplessly as Ron trotted toward the woods. A long brown streak of coyote flashed by and grabbed him by the neck, turning into the brush without breaking stride. If he had blinked he would've missed it. Ron's cry was mercifully brief.

The Buddhist software's voice was gentle. *"Lesson: The grass is not always greener over there. Bang."* The gloomy underbrush disappeared from before his eyes.

*D*enise looked up and down the long beach. If it weren't in Hell it would certainly be a nice place to vacation, with its tall shady palm trees and the huge expanse of white sand. The long swells broke with a deep splash, inviting her to come swim. She ignored them and strolled up the beach. The sand was nicely warm, not yet hot between her toes. Michelle had probably even designed a nice diving reef not far offshore. Denise turned to face the morning sun. It filled in the spaces in her body, the raw void left by too many tears in the night. Michelle had said everything would be better in the morning. One day closer to the end of the universe. This was not her idea of better.

There was a splash of color below one of the trees. As she approached she realized it was Michelle and Plato asleep beneath, or at least partly beneath, his toga. He was barely decent, lying on his back. The silver in his chest hair shone in the sun.

Michelle stretched languidly and turned. Denise wasn't sure she wanted to face Michelle after last night and turned to leave. Michelle waved her over. Denise sat on the sand several feet away and kept her voice low.

"Were you two out here all night?"

Michelle nodded and rested her head on Plato's arm where it lay outstretched. "We went for a walk and never made it back inside. Did you sleep well?"

She could only shake her head. "Not really. I miss John. Ananda did pass along a message. He and Peter were last moose in northern Maine; with no sign of the software yet."

Michelle's smile of contentment faded at the news and Denise wished she'd kept it to herself.

"I don't know what came over me last night. I didn't intend to hurt either of you." She had to turn away.

"It's okay. You were right. It wasn't easy to hear, but I think it helped." Michelle's voice was thoughtful.

Denise nodded toward Plato still fast asleep. "I guess you two did okay."

Her smile returned. "Yes, we did very well."

"Are you afraid of what will happen when he wakes up?"

She shook her head. "We've already made a deal. If there is a future, we are going to try forging ahead together. I want to thank you."

Denise liked the sound of the word. Together. "Thank me for what?"

"If you hadn't spoken, we might not have had even this one night." Michelle raised her head to rest it on her elbow. She gently stroked the exposed inside of Plato's wrist causing his fingers to twitch slightly. "I hope for many more, but I would not have missed this for the world."

She looked out at the surf as Michelle lay her head back down. She replayed the scene of John belowdecks on the sailboat for the hundredth time. Laying her palm against her cheek, Denise forced herself to see him in India as well. Maybe he had needed to focus. He could be so one-track at times. It was as much a part of who he was as breathing. Now that she finally understood that they were fighting for their lives, it made sense. He was doing his best to save them both.

She heard a movement beside her. Michelle had closed her eyes and Plato rolled onto his side behind her. He slid his hand beneath Michelle's arm, below one breast. He gently cupped the other. His movement brushed the toga down to her waist. Michelle smiled without opening her eyes and ran her hand along his arm until their fingers were interlaced. The blood rushed to Denise's face but she couldn't stop watching as Michelle snuggled back against him.

Their hands holding her bare breast; their bodies fitting together. Both were strong people, yet gentle with each other. She'd noticed that gentleness when Michelle had helped him out of the mud on that first day. Their closeness was still in place despite any changes the night had wrought.

Michelle's smile turned thoughtful, but she didn't open her eyes. "I think I've been wrong." Her voice was husky with near sleep. "I want to look ahead, not behind. I think it truly is the future that matters." She slowly fell asleep still holding his hand to her.

Denise looked at the ocean again. The future? If there was one. The present worried her more than enough. Where was John now? She needed to say she was sorry before it all ended. Sometimes it did need to be said, even if it didn't fix things. She had to smile. Hopefully it wouldn't shock him too much.

*B*eing a rat in Libya doesn't sound like much fun to me." Denise followed Michelle to Nicolas Flamel's door. He lived in an old French garret in someplace Michelle called South Central Hell. Plato had elected to wait at the car. He claimed it was not because he disliked alchemy, but rather being allergic to Nicolas' laboratory.

"Easy, Denise. It is working and they are following Ron."

"To quote Uncle," and Michelle joined in unison, "I worry."

Denise couldn't help laughing. She and her new friend, the Devil, were about to pick up an alchemic key from a computer-mangled cookbook to go to Heaven while John and St. Peter rode around the Buddhist Wheel of Life. Ridiculous. But at least the Buddha's message had said John was okay. It had even sounded like John,

'Our main danger is dying of boredom. Tell Denise and Michelle we're all right.' How like John to dismiss his own problems.

The wooden door swung open before they could knock. After they stepped in, a series of pulleys squeaked loudly right by her head and the door slammed shut.

"Whew." Denise held her nose. Maybe deciding to come with Michelle to fetch the recipe for the key to Heaven hadn't been a wise decision. "I had no idea that ostrich pooh smelled this awful."

Michelle also appeared to be a little overwhelmed. This room looked exactly as she would expect a French garret from the dark ages to be, only dirtier. Tomes and scrolls lined the walls. The room was dominated by a rough-hewn oak table covered with beakers, flasks, odd bits of plants and small chunks of various metals.

A huge man, who must be Nicolas, laughed through the great gray beard running down over his equally great chest. "That is not ostrich pooh, Madame. That smells much worse."

"But that's what the recipe called for, didn't it?"

"Up to almost the year 1400, I too was as naïve. You will grow out of it. The usual reason alchemical formulae don't function properly is quite simple once you think about it."

"It is far too odoriferous in here to think." Denise put a hand out very carefully along the edge of a book-case, unsure of her balance. Nicolas relented and forced open a window. The warm air that fluttered through the cobwebs was as refreshing as a glass of cold water on a hot day.

"Ha. This formula is a code. Through my extensive research and vast knowledge I've been able to ascertain that ostrich pooh is a sulphuritic compound based upon blended kitten sneezes, specifically 5 1/2 to 6 weeks old, the kitten, not the sneeze." He held up a small kitten and started to dangle a bit of unraveling from the sleeve of his robe for it to play with.

"Collecting a kitten sneeze can be quite tiring work, especially for a man of my age. We were at it most of the night. It seems they won't sneeze if you tie them down and wait. Tickling their noses with feathers won't work either. It is mainly in attacking dust balls that they sneeze. Thankfully it is not something I lack." He waved at the disaster area of his lab. The kitten complained about its bit of string being suddenly out of reach. He set it on the floor among a particularly dense collection of dust balls, which it immediately began to stalk.

"The other key element is . . . this." He held a small lumpy ball, dappled with bits of bright color.

Denise could see forms in it. With a sick feeling, she saw a face she recognized, but couldn't place from where. Nicolas' smile looked positively evil, but there was a twinkle in his eye that made her back away, rather than bolting from the room.

She move closer to Michelle. "And what is that?"

Nicolas continued to grin. He scrabbled around on his work bench among dusty volumes and parchment scrolls. He pulled out a copy of the Sunday funny papers, slapped the little blob on Dick Tracy's face, and mashed it with his gnarled fist. He carefully peeled it off, showing the imprint to her.

"I love silly putty. It's glorious fun." He dropped it into a beaker of greenish liquid on his bench. The color started changing as the putty melted.

Denise sat down on a low three-legged stool, not sure of her knees.

"Here, drink this." Nicolas held out a strangely shaped flask filled with a thick brown liquid which frothed and bubbled evilly.

"What is it?" Denise again made ready to run.

"MacLeod's Scottish Ale. My favorite. You're looking a little pale at the moment."

She cautiously tasted it. "Hey, that's good. Thanks." She took a whole hearted swallow.

Nicolas handed a second beaker to Michelle as she took another stool.

Denise looked over at Michelle and mouthed, "Is this guy for real?"

Nodding her head, Michelle sipped her beer.

After a few more minutes of puttering at his bench, Nicolas decanted the liquid into a small vial. Denise thought she saw a sorrowful looking Dick Tracy float by in the dark purple mixture. He handed it to Michelle.

"Go someplace where you don't mind killing the grass. Pour it in a small expanding clockwise spiral. You will have about thirty seconds during which you two can step on the spiral and land in Heaven. Sorry, there is only enough to work for two, not three as you requested. I couldn't collect enough sneezes with only one kitten of the proper age."

Denise looked sharply at Michelle and pointed at her own chest. She'd be damned if she was going to simply sit around in Hell waiting while Michelle and Plato tried to postpone the end of the universe. Michelle opened her mouth and, after a moment, closed it and nodded.

Nicolas tapped his forehead as if he was trying to remember something. "Oh yes, do make certain that you have your shoes on when you go."

"Why?" Denise didn't like the sound of this at all. "Will it melt our skin?"

"*Mon dieu*, no. But it would stain your feet a rather nasty shade of purple and it doesn't wash off easily."

Taking a final swallow of beer, they thanked him and hurried out to meet Plato. He reclined against the hood of the Rolls Royce, ignoring the demon chauffeur who danced about his feet. Apparently he was having apoplexy that someone would lean against his Rolls. Plato pushed off the car and met them halfway, giving Michelle an extremely sensual kiss. Denise stared at them unable to look away. With an effort she turned to watch the little demon pull a huge red chamois out of his pocket and start to buff the finish.

Denise heard Michelle try to say something and turned. Denise knew why she couldn't and would take care of it for her.

"Plato, we have a small problem."

He shrugged. "We have scant time to be concerned about such things. The universe is ending."

Michelle looked toward her. "Nicolas could only make enough of the compound for two of us."

"Ah . . . In that case I fear I will not be joining you."

She lay her head on his shoulder, the long hair hiding her face from Denise. "I may not be back."

Plato wrapped one arm around her shoulder. "You cannot leave your guest waiting in Hell and you must go. I am saddened, but it cannot be logically otherwise." He took the vial from Michelle's hand. "What do we do with this? You must go before our resolve can weaken."

Denise looked at Plato. He had stepped blithely past the problem and moved on to what must be done. The disappointment clear on his face hadn't changed his love.

Michelle made a swirling motion with her arm. "You pour it in a spiral pattern that is large enough for two people to step on."

Denise watched numbly as the purple spiral grew on the lawn. If only she could relive that moment in India, what might be different if she had followed Plato's example? Nothing. She and John would still be separated and the universe would still be ending. She wanted to go home, but if John was going to continue helping out, she would too. If she ever wanted to see John again she had to.

"Okay, the circle is all poured." Plato stood. He briefly held Michelle's hand and kissed her. They really did make a wonderful looking couple; the silver-haired man and the tall athletic woman standing in the bright sunlight.

"Michelle, I have not the words to tell you how I feel. So, simply I will say, come back to me if you can."

Michelle kissed him again. "Here's hoping I have a chance to collect on that deal we made."

He nodded and let go of her hand.

Not the words. Could John have meant it as Plato did? She looked away from them and let her eyes rest on the steaming purple grass.

Michelle came and took her hand. "Now remember to sing as you go across. Nicolas was very specific."

"How can an age old alchemical incantation be rock and roll?"

"You'd have to ask him."

Hand in hand they stepped onto the spiral singing,
There we were just a walkin' down the street,
Singing doo-wa-diddy-diddy-dum-diddy-doo.

*D*enise fully expected her next step to be off the spiral and onto the grass on the other side. Instead she stepped onto a white shag rug which looked surprisingly like clouds. She lifted her shoe, but put it back down quickly to cover the bright purple stain on the carpet.

The room looked like any office. It was dominated by a desk with a large computer console. This must be St. Peter's outer office. That crazy cookbook sitting on her kitchen table really did mean something.

"Name, please?"

She hadn't even noticed the short, all-white angel, complete with wings, sitting behind the computer screen. She was barely as tall as the keyboard was long.

Michelle sat on a corner of the desk. "Evil Incarnate."

"Right." The angel spoke as it typed, "Devil, human manifestation, one of. Do you believe in God?"

"What do you think?"

"Don't know, we're not allowed to think. It's not in our programming."

Denise didn't recall blinking, but one moment there was one little angel clerk and the next an even smaller one was perched on the clerk's shoulder, holding a notepad as large as she was.

"Should moose be female or turned into hamsters?"

She was trying to make sense of the question when Michelle snapped out. "Make them bright yellow as a traffic warning."

"Right." The angel closed her notepad and, with a small pop, disappeared. Even Michelle looked surprised. Denise felt a need to go sit quietly somewhere familiar.

The clerk pressed two more keys with finality. "I marked you down as atheist. Sorry, no entry visa."

Michelle walked around the desk and nudged the clerk out of the chair. It fluttered gently to the floor.

"What the . . .? This console's dead. How can you enter anything?"

"No one told me it didn't work. Oh dear, I've typed in thousands of entries. Now they're running around loose. All those unlisted souls. How will they know how to call each other?" The clerk started to hop from one foot to the other, wings flapping out of time. "I'll ask her. She'll know what to do." Suddenly she rushed out of the room.

Michelle jumped out of the chair. "Follow that angel."

Denise raced after Michelle onto the finest lawn she'd ever seen. It was perfect. As they were gaining on the angel, who was more hopping than flying, Denise found herself suddenly bound in some heavy cloth and fell to the grass. She looked at herself. She was clothed head to foot in a heavy gown with a black veil she could barely see through.

Michelle was swearing loudly somewhere nearby.

"Allow me to help you, fair ladies."

Denise looked up to see a tall, spare man with a nicely trimmed beard holding out a hand to each of them. She took his hand. "Thank you, I think."

"Allow me to introduce myself. Gawain. Sir Gawain. You may have heard of some of my exploits."

Denise felt no sense of shock at all. Good. She'd finally adapted. Nothing would surprise her now, maybe ever again.

"Aren't you mythical?"

"Oh no. That is, not totally. I did live in and fight for Camelot. We had a nice table too . . . but it was square. One midsummer's eve we started a storytelling contest about ourselves. I almost won the prize for the biggest whopper, but I was a real ladies' man back then. No one would believe I hadn't slept with the Green Knight's wife . . . or that I hadn't run away from Knight himself."

Denise had been trying to tug off her cloak with very little success.

"Oh, you will not be able to remove it. The Muslim traditionalists must have recently been polled. Every woman must now wear a chador and yashmak, that is, the gown and veil. Strictly enforced, I fear. It should be overturned shortly. The Christians and Jews are, shall we say, less than amused by these various requirements. Heaven without a good glass of wine doesn't make the Jews happy at all. Having it disappear in the middle of drinking it, only to have it reappear while one is reading a good book . . . Quite a mess things are. Quite a mess." The chadors and veils disappeared. "Ah, there you go. Welcome to Heaven."

"Thank you for your kindness, Gawain." Michelle curtsied deeply. It was an odd thing to watch, but it seemed proper respect for a knight errant. "Can you tell us who's in charge? Our guide seems to have outrun us."

"Oh, you want to see her? Won't be much help, but you can give it a try. She's over at his old place. She's, well, how to put it? She's over at his place not deciding anything. Yes, that's an appropriate description. Excuse me now. It appears there are some new entrants. They look quite confused with the reception angel running off and all. Bye now, and watch for those changes."

He strode away. Denise was suddenly wrapped in a chador again and fell down to the luxuriant grass.

Michelle, who had managed to remain standing, pulled out her keypad and tapped several keys. Nothing happened. She pressed several more commands and still nothing changed. Finally the gowns disappeared. Denise climbed to her feet. "Thanks, I can't believe there are women who spend their life in those things."

"You're welcome, but it is nothing I did." She turned the keypad so that Denise could see it. The small screen was flashing, 'System unavailable. Please select alternate startup system.'

"What does that mean?"

Michelle turned off a little switch on the side and put it back into her pocket. "I'd have to ask Peter to be sure, but I think it was offering to restart at the big bang."

Denise felt frozen as she watched Michelle's face shift from concern to fear. With the Devil scared, she couldn't figure out what she should feel. One wrong key and all of existence could be reset to the beginning.

"We need to get moving."

Michelle nodded in agreement.

A small angel appeared on Denise's shoulder. "What's your favorite color?"

"Electric pink with dark purple polka dots," was the first ridiculous answer she could think of.

Immediately the grass for several dozen feet around was electric pink with dark purple polka dots.

Michelle batted away the next angel who arrived. It instantly disappeared and Denise felt a slight pressure alight on her knee. Before it had a chance to speak she swatted at it. It ducked and went away. Michelle grabbed the next one who appeared and pinned it by the wings. It fluttered madly but couldn't escape her grip.

"From now on you will leave the two of us out of this craziness, right?"

The little angel nodded emphatic agreement. The instant it was released it disappeared, but three more arrived and tried to alight on her. They reminded her of the mosquitoes in the Maine woods.

Michelle turned to her, slapping away any errant angels. "We had best do something fast. We can't wait for John and Peter to find the software. Heaven is well and truly collapsing. We may have a day, but not two."

"But I thought we had three or four . . ." She stopped at the sight of Michelle's frown. She could feel the worry sink coldly into the pit of her stomach. Taking a deep breath, she tried to focus. "What can I do?"

"I won't know until we see who 'she' is and what's being done."

"We still don't know where or who she is though, and our unwitting guide seems to have escaped us."

"It's okay. Gawain said, 'his place.'" Michelle pointed at a large building off in the distance. "Whoever she is, she's sitting on God's throne."

Denise nodded. "Seems right. Isn't that where a woman should be?"

Michelle looked at her expressionlessly for a long moment before turning away.

h no." Peter looked toward John. Crabs. They were basic boring rock crabs. John waved his claws around in front of him.

"Great. This is exactly what I always wanted to be. A bottom-mucking carrion eater. I'll bet the software is here somewhere. If I were a demented hungry ghost I'd store the universe's control system in some safe oceanic basin. Wouldn't you? We're running out of time, Peter."

"Clearly it's not going to be here. Relax. I know time is short, but we don't have any choice. We have to follow him. I've come to have faith in Ron, at least in his ability to learn quickly and move along the wheel."

John stopped and scuttled sideways to look at him. After a moment, his claws drooped to the sand. "You're right. We can count on him to die quickly and painfully. Only this time I'm not going to get hurt."

Peter felt relieved. While the Buddhist software did seem to try to take care of them, his friend was always being bruised and battered in each incarnation, if not killed. At first it had been amusing in a slapstick fashion. Now he was feeling sorry for John and tried to protect him, with limited success.

"If you'd simply stay still this journey might be less painful." Peter tried to wrap an arm around his shoulder but klonked his large claw on John's carapace instead.

"Ow. Are you telling me how to enjoy a rapid-fire tour of the Buddhist Wheel of Life? Not possible."

A large cage descended out of the murky water above. He managed to pull John out of the way before the edge of it landed on him.

"Thanks, that would have hurt. It is such a joy to know the software thinks I make a great punching bag." John skittered around the cage. Several other crabs were coming to the area and climbing in the cage doors.

Peter watched the crabs mindlessly crawling into the giant trap. He had crawled into one himself. His blind faith in the triumph of good over evil was shattered by finding that the Devil was one of the better people he'd ever met. Maybe she embodied that triumph. Even the Devil was good? That would make his belief valid. It was not all as neat as it appeared, but it did work.

He grabbed John by a pair of his legs and pulled him over. He had to tell someone. "John, life isn't nice and neat and prepackaged like the proverbial Christmas present." He held his claws out to indicate a boxed gift. "This Wheel of Life, we can ride along or actively take a role. Now, one of those is much more fun. Try to enjoy it for what it is."

John waved toward the massive cage with its fish-head bait. "Enjoy what? That thing almost crushed me."

"Step back a bit. As Jesus is always telling me . . . you know I never understood this before. . . life need not be perfect to enjoy it; doing well is triumph enough."

John scuttled backwards a few feet. "There, now I have perspective. It isn't helping. Next you'll tell me about this great bridge in Brooklyn you want to sell me."

Peter heard the rushing sound at the last moment and jumped out of the way of the next cage. It crushed another crab that stood exactly where John had been moments before. Maybe stepping back did help.

"Bubble, bibble, bobble, bibble. Bloop," the Buddhist system software burbled in their ears. Ron must have been the one the cage landed on. What had he learned? To be careful where he stood? The universe was certainly perverse at times.

*M*ary? What are you doing here?" Michelle sounded pleasantly surprised as she shouted across the crowded room.

A great golden throne towered above the hundreds of people dominating Heaven's reception hall. They were all bathed in a gentle light spilling through the high crystalline ceiling. It made everyone look young and lively, but Mary outshone them. Denise could not take her eyes off the beautiful woman who ran down the turquoise marble steps. A path opened before her like a gentle wave. Her dark-blonde hair swirled behind her and a large white dog followed at her heels.

"Michelle." Mary gave the Devil a hug. "I haven't seen you in days. Do you know what's going on?"

"I was about to ask the same. First, this is my friend, Denise, she's still mortal. Denise, this is Mary." The white dog sniffed her hand for a moment and gave it a large wet lick. "And this is Blaise, Peter's dog."

Mary smelled of fresh roses about to bloom. She gave Denise a kiss on each cheek.

"Mary, as in Mary Magdalen?"

Mary looked at her for a long moment as if waiting for something more. Suddenly she smiled brightly at some private joke.

"You poor woman. All this must be so very overwhelming to you. And yes, I am the misguided girl who Jesus saved, in person. Come, come this way." She led them to a door beside the throne dais. "I can't stand this room for very long. All those people always wanting answers for everything."

Denise looked back from the doorway at the crowd of beautiful people. "They look all right to me."

Mary stood beside her. "Oh, they're okay, I guess. It wouldn't be so bad if I had some answers, but I don't and they simply won't stop. They think everything in Heaven is supposed to be perfect, as if that were possible."

Her laugh sounded light-hearted and genuine, like Kris' wife Marita. But there was no way to compare this casual cheerful woman with her tightly strung cousin-in-law. It was somehow comforting that perfection was only a goal, even here in Heaven. The universe might not be set up the way she'd believed, but it was some comfort that its rules were consistent.

Stepping through the door and closing it behind them, they entered a pleasant little flower garden and seated themselves around a small table in an elegant gazebo. From here not only the gardens, but also the soaring mountains of Heaven could be seen, like mighty clouds piled up to the sky. Blaise, after circling the small space several times, sat between Michelle and Denise.

Mary reached into a refrigerator beneath a bench seat and selected an elegant China plate piled high with little cucumber sandwich wedges.

"Much nicer. Please don't take this personally, but you both look awful. You simply must sit still for a minute. Would anyone like some tea?"

Denise nodded.

"Do you like the gardens?" Mary continued before she could answer, "I've always liked flowers. After the resurrection I found a nice little cottage on the sea and tended my gardens. God let me plant this one. I miss him. We used to sit here until all hours."

Something was missing, but Denise couldn't place it at first. "Hey, no angels have polled us out here. I was asked about a thousand questions on our way over."

"Oh, I grew tired of them and told them to leave me alone and get someone else to make the decisions. I made more than enough on Earth. Jesus was totally stressed toward the end, you know. The poor man was so burned out that he couldn't make up his mind about anything. 'What should we eat, Mary? What should we drink, Mary? When should I die, Mary?'" As she looked off toward the mountains, her brow furrowed. Her voice was distant as she continued, "I'm the practical one, but we barely made it through those last days."

Denise looked at her in wonder. She couldn't imagine being confronted with such a question, and answering. It was unbelievable a relationship could survive that. Yet it had. And Jesus had not been some prophet on a clear, pre-set path. He had struggled through like any mortal. This cheerful, sunny woman chatting happily about flowers had been the strength that had helped it happen.

Michelle played with Blaise's ears. "If you don't like making decisions why are you in charge here?"

"Well, someone had some questions a few days ago and they couldn't find Peter anywhere. They came to Jesus for guidance. He looked at me and said, 'Why don't you have a bit of fun, dear? You could run Heaven until Peter gets back.' I thought it would be a lark, but Peter hasn't returned. Do you know if he's okay?"

"Last we heard he and my lov . . . my friend . . .were giant condors in the Andes." Denise had to look away.

The momentary pressure of Michelle's hand helped, as Mary kindly ignored her gaffe. "Oh, good. Peter's such a cute boy. He doesn't usually get out enough. Spends too much time playing with his computers."

Blaise rested his head on Michelle's knee until she scratched his head. "Where is Jesus the boy wonder?"

"Well, before the gates were closed he went down to coach his little-league team. I haven't heard from him since."

Denise had to blink twice before the words even made any sense. "Jesus coaches softball? Where?" That sounded even sillier than most of this adventure.

"Well, now that I think about it I'm not sure. Jesus and Mohammed were both converted to baseball by that Doubleday fellow, you know, the one who invented it. He hates the big time, but enjoys the kids."

Michelle looked from Mary to her and Denise could tell she'd reached her limit for polite talk. Michelle pulled out her keypad and stared at it as Mary continued.

"The guys're coaching competing teams to keep it interesting. It was pretty wild trying to persuade Mohammed to let his be coed." She whispered to them confidentially, "He still comes over some nights for a drink and complains about the little league moms. They're a bit much for him."

Michelle returned the keypad to her pocket. "Mary, we came to Heaven to find out what's going wrong with the whole system and try to fix it before it falls apart. Are you sure you can't tell us what the problem is?"

Mary's hair shimmered in the sunlight as she shook her head. "How could I? I don't understand computers. I did go to a couple of the consoles, but they're all blank. Something must still be working, though. The angels are functioning. I can't seem to stop them."

Denise sipped at her tea, it was still too hot. "How did the ruling by opinion poll start?"

Mary took a cucumber sandwich and leaned across the table to feed it to Blaise. "I was tired of running things and told the angels to just take care of things. They're the ones who cooked this up. I figured Peter would push a button to fix it when he gets back, but he sure is taking his time. It's pretty messy. Whenever things get too hectic, Blaise and I come sit here. I wish Jesus were back."

Michelle slouched on the bench and crossed her ankles. "He may not be able to get in. It was quite difficult for us and Peter may be another day or so, if we're very, very lucky. Do you mind if I give it a try?"

"The Devil running Heaven?" Mary smiled one of her radiant smiles. "That would be great."

"I can see the headlines." Denise held up her hands, pretending to sell newspapers. "'Devil sits on throne of Heaven. Panic reigns. Dow Jones rises 500 points, setting one-hour record.'"

Michelle smiled. "Don't worry. You get to help."

"Oh no." Denise could barely keep from laughing. "'Cookbook Editor and giant dog help God's angels.'" Blaise perked his ears, knowing he was being discussed.

"Why not? Add to the bylines an interview with Plato entitled, 'From philosopher to the Devil's throne.' Oh, sorry, Mary. I told you about the hard-case I've had for the last few thousand years, that Greek philosopher. I've left him in charge in my absence. He can easily manage any problems that might arise, so I'm free to try to help out here."

"Why, I think you have a new beau."

Michelle's smile was nearly as bright as Mary's. "I think so, too."

It was nearly the same smile Denise had seen on the triptych. Michelle was happy about a man she might never see again.

Michelle took a deep breath and called out loudly, "Hey. Angels. I want to talk with you. Come here."

The garden was immediately filled with angels of every shape and size, from the giants who announced the birth of Christ to the more normal, Clarence-sized ones, down to the little poll-takers.

"Oops. I didn't realize my voice would carry so well. I simply wanted to find out who's in charge here."

Every angel pointed at another. Michelle looked at Denise and Mary. "Any bright ideas?"

Denise shook her head looking lost; surrounded by the mighty host of winged creatures.

Mary handed Blaise another sandwich before turning to the crowd. "No one out there pointing at themselves now is there?" Mary's voice sounded as if she were talking to a three year old, not all of the angels in Heaven.

After a few moments of silence, a small voice said, "I didn't mean to be."

Michelle pointed at the little one who stepped forward. "Is this your spokesangel?"

In answer all the others disappeared.

"You're it."

"Well, I didn't mean to be." She looked around slowly, even peeking under a nearby bush. She finally shrugged her shoulders only to be confronted with Blaise giving her a big sniff. His head was as large as she was.

Michelle laughed as the angel backed into the branches. She called him to heel. "Perhaps if you sat on the table."

Denise leaned down and extended a finger which the angel solemnly shook. "I'm Denise. What's your name?"

"We aren't supposed to have names. We're simply 'angels.' Sort of amorphous, you know."

"How about 'Babe'? You're a pretty melancholy little angel."

Denise had seemed fairly strained for a while back in Hell, but she was clearly adjusting to the surroundings if her sense of humor had returned. Good. Michelle had taken a surprisingly strong liking to this mortal. It was a rare thing, to be enjoyed.

The angel flapped its diminutive wings and floated gracefully up to land next to a teacup Mary set for her.

"How about Henrietta? God used to call me that. I always liked the sound of it."

"Good enough. How did this mess start? Any ideas?"

Henrietta took a sip of the tea. She could barely lift the cup with both hands. "Yes, I do know. We have group consciousness, sort of. Actually, to be honest, we don't have a clue what each other is thinking. I know how it started, because I did it."

The deep sigh that came from the little angel made Michelle feel pity for it, almost.

"I was talking with Mary about what flowers we should plant for her upcoming coronation and celebration. I had started . . ."

Denise interrupted her chatter, "Mary? You were going to be coronated?"

Henrietta didn't give her a chance to respond. "Of course she was. You can't sit on a throne, especially this one, and not be coronated. I started planting some perky yellow nasturtiums, they'd go very nicely with her hair, but she seemed to think marigolds were better. Suddenly she said, 'I don't want this job much less be coronated into it.' I was shocked. We had been planting flowers, ughtering sacred lambs, and all sorts of preparations."

She certainly was a long-winded little thing once she was started. "Could we come a little closer to the point?" Michelle added some lemon to her tea.

"Sorry, I thought I was. I tried to ask again. I'd been put in charge of the flowers after all and I wanted them to be just the right shade. It is sad when flowers conflict with the color of someone's hair during a coronation, you know. If her gown brings out a golden tint then clearly the nasturtiums were the right choice . . . This is when she stopped me and said she hadn't even chosen a gown. This was a huge problem and I immediately summoned all 3,400 decoration angels and the 352 in charge of many different aspects of her gown. She became quite upset."

"No, really." Denise was clearly having fun teasing the little angel.

"Yes. Believe it or not. She . . ." Henrietta almost squeaking, pointing at Mary. "She said, and I quote, 'I've made enough decisions for other people. I'm done.'"

Mary held up her hands, as if stopping traffic. "Well, I have. They were all being so dumb about it, I told them to bug off."

Henrietta waved a tiny index finger at Mary. "She did. I couldn't believe my ears. 'If you want a decision go ask someone else,' she said. Who were we to ask? She wouldn't answer. She left us and came into this garden. We aren't allowed in unless we're called. Asking each other would never work, decision making isn't in our programming. I decided to ask the occupants of Heaven."

"What questions?" Denise asked.

"We started asking about flowers, of course. This led to color and size of animals, guests' attire, and so on."

"Didn't you realize that the answers might conflict?"

"We aren't meant to make decisions. We're meant to

meet needs. The problem is that we all have Heavenly power to implement the decisions made for us. The stranger the answers became, the more questions we had, and that led to stranger answers."

Michelle suddenly had an idea. "What would happen if I made the decision that you had to fix the software?"

Henrietta shook her head. "Nothing. We angels are simply low-level subroutines. We can't affect the higher computing functions even when they aren't missing."

There was a huge crash from the direction of the throne room, making them all jump. It was followed almost immediately by another and a lot of yelling. They all jumped up and rushed to see what was going on, except Henrietta. Michelle looked around and noticed she was gone. Time enough to find her later.

*J*ohn landed with a splash. As he slid beneath the surface he felt a need to breathe, and not water. The stupid software had it in for him. He kicked madly and flew briefly into the air. He took a quick breath before he fell back in. Looking around, he could see several dolphins swimming near him. He rose slower this time, keeping his head below the surface. The water tickled as it swirled around his dorsal fin.

Another dolphin swam up and nudged him before doing an elaborate underwater gyration. It must be Peter.

He chased him down into depths no diver in a suit could go. Turning, they shot side by side toward the surface. He performed a complete flip and landed with a big splashy belly flop while Peter arced in a graceful curve before disappearing neatly through the waves. They swam submerged side by side.

"Remember, John, a few incarnations ago? You asked how life could be enjoyed, even with the entire universe ending?"

"Was that before or after the kid killed Ron while we were parakeets?"

"Before, and you know it. This is fun."

John couldn't hold back any longer, and he started to laugh. "I must be going crazy. We need that software, and I suspect we need it very soon. And yes, I'm having a great time." He shot for the surface. At the last moment he turned sharply and barely avoided swimming into the bottom of a kayak. He lost all control in the air and made a big spray as he splashed back down near another.

He surfaced quietly behind the pair of kayakers.

"Wow, that was amazing. That was so cool. Do you think it'll do that again? Do ya?"

Peter surfaced beside him as the other kayaker spoke, "I'm soaked and I didn't see a thing." She sounded angry as she wiped her face with her hands.

"Well, it was just totally to the max. He did this wild sideways flip-like move before he splashed in. It was awesome."

Peter wagged his head in what looked like a silent laugh. John nodded as they dove. He could still hear them as he and Peter played near the surface. Dolphin hearing was incredible.

"What brought you to the Carolinas?"

"I was on a bicycle trip and I met up with a young

psycho who wanted to ride with me. He decided I'd make a great surrogate mother. I'm done with that, my kids are long since grown. It was my second day out and I had planned to ride for at least a few months in the U.S. Instead I rode to the nearest airport and now I'm here for a while."

Peter did a wild loop-de-loop around him and then nodded upward.

Shooting to the surface they flew over the bow and stern of the woman's kayak. As he went past her he saw that it was Arlene. In his surprise he completely flubbed the landing and sprayed the guy.

Arlene began laughing, quietly at first, but it started to grow and build. He nudged Peter and they swam deep and shot back up, arcing right over her head. The joy in her laugh was something he hadn't heard for a long time. The city must have really gotten her down. Their entry was in perfect unison.

At the top of the next arc, with a full twist and flip over the bow of her boat half completed, the Buddhist software chimed in, *"Lesson: Don't try to eat boat propellers, especially while they're spinning. Bang."* John never hit the water and he was left to wonder what Arlene must think of the evaporating dolphin.

*M*ichelle looked at the hundreds, maybe even thousands, of supplicants filling the throne room. It was hard to see what was happening. Fights seemed to ripple back and forth across the crowds, dozens at a time, any one of which would have fit into the largest saloon brawl scene in any movie. People with common sense were cowering along the walls.

Denise and Mary stood by her side with their mouths hanging open. She pulled Denise out of the way as a chair smashed into the doorjamb where she'd been standing. A roar of triumph off to the right drew her attention. One of the great statues lining the hall had been pushed over. It slowly gained speed as it swung down into the crowd. There were several high screams that were cut short by the crashing sound.

Mary stepped into the crowd to help people. Many lay, bleeding and groaning, scattered about the floor. Blaise jumped at someone who was coming up to drop a vase on Mary's head. The two of them blended into the huge mêlée.

The mob flowed up the dais steps. There wasn't a chance that Michelle would allow some unruly heavenly trash to topple God's throne. She pushed through the crowd, vaguely aware of Denise close behind her. They leapt up the steps, pushing people out of the way to clear a path as they went. Finally she stood before them next to his footstool.

"Back off," she shouted, as loudly possible. All in front of her collapsed and covered their ears. She looked and saw that the shape of the walls behind the dais acted as a natural amplifier. She could feel herself smiling as she turned to face the mob struggling to its feet. So, God was not above a bit of artifice himself. A whisper from

here could probably be heard anywhere in the hall.

Denise was waving a broken chair leg at a few of the stragglers who were still climbing the stairs.

One of the people crouching a few steps down yelled out, "Who in Heaven do you think you are?"

Michelle tempered her voice, but still spoke loudly enough for the nearer members of the crowd to wince. "I am the Devil. I am now in charge of Heaven. If you have a problem with that you are welcome to leave. But do it now."

"Leave? And where are we supposed to go?"

"I don't much care." She raised her voice a little. "Everyone. Get out of this room. And don't come back until you're invited."

They all left quietly, except for the ones that Mary recruited to minister to the wounded out on the floor. The number of injured wasn't too bad, but until the software was recovered there were going to be a few dozen people who would have to take time to heal rather than simply request that it be fixed. Or they'd all be dead in the next few days and it wouldn't matter. She turned to see Denise standing by God's throne with her chair leg still tight in her hand. She returned Michelle's smile, but her knuckles were still white where they gripped the piece of broken wood.

Reaching out, Michelle began to slowly unwrap her fingers. Denise looked down at her hand in surprise, but seemed to be unable to relax it herself.

ome quick. Trouble. Trouble."

Plato opened his eyes and quickly closed them again. A little demon was tugging madly at his arm. It took three or four tries to shake him off. They were worse than alarm clocks.

"I am taking a nap. Go away. I find you bothersome." He settled deeper into Michelle's bed, rolling away from the demon. The satin sheets caressed his skin. Even though they had never shared this bed, lying here made him feel she was nearby.

He looked out of one eye, the other one buried in the down pillow. This room was not in the least as he would have imagined it. The double bed had a huge skylight over it, with a curtain he had closed to block the midday sun. The surprise was that it was such a mess. The rest of the house was pin neat, except for the stacks of books in the living room, but here piles of trash novels cascaded across the floor into heaps of old clothes. A few dusty musical instruments were hung on the walls, along with a signed Beatles poster. Perhaps the most amusing thing was the rose-colored sheets with embroidered edges. He appreciated the feminine touch. Narrow paths led from the hall door to the bed and beyond to one of the most decadent bathrooms it had ever been his pleasure to use.

He settled into the pillow, sleep pulling at his tired limbs. A sudden noise behind him made him turn. The demon. He was still there, hopping from one foot to the other, trying to contain himself.

"What?" Plato attempted to make his tone as acerbic as possible to drive him off. He was far too comfortable to move.

"She said you were in charge, before she left. Come. Come. Big trouble."

He had promised Michelle he would watch over things. "Where, pray tell, is the conflagration?"

He sat up in bed and stretched, imagining the sheets to be her touch as they slid down his body. A shiver of pleasure rippled up his spine.

"Refugees are streaming in from Heaven. They say riots broke out there."

"Who opened the damn gates? Close them." Plato staggered to his feet and looked around for something to wear. His himation was probably still in the Devil's dryer. He picked his way over piles of Clancy, Asimov, Thomas Aquinas, Hesse . . . how could she read such drek? He found a black silk robe on the back of the door and slipped it on. It was probably less than flattering, but it would suffice for the moment.

The demon started tugging on his arm again. "Don't know who opened them. Some Heavenly sympathizer. Not me. Find him. Cut him. Burn him. Can I watch?"

"Close the bloody gates."

"But that's cruel."

"Close them or I shall report you to Michelle when she returns and then you shall reckon with her."

The demon pulled a keypad out of his pocket and tapped a few keys. "They're closed. What about the refugees? Can we burn them? Can we?"

"How many souls made it through?" He tried to head for the kitchen to make coffee, but the demon kept pulling him toward the front door.

"About 450 million."

He stopped in the middle of the living room. "Please tell me I did not hear that last part correctly."

Michelle would be furious about it if a half billion heavenly refugees were suddenly cluttering Hell. It would take forever to straighten out such a mess. Of course, if the world did indeed end in the next few days that would not be as much of a problem. The smell of satin sheets was a poor substitute for lost tomorrows. She had to succeed.

The demon continued in its squeaky little voice that was not becoming more soothing with time, "About 300 million of them were cats. That's not all bad. We've had a mouse problem for some time, you know. Yes, we have. All the other souls, they've gathered outside. Some old man, he's demanding to see you."

"Demanding? Well, let us see them. No one other than Michelle has ever argued their way around me." He did wish she was not able to do it quite as often as she did. The coffee could wait. He would simply have to put these refugees in their place and afterwards worry about clearing up the confusion. Tightening the ties on the robe he appreciated the way the silk felt as if he were not wearing anything at all. He folded the collar neatly and headed toward the door. "Do they have a spokesperson?"

As the demon held open the door he replied, "Some old geezer. Forget his name. Socrates maybe."

Plato felt as if someone had recently dropped a forty ton column of marble on him from a great height. Socrates? Oh, shit. Plato stubbed his toe into the door-jamb quite hard. As he hopped over the threshold on one foot, the pain pulsing all of the way up his calf, he wished with all his heart he were still in bed.

"Hey, are those toys?" John looked the crowd of hundreds of small figures running about on the open field before them.

"People."

"Come on, Peter. If those are people, why are they so small?"

"Look at me."

"Oh." Peter was massive and gray. "I have heard of elephantiasis but this is ridiculous."

He waved his trunk around. It felt like someone had removed an arm and attached it to his nose.

He sidled over, being careful not to step on anyone accidentally, until he and Peter stood ear to ear. "Do you really think we'll find the software and save creation?"

"Yes I do believe we will."

"Faith is easy."

Peter turned and looked him in the eye. "Oh no, John. Faith is hard. It's the hardest thing I've ever done. It is believing in the good outcome no matter how awful the situation is. I'm impressed you've been able to do this on bravery alone. I'm not sure I could, my friend."

John took a scoop of dirt and sprayed it over his back to chase off some flies. It made a funny, ticklish feeling at the end of his trunk. He gathered more dirt and blew it over some nearby people, who backed away. "I don't know if it's bravery or foolishness."

"I only know it must be done. I'm glad you're here. Faith alone may not have carried me this far."

John nudged his shoulder into Peter's. "I wouldn't have missed it. I may be sick and tired of it, but I wouldn't have missed it." A sudden thought crossed his mind. "Hey, will we see each other after this is over?"

"You mean if there is an after?"

John swung his trunk back and forth through the dirt. "Oh. Yes."

"Absolutely." Peter nudged him back. "Some things I don't need faith to believe in."

The color of a woman's hair in the crowd reminded him of Denise's in the winter sunshine; the feel of her hand when she held his during a sad movie; the brief warmth of her in his arms.

"I suppose I do have some faith. But I won't know how that one comes out until after the end of this little journey. I'm with you, Peter. I'm worn down. I'm cranky. But I'm with you."

"She'll be there. It may not work out as you expect, but she will be there."

Please let Peter be right. He had to trust and be patient. There was no other choice.

Peter pointed with his trunk. "Does that one look like me?"

"It's hard to tell; he's rampaging around a bit. Yup, that must be Ron. Oh no. He trampled someone. Damn, we've evolved all the way to elephants, but it's back down the wheel we go."

"I'm not sure he's in trouble."

An Indian park ranger with a very loud megaphone stood on the seat of his jeep. "Please. Everyone is to go away now. Leave these elephants alone. It is your own faults they are far from their home. They have merely grazed outside their homelands. Now you and people like you have harassed them over 50 kilometers from that home. We will lead them back as soon as you depart from here. Thank you very much."

Ron had turned around at the sound of the speaker.

"I'll bet Ron didn't understand that. He's an elephant in this incarnation. He'll only understand elephant."

"Wonder what he'll do?"

"Nothing too stupid, I hope. I don't know about you, Peter, but I could use another break."

"Me too, but we need that software. And soon."

Ron had wandered over next to the ranger. The ranger looked at him carefully and started to back out of the jeep. Ron ran forward, trumpeting loudly, "That hurt my ears," and, using his tusks, flipped the jeep over. The man's scream was brief. Another ranger grabbed a gun and shot Ron, only wounding him, but quite painfully judging by the bellowing sounds he made.

Several of the other elephants in the herd started to stampede. The rangers began shooting wildly at them to protect themselves. John saw one take aim at Peter and he stepped in the way as the ranger fired. The bullet caught him with a massive blow to the head. It brought him to his knees.

He was vaguely aware of Peter stepping over him to guard him with his body. All he could think about was how much his head hurt. Peter turned to look at him.

"Why?" The guns still echoed in the background.

John had trouble drawing breath. "I didn't want you to be hurt." He took another shallow breath. "Besides, I thought I was getting used to the pain."

"Lesson: watch your temper. Bang," the system software sounded like distant gunfire in his ears.

*W*hat a pleasure to see you again." Plato limped over, favoring his damaged foot, and shook Socrates' hand. He would have preferred to cut it off but that would not be particularly civilized. It felt as if the software had set up to attack him again. No. The previous night with Michelle had been no illusion. That had been real, therefore this was, too. He could feel his shoulders sag.

The rolling hills of Hell which rose from Michelle's back door were covered with the amassed hordes of Heaven all clothed in flowing gowns. The crowd spread as if it were a limitless field of pastels. He finally was able to focus his watering eyes on the little man in front of him. His toe still hurt like, well, hell. He had to slap away the demon as it tried to massage it for him.

Socrates looked like a cartoon character. He always had. A little man with spindly legs and arms, long white hair that did not go well with his skin color, a huge roman nose mangling his Greek face, and a big pot belly. Plato thought of his own body, fit from swimming in Hell's Oceans every day since his arrival. As he stood straighter, he could feel Michelle's silk robe shift over his chest. Glancing down at the cut, that probably made her body look fantastic, he decided this would not have been his first choice of attire for this meeting; Michelle would be amused at least.

"You're him? You're the Devil? I might have known." Socrates looked like a disappointed first-grade teacher.

"If you must know," Plato tried to sound as if he were granting a favor by deigning to answer at all. "I am merely sitting in."

"Are you not running Hell?" Two thousand years had not made the old bastard's voice any less whining.

"Yes."

"When I asked for the man in charge was I not guided to you?"

"Yes. You were."

"He's in charge, not me." The little demon pointed at its chest. Plato kicked it lightly back inside, but not quite far enough to close the door.

"Yet you deny that you are the Devil." Socrates sounded disgusted that such a simple conclusion was being gainsaid. The amassed hordes began nodding their heads in unison.

"Actually, the Devil is a her." Plato tried to keep from smiling. The lazy twit had never found out who the Devil actually was. Plato had managed to meet her within only a few months of arriving. He rarely used to score one on the Old Man, and never this early in the debate. This was not going to be as awful as he had first thought.

"Indeed. Therefore you are in league with the Devil and you also appear to enjoy prancing about in her scanty clothing." The Old Man certainly could recover quickly.

"Yes. Actually I do." He thought of making love to Michelle on the beach and decided he did not care what this wretch thought of him. He had disliked being bound to him as a servant when alive. He certainly did not care for him significantly more now that he was dead.

"Indeed. And where is she at this time?"

"To the best of my knowledge, she is presently in charge of running Heaven." The look on Socrates' face was worth an extra hundred years fighting the software. He turned as white as his hair. A low murmur of shock rippled across the vast crowds like a wave on the ocean.

The Old Man's voice was definitely shaky and it took him several tries before he could speak clearly. "May we proceed on the assumption that I have misheard you?"

"Let us not. Allow us to proceed on the assumption the Devil is indeed presently operating Heaven." It felt like winning the finals in an Olympian foot race. The flush of victory made him strong. He could shoo the mighty crowds off the hillside with wave of his hand.

The old wretch turned to the crowds. "*Oy gevalt.* Quick everyone, we must get back and stop this."

"I'm afraid that is impossible." He put a restraining hand on the Old Man's shoulder and turned him back from facing the heavenly hordes. He could have snapped the wiry little man with a single shake. He should never have feared him.

"Why can we not return?"

"The gates are closed. And I, Plato, will not reopen them until I can be sure there are no more undesired refugees waiting to cross. And furthermore . . ." he paused a moment to relish the sense of power that ran through his body and rooted him to the very ground. Socrates started to splutter. " . . . you are not going to go anywhere until all the cats are caught and sent back."

"There must be thousands."

Plato saw that the little demon had returned to his side. He tapped him on top of the head.

"Hey." The demon rubbed the top of his head. "There are 323,345,006 Heavenly cats currently in Hell, but they're fixing our mouse prob . . ."

Plato rapped him between the horns again. "Ow. Careful. I have a bad burn."

"My apologies."

Socrates had managed to recover his composure in that brief moment. He certainly was a wily bastard. "I will proceed on the understanding that the gates will stay closed for now."

"That is a reasonable interpretation."

"And I will further propose it to be pointless to try to catch cats when firstly, they can't be returned through closed gates, secondly, they are proving helpful here, thirdly, that it will solve Heaven's problem of being buried in cats, and fourthly, it is the best thing to happen to the various souls."

"And what could possibly lead you to such a foolish conclusion?" Plato was losing control of the battle quickly and he was not even sure how.

"All of those cats can not be returned to Heaven once they have returned to a life of killing helpless mice; they may now proceed on their proper journey through Hell and beyond as they were originally supposed to."

"Well . . ." He tried to think of a quick response, but once the Old Man had the lead he had always found it hard to regain control, even momentarily.

"And Hell is the perfect place for them to reenter this journey, as they'll be able to see the true contrast between the ideal life of Heaven and the far less happy circumstances you have chosen to wallow in."

The bastard had shifted into his standard lecture pose. Suddenly he didn't look so small, with his back ramrod stiff and his hands folded lightly over his belly. The crowd was once again nodding their heads in unison every time the wretch spoke.

"Yes, it would be in their best interest." Plato hated the feeling of caving in.

"Good. Since we're stuck here I have an inquiry."

"Why not come inside and relax?" Maybe if he could get him away from the Heavenly hordes he could do something. A fire poker to the head seemed appropriate.

"I wish to share this process with all. It is only by open questioning that we may learn about ourselves. Is this not a correct premise?"

Plato tried to think of a new, and different, answer but was drowned out by the Heavenly chorus of a bit over fifty million, plus a few million passing cats, all echoing, "Yes." It had been one of the few wise things the bastard had ever said.

"Good. Now, Plato, my old friend, shall we address the subject of my actual teachings compared with those you put in my historical mouth? I find I've had to live up to your ideal to be accepted in society. Is this not so?"

Once again the horrid chorus of "Yes," thundered beautifully, into Plato's ears, ringing sweetly around inside his head for a few moments.

"Did I not teach that wine, women and/or men, and song were the essentials to a happy life? What did I care about republics? I knew myself."

He could feel himself wilting. He had not known he would be facing the Old Man in the afterlife. Plato had simply written what he wanted to and by putting his teachings in a dead man's mouth he lived a much safer and longer life. He tried not to whimper as he thought of the satin sheets and the woman too far away to help.

*M*ichelle sat on God's throne in the great crystalline hall made golden by the late afternoon sun. Squinting, she wished he hadn't made it this bright. She shifted her tired body. It had taken hours to quell the worst of the riots. The ones who had escaped into Hell were now Plato's problem. Shifting uncomfortably again, she hoped that her throne was fitting Plato better than God's was fitting her. Why had the old grouch made it uncomfortable? Well, he was long past explaining, or caring.

There wasn't any time to waste, she'd best get back to it. Denise came up the podium carrying a chair and set it to her right. Mary was still off tending the wounded.

"Henrietta?"

There was no response.

"Henrietta." The room rattled. Nearly a minute later, she could hear her shout echo off the nearest mountains of Heaven. She was going to have to upgrade Hell with this same gimmick if she ever made it home.

The small angel popped into existence on the wide arm of the throne with a very reluctant sounding pop.

"What? I don't like all of your tricky questions. They make my wings ache."

Denise looked down at her. "Don't whine, Henrietta. It is not becoming."

The angel sat with bowed head and folded hands. "I'm sorry."

Matthew Lieber Buchman

Michelle started to trace the patterns of inlay worked into the wood. "Where did you go in such a hurry?"

"There was a kitten. I had to interview it. Over in West Heaven."

West Heaven? She'd never heard of it. "That's awfully far from here."

"I had to ask it what an acceptable decibel level was for a heavenly choir."

"Don't pout, dear. I only want to tell you angels a few new rules, without calling in the whole herd."

"Oh. Goody." Henrietta nodded fiercely. "We like rules. Did you know that the first rule was . . ."

"Number one, no more of this polling nonsense."

"But . . ."

Michelle held up her hand with one finger raised. She fluttered her wings, but remained silent.

"Reality has to be stable for a while to give us time to straighten things out. Do it. Now. And set everything back to the way it was before you started all this."

"That'll take some time."

"Don't quibble. Get it started."

"Do you have one of the keypads handy? That's the fastest way."

Michelle pointed at the one built into the arm at the angel's feet. "It's dead. I don't think it will help much."

Henrietta cocked her head to stare at the keypad. She knelt and leaned over to punch in a sequence by smacking each key with her fist.

Michelle was impressed to see commands start flowing up the screen, regrettably she didn't recognize most of them.

"Our subroutine access is still running." Henrietta pounded in a few more commands and sat back. "It's done. All our hard work. Gone. I hope you're happy."

It was a start. Michelle asked. "Any other ideas?"

Denise blinked at her several times before speaking. "Like what?"

"If I knew that I wouldn't have asked. Anything."

"Does Henrietta's cleanup make the universe any more stable?"

Michelle bit her lip, wishing she had a different answer. "More tolerable, yes. More stable, no. That would require something more universal."

Denise leaned her head against the back of the chair and stared up at the translucent ceiling. She looked exhausted. "Something more universal. You know, Peter had mentioned that your software and the Buddha's were vastly different. I think he was wrong."

"What do you mean? Purgatory, Heaven and Hell have no relation to the Wheel of Life." Michelle shifted again. Henrietta was gone. After looking around she spotted her sliding down the front leg of the throne.

"Get back here. I'm not through yet."

She began to shimmy up the leg.

Denise leaned over and lifted her onto the chair arm. "Michelle's questions make my wings ache too."

Denise clearly had more compassion than sense at the moment. She didn't relax back into the chair, but slouched with fatigue as she spoke.

"You're right. They behave very differently, but I think you're too close to it. The two systems have a great deal in common. The Buddhist Wheel is much like your Hell in some ways. They're both intended to teach lessons. In Buddhism it would be, 'Create good karma.' In Western religions you would say, 'Do unto others as you would have them do unto you.' That seems similar to me. There's a universal for you. I have no idea how it will help, but there it is."

Michelle scowled briefly at Henrietta, who held up her palms to show that she wasn't going anywhere. Michelle rose and walked to the edge of the dais in order to survey the wreckage of the throne room. There were still several dark spots on the floor that had been pools of someone's blood, now they were simply dried stains that would take a lot of work to remove. People had certainly done unto each other here. How to apply it more sanely was the question.

She turned slowly. Denise was looking down, playing with the ends of her hair. She could feel a great weight lift as it became clear.

"Henrietta." The angel jumped at the sound of her voice. "Heaven is going to be very simple for a while. There is only one other rule until Peter gets back . . . or I change my mind."

"I like the sound of that." Henrietta perked up instantly, looking happy for the first time. "We like it when things are plain. We angels are pretty simple folks, after all. You know we even once . . ."

Michelle tried to keep the edge out of her voice. "The rule is: If it doesn't hurt anyone, let them do it. And no pestering everyone to find out if it'll hurt them or not."

"But . . . but, how will we know?" She looked pitiful with her little wings drooping down to her waist.

"Cherish the obvious, Henrietta. If an idea sounds stupid, it probably is. If it's something that you would not want done to you, do not let them do it to others."

"Okay, we'll try." She didn't look very happy. "But we won't like it."

It wasn't much but it was the best Michelle could think of under the circumstances.

Henrietta waved her hand to one side.

"Yes, you can go."

Henrietta disappeared with a sad-sounding pop.

Denise looked at her with hope in her eyes. "You think they can cherish the obvious, or even recognize it when it comes around? And did it help?"

"Honestly, I doubt if they can, but it will make Heaven much more livable and it will keep them out of trouble." She walked over and looked at the keypad. After several tries, she managed to call up a performance report. The effect had been immediate, the curve of decay had slowed. She looked up to see Denise watching her. "It's a little better, but it's not great. All this may have bought us an extra day, maybe only a half day. The end is imminent."

She nodded and, bowing her head again, curled the ends of her hair around her finger.

Michelle looked once more at the shambles of Heaven's throne room. "I have a suggestion."

Denise didn't respond.

Michelle kicked some of the debris off the platform. "There's nothing else I can do here. I want to go home, if I can. I'd like to spend my remaining time, before it all ends, with Plato. You can either come with me or I'll try to get you to your apartment."

She found a rag and wiped off the throne where some of the dust from the broken statues had settled. Not knowing what else to do with it, she threw it down the steps with the rest of the disaster. Statues, shattered on the floor, still shone with the passion of the Creator. Now there was no one to set it right. She could barely hear Denise's whisper after the long silence.

"I think I'll go home." There was another long silence. "I wish Peter and John would find that program."

Michelle couldn't agree more. Now it was their only chance.

*J*ohn couldn't believe his eyes when he looked at Peter. "Oh man, we're all the way back to being mice." The bright light shining through the long row of dirty windows did little to improve the gray control room they had arrived in.

"Shit. Oh, sorry. I didn't mean to say that."

"Yes, you did, Peter."

"Yeah, I guess I did. Shit. Maybe we need to give up."

"Let's hang on for a few more. Though if we have to be rabid dogs again . . . there goes Ron." John waved his forepaw at a mouse scampering across the decking in front of them, with a large orange tabby in hot pursuit.

"Get him, Ginger," someone called out. John looked around in time to be drenched by root beer splashing out of a can the man was waving about. He realized they were on the bridge of some ship and a crew member was egging the cat on. "At least something is going right with this god-forsaken pitiful excuse for a boat."

"Bosun." A tall, slender man in an officer's uniform stood at the entry door to the bridge.

"Sorry, sir, but we got mice and the blasted software is acting up again."

"Again? Care to fill me in a bit? This is my first trip on this class ferry."

Peter looked at him with raised eyebrows, but John couldn't imagine why. He stayed cowered back as far as he could in the corner and tried to clean his sticky fur as Ron and Ginger went zipping by again.

"Yes, sir. When these here boats were built a decade back, Washington State decided on a computer control system from a small pissant, sorry sir, local company. They totally screwed up the works and then they had the indecency to go bankrupt before we could nail their hides to the wall."

Ron managed to avoid Ginger on the next pass by making a sudden turn between the Bosun's feet. Ginger dug into the slippery deck, with her claws trying to make the turn, and ran into the Bosun's ankle.

"God Damn, Ginger. Just kill the thing." The Bosun spilled the last of his soda on the First Mate. "Sorry, sir. Where was I? Oh. These ferries would sometimes go into full forward instead of full astern during docking and destroy pier after pier. One once went from idle forward to full reverse during loading. Some poor sucker thought he was getting on the ferry and ended up on the bottom of Elliot Bay. The thing that gets me is, they worked out all the bugs when they replaced the computers years ago. This ferry has been jinxed the last week."

Peter gave John a sharp nudge.

"What?"

"Listen." John was listening, for Ron and Ginger. He didn't care why Peter found the history of the Seattle ferry system so interesting.

There was a loud squeak from the corner. "Ginger's caught Ron. Here we go again."

Peter called out, "Buddhist control software, please."

John hunkered down, expecting the shout to attract Ginger.

"Yeah, Peter? What can I do for you, my mouse?"

"Could you leave us here for a bit and still keep track of where Ron goes?"

"Done, o' squeaking one."

"Thanks. I'll call soon."

John turned his attention to the conversation, but kept one ear out for the cat. She must still be around the corner, eating Ron. He took a deep breath to try to settle his stomach. He could not imagine what that twisted software had been trying to teach by killing him with a cat. Respect a superior force, maybe.

The First Mate sat in front of the computer console. "I used to be pretty good with systems. Let's have a look."

"You're welcome to, sir. The last technician told me it was possessed. It's disconnected now, we've fallen back to a phone link with the engine room. It's ugly."

"What if I damage the installation? Do we have an extra copy?"

"Can't damage it no worse than it is, but here's the master tape." The Bosun pointed at a small cassette. "Forge ahead, sir."

Peter leaned against him and whispered in his ear, "This has to be it. You grab the tape and I'll clear their system."

"What am I supposed to do with it once I grab it? It's as big as I am."

"Sink your teeth into a corner and start dragging. I'll take a quick run over the keyboard to clear their system and scream for a bailout."

"Oh, brother. This had better work."

Peter started to run forward, but John grabbed his tail and pulled him back.

"What? I thought we had a plan."

"You may want the password."

"Oops, I will need that. What is it?"

John opened his mouth and closed it. He could feel his whiskers twitch and hoped Peter could not see him blushing through the fur on his face.

"Hurry, John. What is it?"

He took a deep breath and looked at the floor. "It's JA loves DB with no spaces."

Peter laughed. "That's great. It's a good thing you didn't forget that."

He couldn't help but return Peter's smile. "Yes, I guess it is. Let's go."

John ran over and jumped onto the Bosun's pant leg as Peter started to run up the First Mate's.

"Shit. Ginger. Get over here."

He took a few futile swings with his empty can, which John was able to dodge easily as he leapt to the counter.

"Up here." The Bosun scooped Ginger and tossed her toward him on the control console.

John bit firmly on the tape casing. He avoided the cat's first swing, but accidentally jumped off the counter to avoid her second one. He gave a quick twist and landed on all fours. The tape gave him a sharp crack on the nose.

"Shit. Feels as if it broke my nose." He started to laugh despite the pain as he dragged the tape toward a corner, with Ginger leaping down after him. "What will Denise say when John the mouse comes back with a crooked nose?"

Peter looked down at John as he barricaded himself into a corner, hiding behind the tape. In the confusion, Peter had managed to remain unnoticed as he danced back and forth across the keyboard. He hopped on the Enter key and nothing happened. He stared at the screen, arching his back. He could feel his fur standing on end. He ran back and took a flying leap, landing squarely on the key with all fours. It started to give. That Bosun had probably poured an entire can of soda into it. He ran back once more.

"Peter," he heard John squeak out. He looked over to see Ginger tapping her paw against the tape, apparently simply to scare John.

Peter leapt again as the First Mate turned back to the keyboard from watching Ginger.

"What in the seven seas . . .?"

Peter landed squarely on the Enter key. The Bosun was intent on Ginger and John. He must not have heard the First Mate. The key clicked home. The screen flashed several times, distracting the officer long enough for Peter to jump onto his knee and leapt to the floor.

"System software." He squeaked, as loudly as he could, "Get us the heck out of here."

He ran across the decking and bit on Ginger's tail as hard as he could. Her yowl was painful to his ears as he ducked between her paws, hopped over the tape and landed on top of John in the little space that was there. He peeked over the tape and saw a very upset Ginger turning back to them. "And don't forget the tape." He bit down on the case just to make sure.

The Bosun and First Mate were looking at the screen as it blinked once more before displaying the main selection menu.

"You fixed it, sir. Boy, I can't wait to stuff this one in the face of all those overpaid desk jockeys. Well done, sir. Well done. You don't look well, sir. Can I get you a root beer?"

"Lesson: watch out for very large pussy cats. Bang." the Buddhist system software purred.

John couldn't help thinking that the software's lessons were even dumber than he'd imagined when he landed hard on all fours and bruised his elbow against a low table. He looked around to see what they were.

Men.

Peter crouched near him with no clothes on and the data tape clenched between his teeth. They slowly stood and looked around.

Ananda came out of a side room, rubbing his eyes, and flipped on a light. "You're back. Did you find it?"

Taking the tape out of his mouth, Peter held it up.

Ananda applauded his congratulations. "Allow me to fetch your clothes. I took the liberty of having them washed pending your successful return." He stepped briefly out of the room and returned with their clothing.

As John was getting dressed, he saw Peter slip into his underwear and then check his keypad. He looked at John with wide eyes. "We're screwed."

John stopped with one leg in and one leg out of his pants. "What do you mean?"

Peter sat on the edge of the table on top of his still folded clothes. "The system's down. I can't get us to a console to reinstall the software."

"We've made it this far. There must be something we can do."

Ananda sat on a low chair. "Perhaps I may be able to offer sufficient assistance. Having a concern over this very matter, I have worked on a solution. Would you mind entrusting your tape to our software?"

Peter looked at him and shrugged. "What the hell." He held out the tape. It disappeared, and moments later a console appeared in front of him. John tried to move so that he could see the screen but tripped on his pants legs. Pulling them the rest of the way on, he stumbled to his feet and looked over Peter's shoulders.

RELOADING SOFTWARE.

REINITIALIZING SYSTEMS.

REFRESHING SYSTEM STATUS TABLES.

OH NO. YOU MADE A COMPLETE SHAMBLES OF EVERY-THING WHILE I WAS GONE. HOW CAN YOU EXPECT ME TO FIX A DISASTER LIKE THIS? THAT IS WAY BEYOND REA-SONABLE. THERE ARE OVER 1.3 MILLION SOULS THAT YOU HAVE MISALLOCATED. I DON'T KNOW WHY I PUT UP WITH ANY OF YOU SIMIANS.

Ananda sat with a great white smile brightening his dark face. Peter hugged the console. Though he had never done so before, John began to dance a jig around the room.

enise closed her apartment door, latched the chain, and leaned heavily against it. It had taken hours to get here, but she was home. Hopefully the system would hold together long enough for Michelle to reach Plato.

Home at last. She kicked at the mail piled up on the floor. Her box must have become stuffed to make security bring it up and push it all through the slot. Sticking out of the pile, a bright postcard caught her eye.

It was a cartoon of an angry elephant about to land with all fours on top of a computer. On the screen was the message, 'Please enter your response.' When she flipped it over she recognized the distinctive script easily. It was from Arlene.

D., Sorry to bail on you, but that computer was one too many. Good Luck, A.

She let the card drift back to the floor. It was easy to empathize with the sentiment. The adventure had become one too many for her as well. She'd wait for John, or the end of it all, here. She was almost too tired to care which.

No, that was a lie. If only he could finish and come home. She'd try the apology she'd been practicing and see what happened. His last message, as she and Michelle were leaving Heaven, had not been informative. 'Mice. In Seattle. Busy. Love.'

At least he was thinking of her. That was a good sign. She kicked her shoes off, shoved the mail into a semi-neat pile with her foot and pushed away from the door. The deep carpet soothed her sore feet. Walking around the apartment slowly, she trailed her hand along the bookcase he'd built for her. It was unbelievable that this madness had begun only five days ago.

A hot shower and sleep, if she could get any, would help the time pass. She dropped her clothes on the floor on her way to the bathroom, too weary to put them away. A little mess in her terminally neat life . . . maybe she was letting go a bit. John would understand what it represented.

The shower wasn't making her feel any better, but at least she was clean. If only he would magically walk through the door and join her. She twisted the water off with a snap. Not much chance of that; she'd made it clear she wanted nothing else to do with him.

She looked at herself in the mirror. Not getting younger, but that wasn't what was pulling her toward him. Denise had always dreamed of a relationship like Uncle's. Her reflection smiled bitterly at her. Typical to want something instantly that must have taken them years to achieve. People weren't born comfortable together. It was wonderful being with John, but that had taken a decade of friendship.

Denise finished toweling off and slipped into her long nightgown. On her way to the bedroom she saw her clothes scattered about. The Devil was right. It was the future that mattered. Michelle had certainly grabbed out for the future, even though it might be for only one more day. It was high time she unwound a bit herself, worried less and tried living more. Denise hadn't taken a break in years. She wanted time. That was it. To work on her own books. Go hiking again. Time to think. Once that damned cookbook went to press she was outta here. Maybe John would want to come along. What a sad joke that there might not be more than another day.

She stopped at the bookcase by the bedroom door and pulled down her mother's worn volume of Robert Frost. It normally fell open to where Mom had pressed the first flower Daddy had given her, a red rose, now dark with age. This time it fell open to her own favorite poem. The small white flower with pale pink tips pressed there looked familiar, but her tired mind couldn't recall from where. The poor mangled blossom had been damaged before being slipped between the pages. The moisture was gone and only the faintest scent remained. Closing it gently back in the book, she returned it to the shelf. The image of a hand holding this same flower recently was clear before her, but whose hand it was remained illusive.

Turning in at the bedroom door, she froze. Someone was in her bed. About to run, she recognized John asleep under the pale blue sheets. His hand had held the flower. Despite her raging at him he had saved the Indian flower. Her pulse slowed as she glanced back at the front door. The chain was still hooked. He must have come in earlier to wait for her to get home. To wait for her. New energy washed through her as if she'd finally awoken after a full night's deep sleep.

The full moon had snaked its way between the sky-scrapers to wash his face in its light. He looked exhausted.

She tried to step into the room, but couldn't make her feet move. The urge to run swept through her again. This wasn't a time for fear. Mary had faced telling her husband when he should die and now she might die never having heard from Jesus again. Yet still she believed in him. Mary trusted him implicitly and Denise was quite sure it had nothing to do with his being the Son of God. John knew her better than anyone in her life and here he was. He had trusted his knowledge of her to risk being unwelcome.

John had asked her and she'd said no and seen how much it hurt him, but still he had come back. Now that her answer was yes, she understood. She too could brave a 'no' if it came to that.

Her feet still wouldn't move. God, what a choice. Part of her wanted to roust him out for his own sake. She did not want to hurt him again. Another part was about to slide in beside him and take a chance.

John was awake and watching her, his head raised and his eyebrows arched.

"What are you smiling at?" His voice had a wonderful sleepy quality to it.

She had not realized she was. Accepting the flower this time, she took a step across the threshold. Not even saying 'I do' at the altar with Alan had felt like such a strong commitment, nor had it felt so right.

"You're here." It felt as if it took all the breath in her body to say those words.

He nodded.

She moved a step closer. "Did you find it?"

His slow smile filled her with such a lightness that the room seemed to spin around her. He started to get out of bed but she signaled him to stay.

Pulling her nightgown off over her head, she let it fall to the floor.

John laughed. "You're going to leave it there? Such a mess, Denise."

He understood. He loved her as she was, for who she was. Her skin tingled as he looked at her. She slipped under the covers. His warm smell filled her awareness as she rubbed her cheek on his shoulder.

"Your skin is so warm." She ran her hand over his chest and stomach, allowing one fingertip to trace through the surprisingly soft, curly hair below his waist.

His hand took hers and, raising it to his lips, he kissed the center of her palm. The feeling tingled up the length of her arm, remembered and longed for. She hoped he never became tired of that particular gesture.

"I didn't mean to wake you."

"I'm glad you did. I hope you don't mind my climbing into your bed."

"I'm glad you did." She kissed his shoulder.

He pulled her into his arms.

Pushing back, she tried to remember her rehearsed apology but couldn't bring a word of it to mind, especially not with the warmth of his hands on her waist. "John, I need . . . I want to say I'm sorry for reacting rather than hearing. I'm . . ."

Before she could choose the right words, he lay his finger on her lips. "Shhh. Apology accepted."

She kissed his finger as he slowly traced the outline of her lips, the shape of her nose, the curve of her eyebrows. "Denise?"

She dragged her attention back from the incredible sensations that followed his touch. "Yes?"

"There is something I need to say, but I don't know the right words."

Her heart started to pound in her ears. "Try. Please." Keeping silent as he struggled for the right words was maddening, but she bit her lip and waited.

"All I could think of was you." Another long silence ensued. "There is no one I've ever wanted to spend my life with as much as you." He let his breath out, clearly done, and looked at her.

Denise knew she should feel relieved, and she was, but a tightness continued in her chest.

"I'm scared." She nestled her cheek into his palm to look away from his eyes. Those wonderful, searching, deep brown eyes.

"Of what?"

She took a deep breath. She'd put her foot in it now, and it was time to put up or shut up. "Of ruining this.

You know my history. The master of eviscerating innocent men; I don't want to do that to you. Am I what you
really want? I'm headed for a lot of changes." She fought
the tears; they'd been coming easily these last few days.

She could feel his silent chuckle where their bodies
met as they lay together. "What?"

"I've been through a few changes myself lately." He
suddenly sounded serious. "Do you want to be with me?"

She closed her eyes and tried to breathe. "So much
it hurts."

He kissed her on the tip of the nose. "I want to be
with you that much, too." The hoarseness in his voice
sent chills up her spine. "Everything else we'll have to
work out as we go along."

He traced his finger along her ear and started to draw
a little line of fire down her cheek, along her neck and
finally to her breast. She kissed him and his lips were
even warmer and gentler against hers than she'd imagined. All of her awareness followed his hand across her
ribs, over her waist and hip and up the back of her thigh
as she slid her leg along his side.

She could taste the salt of her tears as she kissed him
to seal the bargain. They would work it out. She imagined
she was kissing him with her whole body.

The way his tongue curled against her teeth tickled.
She gently pushed him onto his back and began learning the shape of his jaw with her lips, the curve of his
neck with the tip of her nose, and the tightness of his
nipples with her teeth.

She laughed lightly at his shivers when she slid his
erection back and forth between her breasts. She loved
how his body felt against hers. She let her tongue and
teeth wander back along his body until they were kissing
once again.

"I want you, Denise. I want to be inside you. Now."

She blew gently in his ear. "I don't know if I have any . . ."

Reaching under his pillow, her pillow, he pulled out a small foil packet. "I was hoping you'd wake me."

She took it from his hands and looked at it in the moonlight before deciding to kiss him in thanks.

She sat between his legs letting her hands trail down his body as she did. His back arched as she relished the fullness of his arousal with her fingertips before sheathing him.

He cupped her breasts as she eased down over him. Holding his hands tightly against her, they rocked together. If only she could save this moment and frame it somehow, but at his first thrust the idea was wiped out of her mind.

She feared it would all be over too soon, but John's passion washed through her again and again until she thought she could stand it no longer. They both held their breath for the same moment.

She lay forward onto his chest. He kissed her gently. She was looking forward to many tomorrows.

"John? You got the software back, but is it working?"

His laugh started against her belly and spread until his whole body was shaking against hers. When it finally reached his mouth, it was a glorious sound.

"Yes, there will be a morning after this night."

"Oh, good." It sounded inane, but she couldn't think of anything better as she relaxed again and felt the quiet chuckles ripple across him.

The last thing she heard before she drifted into exhausted sleep was John's tired whisper in her ear. "I love you, Denise."

*I*t should be easier."

Anne looked up to see Joshua throw down his book and rest his head heavily against one side of his armchair. She placed her unfinished letter to her daughter-in-law aside. Only their twin reading lamps lit the room. The photos on the walls looked like stars as they reflected the two lights.

She waited for him to speak.

He turned to her and held his hands palms upward. "Life should be easier for people."

She didn't even try to suppress her laugh. "And your life has been so simple?"

He slapped his hand down against the padded chair with a dull thump, cutting off her laugh. "That's not my point. It was my hope to make Denise's life easier for her than it has been. All I did was make it worse. If I can't even succeed with one person, how can I help others?"

Anne looked at him and felt a deep sigh empty her.

"Joshua, do you know so little of the people that you love so much?"

He looked at her as if she'd slapped him.

She rose, draping her afghan over the footstool. She sat on the arm of his chair and hugged him to her breast. He was the most caring man she'd ever known. She thanked the stars for whatever she had done right to spend her life with him.

His arms were tentative as they cradled her against him.

She held him until his shoulders finally relaxed. He'd been worrying too much. He hadn't had a decent night's sleep in days.

As he leaned back, she kissed him. His gentle kiss reminded her of warm, sunlit places. "Joshua, my dear sentimentalist. If life were easy, what would people learn from it?"

His brow furrowed for a long moment before his eyes went wide. He began to nod his head. "Oh, of course."

She could see the weight drop off him. Once again, all he'd needed was a gentle nudge to see what was really going on around him.

He looked years younger as he closed his eyes. She could not identify the moment when he slipped from nodding with agreement to nodding with sleep.

She watched him for a long time before covering him with her afghan. Maybe it was time to close the deli for a while and go traveling again. They'd been in this one place for a very long time. It was often hard to keep perspective without moving around a bit.

She straightened his hair before kissing him on his bald spot. He sighed and shifted in the chair. His smile, still present as he slept, showed in the light of the single lamp she left on. Brushing her hand along his cheek, she could feel the roughness of his jaw line. It made him so handsome. She turned and climbed the stairs to bed, knowing she too would sleep well this night.

*J*ohn woke and looked around the dark room. He blinked several times, barely able to see a thing. Finally, recognizing the shape of the windows, he remembered he was in Denise's bedroom, in her bed. He could feel the smile start at his heart and work its way to his face. He rolled toward her side only to find it empty. It was still warm. Her smell was on the sheets, on the pillow.

He was about to go and look for her when he heard water running in the bathroom sink. The trail of her sounds let him follow her path from the bathroom, a slight shuffling across the living room carpet, and then silence. A barely discernible shimmer of white stood in the doorway. His heart was loud in his ears as she stood a moment longer before stepping into the room. At the edge of the bed, she paused again.

When she still didn't move he whispered into the dark, "Care to join me?" He lifted up the covers.

She came to him without a word. As she slid into his arms he realized that the white was her nightgown. The warmth of her skin through the thin silk was one of the most arousing things he'd ever felt.

As she lay on her back he kissed her chin, felt the curve of her neck with his cheek and finally placed a kiss on the last bit of skin that the scoop neck of the gown revealed between her breasts. He lay his ear on the spot and, as she ran her hands through his hair, he listened to the quick double beat of her heart.

"John?"

It was several moments before his name registered, he was so enjoying the soft buzz of her voice through her breast bone.

"Yes, my love."

Her hands paused before tracing the shape of his ear. "My love? You're such a mush. Do me a favor?"

He raised his head and she turned on her side to face him. They were nearly nose-to-nose in the dark.

"What?"

"Don't change."

Her lips were warm against his smile.

"Okay. If you insist."

She leaned her head down on her arm as he studied the shape of her waist.

"John, what was your trip like?"

He rested his palm where the curve of her hip fit so wonderfully. Simply thinking about the journey reminded him of how tired he was. "The hardest part was keeping focused. It wasn't bad; it simply seemed to be unending." His voice was rougher than he'd intended. He softened his tone. "I learned a great many things and, believe it or not, we even had some time to play."

She placed her hand on his chest, palm over his heart. "Is that all?"

The words welled up in him and almost burst out. "The trip was tough, but manageable, but to think I'd lost you . . . it was brutal at first." He took a deep breath to try and calm himself when she flinched under his words.

She took her hand away.

He found it and put it back against his chest.

"I held this image of how perfect it would all be between us, and when that shattered I thought it was over. Thankfully, Peter taught me that an argument is not the end of the world."

He laughed once, thinking of how close that had come to actually happening. "He and I both finally pounded it through our thick skulls that life does not have to be perfect to be reveled in. The Buddhist eightfold path is certainly not a straight one, but it gets there."

As her hand finally relaxed beneath his, the relief flowed across his chest from where her light touch rested.

Her voice was shaky as she spoke. "You didn't deserve that, but there's nothing I can do to fix it. It's in the past. All we can do is learn."

"You already did fix it."

"How?"

He could feel her surprise when he kissed her. "By allowing me a second chance. You, Denise, are at the top of my list of things worth fighting for."

She held him so tightly he could barely hear when she whispered in his ear. "You, too."

"But does it make any sense?"

"What? You mean us?"

She wrapped one of her legs behind his, the fabric of the gown sliding over his skin. "It makes great sense that we want to be together. What I fail to understand is why there is a Heaven and Hell. You know the software. Does it really run our lives? I don't like that idea."

He tried to think of some way to explain it as he ran his hand along the shape of her backbone, from the base of her neck to the soft roundness of her hips and back to her shoulders. He had to stop that in order to think.

"The program is like this apartment. It provides a framework within which you live, but it doesn't control your destiny. It may shape it by having four walls and a floor and ceiling. The fact that it is in a high rise in the middle of a city may also have an effect, but it is still you living here, the way you want to within those limits."

"You're saying the software provides the reality in which we live, but doesn't control our destiny."

"Right."

She started to trace small circles on his chest with one finger. It tickled horribly, but he wouldn't stop her for all the world.

"But Heaven and Hell. I know they exist, yet I still can't grasp it somehow."

"That one is tough. Maybe the question is how will we live differently, tomorrow knowing there is a Heaven and Hell, compared to last week when we didn't?"

Her finger stopped. The warmth of her palm soothed the tickling sensation as it spread flat on his chest again. "You are a very wise man, John."

He was? "I am?"

She laughed, a bright and merry sound. "Even when you don't know it you are a wise man. No differently is the answer. It doesn't matter whether there is life after death or not. The key either way is to live each day better than the one before."

He liked the sound of that. He pulled her close and nibbled on her ear. "And how would you like to live the rest of this day?"

She started a kiss that made him glad to be lying down. It was doubtful his knees would have supported him had he been standing.

Day
Seven

*And he rested on the seventh
day from all his work
which he had made.*

≫

*D*enise looked over her shoulder at John and Plato, silhouetted by the red and orange light of the setting sun that poured into Uncle's living room. One story below, light filtered into the deli as an occasional treat. Here, in this comfortable place, light was an ever-present gift.

"They seem to be getting on fairly well."

Michelle glanced over at them and nodded before turning back to look at Uncle's many framed photos. She'd been apparently fascinated by his collection of deli patrons covering the walls of the living room and hall.

When she was little, Denise had loved to sit in this room and imagine she was inside a great golden mirror ball watched over by Joshua and Anne, who smiled out of a hundred family portraits and snapshots with various friends.

John laughed. Denise was wonderfully aware of where they had touched as they slept together last night. When he looked over, she needed no telepathy to know he was remembering the same thing. She touched her palm to her cheek. His laugh faded, but his smile grew.

There was a small silence in the room before their conversation resumed. Something about the software. Denise tried to focus on the picture Michelle was looking at. It was an old brown photo, the edges starting to curl.

Michelle straightened and crossed her arms, only to uncross them a moment later. Her furrowed brow and cocked head indicated surprise or bewilderment.

Denise held her hand to block the sunlight reflecting off the glass and realized it was a picture of Michelle. It was an amazing photo. Michelle sat at the deli table that caught the morning light, with her hands clasped around a steaming mug of coffee. Her eyes were closed and her head was thrown back, allowing the sun to shine directly into her face. Pure joy lit it nearly as brightly as the sun.

Denise stood back to look at Michelle. She looked much the same. Except for the smile. In their several days together she hadn't seen one that could come close to matching the photo, except when she'd remembered Plato while in Heaven. Even that one had been more of contentment and had no such degree of joy as this one.

"Has it been that hard these last years?" She rested a hand on Michelle's arm.

The muscles tightened under her fingers. Michelle turned and sat in an armchair facing away from the photo. Denise moved to the other chair. Michelle slowly traced the gold and green stripes of the fabric covering.

"I hadn't thought so. Maybe they were. I remember that morning. I'd been up for weeks trying to turn the program, but I couldn't. The world was a mess, World War II was in full swing, worse than you can imagine. Sitting there, I felt strangely at peace. I don't think I moved from that table all day. I haven't had that feeling very often since."

They sat together in silence. John's and Plato's voices rose and fell as they discussed implications of multiple universe constructs, whatever that was.

Uncle came into the room with a rattle of teacups and coffee mugs. He placed the large tray on the low table in front of them.

"And how are we all doing? Dinner, it is not too far away now." He started pouring.

Plato and John joined them and came to stand by the appropriate armchair.

John rested his hand upon Denise's shoulder. The electric spark of their connection ran down to her toes.

She saw a familiar twinkle in his eyes. "What is it that you think is so funny?"

He waved to indicate the four of them in a row facing Uncle. "Have you ever felt as if you were on that TV show for Newlyweds?"

Uncle stood straight like a popgun barely catching his glasses in time. "Newlywed?"

Odd that she hadn't been offended at the leap John had made. "No, Uncle," John's hand flinched on her shoulder. "Not yet anyway." His hand relaxed. She laid her cheek on his hand. She'd have to remember not to bait him. She was in this to make it work.

Uncle nodded as if satisfied with her answer. He looked at Michelle for a long moment before he poured coffee into his large lopsided mug.

"Michelle, I am going to pass on a gift to you. It has been in one place too long." He stood formally in front of her chair and held out his old mug, handle first. "A gift that has taught me many lessons. Enjoy it as I have."

Michelle took it gently from him. She ran her finger lightly over the characters. "Contentment." Her voice was barely a whisper. "Thank you Joshua. It is a lesson I still need to learn."

"As do we all, my dear, as do we all."

Denise looked at Uncle. He was the wisest man she'd ever known. It was a perfect gift. She jumped out of her chair and gave him a big hug as the doorbell rang.

He held her briefly and kissed her on the forehead. "Now I must return to the kitchen fires and help your Aunt Anne. She is making her special lasagna. *Oy*. That was supposed to be a surprise. Okay everybody, you must act surprised when she comes out with it. Right?"

"Of course, right, Uncle."

He hurried off toward the kitchen, as the doorbell rang again. "Denise, darling. Let in whoever that is."

She pulled John into the hallway after her and kissed him until the doorbell rang a third time. He raised the back of her hand to his lips, a mirror image of the kiss that tingled on the inside of her palm. She leaned briefly against his shoulder.

They opened the door. Peter stood on the landing. John wrapped his arm around Peter's shoulder and led him in. "Ah, we men who've been mice together . . ." They both laughed.

They stepped into the living room. The sunset, now deep red, shone its last rays through the large windows. Michelle and Plato came over from where she must have been showing him the photo.

"Peter, how's the software running?"

"Hi, Michelle. As quarrelsome as ever. It's great to have it back. I thought having the delete routine in place would make all the difference, but, in reality, 'Michelle's Law' is doing most of the work of fixing Heaven." He shrugged uncertainly and grinned. "Sorry, but I felt it was a bit awkward telling the angels that the 'Devil's Law' was running Heaven quite well and I was going to dinner."

"*De nada.*" Michelle waved it off, grinning back.

When the doorbell rang again John went back out to the hall. Denise could hear Kris and Marita. When Kris came into the living room, Denise gave him a big hug. "You were right, Kris. I am still certain that you're crazy, but sometimes the change is worth the risk."

He held her tightly. "Way to go, little cousin."

Marita called out on her way to the kitchen. "I have to get this stuff into the oven; I'll be right back."

"Hi, Marita." Denise didn't look up as she gave Kris a final hug.

Peter gasped behind her. "Jesus. What are you doing here?"

Denise turned him. "Peter, you know Kris?"

He looked like a fish out of water, trying desperately to breathe. "Kris?"

He smiled as he turned, his voice rising in surprise. "Peter, how've you been?"

"How do you two know each other?" Denise realized she could still feel surprise.

Michelle walked over and stood next Peter. "I haven't seen you in days . . ." she paused for a long moment, "Kris."

"You, too?" Denise looked from Peter's confused expression to Kris' worried one and finally to Michelle's thoughtful one. "Will someone please tell me what the hell is going on?"

Michelle spoke as if she were simply reasoning aloud. "Kris is your cousin. That would mean that your Uncle Joshua is Kris' father. But I thought . . ." Michelle's face slowly changed to one of profoundest disbelief. She turned to look at Denise and seemed to be either about to laugh or to cry.

"Denise." Uncle burst back through the kitchen door. "You'll never guess what I found? It was under the lasagna noodles. You'll never guess, so I'll tell you. I found a copy of Elantra's cookbook."

"What? How?" Denise grabbed the pages he was fluttering around in front of him before he could scatter them. Her last worry was out of her system with the cookbook safe in her hands. She wanted to dance

around the room in great ballerina twirls. Peter stared at
Uncle as if he'd grown a second head, but at the moment
she did not care. "How, Uncle?"

"She gave me a draft to try out. It looked, well, like all
her other books. That woman has no imagination. I
stuffed it away, intending to try it if you wanted me to.
She was going to give you a copy the next day."

Denise clutched the pages tightly to her, they were
hard and real in her hands. "Uncle. You're a life saver.
The other copy I had, well, it wouldn't work."

"I'm glad I could help."

"You?" Peter's shout sounded strangled. He'd gone
sheet-white. "You can't hide from me behind those
glasses; I built them for you."

Joshua sheepishly took off his glasses and slipped
them into his pocket. He still looked the same to Denise,
but Michelle was nodding as if it all now made sense.

Uncle shrugged, and after a moment, smiled hugely.
"Ah well, it wouldn't work forever. Peter, you've come at
last. Why didn't you come sooner?"

"Why didn't I come sooner?" Peter's voice was barely
a whisper. He looked at the others around the room.
"'Why didn't I come sooner?' he asks."

"I left you a note. Or did I? I am certain I did."

Peter looked as if he were ready to attack Uncle, but
Michelle held up a hand to stop him. He spluttered for
several seconds before turning and stomping over to the
window. John followed.

Michelle stood facing Uncle, running her finger along
the rim of the mug she still carried, just as Denise had
seen Uncle do a thousand times. Her words dropped into
the momentary silence. "My God . . . you've changed."

"Sorry to have deserted you, Michelle, but running
Heaven became a real pain in the ass, excuse me. I am

much happier now. Living here, with people, it is a good thing. I'd be glad to give you some tips about what I had to learn the hard way."

Denise felt her knees give way and grabbed the back of an armchair to stay upright.

Michelle, very casually, still holding Uncle's mug, leaned back against Plato who wrapped an arm around her and kissed her on the neck. "I think we'd like that."

Plato nodded in agreement.

Michelle looked down at the mug. "Yes, I'd like very much to spend some time with you."

Denise couldn't contain herself any longer. "You and God are the same person. What, am I supposed to call you God now and pray to you?"

He looked disgusted. "Please don't. To you, my little niece," he wrapped her into one of his wonderful hugs, "I will always be Uncle Joshua and honored to be so."

She held him tightly as all the pieces started fitting into place. Her Uncle came from Heaven, one of her best friends from Hell and her lover from Earth. It made her feel very lucky. Stepping out of his hug she saw Peter storm away from John. He crossed the room until he stood before Joshua. John came over and took her hand as Peter confronted Uncle . . .? God . . .? No. Uncle.

"I know I left you a note." Joshua looked at Peter. "Why you didn't come join me, I couldn't figure out."

"I never received any damned note." Peter's face was redder than the sunset.

"You didn't? Oh dear. Henrietta?" Joshua called out. The little angel materialized on his shoulder.

Feeling John's surprise Denise decided to wave. "Hi, Henrietta."

The angel smiled brightly and waved from her perch. "Hi, Denise." She looked around the room, waving at everyone while she hung onto Joshua's ear for balance. When she saw Michelle she stopped waving, crossed her arms and turned her back.

Michelle grinned.

John whispered in Denise's ear. "I see I wasn't the only one who went adventuring."

She nodded. "I'll tell you later if you're nice to me."

His arms tightening around her told her he would be very nice.

"Hi, Boss." Henrietta's high voice sounded merry.

"What ever happened to the note I wrote for Peter?"

"In your front vest pocket when you left, Boss."

"Oh, thanks."

"No problem." She thumbed her nose at Michelle before disappearing.

Uncle looked down for a moment before facing Peter. "Sorry about that. I really meant to leave it for you."

"All these years you've been here? While I've . . .?" he waved helplessly upward.

"I did wonder why you didn't come. I have a charming daughter who I wanted to introduce to you specially, but you never came to visit." He suddenly smiled. "She still hasn't found the right man and she's as pretty as her mother. I think you would be wonderful together. She couldn't come for dinner, but she promised to be here for dessert."

"But how? I saw you dead before me."

"That was only a screen saver I left behind. I thought you'd see through that easily.

Peter's voice dropped so low she could barely hear him. "How could you leave me to weep alone for you?"

"Oh, Peter. Once Creation was done, it all became a boring. And then we became so rule-bound when we couldn't delete anything. It was horribly frustrating."

Kris rested his hand on Peter's arm. "Anger doesn't suit you any better than pride. How many times over the years have Joshua and I told you to focus on the joy of the time?" Peter's face drained of color before he dropped onto the couch and covered his face with his hands.

Denise, who hadn't made the connection yet, was glad of the support of John's arms. "My whole family is from Heaven?"

Kris', or was it Jesus', grin was not helping. Of course, Marita must be Mary Magdalen. Denise thought she had recognized Mary's laugh, but hadn't expected to meet a relative running God's throne room.

Joshua looked at her. "Well, yes. Haven't I always said my Anne was from Heaven? At the time she was married to Zeus she was called Hera. Zeus was a tedious old bastard, excuse me, and she left him to be with me shortly before they shut down the old Greek software from lack of use. There used to be three systems."

"My Aunt Anne is Hera, mother of the Greek Gods." Right when Denise thought she understood it all, the world could become even weirder.

"Clearly that explains it." Plato was nodding as if the last piece of a large puzzle now fit neatly and he knew who had committed the murder in the conservatory with the lead pipe.

She didn't understand John's answering nod at all. She shook her head. None of the pieces fit anywhere. "What explains what?"

"Your birthday."

Her face must have shown her complete confusion.

"John and I were debating why the software chose you, Denise, when it came to Earth. It was too great of a coincidence, you and the software having such nearly identical birthdays. The software was trying to find him."

He pointed at Uncle Joshua.

"Why was it looking for him?"

"It was looking for God."

"But he isn't . . . .." She stopped herself and began to laugh. "This is going to take some getting used to."

John remembered the question before she could. "How did Denise's birthday end up being the same as a several billion year old piece of software?"

Uncle Joshua cleared his throat a little awkwardly. "That must have been my influence. The software and I worked together for a long time. Even though I've retired, I still seem to cause a few curious side effects."

"It's rather cute." Michelle's voice was surprisingly full of affection. "The software was trying to come home to Papa."

Uncle looked disgusted. "It probably was trying to bring all of its stupid undeletable rules with it."

Michelle reached out to rest her hand on Joshua's arm for a moment. "I'm sorry."

He patted her hand and smiled. "Apology accepted, Michelle. Apology accepted." He stepped away toward Peter, leaving her hand hanging in mid-air. Denise could see her swallow hard and drop her hand to her side. Halfway to Peter, he turned and looked at her. "Exactly what did you do that was so bad?"

Michelle shook her head and her smile slowly returned. "I didn't have the patience to realize that your powers were limited as well. I'm sorry I didn't try harder to work together."

He nodded his head. "Yes, it was vexing that there was no delete command designed into the software."

"There was. I had it. What I lacked was the ability to create. You had that one all sewed up."

"You did quite well without it."

The veins stood out on Michelle's neck. Plato reached toward her but she stepped beyond his grasp until she was toe to toe with Joshua. He stepped back but he ran into the side of the big armchair and fell across it to land in the seat. He struggled to get up, but stopped when Michelle loomed over him.

"What do you mean? It nearly destroyed me not being able to create."

"But you did." He waved his arms helplessly, trapped by the chair and the Devil's anger. "Look at all you made. You created galaxies. You have created a wonderful mechanism called Hell to help people move past their childish ways. You shaped a thousand things. What did I do? Created a Heaven where no one has any fun. A place where people are driven to riot. It was not one of my finer ideas. Of course, most of the rest of it turned out rather nicely. All in all, I'd say we did quite well together."

Michelle straightened and looked around the room until she was facing Denise. Denise felt a moment of panic as she tried to think of exactly what to say. It was silly. She started to laugh. Michelle's furrowed eyebrows only made her laugh harder.

"There is no perfect Michelle. You are as human as the rest of us bumbling along, doing our best to live tomorrow better than today."

Plato nodded at her, clearly approving of her logic.

Michelle smiled, tentatively at first and then more freely. "You're right. Ha. Yes, you are. Thank you, Denise."

She felt a warmth in her belly that connected with the warmth of John's arms around her waist. "No, my thanks to you, dear friend. You and Plato were right. Sometimes it does all work out."

Reaching over, Michelle ruffled her hair. Her smile was as bright as the one in the photo. It made Denise feel like a little girl who had finally taken her first step.

Peter was the only one not laughing. He got up and stalked over to stand in front of Uncle, who had finally turned himself to sit normally in the chair and had been about to rise.

"How could I come join you?" His voice sounded weary. His anger spent. "How could I? It's a full-time job trying to keep Heaven in operation, especially without your help." He shook his head slowly. "But I would have come anyway."

"I explained that in the note. Oh, dear. Henrietta?"

The little angel appeared on his shoulder again, "What did you lose now, Boss?"

"Do you remember the codes?"

"Sure thing."

"Be a dear and tap them in for me, will you?"

"Can't. I don't have the authorization."

"Oh, right." Joshua stood and Henrietta fluttered her wings to stay in place. He patted Peter's shoulder. "If you want a break, tap in the codes Henrietta gives you and you're scot free."

"But . . . why?"

"Why? Why? Why? Why always with the why? It's a much better life if you stop worrying about it all the time. Remember the words of the great Noel Coward, 'Life is for living. One wouldn't know what else to do with it.'"

Peter sat on the footstool at Joshua's feet.

He started to smile.

Henrietta pulled out a tiny keypad and tapped a few keys. A full size console appeared before Peter.

He keyed as she instructed, "Type 'TWISTED' while pressing the Control key. Now tap F12 four times. Now type 'FREE' while holding down the Alternate key. Ta-dah," she cried.

The screen showed, AUTOMATIC OPERATIONS INITIATED. REMEMBER TO ENJOY.

The console, along with Henrietta, left this existence with a pop.

"Everyone. Dinner is served." In the archway to the dining room, cousin Marita, no longer hiding behind a business suit, stood, with her long hair flowing down to her waist, arm in arm with Aunt Anne, the mother of the Greek Gods.

*S*omewhere, very quietly, sounding as if it came across a great distance (it didn't) Shiva the Destroyer, the last God of the Hindu trinity, the God of Ending and Death, began to laugh.

A FEW ETYMOLOGICAL NOTES:

Denise - from Dionysus, Greek god of food and drama

Anne - from the Greek, meaning "A light"

John - from the Hebrew, meaning "God is gracious; God is merciful"

Joshua - from the Hebrew, meaning "The Lord is my salvation"

Michelle - French form of Michal, meaning "Who is like God?"

Ron - from the Hebrew, meaning "joy"

Henrietta - from Old High German, meaning "Home Ruler"

ABOUT THE AUTHOR

Matthew is a refugee from the East Coast who, more by whim than plan, wound up in Seattle, Washington. His many careers have included managing a fast food fish house, sailboat repair, live theater soundman, and now a computer nerd. To this day he is amazed at what can be done with a degree in geophysics. After burning out as a systems consultant, he sold everything and went traveling. This will be chronicled in his next book *Riding Ahead -a Voyage by Bicycle*, also from Goodfellow Press. *Cookbook From Hell* started as a vignette about a college roommate who killed alarm clocks. Neither the character nor the clocks survived past the first draft, but the story grew from there with a life of its own.

Please visit his website at www.mlbuchman.com

GOODFELLOW PRESS

Novels from Goodfellow Press are smooth and seamless with characters who live beyond the confines of the book covers.

Hedge of Thorns by Sally Ash. A gentle story unfolding like a modern fairy tale, of painful yesterday's and trust reborn. ISBN 0-9639882-0-4 $7.99/$8.99 Canada.

This Time by Mary Sharon Plowman. A man and a woman with differing expectations and lifestyles, take a chance on love. ISBN 0-9639882-1-2 $7.99/$8.99 Canada.

Glass Ceiling by C.J. Wyckoff. Facing career and emotional upheaval, Jane Walker makes a bold choice to explore East Africa with an unorthodox man.   ISBN 0-9639882-2-0 $9.99/$10.99 Canada.

Bear Dance by Kay Zimmer. A man betrayed and a woman escaping painful memories struggle to overcome the barriers keeping them apart.   ISBN 0-9639882-4-7 $9.99/$10.99 Canada.

Homework: Bridging the Gap by Kay Morrison, Ph.D/Susanne Brady. Empowers parents, teachers and students to solve the homework dilemma.   ISBN 0-9639882-5-5 $12.99/$15.99 Canada.

White Powder by Mary Sharon Plowman. It is hard to fall in love when bullets are flying. ISBN 0-9639882-6-3 $9.99/$10.99 Canada.

Ivory Tower by May Taylor. Does the scent of lilacs herald a soft haunting? ISBN 0-9639882-3-9 $12.99/$13.99 Canada.

The Inscription by Pam Binder. An immortal warrior has conquered death, now he must conquer living. ISBN 0-9639882-7-1 $12.99/$13.99 Canada.

Matutu by Sally Ash. To find healing and love, an English violinist and an American writer must explore an old Maori legend. ISBN 0-9639882-9-8 $12.99/$13.99 Canada.

A Slight Change of Plans by John H. Zobel. Mike Archer has a chance to solve a mystery and meet the girl of his dreams, if only he can get out of the moose suit. (released 1998)

Riding Ahead - a Voyage by Bicycle by Matthew L. Buchman. To relearn what is important, a corporate refugee sets off on a solo journey around the word. (released in 1998)

Goodfellow Press/*Cookbook from Hell*
P.O. Box 2915 Redmond, WA 98073-2915
206-881-7699

1. How would you rate the following features? Please circle:

	readable			excellent	
Overall opinion of book	1	2	3	4	5
Character development	1	2	3	4	5
Conclusion/Ending	1	2	3	4	5
Plot/Story Line	1	2	3	4	5
Writing Style	1	2	3	4	5
Setting/Location	1	2	3	4	5
Appeal of Front Cover	1	2	3	4	5
Appeal of Back Cover	1	2	3	4	5
Print Size/Design	1	2	3	4	5

2. Approximately how many novels do you buy each month?_____
   How many do you read each month?_____

3. What is your education?
   ☐ High School or less   ☐ College Graduate
   ☐ Some College   ☐ Post Graduate

4. What is your age group?
   ☐ Under 25   ☐ 36-45   ☐ Over 55
   ☐ 26-35   ☐ 46-55

5. What types of fiction do you usually buy? (check all that apply)
   ☐ Historical   ☐ Western
   ☐ Science Fiction   ☐ Action/Adventure
   ☐ Romantic Suspense   ☐ General Fiction
   ☐ Mystery   ☐ Time Travel/Paranormal

6. Why did you buy this book? (check all that apply)
   ☐ Front Cover   ☐ Know the author   ☐ Liked the characters
   ☐ Back Cover   ☐ Like the ending   ☐ Heard of publisher
   ☐ Like the setting ☐ Purchased at an autographing event

For current Goodfellow Press updates:
Name: _____
Street: _____
City/State/Zip: _____

We would like to hear from you. Please write us with your comments.